THE *Senators'* SUITCASE

MITCH ENGEL

A STORY OF LOVE & LEGACY

outskirts
press

Outskirts Press, Inc.
http://www.outskirtspress.com

ISBN: 978-1-9772-2265-7

Library of Congress Control Number: 2019920988

Cover Photo © 2020 www.gettyimages.com.. All rights reserved - used with permission.

Outskirts Press and the "OP" logo are trademarks belonging to Outskirts Press, Inc.

PRINTED IN THE UNITED STATES OF AMERICA

To Robbie, Trista & Madison …
for making our family complete

Prologue

Forgetting her was never an option. The entire country made sure of that. How he chose to remember her was another story.

Introduction

I heard a click. In a literal sense, it signaled the door was unlocked at last. Figuratively, the same could be said because I suddenly was experiencing a rush of emotions I'd been trying hard to suppress. Apprehension being foremost.

Next came the scraping sounds of steel against steel as the young security guard struggled to remove a cartoon-sized padlock from an enormous flange welded to the doorframe. Eventually, he managed to pull back a hefty metal latch that could just as easily have been the keel to a small battleship. All the mammoth hardware looked as though it was crafted for a giant sitting atop a beanstalk.

After so much waiting, I finally could open the door. The moment of truth had arrived.

Before shuffling off toward the elevator, Eric Meyerhoff handed me a plastic box. "Take as much time as you need in there, Mr. Davenport ... and when you're done, just buzz me with that pager there, and I'll be right up to escort you back to the lobby."

Just moments earlier, the eager-to-please Meyerhoff had turned almost giddy while he was reciting specifics on how the locks and hardware at Riley's-On-Raymond were custom-manufactured in Halmstad, Sweden. Thankfully, that had been Point Sixteen in *The Riley's-On-Raymond Sixteen-Point Security Guarantee*, which my new pal was obliged to enumerate in excruciating detail during our trip up to the third floor.

Number fifteen was a dissertation on climate control. "Regardless of the weather outside, your personal possessions are safely preserved at an air temperature that never exceeds seventy-three degrees or drops below sixty-eight."

I probably should have registered a more positive reaction, but what if my mother had been stock-piling ice sculptures or rare orchids? Anything was possible. I had no idea what I was going to find inside the storage locker.

But at least we'd knocked off all sixteen points. After Eric completed Point Fifteen, there had been some doubt. That was when he couldn't find the key I'd handed him in the lobby before we set off on our shared journey – because, of course, Point Four specified "every client must be personally escorted to and from their respective storage units." I assumed these sixteen commandments were engraved on stone tablets somewhere in the vicinity of a burning bush.

After fumbling around, Eric did find the key in the breast pocket of his white button-down shirt – which sported a neon-red logo on one sleeve and a series of food stains on the other.

So, now I was standing alone, pondering what awaited me on the other side of door #34. After all these years, could I possibly be on the verge of having answers? Were there items inside this locker that could fill-in the countless blanks she left behind? Or at least a few of them?

Let me go back. You need to understand what my life had been like in recent weeks – or for that matter, what my life has been like since the moment I took my first breath in the delivery room. It was the second week of September when I received the dreadful call from the White House. Then eight days later, we held a memorial service for my mother – down in Evansville. I use the term "we" rather loosely, since all I needed to do was show up. Her staff took care of everything else.

The following morning, I sat through a lengthy meeting with the family's lawyers, who informed me of my inheritance. Not surprisingly, my mother bequeathed all her tangible assets to yours truly. I was her only child – in fact, her only living relative. The solemn attorneys lining the other side of a long wooden table went on to apprise me of a great deal more, but I'll get to those details later.

Included in her estate was the condo in downtown Indianapolis where I'd spent most of my youth. I wouldn't say I was raised there, because I'm not sure I was raised. Mostly, I was molded. Molded into what she had needed me to be.

With the condominium and its contents now fully in my possession, I had every legal right to open drawers, cabinets, and closets previously deemed off-limits. More than a right, I had an obligation. As the dutiful son, it was my responsibility to make sure her final affairs had been left in proper order.

But whom was I kidding? No facet of my mother's life ever had been out of order. She wouldn't have allowed such a thing.

No, what I really had been granted was a search warrant. Upon returning home to Indianapolis, I devoted every spare moment to unearthing her earthly past. If I wasn't on campus at Wabash, I was back in her condo boxing up personal effects or sifting through file folders. At last, I would find answers to the seemingly basic questions she evaded throughout my childhood and subsequent adulthood. But after nearly two weeks, I was as perplexed as ever. Maybe more so. What few items of interest I uncovered only added to the mysteries surrounding her.

Then on Friday evening, while rushing out to meet up with a female acquaintance, I accidentally knocked over a pewter lamp in my mother's bedroom. Picking it up, I heard something rattling inside. It turned out to be a key. One side was blank. On the other, a lone number stamped in brass – "34."

For the balance of my weekend, I played Sherlock Holmes,

completely obsessed with key #34. Eventually, I connected a few dots from her credit card statements. For each of the prior three years, she had been billed $1,624.50 by some entity called Riley Enterprises. I couldn't determine if this recurring charge might go further back because my mother tossed all her records from earlier years. She always had been proficient at discarding the superfluous from her life – but I needn't bore you with those particulars. Anyway, according to good-old Google, Riley Enterprises owned and operated a regional network of storage facilities, including one not far from the downtown condo – Riley's-On-Raymond. So presto, there I was, ready to enter my mother's storage unit.

Okay, it wasn't exactly "presto." In typical fashion, my mother had specified that she and she alone could be granted entrance into her storage unit. Accordingly, those family lawyers I mentioned, they needed to fax letters back and forth with a bunch of other lawyers before I finally gained access.

You see, dealings involving my mother rarely came easily. The mere sound of her name evoked a certain wonderment and prompted otherwise normal individuals to behave strangely.

I guess I should step back again. You need to know who my mother was. Beth Davenport. The late great Senator Beth Davenport. Ever since the accident, "late great" seems to have become permanently affixed to her name. With the passage of a few more years, I imagine "legendary" will be substituted. Yeh, that sounds about right. The legendary Senator Beth Davenport.

So now I'll jump ahead. The contents inside the storage locker would change everything. Not at first, and not for the reasons I might have guessed. But that's where this story begins – or at least my part in it. As for my mother, one could argue that unit #34 is where her story finally drew to its proper close.

Part I

Unanswered

Chapter 1

According to the security log, not a soul had entered Unit #34 for more than a decade. Not even my mother. Nothing in her personal files suggested anyone else knew about the lease she'd been renewing with Riley's-On-Raymond for more than a quarter-of-a-century. The family's attorneys were caught totally unaware when their assistance was required for me to gain entry. Only one conclusion could be drawn. The "late-great" Senator Beth Davenport had wanted her storage locker to remain a secret. Logically, I figured the same must be true for whatever she kept inside – if logic still existed in a world like hers.

The secured space turned out to be empty except for two ordinary-looking items pushed into the far corner – a small wooden table and an old leather suitcase resting on the top of it. What I found inside the suitcase was anything but ordinary. The contents numbered five-and-a-half million.

Who hasn't fantasized about discovering an outlandish sum of hidden cash? Who hasn't dreamt of faraway places and offshore bank accounts? But as I pulled out the endless packets of currency, my thoughts traveled elsewhere. Back to Evansville. Two weeks before.

"Saying our Beth will be missed by those fortunate enough to call her a colleague, is an understatement of epic proportions. Senator Elizabeth Davenport will be missed by entire generations who admired and respected her. As this remarkable woman blazed a trail for other women with aspirations for positions of leadership, she also helped make us a more inclusive nation for persons of every ethnicity, every economic stratum, and every political persuasion. She was, and will remain, a statesperson of the highest order. In my forty-three years of public service to this great country, I've rarely met a person with so much ..."

I was seated in the front row, watching as another national figure fell deeper and deeper in love. I had been observing public officials at close range since I was old enough to walk. At thirty-five years of age, I knew full-well how seasoned politicians could find romance in any circumstance. Romance with the sound of their own voices. Not to mention the love affairs they carried on with the batteries of cameras forever trained upon them. Funerals were no exception – especially a funeral for one of their long-time Capitol Hill compatriots. The hordes who had flown in from Washington to pay their respects were now staging an unmitigated orgy.

"... and what she meant to this country. In today's political climate, we often wonder whether persons of strong moral character can climb to the top in our government and succeed. Beth Davenport's celebrated career proves they still can ... and still do. How fortunate we are to have people with genuine honor and nobility wielding such powerful influence on our lives. The landmark legislations that have Beth's name attached to them will stand as lasting monuments to her unyielding dedication to social reform during her thirty-seven years as an elected representative of this great state. Beth Davenport was one ..."

The leather-skinned face behind the lectern at the front of the church had hit the five-minute mark – his designated time limit. But the majority whip was barely warming up, so I allowed my mind to wander. His comment about lasting monuments had struck a chord. Or maybe it was a nerve. My mental state was riding a rollercoaster, so I'm not sure I could have recognized the difference. Regardless, I wracked my memory bank.

'Monuments.' What was it that guy had said? It was rattling around somewhere in the back of my head. I was pretty sure I'd even tossed the quote into a term paper for one of my ancient history classes. *Something about wanting no monuments. How did the damned thing go?*

No matter how hard I tried, I couldn't make the words fall into place. Perhaps too many brains cells had been squandered since I last contemplated the musings of Cato.

Nonetheless, Indiana's senior senator would have appreciated how the occasion of her funeral was conjuring up thoughts of famous Roman statesmen. How often had I heard her utter those words? "People will be judged by the individuals with whom they are associated." Cato, Caesar, and now my mother. She would have liked being placed in such esteemed company.

After someone has been dead, it is better to have people wonder why there are no monuments erected in their name, rather than ask why they deserve to be remembered at all. Bingo. Maybe that wasn't exactly right, but close enough. Translating Latin was never a strong suit. It didn't matter.

I was going to keep this latest surge of cynicism to myself. I'd already prepared enough raindrops to disrupt the afternoon's well-orchestrated parade – the endless procession of suitably sober faces blathering on and on about their beloved comrade. On this September afternoon, each of them was dutifully paying forward, so that at some future date, similar Washington hordes could airlift into their respective hometowns and produce a communal silk purse at their own memorial services.

"Honor." "Nobility." Those high-bound words had oozed so effortlessly from the man's lips. What did the majority whip know about Beth Davenport? What did any of them know about my mother? All they cared about were the camera crews perched in the choir loft, capturing soundbites for the next 24-hour news cycle.

Hell, a few weeks later I found myself staring at a mountain of cash extracted from a suitcase. How much did I truly know about Elizabeth "Beth" Davenport?

I had been slated as the final speaker at her service – that was if some unscheduled bastion of democracy didn't leap to the microphone and deliver another seemingly spontaneous tribute. Anything was possible in a church bursting with politicians.

Every portion of the afternoon service had been planned by her staff, in the precise manner Madam Senator would have instructed if she'd still been alive. For more than three decades, her teams in Washington and Indianapolis had functioned as a seamless extension of my mother. In her absence, both offices likely could function into perpetuity without missing a beat. Why should her son and sole-surviving relative be allowed to weigh-in on something as routine as her funeral?

That morning, I'd pulled to the side of the highway and watched the tarmac at the regional airport be transformed into a parking lot filled with private jets. The local news broadcasts predicted the funeral would bring the largest throng of dignitaries to the city of Evansville since its founding – which had taken place more than two hundred, mostly unmemorable, years earlier.

If all the visiting hot air could have been collectively harnessed, we might have lifted the whole of Evansville's downtown commercial district with a single balloon. No doubt, Beth Davenport would have been overwhelmed with humble gratitude by an outpouring of this magnitude. At least publicly. Privately, my mother would have expected nothing less – though that wouldn't have stopped her from grousing about the amount of time and taxpayer dollars such a gathering consumed. Outward humility and inward contradiction were just two of the more notable hallmarks to her personality.

As the longest-serving female independent in the history of the United States Congress, Senator Beth Davenport's death had been certain to draw national attention regardless of the circumstances. But the fact that she died in a helicopter crash while visiting a military base outside Doha, Qatar, had magnified the significance of every detail from her life. During the week since the accident, video clips recapping her distinguished career had been running round-the-clock on cable news channels, with even the most inconsequential aspects of her voting record and committee appointments now being portrayed as towering acts of patriotism. Since the time I stopped crawling, I'd been unable to step outside the shadow she cast. From this point forward, her legendary profile might as well be carved onto the side of Mt. Rushmore.

When it came to my own paltry accomplishments, I recognized most people in attendance at her funeral service would ascribe to me but one noteworthy deed. Birth. Weighing in at six-pounds-twelve-ounces, Little Troy arrived just two months into Beth Davenport's first term in the House of Representatives – shortly after she had unseated a Democratic fixture by campaigning nose-to-nose right up until November's election day while carrying a first child at the age of forty-two. It wasn't the only time I would become a convenient prop in the molding of my mother's public image.

A few days before the funeral, I had been handed a script containing personal recollections of what it was like to be raised by a political icon. The series of anecdotes struck a perfect balance of humor, humanity, and poignancy … and for the most part, they were true, as best I could remember. One of the speechwriters even thought to include a reference to my father, since this man, long-forgotten by most, presumably had played some role in Little Troy's early development – or at a minimum, my conception.

My father died from a rare blood disease in 1988, at age fifty, and his name still appeared as an occasional footnote in news stories related to my mother. At the time of his death, I was five. By then, the unflappable widow, Beth Davenport, had progressed upward to the Senate. She was a year into her first term. Her vigilance during those final months of her husband's life, combined with the grace by which she coped with the tragedy and transitioned into single parenthood, eliminated any question about my mother winning a second term. So, I guess through the sheer act of dying, my father also had contributed to the Senator's historic rise.

Over the eight days since the fatal helicopter crash, and that ominous call from the White House, I had struggled to draft my own version of a eulogy. It was tucked into the coat pocket of my dark blue suit – the exact suit I'd been instructed to wear. White shirt, patterned tie, black oxfords. Of course, the black oxfords. *"Troy, why do you and the young men of your generation insist upon wearing those dreadful brown shoes with dark suits? They look perfectly horrid."*

The majority whip was working up to a crescendo. His voice was cracking at just the right moments, and he'd pulled a handkerchief out of thin air to daub his eyes. Shortly, it would be my turn. I patted the bulge inside my coat and smiled, thinking about the entirely different set of anecdotes I'd scribbled onto notecards. Perhaps it was time for the rest of the world to gain new insights into their beloved Senator Beth Davenport. What purpose was to be served by perpetuating a façade?

Shouldn't the electorate know what type of person the nation really lost in a helicopter crash? Shouldn't they know that those ever-present warm smiles merely were masking a deep-seated aloofness? My mother was a political automaton. Out of the public eye, she kept her emotions in a closet, just like the fashionable suits and dresses she pulled out every morning. All part of her well-crafted façade. In private, genuine human interactions often appeared to be drudgery. She constantly erected new walls, uncertain boundaries that forever were shifting. To Beth Davenport, maintaining control was paramount.

But once I stepped up to that lectern, I would be outside her reach at last.

Chapter 2

"I wanted you to know how truly sorry I was to hear about your mother, Troy. I watched the whole thing on TV this afternoon. She would have been proud of you ... so incredibly proud of your impeccable delivery."

Before responding to the other end of the phone, I allowed a few seconds to pass – stifling the urge, the low-hanging temptation. I wanted to deny her the satisfaction of knowing she'd scored. "Thanks, Vic. It was nice of you to call."

Vicki Richardson had known exactly what to say. She always could find just the right words. It had been fourteen months since she moved out of my apartment. To be fair, I did miss the fun and sex we once enjoyed, but fun had vacated the premises long before she and the sex did. At first, I'd believed this live-in relationship might be different, more adult-like than my prior attempts. But by the time we finally separated, the once intriguing *"Vicki-with-an-i"* had morphed into a dark cloud that hovered around my every waking hour. The two of us managed to uncover all kinds of hot buttons during our time together, but she was the most adept at digging under the skin. She was especially skilled whenever the subject of my mother arose.

"The perfect, obedient son right til the very end." She made a second attempt at goading me.

I refused to take the bait. "I was okay with what my mother's speechwriters prepared." I decided not to pretend the words in the eulogy had been mine. "Now I can move on with the rest of my life, and maybe you might do the same."

This parting shot was my retribution. Vicki had been the one to pick up and leave, without any warning whatsoever, in the middle of a spring afternoon while I was in front of a classroom fifty miles away. But she also was the one who'd phoned at least a dozen times since to suggest we give living together a second shot. At moments like this, I was thankful my masculine pride had prevailed.

After hanging up, I laid on the couch and pondered what I had said to my most recent ex-girlfriend. All in all, it was truthful. By the time I made my way to the lectern at the front of the church, I did feel okay about delivering the eulogy given to me by her chief of staff. Just carrying my own version to the front of the church had been enough. That very act was cathartic. Right up to the last second, I retained the option of withdrawing that alternative script from inside my lapel and exploding a few myths about the esteemed Senator Beth Davenport. No one could have stopped me. But it was me, on my own accord, who made the choice not to stir things up. To permit the myths to live on. It wasn't my mother. It wasn't anyone from her loyal entourage. It was just me. That knowledge alone had felt adequate.

But as I sat on the bare concrete of a storage locker, surrounded by tightly wrapped bundles of hidden currency, any semblance of satisfaction had vanished. Vicki-with-an-i was right all along. Little Troy had been obedient to the very end.

Chapter 3

B y the time I discovered the suitcase, three weeks had passed
since the call from the White House. I almost didn't answer
because the number on my screen was unfamiliar. Expecting a sur-
vey or sales pitch, I was poised to hang-up. But then I heard an offi-
cial-sounding voice that couldn't possibly be faked. "Mr. Davenport,
please hold for a moment … the President would like to speak with
you."

From that day forward, no one with a sense of decency would
have dared to utter a negative word about my mother. At her memorial service, I was on the verge of becoming that lone exception. Now
I was second-guessing my decision. Maybe the bubble of rarified air
protecting Beth Davenport should have been punctured long ago.

What reason other than a nefarious one would a career politician
have for stashing away millions of dollars in cash? Before entering
the storage locker, I'd already begun questioning other aspects of
my mother's past due to a couple of surprises discovered during the
intervening weeks. The first jolt came on the day after the funeral
when I met with the attorneys to review her will. I had presumed I
would be heading back to my job in Crawfordsville with a healthier
bank statement, but I was unprepared for the totality.

I considered my teaching salary more than adequate for the less
complicated lifestyle to which I'd become accustomed – especially

if I threw in the $5,000 each month I still received as a "living expense stipend" from the trust fund my grandfather set up for me on my thirteenth birthday. In more recent years, I hadn't even touched those checks and instead was heeding the advice of the financial mavens who staffed the Davenport family office. The monthly distributions from the trust were accumulating, compounding, and accruing in some fancy investment account they managed on my behalf.

As a senator, my mother pulled in a decent salary – though she'd never been shy about spending excessively on herself. But she'd also enjoyed a lucrative business career before launching into politics. Plus, there was whatever money my father had left her. So, when I met with the attorneys, I would hear the final tally that could be assigned to her seventy-eight years of material existence. I didn't much care.

The almighty dollar once had been a huge priority for me – at times, my only priority. As a high school teenager, and later as a college student, I couldn't spend money fast enough. Having five-grand deposited into my checking account each month by a wealthy grandfather was like holding the keys to Fort Knox. I immersed myself in the latest sound systems, computer equipment, and electronic games. I leased a new sports car every two or three years. I spent spring breaks and long weekends in the Caribbean. I picked up endless bar tabs with my drinking crews. My girlfriends were treated to the most popular clubs and restaurants. At sold-out concerts, I usually could be found in the front row with my latest conquest sitting next to me. The money poured in, and with a billionaire grandfather tending to my needs, I had every reason to believe this golden goose would someday deliver an untold fortune.

With my financial future ostensibly secured, my approach to looming adulthood had been carefree. Some might say reckless. I passed through those formative years rather whimsically. Guaranteed affluence allowed me to flip my ambition on and off at will. Schoolwork. Sports. Dating. Career directions. My life experiences were nothing more than a sample pack. A little of this, a little of that. Picking and choosing when to apply my energies and talents. For the sake of my mother's reputation, I was careful not to cross lines that could be deemed as overt bad behavior. Apparently, aimlessness and apathy were acceptable to her – eliciting only mild rebukes when I might happen to cross paths with the good senator amidst her overbooked appointment calendar.

But my built-up expectations for the years ahead came crashing down after my grandfather died. My anticipated benefactor left me out in the cold. My mother and I weren't even invited to the reading of his will. Instead, a few days later, one of the junior associates from the family's legal firm contacted me. "Troy, you'll be happy to know the $5,000 monthly stipends will continue indefinitely." No other provisions had been made.

In an instant, my view of the world evaporated into thin air. Barely twenty-five, I had lost a fortune that was never mine to begin with. Thoughts of work, or pursuing an actual occupation, suddenly took on greater meaning. Notions of wealth and privilege soon turned alien to me – and over time, borderline repugnant. In retrospect, I guess I chose resentment as a suitable coping mechanism. But I don't regret those feelings, because eventually I recognized money was not my friend.

At the time of my mother's death, I was early into my fourth year as an associate professor at Wabash College, where I'd been told I was well along the path toward tenure and a full professorship. My chosen field was sociology.

When I'd declared sociology as my major half-way through college, I essentially was making a statement. Nobody serious about preparing for a legitimate occupation would dedicate their college years to the study of sociology. It was a discipline that frolicked in the gray areas – if sociology could be considered a discipline at all.

The degree on my diploma was meant as a badge of honor. I was clarifying for anyone who doubted that Troy Davenport had no intention of ever charting a serious career. I instead would hopscotch through college, learning about the arcane and the abstruse.

But this blithe approach to academia dramatically narrowed my options for finding a job when the prospect of independent wealth disappeared in a flash. So like thousands of other sociology majors, I pursued the one profession for which I was suitably qualified. Instructing other young minds on the idiosyncrasies of human society. I would guide new generations of wandering souls through their weekly escapes from the finite world.

Wabash College was a well-regarded school with nine hundred students and eighty-one faculty members. The institution carried the distinction of being one of the country's three small liberal arts colleges still offering enrollment to males only. My fellow faculty members appeared to place great emphasis on the vaunted history of Wabash. Pedigrees mattered little to me. This picturesque campus of higher learning was merely a place to work, a job – just like the two that preceded it.

I'd been lured to Wabash by a phone call from a headhunter, informing me of a recently vacated position. I was immediately receptive. Similar calls had led me to teaching positions at Wooster College, in Ohio, and Truman State University, in Missouri. A rolling stone needed to keep rolling. Surprisingly, a few weeks later, this latest open slot was mine.

Like other faculty members at Wabash, I was encouraged to take residence in Crawfordsville, a bucolic town of 16,000 people, fifty miles to the northwest of Indianapolis. I considered the suggestion but ultimately decided on an apartment on the northside of Indianapolis. I'd spent much of my youth in the state's capital and preferred the city's size and familiarity. My decision left me with a two-hour round-trip commute – five days a week, plus random

Saturdays for football games and glee club performances.

All the while, I had no idea whether the job offer from Wabash or either of the two prior schools had resulted from strings being pulled by loyalists to my mother. In each case, I was told I received superior recommendations. Could there really have been students in my past who were motivated by the approach I took in the classroom? I had no idea. I'd learned long ago to stop worrying about such things. I'd grown accustomed to these types of uncertainties since my earliest memories, when I routinely was assigned to the best play groups or placed on the most competitive little league teams. The deck always seemed to be stacked in my favor and there was little I could do to even the odds. Because of the influence that a celebrated mother and a powerful grandfather could wield, success had been assured in virtually every aspect of my life. I rarely had seen much reason to try very hard. Any sense of achievement only would have been tainted with ambiguity.

My grandfather, the original Joseph Elwood Davenport, had passed away at the anything-but-ripe old age of eighty-seven. This business titan had planned to live another thirty or forty years, but I guess his weakened heart had other ideas.

My father was Joseph Elwood Davenport, Jr., and I would have become Joseph Elwood Davenport III, if not for my mother, who insisted upon a name that carried linkage to her side of the biological equation. Troy, Ohio was where her maternal grandparents resided, and where Elizabeth had visited every summer as a young girl. Hence, the negotiated compromise resulted in the official identity imprinted on my birth certificate – Troy Joseph Davenport.

My grandfather began calling his own son "Junior" from the moment he was born. He insisted everyone else do likewise. The name stuck and followed my father into adulthood. For the entirety of his life, he was known only as Junior. That always seemed kind of sad to me.

In an act of punctuational overkill, my grandfather adopted the nickname "Senior" for himself – in theory, to eliminate any potential for name confusion within the family. But others familiar with my grandfather had suggested the elder Joseph Davenport preferred the authoritative ring to his new moniker. "Senior." It left little doubt about who was in command. Over the balance of his lifetime, no one called him anything else. Even his grandson. I never dared to call him anything but Senior.

Now they were gone. One by one. My father, my grandfather, my mother. I was left alone to fend for myself. The sole surviving Davenport.

Chapter 4

The meeting was slated for 8 a.m., and since it was scheduled solely for my benefit, I figured I should try to be punctual. Most of the civilized world operated under the premise that business days started at nine, but this was Evansville. If I'd chosen the faster line at Donut Depot, I might have arrived on time. Or at least on time-ish.

The law firm was in the same building where my grandfather, father, and mother once worked together. Davenport Industries had ceased to exist in 2005, when its shareholders accepted a tender offer from a Canadian mining conglomerate. The new owners paid $23.6 billion – nearly thirty percent more than the company's market cap at the time. And at that time, I had no idea what a market cap was. This hefty premium still didn't stop my grandfather from trying to kill the deal with the board of directors at the eleventh hour. As consolation prize for his failed attempt, Senior Davenport walked away with $2.3 billion in exchange for the ten-percent ownership he'd held onto since taking the company public in 1993.

A last-minute concession from the Canadians allowed the Davenport family – meaning my grandfather – to retain full ownership of the headquarters building on Water Street, overlooking the Ohio River. The seven-story structure in the heart of the city had become a landmark of sorts in Evansville, with locals still today referring to it as The Davenport Building. After the sale, my grandfather leased its space to other local businesses – except for the northeast corner of the top floor. Housed there was the Davenport family business office. Occupying the balance of the seventh floor was The Law Partnership of O'Keefe & O'Keefe. For more than fifty years, Gerald O'Keefe was the primary legal counsel to Senior Davenport in both business and personal matters. Gerald's son, Daniel, was handed the reins to the firm just a year after my grandfather died. Thus, Daniel O'Keefe and two of his junior attorneys were standing in the lobby as soon as I exited the elevator.

Waiting in the conference room was Calvin Stratton, who was designated trustee to my mother's estate. "Uncle Cal" had been a positive and steady presence throughout my life. My father met Cal as a teenager, at boarding school, and the two remained best friends until the day Junior Davenport died. I was too young to remember many details from those final weeks, but Cal apparently sat at the bedside with my mother, as my father's body and spirit withered away in unison. Over the years since, Cal had maintained a close relationship with my mother and me. Many birthday and holiday celebrations were made a great deal more memorable by this outgoing and personable gentleman. Due to Cal Stratton's connections across the state of Indiana, he also was the perfect individual to head-up fundraising for several of my mother's election campaigns.

In more recent years, contact with Cal had tapered off due to busy schedules and geography. We traded periodic phone calls, but the last time I'd seen Uncle Cal in person prior to my mother's funeral was a lunch in downtown Indianapolis, back in June. We briefly hugged before the memorial service began, and that's when I noticed how much Cal was struggling with his emotions. As soon as the service was over, Cal left the church before we could talk further about our shared loss.

Calvin William Stratton was a retired banker, having enjoyed a long and prosperous career as a senior executive with Indiana Federated Bank. He had served on too many corporate and non-profit boards for me to keep straight. Cal now split his time between Indianapolis and John's Island, in Vero Beach, Florida. Based on appearance, retirement and life in general continued to agree with him. Cal was reputed to have been a ladies' man of the highest order inside the social circles of Central Indiana. He'd never married, and I suspected senior citizenship hadn't noticeably diminished the number of women willing to tie the knot.

My father would have been eighty if he had lived, which meant Uncle Cal was about the same age. This hardly seemed possible as I studied the man who stood to greet me. Tall and fit, with ever-perfect posture. He had a full head of neatly-trimmed silvery hair that still harbored a few speckles of stubborn darkness. His bronzed skin, glowing from the sun, provided a perfect backdrop for the bright teeth revealed by his familiar smile.

"Good morning, Troy. You spoke well yesterday ... it's easy to see how you've gained your reputation in the classroom." His handshake was firm. Then the handshake transitioned into a hug. "She was a great woman and a special friend," he half-whispered to me with a slight quiver in his voice.

"I know, Uncle Cal ... as you were to her ... and to my dad." The realization hit me for the first time. Cal was my strongest remaining link to my parents.

After we separated, Cal stepped back and raised his open right hand to capture the attention of the three attorneys who were doing whatever it was attorneys did as they shuffled through their stacks of file folders.

"Before we begin, I want to clarify something. We all recognize my participation here today is rather superfluous at this point, but when Troy's parents drew up their estate plans those many years ago, their pride-and-joy had yet to turn a year-old and they thought it wise to name a third-party fiduciary. After Junior's premature death, there was nothing we could do to remove my signature from the string of legal documents that locked into place for time and memoriam. Rest assured, I will not be an impediment to any decisions you folks need to make."

Someone from O'Keefe & O'Keefe had alerted me in advance to the need for Cal Stratton's attendance, but until his opening comments, I hadn't considered the possibility that my parents' closest friend could become an impediment. With a grandfather who was a ruthless billionaire, and a mother who was a popular U.S. senator, my life to-date already was playing out like a soap opera script. All I needed now was a sinister plot over inheritance.

"Hey, I teach sociology ... you remember, esoterica. Believe me, Uncle Cal, I'll take whatever assistance you can provide once our friends here start clicking into legal-speak. If you see my eyes rolling toward the back of my head, that's a clear sign my brain is shutting down."

The first part of the meeting lasted most of the morning, and indeed, I did need assistance from Cal to understand the complexities of my mother's estate. For some incomprehensible reason, the trio of attorneys decided they should methodically dissect the origin and evolution of each of her traceable assets. There was the money that a young Beth Davenport had saved from her brief and successful career as an investment advisor. Then, the money my mother had socked away from her tenure with Davenport Industries, where she served as a senior executive. Plus, the money bequeathed to her by my father.

All those funds were invested in accounts to which specific values could be ascribed. In addition, there was the sizable home in Evansville that my mother had maintained but rarely visited. There was the condo, a block north of Monument Circle in Indianapolis, that served as her primary residence for more than thirty years. Then there was the two-bedroom townhouse in Georgetown, where she stayed whenever Congress was in-session. And lastly, at some unspecified date in the future, an unnamed federal bureaucrat would be sending me a lump sum check for the portion of her government retirement account to which I was entitled as her designated descendant, combined with the pay-out from a term-life insurance policy she'd purchased at favorable rates as a member of Congress.

While this whole wearisome ordeal crawled ever-onward, I was pretty sure I experienced a personal epiphany. For the first time in my life, I recognized that sociology was more than a convenient career choice I'd happened upon during college. I finally understood that sociology had been a deeper calling. Somewhere in my youth, or maybe in the womb, God must have spoken to me about a righteous path to eternal happiness that was devoid of market volatility, net present values, imputed interest, unrealized gains, and all things numeric.

The two junior lawyers patiently led Cal and me through a neatly bound booklet that likely was prepared by an even more junior staff member who might go weeks at a time without seeing sunlight. If I had been keeping a running total in my head, I wouldn't have been surprised when they finally reached the dollar amount on the last page of the booklet. But again, my field was sociology. I never kept running totals of anything.

It was Daniel O'Keefe who delivered the coup de grace. "After assigning net present values to the deceased party's real estate holdings, based on fair market appraisals conducted last week, we calculate the final estate of Elizabeth Monroe Davenport to be worth $20,933,627 – with all said properties and assets transferring to Troy Joseph Davenport, in accordance with the directions set forth in her last will and testament, originally filed and notarized in this office on April 23, 1985, and last revised on July 17, 2015."

When he was done, the firm's namesake principal removed his

reading glasses, sat back in his chair with arms folded loosely across his chest and eyes fixed in my direction, as though he expected me to give him a standing ovation – or at least let loose with an exultant gasp.

I wasn't inclined to offer either. I instead closed the booklet in front of me and thanked the team for their thoroughness and, more importantly, their diligence in representing the Davenport family over so many years. The gratitude was genuine. Otherwise, I was experiencing little emotion as a newly-minted millionaire. The events after my grandfather's passing, more than a decade earlier – my "inheritance lost" – had tainted my views on money. With time, I'd resolved this change in perspective was a good thing. Now I would need to revisit my attitude about wealth.

I leaned over to Uncle Cal, "Can I interest you in lunch?"

He was instantly receptive. "I'd love some time alone with you, Troy … but I need to give you fair warning. As of this morning, your days of freeloading off me are officially over. Bring your credit card, moneybags."

Chapter 5

Daniel O'Keefe overheard my conversation with Cal. "Sorry, Troy, but we require a bit more of your time." The lead attorney hesitated, looking somewhat sheepish. "And I'm afraid we are bound by very specific instructions … our next discussion must be held in private. Mr. Stratton, I hope you understand."

The request caught me off-guard, but Cal was unfazed. "No problem here," he said. The distinguished octogenarian stood, straightened his fashionably narrow tie, and prepared to leave.

I grabbed his sleeve. "Why don't you grab us a table at Angelo's … I'll catch up with you in a few minutes?"

But escaping was impossible, as O'Keefe interjected again. "Excuse me, Troy, but the items we need to cover are likely to take a while. We've arranged for lunch to be brought in."

All I could do was shrug. I still hadn't caught up with Cal or talked about the whirlwind surrounding my mother's death. Unfortunately, he had an appointment in Indianapolis for that evening, so we hugged a quick goodbye and agreed to regroup up north.

After one of the younger associates escorted Cal from the conference room, I turned to the others and threw up my arms in surrender. "I guess I'm all yours, gentlemen." I was bracing for whatever surprises were to come my way. It would have been just like my mother to stay two or three steps in front of me. Perhaps I was about to receive some handwritten exhortation about living up to my full potential. Death didn't mean I couldn't continue to fall short of the Senator's expectations. Maybe through her last will and testament, my mother finally would express the unspoken disappointments she couldn't quite voice while alive. Or maybe she would provide a few answers to questions that any son would have had. The kinds of questions I'd been asking to no avail since I first started stringing words into sentences.

But regardless of the possibilities running through my head, nothing could have prepared me for the real purpose of this second closed-door meeting. One of the young associates quickly distributed another freshly-minted binder as Daniel O'Keefe opened the conversation with a bombshell. "Troy, pursuant to the unfortunate loss of your mother, there is an unresolved portion from your grandfather's estate that now can be distributed, per the terms of his will and testament as last amended … and that is the subject we've been instructed to discuss with you."

When my father passed away, my mother had been a part of the Davenport family for twenty-five years. She survived another thirty years as Junior Davenport's widow and mother of Senior Davenport's only grandchild. Thinking back, I couldn't recall her ever saying a disparaging word about Senior – or likewise, Senior about her. But despite this outward civility, something in their body language always had suggested a gnawing animosity.

With both now departed, the family's attorneys were left the unpleasant task of confirming this unspoken hostility. Based on what Daniel O'Keefe and his associates disclosed over the next two hours, it sounded more like unmitigated disdain. Consequently, Senior Davenport went to great lengths to make sure my mother didn't benefit in any manner from his accumulated wealth following his death. My grandfather refused to allow mortality to impede his absolute authority.

Since this powerful man was my grandfather, I supposed I'd loved Senior while I was growing up. As an adult, I wasn't sure how I felt about him. I couldn't help but respect his drive and persistence. But what I mostly remembered were the fears I experienced whenever we were together. My trepidations about doing something wrong and igniting the volatile temper I'd witnessed when situations weren't to his liking. My anxiety about coming up short when we were fishing, hunting, or target shooting. The discomfort that my presence could somehow exacerbate the pervasive tension among people who worked for my grandfather and catered to his every whim.

My parents had relocated their primary residence from Evansville to Indianapolis before I turned five. After the move, I saw my grandfather only a few times each year, and almost always in Evansville. His trips to Indianapolis were infrequent and even on those occasions he was usually in town for business rather than family visits. Our principal times together were the two weeks every summer that I was shipped down to the southern part of the state. There, we shuttled between Senior's in-town mansion and his various getaway properties out in the countryside.

By age seven or eight, I could recite all the chapters and fill in most of the verses to the self-made success story of Joseph Elwood Davenport, Sr. – not that my grandfather ever took the time to regale his grandson with details. He didn't need to. The people surrounding Senior did that for him. His friends, his business associates, his sizable household staff. They all vied for his favor and building him up to his lone grandson was sure to score points. The ways in which my grandfather exuded power and commanded loyalty couldn't possibly have been learned behaviors. Joseph Elwood Davenport must have stomped out of the delivery room with the innate ability to domineer and intimidate.

Three years after graduating from high school, Joseph Elwood already had moved up to night crew foreman in the Eastern Kentucky coalmine where he, his father, and two of his uncles worked. Two years later, he was put in charge of day-to-day operations. That year was 1942, just months after Pearl Harbor and the outbreak of a second world war. This latest promotion meant young Joe was now part of management. His position exempted him from the draft for the duration of the war because an uninterrupted coal supply was deemed vital to the nation's military effort.

As other younger men shipped overseas, Joe stayed home and put in double shifts. Due to his tireless energy, he stood out among the older and timeworn miners who were left behind. With youthful vigor, he stepped up to the most challenging assignments one after another. By war's end, Joe Davenport was a central figure in anything meaningful that took place in or around Pikesville, Kentucky. So when the calendar flipped to 1946, and the owners of the coalmine began negotiating a sale of their operation to a wealthy mining family from West Virginia, Joe stepped in and convinced a group of local businessmen to finance a deal that would match the offer on the table, keep the ownership in Kentucky, and hand him the full responsibility for running it.

Within six years, Joe bought out his original group of investors – and by then my grandfather was overseeing a company comprised of eight coalmines across a four-county region. By the late 1960's, Davenport Mining owned dozens of mines scattered about Kentucky, as well as portions of Southern Ohio and Southern Indiana. During one of those years, Joe elected to relocate his base of operations to a larger city. Strategically, he'd always wanted to be situated on the Ohio River, but he passed on the more obvious choices of Louisville or Cincinnati – choosing instead to become a bigger fish in the smaller pond of Evansville, Indiana. The site he selected for the headquarters building offered a panoramic view of his home state of Kentucky, just across the river.

Over the two-plus decades that followed, my grandfather and

his bankers continued to pick off coalmine after coalmine, usually at distressed prices. Eventually, Davenport Mining diversified into so many other businesses that the company's name was changed to Davenport Industries in 1980. When Davenport Industries went public seven years later, Wall Street welcomed Joe with open arms and even more open checkbooks.

Missing from this oft-told story about my grandfather's rise from rags to riches was any mention of a woman – which always had puzzled me, because somewhere along the trail I must have had a grandmother. But that chapter long ago had been redacted from the family narrative. From what I was able to piece together through secondhand sources, my grandfather had married a young woman when he was twenty, as the result of an unforeseen pregnancy. She was a local girl who knew her way around mining camps, and little else. By the time their son, who was my father, reached kindergarten, Senior easily could write a check that bought him full custody and a vanishing act from his young wife.

Soon after my grandfather's death, I hired a specialized investigator to track down this woman who had brought my father into the world. I was hoping I might connect with my mysterious grandmother. I wouldn't have dared to attempt such a blatant act of betrayal while the family's patriarch was still roaming the earth.

The report I received was disheartening. Anna May Wilder, the former Mrs. Joseph Elwood Davenport, had died of alcohol poisoning in 1954. Her obituary made no mention of a son or her short-lived marriage. Whatever deal was struck with her one-time husband, Anna May had honored it to the end. My grandfather clearly knew how to get what he wanted.

Now, the family's attorneys were affirming this fact. Daniel O'Keefe tried to be delicate, but the truth was inescapable. Through his final will and testament, Senior Davenport had taken every conceivable precaution to make sure his daughter-in-law couldn't touch a dime of the wealth he accumulated over the course of his lifetime, which seemed to be the standard by which my billionaire grandfather measured a person's importance.

"Troy, you probably recall that upon your grandfather's death, his will designated that 750 million dollars be given to the City of Evansville for the construction of the Davenport Civic Center ... and that a larger amount, in excess of 2.5 billion dollars, be transferred into the Davenport Foundation. People naturally assumed these two sizable sums represented the totality of Senior's estate. However, since that time, my associates and I, along with the IRS, have known otherwise. With your mother's passing, we now are at liberty to bring you into this circle of knowledge."

The expression on Daniel O'Keefe's face was a mixture. He seemed unusually relieved, as though maintaining such a bizarre confidentiality agreement had taken some personal toll on him. But there also was an awkward look of distress. "Troy, please understand, we are restricted from disclosing any background details beyond the directives specified by your grandfather."

From across the table, I nodded apprehensively. The issues surrounding my high-profile family always had been complicated. Now I feared I was about to enter a whole new frontier of convoluted Davenport realities.

O'Keefe continued, "Let's start with the biggest headline for the afternoon. You soon will become an extremely wealthy young man, Troy Davenport. The money from your mother's estate pales in comparison to the inheritance left to you by your grandfather. According to the most recent account statements compiled by the Davenport family office, the amount comes to slightly less than four hundred million dollars – which, due to recent stock market performance, is approximately fifty-five million dollars more than when Senior died. So, I would say congratulations are in order."

The three attorneys leaned forward in their seats, expecting a celebratory reaction of some sort. The best I could give them was a smile – and a rather forced one at that.

Two hours later, the elevator doors closed, and I began my descent to street level, desperately hoping normal people still populated the planet. I now was convinced normalcy didn't exist inside the Davenport family.

So much about my mother remained an enigma, and the day's proceedings had added another layer of intrigue. But this latest chapter also involved my father. Over the decade since my grandfather died and seemingly left us out of his will, my mother had refused to discuss what possible reasons he might have had for disinheriting his only living relatives. I eventually resolved that Senior Davenport must have been the cold-hearted, self-centered tyrant his detractors claimed him to be – that he was more committed to shrines bearing his name than his own flesh and blood. But as it turned out, my parents had done something to alienate and provoke my grandfather to the point where he wrote them, and not me, out of his will.

"In April of 1988, your grandfather instructed us to nullify his previous will and institute a new one stipulating that his son, Joseph Elwood Davenport, Jr., and the wife of said son, Elizabeth Monroe Davenport, were not to receive a single proceed from his estate. Over the subsequent twenty years, we effectuated a series of amendments and codicils to distribute assets according to his wishes. With one of those modifications, in 1996, your grandfather wanted to ensure that any funds distributed directly to you could under no circumstances benefit your mother. He was concerned that after his death, you might turn around and gift a portion of your inheritance to her or one of her political campaigns."

To the surprise of the attorneys, I chuckled. I couldn't help myself. The whole scenario sounded ludicrous. I posed a question to them. "So, the grandson has to wait until the daughter-in-law dies to learn that he has inherited hundreds of millions from his grandfather

… so what if my mom had lived for another twenty-five years?"

Daniel O'Keefe gave an understanding nod. "Troy, please trust that we covered every possible scenario with your grandfather. But he was adamant. Not to speak ill of the departed, but Senior Davenport was a clever and sometimes ruthless businessman. Accordingly, it wasn't uncommon for Senior to insist on convoluted legal stipulations to protect him from the cleverness or ruthlessness of others … especially when his relationships became discordant. As to your inheritance, he wasn't concerned about when you received the benefit – or frankly, whether you personally received benefit at all. Senior just wanted to be certain that the remainder of his wealth was passed along to a rightful next generation in his family … and if this money skipped by you completely, he was content with such an outcome … as long as your mother didn't benefit."

Chapter 6

The meeting at The Law Partnership of O'Keefe & O'Keefe had delivered me a bombshell – and it had nothing to do with the four-hundred million from my grandfather, or the twenty million from my mother. Those boxcar numbers were too abstract to absorb. Besides, according to the attorneys, any actual transfer of funds would take months to effect. No, the more astounding revelation concerned the animus that must have existed between my parents and grandfather. For nearly a decade, my mother chose to withhold any and all pertinent details from me after I seemingly had been disinherited by that same grandfather. I had probed her numerous times about what I might have been missing. Yet, she repeatedly assured me she wasn't aware of any issues that would explain his behavior. My own mother purposely had lied to me. But why had she refused to divulge this reality? What had my parents done to incur Senior's wrath?

A second jolt came a few days later. The details weren't nearly as consequential, but once again I realized my mother had made a conscious choice to lie to me.

The dean of my department had granted me a two-week leave of absence to deal with my mother's passing – which following the news of my inheritance, left me five unencumbered days to roll up my sleeves in Indianapolis.

Going through her possessions in Evansville had taken no time at all. I packed up several framed photos hanging from the walls of my parents' one-time home, along with a few of the more significant mementos that local organizations had presented to my mother. I threw those cartons into my SUV and headed north just hours after leaving the law firm.

The limited wardrobe that Madam Senator kept downstate would go to charity, and the furniture and other remaining contents could be sold with the house. The family business office was taking care of those details.

Since her first senatorial election, over thirty years earlier, Evansville had been little more than an address to my mother – albeit, an important one that reinforced an image she relished. Beth Davenport was perceived as a hard-working and sometimes "feisty gal" who never stopped fighting for the local folks who first put her into the House of Representatives. But since 1987, she had spent only random days in Evansville. Soon after her first election to the upper chamber of Congress, my parents purchased their condo in Indianapolis and my mother quietly transitioned her political operation.

As people inquired, she and her staff offered suitable explanations about where Senator Davenport needed to spend her time. As the state's capital and largest city, Indianapolis afforded her better access to government resources, support agencies, fund-raising, and airline schedules. But I now perceived an added benefit. Indianapolis placed 175 miles between my parents and my grandfather.

I wasn't even six when my father died, so my memories of him in many situations were distant and sketchy. I did remember him being more quiet than usual whenever my grandfather was present. Or often, he simply disappeared from the room. My mother put noticeably more effort into her interactions with Senior, but I could tell there was an unspoken awkwardness.

It was ironic that so many Washington colleagues had felt obliged to travel to Evansville to pay final respects to my mother, when she traveled there so infrequently herself. By selecting the city which first elected her to Congress as a final resting place, she stayed true to that local girl image until the very end. Besides, a cemetery in Evansville was as good a spot as any for interring her body. My mother's deeper roots had been incidental at best.

Unlike most politicians out on the stump, Beth Davenport never felt a need to dust off convenient stories about her parents, siblings, original hometown, or anything else connected to her youth. She wouldn't even make mention of her childhood in casual conversations. As far as anyone knew, my mother's life began when she met my father as an undergrad at Oberlin College.

I was aware she'd been raised in Findlay, Ohio. Her father worked on the maintenance crew at the central facilities of Marathon Oil, where her mother was a switchboard operator – that is, until her older brother fell asleep one evening with a lit cigarette. My mother had been a teenager when the house went up in flames, but she was spending her annual month during the summer with her grandparents in Troy, Ohio. She went by Lizzie back then, and after losing everyone in her immediate family, Lizzie had no choice but to move in with those same grandparents and finish her last year of high school in Troy.

Her parents had left her no savings. The insurance policy on her dad's life barely covered the cost of the burials. Whatever worldly possessions they owned were destroyed by the fire. Her grandparents were eking out a living, so Lizzie was forced to work multiple odd-hour jobs. With no close friends in her new town, Lizzie devoted most of her free time to schoolwork and earned a full scholarship to Oberlin College.

That's about all she'd ever told me about her childhood. Her grandparents in Troy died long before I was born. I'd never met a single relative from my mom's side of the family.

On my own, I'd tried repeatedly to dig up additional details about my mother's early years. Myriad internet searches proved fruitless. Journalists never delved into Beth Davenport's more distant past – not wanting to be vilified for prying beneath the scar tissue. The Senator not once had exploited or dwelled on the horrific tragedy that struck her family. Nor had she manipulated misfortune to gain political advantage. Thus, it was tacitly understood. The childhood of Senator Davenport was off-limits. I sometimes wondered if her stoicism on such matters merely was just another piece to her well-crafted public persona.

Upon returning to Indianapolis, I planned on splitting time between her downtown condo and my own apartment twelve miles to the north. Stringing together remnants of my mother's life was bound to be arduous. But after thirty-five years in the dark, I could be patient.

The news of her death had been a devastating blow. In the ten days since, I'd mourned her passing in my own way, and surely would mourn her again at various points in the future. But for now, I was feeling a rush of energy. A curtain finally had been lifted. I was eager to learn things that would make my mom a more complete person, instead of the cardboard cut-out she propped up in front of voters.

Specific details that might have helped me understand my mother's inner thoughts always had seemed just out of reach. It wasn't that she imposed categorical restrictions on what we could or couldn't discuss. No, her boundaries were drawn by guardedness. Open, rambling conversations never were part of our shared existence. I felt like I'd known more about Aleena, the woman who lived with us for many years and looked out for me while my mother shuttled between Indianapolis, Washington, and anywhere else she could stand before a crowd or a camera.

The private study adjoining her bedroom really hadn't changed much since my last summer break in college, which was the last time I'd lived with my mom in the condo. She hadn't even installed a personal computer during the intervening years. Madam Senator intentionally had remained as "old school" as possible – assigning all cyber duties to members of her staff. She did use a laptop for work-related emails, but nothing else. It was a decision she never regretted as she watched more and more public figures wreak havoc upon themselves through their digital impulses and miscues.

Added photographs had been hung in the study – shots of her shaking hands with two more presidents, and side-by-sides with a few of her more recent colleagues. The lone picture of me was still an action shot from one of my high school basketball games. New awards she'd received had been inserted into the array she frequently rotated within the floor-to-ceiling shelves covering one entire wall. The furniture and its arrangement were unchanged – each piece frozen in time. Any congressperson since the dawn of the Colonies would have felt much at home amidst her expensive mahogany.

The room was part of an elaborate master bedroom suite I'd never dared to enter unless my mother was present. Even now, I felt like I was trespassing as I took the seat behind her desk. Her leather desk chair was a gift from Washington staff members on her seventieth birthday. The very next day, the chair had been shipped from the Dirksen Senate Office Building to her Indianapolis address – where no staff person was likely to see the brass plate was removed. The inscription on said plate commemorated the advent of her eighth decade among the living. Age was a sensitive subject with my mother.

As I set out upon my grand exploration, the first surprise came quickly – the moment I opened the top drawer to her desk. Next to a tray that neatly arranged her pens and pencils was a small hand-painted ceramic dish filled with paperclips. I had made the piece in second grade art class and given it to my mom as a Christmas present. For several years, the misshapen glob of clay sat atop her desk, tucked behind the phone, until one day I noticed it was gone. I'd always assumed Mom threw it away.

Built into either side of her desk were file drawers. Inside, the contents were efficiently arrayed. Clean manila folders, standing upright in alphabetical order. Their labels typed neatly in all-caps. Precisely the way my mother liked things.

ACCESS CODES. ACCOUNTANT. AIRLINE CLUBS. ANTIQUE DEALERS. AUTOMOBILE RECEIPTS. It came as no surprise that my mother's personal affairs were organized into nameless, faceless categories. CABLE TV. CATERERS. CELLPHONES. CHARITABLE GIVING. CLUB MEMBERSHIPS. COMPUTER TECHS. CREDIT CARDS. Each file economically thin.

I found nothing out of the ordinary as I progressed through the alphabet. That was, until I reached the M's. MAGAZINE SUBSCRIPTIONS. MAINTENANCE AGREEMENTS. MEDICAL BILLS. MONROE.

MONROE. Finally, a file that smacked of humanity. The lone item inside the folder was a large cream-colored envelope sealed with cellophane tape. It looked old. Monroe had been my mother's maiden name. Perhaps the envelope contained a copy of her birth certificate. Whatever the contents, my mother clearly hadn't opened the envelope in quite some time. The tape on the flap practically disintegrated as I ran my hand over the edge.

I tilted the envelope and shook lightly. The corner of an old black-and-white photograph peeked out. Pulling the photo further into view with my fingertips, I discovered two more pictures stuck to its back. I carefully pried them apart and laid all three across the desk pad. That's when it registered that my mother again had lied to me.

She had told me every picture from her youth was destroyed when the family's house burned down. But there she was as a young girl. The large, round eyes. The high cheekbones, the deep dimple on the right side of her face, and the shallower one on the left.

In the top photo, she was standing on the front porch of a small frame house that badly needed paint. She looked to be in her pre-teens – thirteen, at most. Next to her was a slightly older boy. A man and woman stood behind them. Nothing was written on the reverse side, but these people had to have been her family.

The second photo was a close-up of the same adult couple whom I presumed to be her parents – ergo, my grandparents. This picture looked to have been taken the same day, on the same porch, in the same clothing.

The third photograph was taken a few years later at a different location. My mom was maybe fifteen or sixteen, and she was sitting atop a picnic table with another girl. Both were laughing and mug-ging for the camera.

Studying the pictures spread across the desk, I noticed two things. First, the only trace of joy exhibited was in the shot featuring the two young girls. The faces in the other two photographs were completely devoid of emotion – as though strangers had been pulled randomly from a crowd and posed next to one another.

The second observation made me rather uncomfortable. Over the years, Beth Davenport often was described in the media as at-tractive – especially back in the early phases of her political career, when referencing a woman's physical appearance had been consid-ered fair game. Her looks, no doubt, heightened her appeal among many male voters. For me, however, this woman was my mother. I hadn't paid much notice.

But I saw something in that picture taken at the picnic table. Any man would have. Even in an old black-and-white photograph, my mother exuded a sensual energy, a vibrancy that only could be described as raw beauty. Her hair was long – probably light brown in color. There was an obvious shapeliness beneath her t-shirt and cut-off jeans. No son wanted to verbalize what I was thinking. The teenaged girl in the photo was not only "hot" … she was sexy as hell. I quickly banished those thoughts to a remote recess of my brain – hoping never to stumble upon them again.

I took a closer look at my presumed grandparents and uncle, who had died a quarter of a century before I was born. For some reason, my mother had not wanted me to know what they looked like. Appearance-wise, I saw how much I resembled this pictured family.

When I finally stopped growing, I'd topped out at six-foot-four. In the front porch photo, the father and brother towered above the two females – noticeably taller than the men on the Davenport limb of the family tree, since both Senior and my father would have been categorized as average in stature. I didn't remember my mother ever mentioning how my height was passed down from her side of the family. Also, like my mother, I had lighter hair and skin color than the Davenports – traits that appeared to be common among the Monroes.

Almost instinctively, I ran the fingers of my right hand over the faces in the porch photo. Perhaps I was seeking some sort of spiritual connection. Either way, the realization struck me. I, and I alone, comprised the sole surviving generation of two disparate families. Two disparate families with secrets my mother purposely had kept from me.

Chapter 7

To me, love always had seemed more a concept than a feeling. But, of course, cynicism was a prerequisite to becoming a tenured college professor. Thanks to all the published pieces foisted upon academicians by fellow social scientists, I possessed a reasonable grasp of love's ethereal nature with its various mutated forms. Mother-son relationships were especially thorny, and I was learning they didn't get any easier post-mortem.

During my first week back in the classroom, I couldn't stop thinking about my mother as I made the long drive to and from Crawfordsville. Such single-mindedness probably wasn't unusual for a son who recently lost a parent. But I wasn't ruminating over the unexpected tragedy of her death. Nor was I contemplating the quality or substance of her life. Instead, I couldn't get the three old photographs out of my mind.

After discovering them, I rummaged through the rest of her condo for several days. But my search produced nothing else of consequence – leaving me with the same haunting question. Why would she have told me that no such pictures existed? Okay, maybe my mother loathed her family, or even her childhood in total. Maybe she'd wanted to bury all the wreckage from her past. Yet she'd retained those photos and kept them to herself. On some level, she must have wanted to remember what those people represented to her. She had carried some emotional connection to the stony faces on that porch and the girl sitting next to her at a picnic table.

Even if she despised her parents and brother, wouldn't a normal mother have felt obliged to show her own son what his grandparents had looked like? But, of course, Senator Beth Davenport was wired differently than other women.

In the broadest sense, I loved my mother while I was growing up. I supposed I still did. Over the entirety of my childhood, not once was I mistreated or taken lightly. During each successive stage of my upbringing, she'd made certain every opportunity was afforded and every physical need met.

In return, I was expected to be that "dutiful son." The dutiful young son who shook hands with adults and looked them squarely in the eyes – speaking clearly and referring to them as "Sir" and "Ma'am." The dutiful young son who stood by his mother's side at public events – straight posture, smiling pleasantly.

The hugging and kissing phase with my mother ended around age seven or eight. From then on, outward emotions remained in check. Lightheartedness and silliness were reserved for friends on the playground. At home, our shared demeanor was respectful. Forever respectful, regardless of the situation. We took an interest in each other's activities and accomplishments. Criticisms rarely were exchanged. I was free to raise any subject whenever we were alone – just as she was free to engage or not engage in pursuant discussions.

Over the years, I had studied parenting and the nurturing bonds that formed out of maternal instincts. With my mother, those inclinations barely were evident. The feelings between us were more platonic. Whatever impulses propelled most females into embracing motherhood, Beth Davenport didn't possess them.

When the next weekend rolled around, I was back in the condo. But now, I was planning to cut off my search for answers. Thus far, all I'd done was uncover lies my mother had told me and they were weighing heavily, so I simply wanted to pack up her possessions and put the pricey downtown residence on the market. I needed to move on with my life and not be bogged down by deficiencies in a relationship that no longer couldn't be rectified.

Then, on Friday evening, everything changed. I had been working in my mom's study, boxing and labeling more of her favorite mementos. I planned on sending them to long-time staff members, loyal campaign workers, and significant donors. I'd lost track of the time when my phone rang. It was Shelly – a spirited young shortstop I'd met in a co-ed softball league during the summer. She was seated in the sports bar where we had agreed to watch a pre-season Pacers game. The first quarter was almost over.

My hands, arms, and blue jeans were streaked with markings from a felt-tip pen. I made a mad dash into the master bathroom for a quick clean-up. Hurrying out, I knocked over an antique pewter lamp on the nightstand adjacent to my mother's bed. Lifting it back into place, I heard a rattling noise from inside the base. The fall to the floor must have broken something. I instantly was overcome by a feeling of dread, but then remembered my mother wasn't likely to notice.

Hoping to make a fast repair, I grabbed the boxcutter from my nearby work pile. I slid the blade beneath the felt-covered cardboard on the bottom of the lamp, anticipating this square piece would be stubbornly affixed. Instead, it fell away with minimal effort. Clearly, this wasn't the first time the bottom had been removed. Peering inside, I saw what had been rattling around. A key ... a brass key.

As soon as I removed it, I saw one side was blank. On the reverse, two digits were engraved in the center. The number "34."

For several moments, I stood there pondering what reasons my mother might have had for hiding a key. Then a pulsebeat of light drew my attention to the clock sitting next to where the lamp belonged. The digital display had advanced another minute, which brought my thoughts back to Shelly and the nimbleness with which she fielded groundballs. Key #34 could wait.

Chapter 8

The next morning, the key was there on the nightstand alongside the up-righted lamp. With my mother's kitchen restored to immaculate order, I could give it my full attention. Earlier, I'd fried eggs, hash-browns, and sausage for two. Earlier still, I had checked-off an item from a mental bucket list that must have resided somewhere in my subconscious. For the first time, I had dared to bring a female into the condo. Alone. And Shelly proved to be every bit as interesting as I imagined. We spent the night in the very bedroom, as well as the very bed, where I frequently fantasized about such possibilities as a teenager.

But now I needed to focus on the mysterious key. It looked generic enough to open most anything. A safe deposit box? A post office box? Maybe a special room reserved for senators at some fancy private club? If I let my mind go wild, I probably could have come up with thousands of places where a corresponding lock might be found. A file cabinet in a Washington basement where photos of actual alien landings were concealed from the public?

Suddenly, another possibility dawned on me. What if my mother had other hiding places? Other secret items?

I quickly moved from room to room, gently shaking the remainder of her expensive lamps. For the next hour, I crawled around on my hands and knees – reaching under beds, peering under sofas and chairs. I flipped cushions and hoisted up mattresses. I climbed on tables to peek inside chandeliers. I looked behind pictures and mirrors. I pulled out drawers to see if anything was taped beneath them. I checked for loose edges to carpeting. I ran my fingers over the tops of door frames. I tried every trick I'd learned in prime time. But there was nothing. My attention shifted back to key #34.

The logical thing for me to do was to contact members of my mother's staff. Her senatorial offices in DC and Indianapolis were to remain intact until Indiana's governor named a successor who would serve until the next scheduled election. Maybe someone from her team might know something about a key. Or better yet, maybe they'd offer to root around. After all, they always managed to dig up answers for Madam Senator. But those offices were closed for the weekend, so my calls would have to wait until Monday. In the meantime, I would pick up where I'd left off the previous evening – boxing and labeling.

No matter how hard I tried busying myself with menial tasks, my mind kept drifting back to the curious brass key on the nightstand. I'd vacated her premises fourteen years earlier and my mother had lived alone ever since. From whom would she need to hide a key? Her cleaning lady? Certainly not houseguests. She never had any. What's more, she had hidden the damned thing right next to her bed so that even a late-night interloper couldn't have stumbled upon it without her knowledge.

Eventually, my curiosity prevailed. I called one of my drinking associates and informed him that the streets of Indianapolis were to remain a great deal safer on that particular Saturday evening. I was staying in. I poured myself a tall glass of sparkling water, of all things, and made my way to the study.

The first time I'd gone through my mother's files, the week before, I had given the contents a cursory glance. This time would be different. I was a man on a mission – a trained academic pit bull in search of relevant facts. Or maybe I was just stubborn. Either way, if there was anything in my mother's files that might offer the slightest hint about a key, I was hellbent on finding it.

Most normal human beings would have started from the front of the alphabet. On impulse, I elected to work backward. As often the case, my iconoclastic tendencies led me astray. If I had started with the A's, I could have saved myself many hours of tedium.

I sifted through each scrap of paper inside each successive folder, looking for a clue. Correspondence. Service contracts, warranties, and sales literature. Random business cards. Purchase receipts. I was sidetracked by all sorts of peculiar tangents but didn't find anything that might connect to a key. Until I worked my way back to the letter "C." CREDIT CARDS. That's where I noticed the recurring charge from Riley Enterprises. The Google gods took over from there and landed me at Riley-s-On-Raymond.

Chapter 9

The Riley's website promised round-the-clock access, so key in hand, I'd practically sprinted out of the condo. I made it to the converted warehouse at just past 10:30 on Sunday night. That's when I first met Eric, the lone person on duty. He seemed grateful for human contact.

The front entrance was locked, but as soon as I held key #34 up to the glass, he smiled and began working his way down a series of deadbolts. *Eureka, I'd struck gold.*

"Any chance I can get into my storage unit?" I asked as the door swung open.

The nametag alleged that Eric Meyerhoff was a security guard, but the pudgy-face in the uniform couldn't have been more than twenty-two or twenty-three. His shirttail was mostly hanging out and his untied shoelaces were dragging behind him. I figured I'd caught him napping, but then I noticed his cheeks. They puffed out and his jaws were working double-time on whatever he had inhaled from the fast-food bag jammed into his hip pocket. After a last hurried swallow, he responded, "Sure, that's why I'm here. For valued clients, Riley's-on-Raymond is never closed. I just need to see an ID, so we can get you signed in." If nothing else, the unkept Mr. Meyerhoff had mastered the section on helpful enthusiasm in his training manual.

Once I handed him my driver's license, the amiable guard logged onto a computer station at the front desk. A few moments later, he began awkwardly shuffling the mouse. "Uh, Mr. Davenport, I'm sorry … but only one person is authorized to access unit-34. And since you're holding the key and share her last name, I'm guessing you must be related to that person – Elizabeth Davenport."

Her name didn't seem to hold any meaning to Eric Meyerhoff, which was rare for a person of voting age in the Hoosier State. I replied politely, "She was my mother. She recently passed away and I'm trying to wrap up her affairs, so I was hoping to inventory what she kept here in storage."

Hearing of her death added to Meyerhoff's uneasiness with playing the bad guy. "I'm sorry for your loss … and really, I wish I could help … but there's nothing I can do … honest. You'll have to speak to one of our senior managers during normal business hours. Is that okay?" With the question, his face went full puppy dog on me.

I quickly let him off the hook. "Completely understood … I'll take care of it tomorrow morning." He looked relieved, so I offered him a chance to be more accommodating. "Might you be able to tell me when my mom started renting her storage unit? I'm just curious."

Eric Meyerhoff paused as though trying to remember the relevant passage from his Riley's-On-Raymond employee bible. Finally, he shrugged, "Sure … why not?" He hurriedly scrolled to another page on the computer screen. "It says here your mother was assigned unit-34 shortly after we first opened … which was 1992."

I thanked him and exited. The attorneys took over and by Tuesday afternoon, Riley Enterprises had received a copy of my mother's death certificate and a letter transferring rightful ownership to yours truly. The delay gave me two more days to ponder what had been stashed away inside a storage unit for more than a quarter of a century. I was convinced the secrecy surrounding the key and locker meant I finally would find some of the answers my mother had been unwilling to share.

As soon as I entered the lobby for the second time, a neatly dressed woman at the front desk stood and extended her hand. "Good afternoon, Mr. Davenport … and let me be the first to offer you an official welcome as a treasured client of Riley's-On-Raymond. We deeply regret our relationship is starting under such tragic circumstances. Your mother truly was an inspiration to everyone at Riley Enterprises."

I was accustomed to overdone greetings. They'd become part of everyday life as Senator Beth Davenport's son. If anything, I felt sorry for this well-meaning receptionist who likely was doing exactly what some stiff suit at headquarters instructed. I often wished I could wear a sign that let people off the hook. *No hyperbole required.*

"Thank you for your kind words. My mother would have appreciated them." I hesitated for the obligatory moment these exchanges demanded, then moved on. "How can I find unit-34?"

"You don't have to find your unit, Mr. Davenport. Our policy at Riley's-On-Raymond specifies we accompany …" That's when she'd launched into her portion of the requisite spiel. As she was wrapping up, Eric Meyerhoff emerged on cue from a side door, tucking his shirt into the back of his pants and flashing a sheepish smile.

Ten minutes later, it was just me and door #34. I gripped the knob and slowly pushed inward. Nothing came into my immediate view – just plain gray walls and a pristine cement floor. Not until the door was completely open, did I see the wooden table, about three-feet in height. Resting on top was the brown leather suitcase, laying on its side. I entered the unit and closed the door behind me. The suitcase showed few signs of use, but the straps, buckles, and exterior stitching suggested a bygone era. It looked to be standard size – maybe twenty-four inches from front-to-back, thirty-six from side-to-side, and fifteen inches in thickness.

I placed a hand on either end and lifted it just enough to gauge the weight. Whoa. Probably a hundred pounds or more.

I suddenly felt like I was living inside some sappy old movie. I could almost hear the organ music building to a crescendo. I took a deep breath, undid the leather guards protecting the tarnished hardware, pushed open two rows of metal buckles with my thumbs, and carefully raised the lid.

I had readied myself for secret government documents. Possibly fake passports. Of maybe even bones and a murder weapon. Instead, all I could do was stare at the oddity before me.

A sea of white stared back. As my eyes adjusted, I noticed narrow gaps. It was a grid of white rectangles – vertically aligned in columns and rows that spanned the entirety of the suitcase in either direction. Eventually, my brain began processing. The white rectangles looked to be envelopes – and each envelope looked to be filled. I was seeing only the top layer of what appeared to be stacks of them. Three deep and ten across. Thirty stacks in total.

Someone, presumably my mother, had arranged the envelopes with fastidious care. All the columns and rows were separated by maybe a quarter-of-an-inch of space. The suitcase couldn't have been moved since it last was closed because, otherwise, the stacks would have shifted.

The orderliness was so imposing that I was hesitant to touch the envelopes. But after several moments, I reached inside and picked one up. It was bulkier than anticipated. For some inexplicable reason, I began moving in slow-motion, rotating the envelope in my hand and gingerly examining both sides. The flap was sealed. There were no exterior markings.

I was postponing the inevitable, as though this lone remaining act would transport me across some threshold of no return. I noticed one end of the envelope's flap was loosened with age. I swallowed hard and gently slid my forefinger under the remainder of the flap. There could be no turning back now, I slipped my hand inside the envelope and withdrew the contents.

"Holy shit!"The words echoed inside the confined concrete space.

My heart began racing and my eyes felt like they might pop out of their sockets. I was holding a packet of money with a hundred-dollar bill on top. A band of heavy paper was wrapped securely around the bundle and an amount was printed boldly in the center. "$10,000." Grasping one end of the tight bundle, I slowly thumbed through the bills from the other end. All were of the same denomination. I wasn't a math genius, but if the sum on the wrapper was to be believed, the packet contained a hundred of these hundred-dollar bills. I'd never held that much actual cash at one time.

I looked back inside the open suitcase. The rest of the envelopes couldn't possibly contain similar contents. There had to be hundreds of them stacked side-by-side. Beads of sweat started forming on my forehead, hands, and God-knew where else. I stood motionless, afraid to pluck another envelope from its resting place.

I forced myself to reach down and remove several more from one of the orderly piles. I took several steps away from the suitcase and tentatively opened a second envelope. The passing years had weakened the seal and a second bundle of cash soon was revealed. The amount imprinted on its paper band was the same. "$10,000."

I opened another, followed by three more. The bundle of currency inside each was identical. I stepped closer to the suitcase again. I'd barely made a dent into the stacks of envelopes, and already the total had reached $50,000.

What the hell had I uncovered? Lying to me about family issues was one thing. But hoarding cash in a secret storage locker? Had Senator Beth Davenport been just another dirty politician? First it was dismay, then dread. The feelings moved in like thunder clouds.

But I was getting ahead of myself. I needed to gain control of my emotions and put a stop to the doomsday scenarios playing out in my head. I would concentrate on what was tangible, the contents of the suitcase. For the moment at least, I couldn't fixate on the whys or the hows.

I braced myself for the weight of the open suitcase and carefully lowered it onto the floor next to the table. I took an adjacent seat on concrete and began my arduous count. One by one, I carefully opened the envelopes' sealed flaps and removed the tightly wrapped parcels. A green mountain took shape in front of me. I was living some bizarre nightmare.

I noticed variations in the paper wraps that held the bundles together. The borders on all these narrow strips were yellow, but the shades of yellow often differed. The same was true for the thickness of the paper, as well as the dollar amounts printed in the center. On some, the label read "$10,000," while others read "Ten Thousand Dollars," or simply "Ten Thousand." The variations suggested the bundles might have originated from disparate sources, or that they had been collected over an extended period.

I randomly leafed through a few. It was hypnotic to watch "100" flash by in block numerals from the upper corners as Ben Franklin's smiling face glanced up from the center.

Further down in the suitcase, the packets of hundred-dollar bills in the envelopes no longer were wrapped by paper straps. They were held together with thick rubber bands.

Nearing the bottom, the envelopes suddenly appeared thinner. I figured they might hold lesser amounts of cash, but I was mistaken. Inside were thousand-dollar bills – ten to an envelope. It was a denomination I'd never known existed. Who would have guessed that the featured president on a thousand-dollar bill was a stone-faced Grover Cleveland?

Once I removed the final envelope from the suitcase, the total in my head had soared so high I was doubting myself. It didn't seem possible. A recount was necessary, so I hurriedly separated the packets into smaller piles of ten each, spacing them around the empty storage locker. When I was done organizing, there were three leftovers. I held those in my hand and began slowly pacing the small enclosure to count the piles. To my amazement, I'd been correct.

Fifty-four mounds of ten, plus three orphans still in my hand. In all, 543. Five-hundred-and-forty-three bundles, each comprised of $10,000 in legal tender. I was standing in the middle of $5,430,000. I tried to let the staggering amount sink in. I think I even blanked out for a while, because when I finally looked at my watch, over an hour had passed since my arrival.

Until I came up with a plan, I had no intention of walking out of a secured storage unit carrying five-and-a-half million dollars in spendable currency. I began hurriedly tossing the exposed bundles of cash back into the suitcase, but then experienced pangs of impropriety – as though I might be violating some sacred protocol practiced my mother, the late and maybe-not-so-great Senator Beth Davenport. I emptied the suitcase and started over, this time sliding the packets back into envelopes and stacking them into thirty neat columns as best I could.

My head was spinning. My mother had earned plenty of money. She'd possessed the means to sustain an enviable standard of living for a dozen lifetimes. Plus, when or if Senator Elizabeth Davenport might have retired from politics, she could have collected hundreds of thousands a year in speaking fees and honorariums – on top of a generous government pension. She would have had no reason to put aside money for a rainy day. Financially speaking, her life had been pure sunshine.

The interior to her storage locker looked almost new, with only a few minor scuff marks in the vicinity of the suitcase. Its physical condition suggested my mother had rented the unit for the sole purpose of securing one item – which meant she had been hiding substantial sums of cash in a suitcase for over twenty-five years.

No answers. Just more and more questions. But this time the implications weren't just odd or hurtful. They were scandalous.

Chapter 10

What would moving on with the rest of my life actually look like? What did that whole concept even mean? For three weeks I'd been debating whether the time had arrived. My mother's enormous presence was gone. So obviously, I needed to turn the page. Start fresh. Chart a new course. Explore new horizons … and all those other bullshit clichés people had been tossing my way for the last twenty years. Everyone except my mother. She had been completely content with her son's complacency. His mediocrity. Living an unremarkable life, well inside the guardrails, was what a politician's son was supposed to do.

"Troy, I'm counting on you to respect the law and stay out of trouble. We live under the public's microscope … you don't want to draw negative attention to yourself or our family." Her familiar words had started as a whisper as soon as I exited Riley's-On-Raymond, but soon they were screaming inside my head. Talk about bullshit.

I was heading home to my own apartment. I couldn't stomach the thought of being back in her condo. As I drove, I tried calming myself with slow, deep breaths. To no avail. I was reeling from the shock of finding millions of dollars in a suitcase. I was reeling from the hypocrisy.

If I truly wanted to abide by the law, I knew I should discretely contact the authorities. The FBI. Some committee of Congress. But the repercussions were obvious. Washington was a sieve, and this was the revered Senator Beth Davenport. Her public and private life would be dissected down to the smallest detail. Her towering reputation would topple like dominoes. Guilty until proven innocent in the eyes of a cynical public. And my life would become a living hell.

Maybe she deserved it. Maybe we both did. For thirty-five years, I'd been content to have it both ways – resenting her celebrity and influence, while playing them like show cards under a guise of indifference. But for the time being, I decided, the existence of this suitcase needed to remain a secret. Out of respect for my mother's legacy. Out of respect for my own sanity.

Five-and-a-half-million dollars didn't fall from the sky. Somewhere, there had been a money source. And from that source, a money trail. I was convinced I could find one or the other, and maybe both. At least that's how I felt when I reached my apartment later that evening.

By next morning, I wasn't so sure. Money source ... money trail? In what fantasy universe had I been envisioning my own capabilities? I barely could balance a checkbook. I just needed a foothold – some accessible fragment of information to give me hope that my mother hadn't lived her life as a total fraud.

During my spare hours over the next few days, I focused first on the currency itself – starting with the thousand-dollar bills. Those bills from the bottom of the suitcase had seemed more dated than the others. Their color and texture were different. After a little search time on the internet, I understood why.

The U.S. Mint had stopped printing thousand-dollar bills in 1945. Then in 1969, the Federal Reserve officially suspended their usage, which meant banks no longer could issue them. Any bills already in circulation were still to be treated as legal tender, but usage essentially ceased with collectors gobbling up the remainder. Based on a few articles I found, the ninety-one paper-clipped packets inside the suitcase were worth a great deal more than face value. Such a sizable quantity of thousand-dollar bills suggested my mother had begun amassing her cash long before she rented the storage unit in 1992.

This probability was confirmed by what I learned about the paper bands holding most of the bundles of hundred-dollar bills together. In banking jargon, these official-looking narrow sleeves were referred to as "currency straps." I figured they'd been around since the days of J.P. Morgan and Andrew Carnegie. But to my surprise, their standardized usage didn't start until the mid-1970's. The American Bankers Association designated yellow as the color for hundred-dollar bills, with a packet of one hundred becoming the accepted unit.

Logic therefore suggested that the envelopes filled with hundreds held together by rubber bands traced back to a period before the introduction of currency straps in the mid-70's, and after the suspension of thousand-dollar bills in 1969.

Next, I placed a call to Riley's-On-Raymond, hoping the cooperative Eric Meyerhoff might again be on duty. He was.

"Eric, I was wondering if you guys keep a log of when your clients visit their storage units."

"We sure do, Mr. Davenport ... a permanent record of every visit is maintained in our computer system." As usual, the young security guard was eager to help, "If you want to know when your mother was here last, I can look that up for you."

"Well, actually, I'm looking for a bit more than that, if you don't mind. I was hoping you could provide me with the dates of every visit she ever made to her unit. Do you think that's possible?"

"I don't see why not ... just hold on." Meyerhoff paused and I could hear him working a keyboard in the background. When he finally spoke, his voice was more hesitant. "Uh, Mr. Davenport, your mom came here a lot ... or at least she did for many years. You may want to give me your email address ... this list here is pretty long."

Ten minutes later, I was scanning through a file with all the dates and times of my mother's trips to her storage unit. In early 1992, she began signing-in to unit #34 on a regular basis – essentially once a month. But during the summer of 2008, after a hundred-and-ninety-seven visits, she stopped. Since then, she had not signed in a single time. If the company's records were accurate, my mother hadn't bothered to check on five-and-a-half million in cash for more than nine years.

I scrutinized the dates of her visits over those sixteen years between 1992 and 2008. From October of each year through March of the next, she logged-in like clockwork during the first week of every month. But during the spring and summer months, her visits occurred more randomly throughout the month. At first, those seasonal patterns baffled me, but then I remembered her travel schedule. Senate typically was in session from April through September, which meant my mother mostly stayed in Washington, fitting in trips to Indianapolis only when her calendar allowed.

The predictability of my mother's routine during autumn and winter, when Congress was out-of-session, suggested something took place at the beginning of each month that correlated with her trips to the hidden suitcase. Presumably, she was adding or withdrawing cash. But whatever interactions had prompted these monthly visits, they apparently came to an end during the summer of 2008.

Chapter 11

Had the late-great Senator Davenport been peddling influence during her years in Congress? What deals might she have struck to gain her powerful committee positions? What promises had she made for how she would assert them? Whatever she had done to collect bundles of cash, she had done it over an extended period. The protracted nature of this unknown arrangement was the next thread I hoped to grasp. If that thread was to lead anywhere, I had a pretty good hunch as to who might point me in the right direction.

Annabelle Jenkins had retired in 2015, when emphysema finally forced Byron into assisted living. The two of them recognized the looming probability of hospice, and he wanted to spend whatever time was left in his hometown of Logansport – an hour-and-a-half northeast of Indianapolis. Annabelle would have done practically anything for my mother, as she'd proven time and again for twenty-seven years. But three hours of commuting, on top of her already long hours in the office, would have left little time to spend with the man she loved.

My mother understood completely. In fact, after a few well-placed phone calls from Senator Davenport, Byron Jenkins gained immediate admittance into Logansport's most desirable healthcare facility.

The strong bond between these two women first formed in 1988. Annabelle had confided the details to me at her retirement party, when I asked her how she'd become such a trusted friend and confidant to my mother. In retrospect, I couldn't think of anyone besides Cal whom the Senator would have placed in that category.

Annabelle described how she was toiling away at her desk one morning when the phone rang. Oddly, the light indicated it was her line rather than her boss's. That boss went ballistic whenever he caught his office staff having personal conversations, so Annabelle's family and friends knew not to call during normal work hours.

"Mrs. Jenkins, this is Beth Davenport. Could I possibly interest you in joining me for lunch this afternoon?"

They met and later in the day, a messenger delivered Annabelle Jenkins the letter that formalized her job offer.

The previous night, my mother, who was then a first-term senator, had been sitting with a group of assembled deep pockets at a weeknight fund-raiser. The affair spiraled into its "scotch and cigar" phase. Kirk Bellingham, a congressman from the Indianapolis area, and a man whom my mother inwardly detested, also was seated at the table.

My mother was the sole female among those gathered and the conversation eventually landed on women in the workplace – which often happened late in the evening at such events. But these types of discussions rarely dealt with women's rights or gender equality. Far from it.

A boisterous local business owner commented, "We just hired ourselves a new administrative assistant ... and she sure as hell better know the letters on her keyboard by heart. Because there's no way she's ever gonna see em' beneath those two championship trophies she's totin' around underneath her blouse."

When the obligatory laughter subsided, Congressman Bellingham kicked in, "I don't know about the rest of you, but this whole title thing among all these gals is getting to be downright foolish. Who took it upon themselves to decree that a secretary needs to be called an administrative assistant? You take my girl, Annabelle. She's gonna stay a secretary for as long as the people in my district see fit to elect me ... and besides, I'm sure a lot of my constituents wouldn't take to the notion of a person with her skin color being called an administrative anything."

My mother noticed how this time the obligatory laughter was no less restrained. During lunch the next day, she shared the prior evening's conversation with Annabelle. A mutual trust formed immediately. Close friendship soon followed.

This story was one of my favorites about my mother – though I never got around to telling her. Annabelle swore me to secrecy. To think, a freshman senator took it upon herself to see that a hardworking minority female was no longer subjected to the bigotry and chauvinism of an oily glad-hander like Kirk Bellingham. She'd shown the kind of mettle that made a son proud.

Annabelle Jenkins moved offices the next week, with a twenty percent bump in salary and the title of senior administrative assistant. Two years later, Annabelle was managing my mother's entire office staff in Indianapolis.

I'd seen Annabelle a few weeks earlier at the memorial service in Evansville, where she sat next to me. Growing up, she and Byron had been like family.

When I phoned about paying her a visit, Annabelle invited me to lunch on Saturday. I instantly recognized what that would mean. Byron's "fire-breathing chili." Byron had concocted his marque meal as a cook in the army. Early in their marriage, Annabelle helped her husband fine-tune the secret formula to perfection. Over the ensuing years, they together served up thousands of gallons. To family and friends. To homeless families in food shelters. To volunteers and donors at political rallies. No matter how many times I would

overeat and swear off ingesting another spoonful of Byron's specialty, a few days later the anticipation would begin anew. At noon on
Saturday, I arrived on the doorstep of Annabelle's familiar Cape Cod
in Logansport, armed with a pint of peach gelato – the prescribed
remedy for fire-breathing after-effects.

We hugged, as we always did, but the sustained embrace was
more than a warm welcome this time. When we parted, I could see
tears trailing down Annabelle's cheeks. "I can't believe she's really
gone. Your mother was so much larger than life. It doesn't seem
possible."

Clearly, my mother's most trusted confidante had been holding
back in Evansville, projecting the type of controlled emotion that
Senator Beth Davenport would have expected from the people closest to her. Now alone with me, she was free to display the genuine
sorrow she still carried.

For several days, I'd been thinking about the best way to approach Annabelle – contriving all sorts of shadowy explanations as
to why my mother might have kept millions of dollars stowed in a
suitcase. I wanted to be careful. I didn't dare say anything to dimin-
ish the admiration Annabelle held for her former mentor. At least
not yet.

My mother always refused to reveal Annabelle Jenkin's exact age
to me, though once she'd suggested Annabelle was about ten years
her junior. It seemed unimaginable. This special soul couldn't possibly be approaching seventy. The firmness and smoothness of her
dark skin suggested an age twenty years younger. Her hair may have
been the singular giveaway. Annabelle had worn the exact same style
since she was a teenager, a loosely kept Afro from a bygone era –
with a few strands of silver and white spoking out at random in more
recent years.

Tall and graceful, Annabelle was attractive by most anyone's definition. When she smiled, however, Annabelle Jenkins transformed

into a woman of extraordinary beauty. Her face gleamed, her eyes glittered, and the world instantly seemed a better place. The radiance in her countenance was matched only by the joy and optimism in her voice – the deep tone, the melodious cadence. So soothing were the words from her mouth, that even the most casual of conversations felt like the absolution of sin. If eternal peace were to be given a voice, I was sure it would sound like Annabelle Jenkins.

Once we were seated at the small island in her kitchen, the casual interrogation began. Unexpectedly, it was Annabelle who took the lead. "What's troubling you, Troy?"

The question caught me off guard. "Why would you ask?"

She chuckled. "Don't get me wrong ... I'm always glad to have you stop by for a visit. But when was the last time you called two days in advance ... instead of just texting me on the spur of the moment? You've got something on your mind ... and I'm guessing it has something to do with your mom."

That was the other thing about Annabelle Jenkins. She had this eerie sixth sense about human behavior – a characteristic which made her even more indispensable to a busy senator with persons coming at her from every corner at all hours of the day.

I was slow to respond, choosing my words judiciously. "You're right ... just like you always are when the subject pertains to Madame Senator. Since her death, I've been giving a great deal of thought to her incredible career ... and I now realize I know little about the people or organizations who most influenced my mother. Obviously, I know which issues were important to her ... most of Indiana's voting populous could tick those off. I recognize who her official inside advisers were ... as well as the unofficial ones like you. But who were those outside voices that could sway her thinking ... especially the ones from twenty and twenty-five years ago ... or even further back ... when she'd been an up-and-coming senator?"

After finally posing the question, I recognized how I'd rambled too long. If Annabelle wasn't already suspicious, she would be now. Snooping was not going to come naturally.

"What has prompted this sudden new interest, Troy?"

In preparation, I had muddled together a cover story. "I've been invited by a number of groups to speak about my mother ... and I imagine other requests will follow. I don't intend to accept many of the invitations, but I may agree to a few ... you know, with audiences that would have been important to her."

My response was rooted in truth, as I indeed had received invitations to speak about my mother. I also knew the part about choosing audiences important to my mother would sit well with Annabelle. She didn't need to know that I thus far had turned them all down.

Seeing her smile, I continued, "I just want to be certain I have answers for questions I'm apt to face ... so I don't wind up standing in front of a crowd looking like I didn't know my own mother very well. I have a hunch people are going to be curious about which folks carried the most influence with the revered Senator Davenport."

I forced myself to stop, trying to avoid going overboard again. I watched for Annabelle's reaction. Her smile was gone, and she was staring at me. I suppressed an urge to resume my blathering and after a few moments, she responded. "That makes sense ... and we definitely don't want to stand our young professor in front of a hungry crowd without answers."

This time Annabelle Jenkins flashed one of her signature smiles and, for me, all seemed right with the universe. She was buying my story.

But I soon learned that even with her closest staff member, my mother had been reticent to share many details about her personal and professional relationships. For the next ninety minutes, Annabelle passed along vagaries related to individuals and organizations to which Senator Beth Davenport had demonstrated some degree of loyalty or gratitude, as well as persons and groups who managed to alienate her. Repeatedly however, Annabelle reminded me that all she was offering were her own observations. "The Senator wasn't one to talk much about folks she trusted ... or the ones she didn't."

I'd pulled a stack of index cards from a jacket pocket and was jotting down the names as Annabelle ticked through them. To cover my tracks, I also probed her on other subjects that an alleged audience might raise. Our wide-ranging conversation took a series of unexpected turns. She described various acts of kindness my mother had carried out over the years – none of which I'd known about.

When Annabelle Jenkins eventually saw me to the door, my emotions were mixed. This woman was like an aunt. Spending a few hours with her always had been a treat – chili or no chili – and this Saturday afternoon was no exception. Still, I felt uneasy about the duplicitous manner by which I'd exploited our special relationship. But then, without warning, she alleviated my guilt.

As I was stepping off the front porch, I leaned forward to give Annabelle a peck on the cheek. In anticipation, she reached up and gently pulled my head close to her face. In a teasingly soft tone, she whispered into my ear, "Troy, whatever it is you're up to ... I'm sure I could be a lot more helpful if you'd just tell me what you really want to know."

Chapter 12

By spring, I was to become one of the wealthiest persons under the age of forty in the entire state – at least according to Cal Stratton, who was a walking encyclopedia on matters pertaining to money. If not for my grandfather's affinity for giving away buildings with his name emblazoned across them, this pending inheritance would have been even more astronomical.

Perhaps the late Senior Davenport always had harbored a penchant for seeing his name over doorways, but he waited six-and-a-half decades to act upon this desire. In celebration of his own sixty-fifth birthday, he staged a media event to present the University of Evansville a check for fifty-million-dollars. Six months later, he was front and center again at a groundbreaking ceremony for the state-of-the-art recreational center that just happened to be called Davenport Hall.

Then, after Davenport Industries went public in 1984, he donated eighty million to Eastern Kentucky University – presumably the college a much younger Joe Davenport would have attended if he hadn't gone to work in the coalmines right out of high school. Soon thereafter, that campus's version of Davenport Hall was under construction. This building eventually housed the School of Geology and upon completion, Senior received an honorary degree in earth science.

More Davenport Halls followed in other locations. Each new

edifice came wrapped in publicity. Each would carry my grandfather's name into posterity. The media assigned him the convenient designation of philanthropist – a label he enjoyed immensely.

The prospect of my imminent wealth produced an odd prism through which I struggled to figure out how I might want to alter my regular routine. I don't mean to suggest my life was perfect. Not by a long shot. But overall, I was reasonably content – especially with Vicki in my rear-view mirror.

To succeed as a professor, outward indifference was a tacitly understood requirement. I routinely flaunted my half-hearted attitude about careers – mine or anyone else's. Soon I would have the option of not working in any capacity whatsoever. Oh, the ironies of human industry. I was being forced to confront my truth and accept that I truly enjoyed the classroom. If I were to quit, I would miss the imprecision of sociology and my frequent opportunities to stir things up with students. Shockingly, I even liked most of my fellow faculty members. But not all.

This degree of introspection was unprecedented. As my chosen field might suggest, I was fascinated by the science of behavior. Just not my own. I'd never been one to assign deeper meaning to anything I did or didn't do. Though I admired people who absorbed all of life's experiences with open arms, I really couldn't relate to them. The best I could do was carom from one moment to the next and occasionally find interests or persons that held my attention for brief slivers of time.

For me, growing up had been less a journey and more a guided tour – a tour approved and paid for by Senator Mom. Rarely had I seen much reason to exert myself. Amusement and novelty sufficed. I grew up believing the golden goose was a birthright. By the time I learned otherwise, it was too late. My happy-go-lucky approach to life had become patterned behavior.

In younger years, there had been one notable exception to this engrained indifference. Basketball. At an early age, I'd gotten hooked on the game. Like most kids, I sampled a wide array of junior sports. Aleena, my mother's housekeeper and all-purpose surrogate was charged with transporting me to endless gymnasiums and playing fields across Central Indiana. I turned out to be reasonably coordinated and probably could have made several teams at Park Tudor High School – an exclusive private institution on the northside of Indianapolis. Park Tudor was where a senator's kid could unobtrusively weather his secondary school years and rub elbows with the daughters and sons of the city's elite.

Despite urgings from the school's other coaches, I elected to play only basketball. I was tall and liked battling for rebounds. I earned a reputation for playing tight defense and was relatively quick at driving the lane. Plus, I happened to live in a state that was rabid about its basketball. And most importantly, I loved playing the game. For me, fun always trumped hard work. Ergo, I elected to make my mark on the hardwood.

Quite fortuitously, basketball wound up giving me the one thing I'd always wanted. My own identity. My own identity among the newspaper reporters who covered the local high school sports scene. My own identity among teammates and guys I hung around with. My own identity among girls who attended Park Tudor – and most notably, the ones I dated, used to date, or planned to date. I had wanted to live inside this ecosphere forever because within this protective bubble I was Troy Davenport, the basketball player. Not Troy Davenport, the senator's son. Not Troy Davenport, the grandson of Senior Davenport and member of the powerful Davenport family. I was just Troy Davenport, the basketball player.

Regrettably, this bubble burst during March of my senior year, just a few weeks after the high school basketball tournaments ended. I was hoping to continue carving out a niche for myself at the Division III level, and my decision on where to enroll in college was down to three small schools that had shown interest in my abilities. During spring break, most of my classmates headed south to island beaches. I felt the week could be better spent doing a final tour of the three campuses and once more meeting with the respective coaching staffs. To my delight, the red carpet was rolled out for me at the first school – Williams College, in Massachusetts. Most of the basketball team was waiting outside the head coach's office when I arrived. At lunch, we were joined by the school's president, as well as some gray-hair with the title of provost.

At the end of the day, one of the assistant coaches drove me back to the airport. He evidently had been charged to pour on the enthusiasm, and during our conversation he made a statement that changed everything. "Troy, you probably have the grades to get into Williams on your own ... and based on the tapes your high school coach sent us, you appear to have enough game to make the team. But asking your mom to call the college president was a smart move. That was a clincher. Having a senator's son on the team is sure to draw a lot of positive attention to our program."

Once he dropped me off, I pulled out my phone and canceled the appointments at the other two schools. I returned to Indianapolis, packed my swimsuit, and booked a flight to St. Thomas. The following fall, I started classes at Oregon State – slipping identity-less into its large student body, two thousand miles from Senator Mom.

For much the same reason, I was selling her eight-room condo. Every square inch of the place was hers, and always would be. I had gone to the folder in her drawer marked REAL ESTATE AGENTS and phoned the circled numbers. Soon prospective buyers would be traipsing through and overbidding for the privilege of living in the former residence of a genuine national treasure.

But first I wanted to make sure all my mother's prized possessions were distributed to their rightful destinations. Since the funeral, the personal effects inside her condo had multiplied substantially with the arrival of two truckloads of additional boxes. The initial shipment was sent by my mother's long-time assistant in Washington, who hand-packed the senator's personal items from her office, as well as the Georgetown townhouse. For the time being, I was renting that townhouse to a freshman congresswoman from Wisconsin. The second delivery arrived a few days later and it contained items from her Indianapolis office, just a few blocks away.

Over her distinguished career, Madam Senator had collected hundreds and hundreds of awards and mementos. Most would go to schools, charities, or public venues throughout the state. A few artifacts would be displayed in local museums. Several dozen others already had been sent to individuals. I'd yet to determine which of her possessions I might keep for myself, though I was leaning toward none. Keeping her memory alive hardly required material objects.

I donated the sizable wardrobes from her two principal residences to the Salvation Army. This woman who fought tirelessly to advance the plight of the underprivileged, always was outfitted in the latest designer labels when she took her battles to Capitol Hill.

Then there were the books. Volumes and volumes and volumes and volumes of books. My mother had loved reading since she was a little girl. What few spare moments she could enjoy as an adult were usually spent with a hardcover book in her hands. Leather-bound whenever possible. Especially the old European classics. As a kid, I wasn't permitted to watch television on school nights – unless, of course, my mother was in Washington. Instead, I was encouraged to bury myself in one of the countless editions that occupied endless shelves lining endless walls inside the condo. My mother would do likewise, usually in a separate room. Her time alone with Chaucer or Voltaire apparently had been more important to her than playing cards or shooting the breeze with her son. Several hundred books from Washington had been added to the considerable collection being shipped off to various senior centers around the state.

Chapter 13

While learning her way around Washington in the early Eighties, my mother soon realized she had little choice but to declare herself an Independent. The newly elected Beth Davenport had entered the fray as a Republican, only to bounce into impenetrable walls at every turn – walls that separated the two major parties on virtually every issue of importance to her. An ambitious idealist, she treated the political divide as nothing more than a ping pong net, serving up earnest and vocal perspectives from either side. On fiscal issues, she sounded like a staunch conservative, decrying deficit spending, mandated union memberships, imbalanced trade sanctions, and unchecked welfare reforms. Yet, on an ever-growing list of social issues, my mother was like a poster child for bleeding hearts. She was pro-choice when most politicians wouldn't dare utter the word 'abortion' within earshot of a journalist. She likewise had been out front on healthcare for the indigent, affirmative action in the private sector, and gender equality across the board. As years passed, she advocated same-sex marriage and fought hard to protect the rights of every hue across a widening rainbow of sexual identities.

By the end of her first term in Congress, she had turned into kryptonite with the big brass from both parties. Neither side wanted to touch her as she mounted her first reelection bid. She refused to steer away from third-rail topics that party stalwarts instinctively avoided. On the contrary, she ran toward them at ramming-speed. Once her station on the political landscape became secure, either of the major parties gladly would have donned blinders to bring her into its fold, but by then my mother had neither interest nor need. Her independent positions had become a calling card.

With time, she achieved icon status among the Hoosier State's electorate. The month of November meant landslide. In her last three elections, neither the Democrats nor the Republicans bothered to put up a serious opponent – keeping their powder dry for more winnable races. National leaders of both parties contented themselves with the knowledge that Beth Davenport's votes on Capitol Hill would land in their column about half the time anyway.

Her mounting successes and storied popularity formed the familiar refrain for the modern-day ballad of Senator Beth Davenport. I'd heard or read the oft-told narrative too many times to count. So much about this woman always had amazed me. So much of her journey had made me proud of what she accomplished. Now I feared she'd been a phony. By chasing down names elicited from Annabelle Jenkins, I hoped to discern which individuals might have lured, steered, or joined my mother along a less noble path.

To kick things off, I cross-referenced the names on the index cards from Saturday's conversation with a master list of political donors that I'd found among the materials sent by her Washington office. It catalogued the people and groups who supported my mother's various election campaigns. I focused on individuals whose contributions dated back to 1992 or earlier – figuring portions of the hidden cash dated back to that same period. There were six matches to persons mentioned by Annabelle.

According to Annabelle, my mother scheduled a meeting each spring with a woman named Sophie Mullins but never divulged her reason for doing so. "Your mom was adamant about getting that appointment on her calendar." This woman's identity meant nothing to me, so when the name of Sophie Mullins also showed up on the regular donor roster, I went to my computer – since Google searches now had become a reflex action. In a matter of minutes, Mrs. Mullins shot to the top of my suspect list. Sophie Mullins had been married to the former head of the Indiana State Teachers Association, a union representing more than 40,000 educators in the state's public-school systems. Bingo. Illicitly financed coalitions between powerful unions and influential politicians were a recognized part of the American fabric.

In 2013, Sophie Mullins' husband had forfeited the powerful position he held for twenty-four years, when reports of frequent off-hour dalliances with female union representatives went public. Divorce followed and this former wife wound up with their five-bedroom Victorian in an upscale neighborhood on the near north-side of Indianapolis – which was where she consented to sit down with me.

Walking up the sidewalk toward the large wrap-around porch, it was hard not to notice the imposing front door crafted from carved walnut, as well as other custom features everywhere I looked. Maintenance alone for this home would have chewed up an average teacher's salary. Fighting for the welfare of public educators apparently had provided a lucrative career. And during the entire period he held his coveted position, the man's wife donated generously to keeping Senator Beth Davenport in office.

In person, the sixty-something woman was much more pleasant than on the phone, when Sophie Mullins had sounded suspicious of my call. Six o'clock in the evening was cocktail hour inside most homes along the tony block of Washington Boulevard, so she offered me a drink. After bringing me a beer and herself a glass of iced tea, formalities were complete. She wasted no time in getting down to business. "How can I help you, Troy?"

This time I jumped right into the deep end, not bothering to wade through another contrived preamble. "For many years you met privately with my mother. I was hoping you might share the purpose of those meetings."

She didn't flinch. "I enjoyed a friendly and respectful relationship with the Senator. Our discussions were private and personal."

I wasn't flinching either. "I'm sure they were, but for reasons I can't yet disclose, it is paramount I understand the nature of dealings with anyone who made significant contributions to her campaigns." I stopped to allow the seriousness to sink in. Then I added, "Especially someone like yourself, who was married to an influential union head."

An awkward pause followed as Sophie Mullins processed what I'd said. She studied me while I waited silently. Finally, she must have decided that she didn't want to become embroiled in any ugliness related to campaign financing. "I assure you, my contributions to your mother had nothing to do with either my husband or the teachers' union. Nor did my contributions even relate to the substance of my meetings with her ... except for the fact that I gained immense respect for Beth and wanted to see a person with her character continue to represent our state."

One more nudge should do it, I figured. "Please go on ... whatever you tell me will stay between us."

The floodgates opened. "Your mother reached out to me just weeks after we lost Jamie, our five-year-old son, in 1989. She was in her first term as a senator, and I didn't even recognize her name when she called me here at home. I was out-of-touch ... my attention had been focused almost exclusively on Jamie for many months. He'd been born with an abnormal heart that required a series of corrective surgeries. During one of those operations, he received a transfusion of tainted blood ... he was diagnosed with AIDS in 1987."

She stopped and looked at me. "You're too young to remember

how unprepared the healthcare system was in those days for dealing with that frightful disease." Her eyes began to tear up. "We did everything we could for two years, but it was only a matter of time. He spent the last ten weeks of his life inside an isolation ward."

Her tone suddenly turned indignant. "Jim, my husband, wanted to keep the whole thing quiet. AIDS was associated with homosexuals and drug addicts. Because of his role with the union, he wanted to be hyper-cautious so that people wouldn't make any wrong assumptions about our private life. As a result, we allowed everyone to think Jamie died from his heart condition … when we should have gone public about the real situation surrounding his death … to help advance the understanding of AIDS and the necessary precautions parents and medical workers needed to take."

Sophie Mullins softened again. "Your mother recognized that … but she never laid a guilt trip on me. To this day, I don't know how she learned the true cause of Jamie's death. But that's why she called … to invite me to coffee … to express her sympathies in person. She was a godsend. She could sense how much I was hurting inside … not just from Jamie's death, but from having to lie about it. A woman needs to mourn the loss of a child in full … not cloaked in secrecy. Your mother allowed me to do that. I always will be grateful to her."

I had read too many paperbacks. I'd arrived at the Mullins home anticipating some quid-pro-quo deal struck between a corrupt politician and an unscrupulous union boss. Now I was struggling to keep my composure as the woman in front of me bared her soul about the darkest chapter in her life, and the role my mother had played in helping her maintain her sanity. My apprehension had been replaced with curiosity. "No doubt, Sophie … my mother could be an amazing person. How was it that the two of you continued meeting for all those years after the loss of your son?"

Sophie Mullins shook her head and smiled. "Troy, I have no idea … I can't explain it. Staying connected was something your mom initiated ... I wouldn't have dared to impose on her busy schedule. Every year, I'd receive a phone call from someone on her staff. Then we'd meet and talk about life. Nothing more. She was just checking on me ... the way a real friend would. To me, she was more than a friend. She was a saint."

She stopped, retaining a reflective smile, then added a final comment. "You should know, I never once was solicited about donating to her election campaigns. That was something I did on my own ... for reasons I hope you now understand."

Chapter 14

N ext up was a lengthy association my mother cultivated with a man named Ulrik Jorgensen. According to Annabelle, she often reached out to him when matters of budget and finance hit the floors of Congress. The Senator would contact Jorgensen by phone, or occasionally book a flight to see him in person. After reading through a slew of articles, I understood why she sought his input. This transplanted Norwegian was a widely acclaimed professor of economics at the University of Chicago.

Jorgensen happened to be in his office when I phoned. "Such a tragic loss ... I admired your mother immensely. I will miss her." His Scandinavian accent somehow made the words sound more somber.

Ten minutes later, I was convinced the private conversations between this erudite professor and a popular senator were borne out of mutual admiration and nothing more. Unlike many in the field of academia, Jorgensen had insisted upon confidentiality with whatever counsel he offered my mother, because he didn't want to draw attention to his politics and lose any perceived objectivity among students. Not once did my mother violate this trust by citing him as a source or referencing his well-informed opinions. She remained true to her word. "Your mother wasn't interested in exploiting my name or credentials to garner support for whatever point of view she might be expressing. From the onset of our friendship, she merely sought my views to help shape her own."

Since sitting on a panel with my mother in 1990, the professor had been drawn to her approach to public service. Through the years, he quietly sent checks of support to the maximum level allowed by law. "I always had hoped she might someday change her mind about running for the presidency. How fitting it would have been to see her as the first female in the White House."

After hanging up, I put a line through a second name on my list. Thus far, in trying to determine what sinister motives had allowed my mother to fill a suitcase with cash, I instead was uncovering laudable aspects to her personality that I'd known nothing about. She had no reason to conceal her dealings with Sophie Mullins or Ulrik Jorgensen, yet she'd kept her most trusted staff person, Annabelle Jenkins, almost completely in the dark. To say the least, the Senator was a complex individual.

I often had questioned whether my mother's true personality matched its lustrous veneer. Now, after just a few days of probing, I'd heard two heartfelt testimonies about the profound impact she could have on people in private. Because of her frequent detachment at home, maybe I'd been too quick to assume she was driven solely by public image. Could she possibly have suffered from occasional bouts of altruism? It was an unthinkable proposition in her line of work. Nonetheless, I would try to keep a more open mind.

This new outlook would be tested soon enough, when I jumped to the third name on my list. Elliot Reynolds. According to Annabelle, my mother had nurtured an especially close relationship with Dr. Elliot Reynolds. "She reached out to him whenever healthcare issues made their way onto the docket in Washington ... but there were other times, too."

I also had interacted with Doc Reynolds – on maybe a dozen or more occasions during visits to Evansville. This respected physician was one of my grandfather's closest friends. Considering the strong family connection, I hadn't been surprised to see this soft-spoken gentleman listed as a regular contributor to my mother's campaigns. What I didn't expect was a footnote signifying he'd also been one of her largest political bundlers. He had raised hundreds of thousands of dollars from others in the medical field, and this heightened level of financial support warranted a deeper look.

Elliot Reynolds had passed away several years after my grandfather. Before retiring from medicine, he devoted the final chapter of his career to serving as the chief medical officer for Southern Lowlands Regional Hospital. Building such a hospital had been a lifelong passion and securing the senior position a lifelong dream. Achieving both was made possible by none other than Senator Beth Davenport. My mother didn't often deal in pork, but she'd made an exception in 1993. Due to her behind-the-scenes legwork, funding for the hospital was slipped into an omnibus budget bill at the last minute.

To anyone paying attention at the time, my mother's unusual action would have appeared to be nothing more than a senator looking out for the people in her home state. But now, I wasn't so sure. A self-acknowledged introvert, Elliot Reynolds had practiced reticence as though it was religion. He often admitted to having only three interests in life. His family. His total preoccupation with the field of medicine. And the fishing cabin he shared with Senior Davenport. Irrespective of the gratitude the good doctor must have felt toward my mother for funding the hospital of his dreams, he hadn't been the type to get mixed up with politics. Even more out of character was serving as a bundler and thereby hitting up others to write checks.

I wasn't optimistic about ferreting out a reasonable explanation for Elliot Reynold's unexpected behavior. Both he and his wife were deceased, but they had raised three children. So, I decided to give them a try. After a modicum of online surfing and scrolling, I discovered one of the three still resided in the Midwest – Melanie, their youngest. She lived 140 miles to the west of Indianapolis, in Effingham, Illinois. After a few rounds of telephone tag, I set out on a road trip.

I arrived in the early afternoon. Totally unprepared.

I had remembered Doc Reynolds as a pleasantly affable soul. But, in many ways, he also came across as your prototypical nerd. I recognized that outward appearances could be misleading, but on first impression alone, I was dead certain the doctor's daughter, Melanie, never had been called a nerd or anything in the same quadrant.

Her bio said she was forty-one years old. Seeing her in person, I wasn't buying it. She looked mid-thirties, tops. My mouth went slightly dry as soon as she opened the door. I immediately was caught off-guard by her attractiveness, and how much of it was exposed.

"Melanie Reynolds?" My voice cracked as I spoke her name.

"The one and only," she responded.

Of that, there could be no doubt. She was wrapped in a towel and nothing else.

She ushered me inside, "Make yourself at home. My spin class ran late, so I just got out of the shower. I'll be right back."

In a flash she was gone, leaving me in the middle of an enormous room that occupied almost the entirety of her one-story ranch house. I assumed there was a bedroom behind the door into which she'd disappeared as a bare-skinned blur. Other than what looked to be a powder room in the opposite corner, there didn't appear to be any additional rooms. Someone, presumably Ms. Reynolds, had removed the interior walls to create an expansive living space comprised of free-flowing sections. A kitchen and dining area. A contiguous area filled with easels and an art table. Another with mats and exercise equipment. In the middle was a collection of randomly-styled easy chairs and ottomans that somehow made sense together. On the back wall was a large stone fireplace flanked by floor-to-ceiling shelves that were filled with books and electronic equipment. The other walls were covered with scores and scores of framed photographs.

That Melanie Reynolds was a free spirit had been immediately obvious. This first impression intensified as I started making my way around the room, taking in pictures that reflected a rather adventurous lifestyle. Whitewater rafting. Scuba-diving. Heli-skiing. Safaris. The finish line at the Boston Marathon. The New York Marathon. What looked to be the London Marathon. Trekking along the Great Wall of China. Scaling the steps of the Acropolis. Machu Piccu … Angkor Wat … Antarctica. The good doctor's daughter most definitely was a woman who made good use of her days off.

Besides wanderlust, fearlessness, and athleticism, two additional qualities about Melanie Reynolds were evident from the photos. First, she clearly was social. Extremely social. In almost every shot, she was part of a group or arm-in-arm with some other person – often male. Interestingly, I observed none of these males showed up with recurring frequency. And no matter how many individuals were assembled, everyone around her seemed to be smiling, laughing, and having a great time.

Second, I couldn't help but notice that regardless of what she was doing, or with whom she might be doing it, Melanie Reynolds always looked incredible. The sensuous eyes and lips. The smooth complexion. The toned fitness of her legs and arms. Her physical features were almost unchanged over the years. The only significant variation seemed to be hair color – which sometimes looked brown or blond, and others almost jet black. Even red, on occasion. I had no idea what color those long flowing locks might be currently, because her hair had been soaking wet when she'd met me at the door.

I had pulled into the driveway less than ten minutes earlier, seen Melanie Reynolds for a matter of seconds, yet already was completely intrigued by this woman. Moving slowly from picture to picture, I tried to imagine the pleasures of exploring the furthermost reaches of all seven continents with someone like her. My mind was drifting thousands of miles from Effingham.

"See anything you like?"

With the thoughts churning through my head, this question from behind couldn't have caught me at a more awkward moment. When I turned, I was sure I was blushing.

She didn't notice, or at least didn't mind if she did. "I'm sorry to keep you waiting."

Faded blue jeans. Flannel shirt with rolled-up sleeves. Barefoot. All I could do was stare, which she also didn't seem to notice. Finally, I spoke. "Ash blond ... maybe dishwater."

She looked at me, utterly perplexed. "I'm sorry?"

"Your hair ... I had been wondering what color your hair might be today."

Melanie laughed, which was an entirely new erotic experience for me. "Oh that ... sometimes I get bored with how I look."

"You mean you get tired of being gorgeous?" An alien presence had taken control of my faculties. I never would have said something that forward, that cheesy, to a woman. But I'd been unable to stop myself.

Now it was her turn to blush. She didn't say a word, and instead ambled over to the refrigerator and grabbed two beers.

We moved to the easy chairs in the middle of the room to begin the conversation to which she'd agreed over the phone. She was a therapist who specialized in couples and family counseling. I soon found talking to her came easily. I could envision a discussion going late into the night, but I was determined not to allow that to happen.

After the way things had ended with my most recent mistake, Vicki Richardson, I had sworn off eccentrics. No more free-spirited thinkers. No more iconoclasts or rebels. No fringe elements of any kind. From this point forward, I only was interested in pursuing relationships with females who lived safely inside the boundaries. The exact sort of women my mother had hoped I someday might start dating.

Hitting it off with the opposite gender wasn't something I'd ever given much thought. As I went about life, the connections just happened. Arguably, this ability was my most natural talent – and at times, my greatest curse. I couldn't begin to explain the chemistry that formed when I met a woman who interested me. But for sure, there'd been a steady stream of those since passing through puberty.

Now, though, the wild days were behind me. That bad-boy stage had lasted too long. Way too long. The reckless partying. The exploration of new sexual frontiers. The random alcohol and marijuana binges. The morning hazes. Whatever realities I'd been trying to escape, whatever secrets to eternal happiness I had hoped to discover, I unequivocally was done with all that.

"Melanie, I'm trying to make sense out of some of the pieces to my mother's life, and I was hoping you could help me understand the relationship she and your father enjoyed for many years. I know he was a family friend … but he also was a significant contributor and fundraiser for her election campaigns. In no way do I mean for this to sound inappropriate, as I respected Doc Reynolds a great deal, but this level of involvement in politics somehow seems out of character. Would you happen to know the history between them?"

I'd been unable to come up with a better starting point than sheer honesty. I paused, anticipating that she would throw a barrage of questions back at me. How else would a person react to such a brash inquiry about a beloved family member from someone she'd never met?

She smiled calmly, maintaining eye contact but saying nothing – seemingly considering how best to handle my tactless invasion of privacy. But then, she totally surprised me by offering a straightforward response – and I soon learned unbridled straightforwardness was the approach she took toward most everything in life.

"Yes, they were friends ... but my dad also was your mother's physician ... that is, until your family relocated to Indianapolis."

I was unaware of the doctor-patient relationship. "Impressive. Did you memorize your father's entire patient list?"

She shook her head, still smiling. "Not many doctors could claim to have a famous congresswoman as a regular patient. My dad was proud of that fact ... so he liked to remind us."

"Do you remember him saying anything else about my mother?"

Melanie's smile disappeared in an instant. She was struggling with something. She closed her eyes and bit her lip as she weighed my question. Holding back did not come naturally. Finally, she decided to let go and divulged, "Troy, I do recall one other conversation. My father didn't want to have it with me ... but I'd overheard my parents in the kitchen one evening while I was home from college. I think I should stop though. What he ultimately told me was privileged information."

I hestitated, trying to be sensitive to her uneasiness. "Melanie, I wouldn't be asking if this wasn't really important. My mother is no longer alive ... I'm her only remaining relative. Your father is deceased ... and you weren't her doctor.. Could patient privilege really apply in this situation?"

She obviously had been wondering the same thing. "Probably not, but I want to stress ... my father wouldn't have said a word to me if I hadn't been eavesdropping."

"Thank you for understanding. Please ... go on."

"Okay, we're talking early 90's. My dad was getting raked over the coals by my mom because he had committed to raise money for your mother's next election campaign. Both of my parents abhorred politics ... and I heard my mother ask, 'Don't you think you've already done enough for Beth by handling those miscarriages the way she wanted? It's time you start saying no to her.' Well, as you might imagine, I couldn't ignore something that juicy ... so when Mom wasn't around, I confronted Dad a day or two later. I was his little girl ... and he always would cave if I pestered him enough. He eventually confided that your mother had asked him to make entries into her medical files on three different occasions during the 1970's. Each time, she had asked him to document a miscarriage."

Melanie paused to take a breath. Her revelation had thrown me for a loop. "I was unaware my mother was ever pregnant before I came along. Did your father figure out why she kept losing the babies?" Then I caught myself. "I guess he did ... since I'm here."

The look on Melanie's face suggested I wasn't going to like the rest of what she had to say. "No, Troy ... it was just the opposite. Based on her regular physicals, my father strongly suspected your mother didn't lose any of those babies ... that she'd never been pregnant at all. But in fairness to your mother, he didn't conduct a thorough pelvic exam after any of her claimed miscarriages. He chose to take Beth Davenport at her word ... I assume because he wanted to avoid possible claims that he knowingly falsified her medical records. If she had been anyone besides your mother, I'm sure he never would have consented ... so that gives you an idea of how much my father admired her."

I was stunned. Reflecting on the suitcase and my mother's propensity to hide matters of finance, I asked, "Did you ever get a sense for how much she paid your father for his complicity?"

Melanie quickly jumped to his defense. "There is no way he would have accepted payment. Whatever favors my father did for Beth Davenport ... whatever money he went on to raise on her behalf ... she repaid him many times over by making his dream come true with the hospital."

Melanie Reynolds was perhaps the most uncomplicatedly honest person I'd ever met. I was amazed by what she'd been willing to share. She hadn't shied away from a single question.

I still had one follow-up, before we hopefully could move on to more congenial topics. "On the issue of raising money, I want to go back to that kitchen conversation you overheard. Considering what your father already had done for my mother with her medical records, I'm amazed she would ask him to fundraise. She rarely made requests like that ... especially with friends. She was popular with voters ... she had more than enough money pouring into her campaigns. Why didn't he simply say no?"

Melanie smiled. "I had a great deal of respect for your mom ... and I agree with you. I doubt she did ask my father. But your grandfather ... he was a different story. Senior was my father's closest friend and he could be very persuasive. Senior loved seeing the Davenport name gaining prominence in Washington, thanks to his daughter-in-law. His posturing was relentless ... and I have a pretty good hunch he was putting the heavy hand on everyone around him. If Senior asked, my dad would have swallowed his pride and solicited his friends in the medical community."

I thanked her profusely for entrusting me with so much sensitive information. From her matter-of-fact reaction, it was obvious that full disclosure was nothing new for Melanie Reynolds.

The discussion about our parents was over and done. I would process the startling revelations later. For now, Melanie and I had other things to talk about. The hours flew by as we landed on one shared interest after another. The sun had been down for quite some time when I finally remembered my long drive back to Indianapolis.

As she was seeing me out the front door, Melanie said something completely unexpected. "Call me." She then leaned up and kissed me – right on the lips. She held the kiss for several seconds, letting me know she was serious. I didn't know what to say, so I simply nodded. This astonishing creature genuinely wanted to see me again.

For several moments, I stood motionless, staring into the door she had closed behind her, wondering about the train that just struck

83

me broadside. Eventually, I forced myself to turn and move my feet in a slow, forward progression toward the car. During the two-and-a-half-hour drive east to Indianapolis, one single thought kept ricocheting around my skull. *What the hell just happened?*

Chapter 15

Five-and-a-half million dollars hidden in a storage locker. Three recorded miscarriages that likely never happened. My mother had left me a lot to think about.

When it came to why a famous politician might have stockpiled cash on the side, I'd been able to dream up a whole bunch of reasons. But I couldn't conceive a single explanation for why a woman would counterfeit miscarriages – let alone, a series of them. I hardly could wait to discover what other surprises awaited me.

Over the next week, I did enough searches and made enough calls to check-off the remaining names from the list compiled with Annabelle Jenkins. At times it got a little monotonous, hearing all the remarkable things my mother had done for people.

Since the beginning, I'd been procrastinating on the most obvious person I needed to contact – Cal Stratton, who had known my mom longer than anyone. I wanted to call Uncle Cal from the moment I discovered the suitcase. I couldn't think of a living person I more trusted, or whose counsel I more valued. But involving this man who had bounced me on his knee would be a risky proposition. If Uncle Cal were to sense I'd uncovered something with the potential of besmirching the Davenport reputation, he would come riding in like the cavalry. For as long as I remembered, Cal Stratton had been the self-appointed protector of my parents.

I admired his devotion and even loved Uncle Cal for such un-wavering loyalty, but I didn't want to invoke his full participation. At least, not yet. Still, he was the only person who might be able to explain three false pregnancies. For now, I would limit my questions to that one subject. As a banker who ran the finances for some of my mother's campaigns, I didn't dare step into the minefield of asking him about money, hidden cash or otherwise.

With the changing weather patterns of October on the hori-zon, Cal was apt to be chasing golf balls and marlin in Florida. I texted him on Monday morning to set up a time to chat by phone, or suggest we meet for lunch or dinner if he hadn't migrated south. Cal promptly responded, wondering whether I was free on Thursday evening. A subsequent text confirmed, "7:00 at St. Elmo's. Rich kid buys."

When Thursday rolled around, I was my usual ten minutes late, so Cal already was seated at a table, nursing his customary Old Fashioned. Rising from his chair to give me a hug, the first thing I noticed was the dark tone of his skin. "What brings you back north?"

"Why … dinner with you, of course."

I chuckled, waiting to hear the real reason. But Cal offered noth-ing further, instead signaling for the waiter so I could place a drink order. Ever the gentleman, Cal waited for me to sit down before reclaiming his own seat.

"How good it is to see you, my boy. Last time, we didn't have much chance to enjoy one another's company." He was referring to Evansville, when we'd been unable to connect at the memorial ser-vice, and barely exchanged pleasantries when we met with the attor-neys. I hadn't gotten around to scheduling the lunch I'd promised, so any communication since had consisted of emails and texts.

"You look fantastic, Uncle Cal … but, of course, you always do." I wasn't being the least bit gratuitous – and two middle-aged women at the adjacent table evidently agreed with me. Their eyes followed

Cal's every move as their husbands kept shoveling down steaks and baked potatoes. Regardless of the passing years, Cal Stratton continued to look like a Hollywood leading man.

"So, it's still 'Uncle Cal' is it?"

At once, I felt like a small child. I was thirty-five-years-old, for God's sake. I surely should have outgrown this throwback from my youth. "I'm sorry … how stupid of me."

"Stupid, my ass. Don't you dare stop calling me Uncle … it's better than any of those fancy titles I earned at the bank." My beer arrived, so Cal raised his glass and added, "You know, with your mom's death, we've got something in common. The nearest thing either one of us has to family is sitting right here."

Feelings of childish embarrassment were one thing. Now, I was feeling stupid and insensitive. I had known Cal Stratton's history. This man I called Uncle never had married or fathered children. Before the age of thirty, he had lost both parents to cancer. His lone sibling, a younger brother, was killed in Vietnam. Yet until this moment, the net result had been lost on me. No wonder Cal had invested so much energy into his friendship with my parents and eventually me. We had become his replacement family.

I was silently berating myself when Cal moved the conversation along, "What is it you want to discuss?"

There was no way to soften the intended subject, so I moved right to the point. "Some aspects of my mother's medical past have come to my attention for the first time. Would you happen to know about any miscarriages before she became pregnant with me?"

Cal stared forward with a slight smile, not really gazing at anything as he gathered his thoughts. "That's a difficult question … and I can't imagine how information of this sort might have found its way to you." Retaining his smile, he paused before calmly offering the advice of an elder. "Troy, your parents made a conscious decision to keep details about their efforts to conceive children between the two of them. Nothing is to be gained by digging into such private matters now. I suggest you honor their wishes ... as I will."

Just like that, the main purpose for my initiating the dinner had been declared off-limits. As far as Cal Stratton was concerned, the issue was closed. Further efforts on my part would have been futile.

However, the abrupt roadblock did produce residual benefits. The evening turned into a relaxed and joyful reunion – ending with live jazz and a nightcap at the Slippery Noodle. For me, a conversation with Uncle Cal was like an easy stroll down a country lane. Cal wanted to hear about the classes I was teaching, the plans I was making for my pending wealth, and the latest women in my life.

I didn't disclose anything about my visit with Melanie Reynolds. Cal Stratton had spent plenty of time in Evansville and was sure to have known her father. Blurting out the Reynolds name would have immediately identified my source related to the miscarriages. Secondly, though, I didn't know if Melanie could be categorized as a woman in my life. She most definitely was a woman. In fact, an otherworldly woman who, since Saturday, had consumed a significant portion of my idle thoughts. The possibility of her becoming a more significant part of my life was frightening as hell.

Cal Stratton was the master of conversation he'd always been. No matter how many times I tried to shift our meandering dialogue away from me, the focus somehow worked its way back.

Shortly after midnight, the tireless octogenarian threw in the towel. "Hate to be a short-hitter, but I've got a 7 a.m. flight back to Florida. Friday afternoon means cocktails by the pool ... and I've got hosting duties this week."

As we separated, I was left wondering whether Cal Stratton truly had traveled north for the sole purpose of having dinner with me.

Chapter 16

The next morning slogged in like yesterday's oatmeal. Hanging out with eighty-year-old veteran revelers came with a price. Fortunately, I'd had the foresight to cancel classes for the day – having cut a deal with my students earlier in the week. No class-time on Friday if they agreed to attend a guest lecture on Wednesday evening – "Face-to-Face Conversations, The Original Social Media." The speaker apparently made an impression, because by the time the session was over most of the audience had put down their iPhones.

After a third cup of coffee, I headed south toward Evansville for a series of meetings with the financial professionals who comprised the Davenport family office. Under normal circumstances, a specialized staff of this nature might be fearful of losing their jobs, seeing as how the lone remaining family member was an academician who had dedicated his career to esoterica. But normal rarely applied to the Davenports.

The family office opened shortly after the sale of Davenport Industries. To no one's surprise, the Canadian conglomerate that bought the company started downsizing the corporate staff in Evansville almost immediately. Per terms of the transaction, significant severance payments were made to anyone who lost their jobs – Senior had seen to that personally. But he'd made alternative plans for his CFO and a few hand-picked members of the finance team.

Moving forward, they would focus their energies on the monetary interests of one mega-wealthy individual and his family. In the years since Senior's death, they had dedicated a portion of their time to my mother and me, but most of it was spent overseeing my grandfather's beloved Davenport Foundation.

With my mother gone, the four-person team only needed to tend to one breathing Davenport. They'd been left with a college professor whose idea of a diversified portfolio was having ones and fives in his wallet at the same time. But regardless of how many family members did or didn't survive, job security wasn't something to which the folks in the family office paid much attention.

In his will, my grandfather had decreed, "the Davenport family office shall remain intact until such time as Kendall Ackermann is deceased or voluntarily retires." Living or dead, Senior Davenport continued to hold onto the reins of anything important to him. Kenny Ackermann had been my grandfather's most loyal crusader during the early years, when the Davenport coalmining empire took shape. Ackermann served as the linchpin with Kentucky banks as Senior built his regional network of mining operations through hostile take-overs and highly leveraged acquisitions. In return, Kendall Ackermann had been guaranteed a generous salary for heading up the family office for as long as he registered a pulse.

Because of the clumsy start to my day, I arrived ninety minutes after my appointed time. The plan was for me to start with the most junior person in the office, and over the course of the afternoon, work my way up the line and end with the crusty Kendall Ackermann. I felt obliged to learn more about the day-to-day operation inside the family office, but mostly I hoped to glean insights into my mother's financial dealings. Perhaps a member of the team would inadvertently expose some reason why she might have kept a separate supply of cash.

The schedule allotted me an hour with each of the dedicated

professionals. The first was a robotic middle-aged woman who had been programmed to describe every nuance of her functional duties. The second, a middle-aged gentleman, did much the same. Third was a younger, more energetic woman whose title suggested she was the number two person on the org chart, but it quickly became apparent that she was the one truly running the show while Kendall Ackermann logged limited hours and collected his annuity.

All three sessions ran well over their prescribed times – in part because I kept interjecting questions about my mother's spending habits. But everything I learned merely confirmed what I already knew. Funds never had been an issue for Beth Davenport. From a financial perspective, the money in the suitcase was superfluous.

It was after five when I knocked lightly on the doorframe to the corner office. Kendall Ackermann was seated behind his desk, eyes downward, and doing absolutely nothing. His workday had ended. And for all I knew, it may never have started.

I'd spotted Kendall at my mother's funeral service, but before that, it had been six or seven years. It didn't matter. Appearance-wise, the passage of time was irrelevant. Kendall Ackermann was one of those persons who always had looked old and never seemed to change.

His thin veiny hands were folded as they rested atop the polished surface to the oversized and empty desk. His bright green suspenders and polka dot bowtie were perfectly in place, as usual. His bald head was as shiny as ever.

"Come in, Davenport … let's get started with our three o'clock … shall we?" He didn't bother lifting his head as he raised one finger above the others and pointed toward the wall clock behind me. I turned. 5:52.

His personality hadn't changed. I remembered him as a perpetual crank.

"Sorry about the late hour … the discussions took longer than anticipated. You've assembled quite a staff here, Mr. Ackermmann. You are okay if I call you 'Mr. Ackermann' … aren't you, Kendall?"

He continued to stare at his hands, showing no reaction whatsoever to my attempted light-heartedness. My grandfather's stoic moneyman had retained his aversion to normal human contact.

I figured I might as well have a little fun. "Since I'm already cutting into your evening, why don't we just move our conversation to the bar across the street … where I can buy you a drink?" I hoped my ridiculous suggestion might at least elicit a scowl.

Instead, Ackermann rose from his chair without saying a word, moved past me, grabbed his overcoat from the back of the door, flipped off the lights, and walked out of his own office. I was left standing in the darkness, embarrassed for having pushed my teasing over the line.

Moments later, from down the hall, I heard, "Come on, Davenport, I haven't got all night."

As soon as we were seated inside Riverbank Tavern, I was greeted to a second surprise. Ackermann simply looked at the waitress and gave her a nod. In a pleasant voice, she responded on cue, "Double martini. Grey Goose. Three anchovy olives." He gave her a second nod. Then, for the first time that evening, and conceivably the first time in his life, Kendall Ackermann flashed a smile.

I didn't really care for martinis but ordered the same. Then I started to launch into my first question. Ackermann held up his hand and cut me off. "Not yet." The two of us sat in silence until our drinks arrived.

Intrigued by his persnickety comportment, I found myself studying the man's every move. Ackermann slowly picked up his glass, brought it to his lips and paused, allowing the anticipation to build for one last moment. He took a prolonged sip, hesitated, then took a second. Finally, he placed the glass on the table in front of him and looked me straight in the eyes. "You may begin."

I figured the best approach was to open our conversation on safe turf. "You went way back with my grandfather. You two must have been extremely close?"

"Your granddad was a ruthless son-of-a-bitch."

Not the answer I had expected, but I was getting a feel for the rhythm of Ackermann's behavior. I understood it was best to say nothing. I waited.

After another slow taste of vodka, Ackermann spoke again. "But that ruthless son-of-a-bitch always stayed true to his word ... and he always looked out for the people who looked out for him. I miss Senior a great deal."

And so it began. A transformation I hadn't anticipated. The curmudgeonly Kendall Ackermann derived far greater satisfaction from journeying through the past than he ever could from dwelling in the present. He came alive as he recounted the memorable deals that he and my grandfather had pulled off during the company's early years.

His dedication to Senior Davenport remained as steadfast as ever. If my grandfather had asked this trusted lieutenant to sacrifice his life for the enterprise, Ackermann no doubt would have dragged a knife across his throat at high noon in the lunchroom.

The descriptions from Ackermann confirmed what I had heard about the manner by which my grandfather conducted business. Hard-driving. Results-oriented. Intolerant of weakness in others. Cutthroat whenever the situation dictated. Regardless of the odds, one never should have bet against Senior Davenport.

But there also was the other side to his personality. He was a man of his word and fully dedicated to the people who worked for him. Kendall relished the stories he told me about my grandfather's loyalty and compassion for hard-working coalminers and their families ... about how Senior had paid for funerals and medical procedures out of his own pocket. How he made sure his mines were the safest in the country.

It was awkward to have ambivalent feelings toward the only grandparent I'd ever known. But a fine line always separated the respect I felt for what Senior accomplished over the course of his lifetime and the repugnance I experienced whenever I heard the extents to which he was willing to travel in order to claim victory.

None of my grandfather's methods for conducting business seemed to bother Ackermann in the least. He spoke about Senior's triumphs with a reverence typically reserved for biblical prophets. But when the conversation shifted into my grandfather's private life, so did Ackermann's attitude.

"It was never my place to say anything to him directly, but Senior … he could be a hard-headed fool about the people closest to him."

I could see the man's mind at work. He didn't mean 'people,' he meant 'person.' I waited, knowing more remembrances would follow.

Ackermann's eyes now showed signs of sorrow, as his head wagged slowly from side to side. When he finally spoke, his voice sounded softer, more somber. "Your daddy … Junior … that poor kid never had a chance growing up without a mother. Your granddad didn't have the proper temperament to raise a son on his own. He would hire one nanny after another … then fire them one-by-one after Junior failed to live up to Senior's standards."

He took a sip of a second martini that the waitress had discretely dropped off at the table. "Whatever that boy did, it never was good enough. Senior brought in all the best tutors … all the best coaches … but to no avail. As a kid, and then later as an adult, Junior didn't want to live in Senior's shadow … he wanted to be his own person. Was that too much to ask? Who knows …"

Ackermann stopped himself mid-sentence and looked mournfully at me. "I'm sorry, young man … you don't want to hear about all this."

Just the opposite. There was a ring of familiarity to what I had experienced during my childhood. I wanted to hear every detail about how my father was raised. Living in the shadow of a successful, powerful parent – and a single parent, at that. Having all the best tutors and coaches. Time and again, coming up short. But still, there'd been a difference. Somehow my mother ultimately had encouraged me to become my own person, regardless of whatever disappointments she might have harbored along the way.

"Please, Kendall, what were you going to say? My mom rarely talked about my dad ... so I don't know much about the relationship he had with his own father."

Ackermann sighed. "I'm not surprised. It wasn't easy for Bethie either ... you know, being dropped into that situation and getting caught between the two of 'em. I guess I was just pondering ... wondering what your dad might have done or accomplished if he'd been allowed to chase his own dreams. It's too bad he didn't pull himself away from Senior sooner. Getting out of Evansville was the smartest thing your folks ever did ... but sadly, that happened only a couple years before poor Junior got sick."

He seemed ready to change subjects, but then realized he had more to say. "I truly believe Junior could have been quite successful in his own right ... he liked helping people. He was softer than your granddad ... more sensitive. Yet, just as smart in a different kind of way. I guess we'll never know."

I called an intermission by excusing myself to the men's room. When I returned, Ackermann had drained his second drink and was stirring a cup of coffee – ready to keep going.

"Okay, Davenport, I suppose I should offer you my perspectives on the family office ... seeing as you now represent the entire family."

I smiled, assuming the man's humor was intended. "If you don't mind, Kendall, can we go over all those details some other time?"

Ackermann's expression went blank, as though he'd rebooted to his former self. He reached for the overcoat draped over the empty chair next to him.

I quickly spoke up. "That's not what I meant. I was hoping we could defer the family office conversation for now, and just keep talking the way we were."

Ackermann let his coat fall back in place, pushed the coffee aside with a slight gleam in his eye, and signaled to the waitress.

Chapter 17

According to Kendall Ackermann, the interactions between my mother and Senior were every bit as complicated as the dealings between my father and grandfather. Whereas the father-son relationship could be fragile and, at times, openly hostile, the one between Senior and his daughter-in-law sounded more like a high-level chess game. Harsh words never were exchanged. Instead, they seemed to operate according to unspoken ground rules which evolved over time as they vied to outmaneuver one another.

Ackermann took me through a total history from his vantage. For eight years, my father had gone away to school – four years at Culver Military Academy, and then Oberlin. After he turned eighteen, each summer was spent in a different city or town, rotating through assorted coalmining jobs that would prepare him for a full-time position upon graduation from college. Once he earned his diploma, my father continued his rotations, returning for weeks at a time to Evansville, where he was subjected to a daily grilling from Senior. Two years later, my father surprised everyone by announcing his engagement to a college sweetheart.

"None of us had any idea that he'd left a serious girlfriend behind at Oberlin … and we sure couldn't figure out when he'd found time to see her. But Senior was plenty happy with young Junior's choice. Your momma went by Liz or Elizabeth back then, and when she finally moved to Evansville, your granddaddy shuffled her around town like she was the Queen of England … showing her off to all his friends. In those days, she would have been described as a 'knock-out,' and Senior seemed especially proud of her looks … as though his son getting married to a gal that pretty was somehow a reflection on him."

For the next year or so, everything appeared to be going along fine, according to Kendall. But then Senior started complaining to people around him that my father was screwing up on the job. "College degree, my ass. I can't count on that thick-headed son of mine to get anything right. How the hell is Junior ever gonna run this company when I'm gone?"

Ever since Junior's birth, Senior had gone on and on about the plans for his future. Whether he was hunting or fishing with Ackermann and their cronies, or just out drinking in a pool hall or tavern, Senior would preach about how important it was that future generations of Davenport men hold onto the reins of the company he was building for them. Senior was hellbent that the family name be recognized across the region, if not the whole country, long after he was gone.

What soon became apparent, however, was Junior's lack of passion for mining, acquiring companies, or even making money. A few years later, Senior moved him into human resources and named him a vice president. "He likes all that touchy-feely crap, but what he does in that job won't mean squat to growing our mining business … I guess we'll have to count on Beth for taking over all the really important stuff."

These many years later, Ackermann still marveled about how my mother turned out to be the wild card in the equation. During her earliest years in Evansville, she worked for an investment brokerage firm. In no time at all, she had built up a sizable client base – in great part because she knew how to leverage the Davenport name. Senior didn't resent this blatant exploitation in the least. "If anything, I'd say he got a huge kick out of it." So, when she eventually went to her father-in-law in private and requested a role in the company, he jumped at the opportunity. She first was assigned to the finance team, reporting directly to Ackermann.

Over the next decade, my mother was like a rock star inside the male-dominated mining industry, changing positions often, and routinely taking on the toughest tasks. No one doubted she was being groomed to lead the company whenever Senior stepped aside – or that she would be every bit as capable as he had been.

A big curve ball was thrown into the mix in early 1982, when my mother informed Senior she was interested in running for office. Amazingly, he didn't balk at the idea. Senior told Ackermann that his daughter-in-law had been planning to run for city council, convinced she someday could become mayor of Evansville. That was the part that made my grandfather balk.

"He told Bethie she needed to set her sights a lot higher. Senior said he wasn't going to waste the family's money or energy playing penny ante poker. On the spot, he vowed to get her elected to the United States Congress ... which he saw only as a stepping-stone. Then, damned if he didn't' live up to his promise"

Kendall Ackermann had turned out to be a fountain of information. Despite countless conversations with my mother through the years, I'd known virtually nothing about her business career or subsequent transition into politics. Maybe I should have treated her to a few martinis at the Riverbank Tavern.

Returning to Indianapolis on Saturday morning, I had much to think about. But thirty miles onto the highway, I started feeling a westward tug on the steering wheel. The SUV was functioning fine, but my mind was a different story. I waged an internal debate for another thirty miles before finally making the inevitable phone call.

I arrived in Effingham around noon. When Melanie came to the door, she was even more stunning than I'd remembered.

"I wanted to see if, on occasion, you wore clothing when you met guests at the door."

She raised an eyebrow. "If you had given me proper notice, I would have changed my hair color."

My cheesy alter-ego kicked in again. "And whatever color you might have chosen, you would still look spectacular." I then stepped forward, put my arms around Melanie Reynolds, and kissed her with a passion unlike any I could remember.

For a solid week, I had been thinking about kissing this woman a second time. Over more than a hundred miles of highway, the anticipation had been building. No kiss possibly could have lived up to such eager expectation. But it did. And a whole lot more.

In that moment, we both knew we were going to have sex. But instead of rushing to bed, she threw on a coat and we went for a long walk. The talking between us still came easily, as did the laughter. At dusk, we worked in tandem to produce a chupe andino – a stew she'd learned to make while trekking through the mountains of Ecuador. More hours were spent in front of the fireplace. Those afternoon and evening conversations were the most sustained and exquisite form of foreplay I'd ever experienced. Around nine o'clock, she gave me a look that only could mean one thing.

Once inside her bedroom, I made love like a teenager. But not in the fashion a thirty-five-year-old male would have hoped.

I was still panting as I trundled to her side. "I'm sorry … I guess I got too excited."

She pulled up the sheet and shrugged – her expression at first suggesting our lovemaking hadn't mattered much to her one way or the other. Then she gave a teasing grin. "There is something to be said for explosive enthusiasm."

After we stopped laughing, I tugged the bedsheet down and gazed playfully at her nakedness. "You definitely deserve better." My eyes completed another quick tour of the mind-staggering land-scape. "In fact, you deserve much better. I won't let you down … I promise." Fortunately, I was true to my word the second time. As well as the third. I finally watched her drift off and allowed myself to do the same.

As a rule, my body refused to function without a morning cup of coffee. Sunday was an exception. Melanie and I awoke early but didn't roll out of bed until sheer hunger kicked in. We enjoyed a leisurely brunch at a roadhouse just outside of town, before heading out on another lengthy stroll. Every second with this breathtaking woman was dreamlike. I now had glimpsed paradise and dreaded the resumption of mortal existence.

Chapter 18

Kendall Ackermann had filled in a lot of the blanks about my mother's life in Evansville, but I still knew little about her years before – and I wasn't getting any closer to solving the puzzle surrounding the suitcase. If anything, I was more confused than ever about what made my famous mother tick. It was time to pursue an alternate approach.

I would start with her childhood and try plotting her sequential path to Evansville, and ultimately into the innermost circles of the United States Senate. If I was lucky, I might discern the point at which she intersected with an opportunity to stash away millions of dollars. This new plan seemed perfectly logical, except that I was clueless on where to begin. I didn't know a soul in the town where she was raised.

Grasping at straws, I went back to my mother's donor list. The chances were slim that she would have attracted many campaign contributors from Ohio, as I couldn't remember her ever making a single reference to her geographic roots during a public appearance.

Page by page, I ran my finger down the address column. I was moving through the list so rapidly that I almost missed it. Findlay, Ohio. I slid my finger over to the adjacent column. The donor was identified as "Lizzie's Girls" and the amount was coded as a group contribution.

Their donations were small, at fifty dollars, but Lizzie's Girls had contributed this same amount to my mother's first seven election campaigns. Then two cycles ago, the amount dropped to $40 – and then $30 for the most recent election. Whoever these "girls" were, they surely had known my mother. Not as Beth Davenport, but as Elizabeth Monroe, or 'Lizzie' to her friends.

My daytime hours still were consumed by teaching and prepping for class. Until I had answers about the suitcase, I was left no choice but to sacrifice the spontaneity of my evenings – the pick-up basketball games or last-minute calls to meet up with friends. Weeknights now were designated as uninterrupted "Sherlock Time" – but I did manage to pull away from my amateur detective work long enough to place calls to Effingham, usually on FaceTime. I quickly became addicted to hearing Melanie's voice and seeing her amazing smile on a nightly basis.

By the time the next Saturday rolled around, I had lined up another weekend getaway. I invited Melanie to join me, but her calendar posed a conflict. One Saturday each month, she scheduled office hours. The disappointment on her end of the conversation was overwhelming. "But truly, Troy, I am touched. You're the first person ever to invite me to Findlay." After a pause, she added, "I hope you'll take lots of pictures."

Based on the address assigned to Lizzie's Girls, I was able to identify a name, and eventually a phone number. Grace Winfield was the woman who'd kept the "girls" connected for nearly sixty years – since their high school days. Once I convinced her I wasn't selling reverse mortgages or cemetery plots, Grace agreed to meet with me.

The woman who greeted me at the door couldn't possibly have been a contemporary of my mother. Senator Beth Davenport had maintained a photogenic Washington agelessness through exercise and diet – plus occasional visits to her trusted surgeon. Between my mother and Cal, I had lost perspective on how the forces of atrophy and gravity conspired against humanity. Grace Winfield stood slumped to one side, bordering on obese. Her hair was stark white, and her wrinkled skin looked leathery. Still, Grace's most noticeable feature was a pleasant smile. She had resided in the same frame house for half-a-century, with every intention of someday getting wheeled out on a gurney. In theory, she lived there alone – a widow since 2004. But one of her granddaughters kept a room in the basement and periodically stayed there when her husband "took to gambling and drinking again."

Grace didn't have many opportunities to talk to people anymore, so I was obliged to sit back and mostly listen. I heard a litany of stories about the years she worked the cash register at a local grocery store – which had resulted in the back flare-ups that still bothered her from time to time. "Or I guess I should say, most of the time." I gained candid perspectives on the challenges of staying current with three kids, five grandkids, and two great grandkids. They were the joy of her life. At least on their good days. At seventy-nine, she'd learned to take what the Good Lord dealt her.

I arrived armed with questions, and despite the many tangents in our conversation, I was able to get answers to most of them. 'Lizzie's Girls' had originally consisted of five of my mother's classmates who wanted Beth Davenport to know they were rooting for her when she first ran for Congress. None of them had much money back then, or since, so they kicked in ten dollars apiece toward her campaign in 1982. "We agreed the show of support was more important than any dollar amount ... and the note she sent back told us we were right. Then after she won, we decided to stick with her in all of her future elections ... and darned if she didn't send each of us a personal note every time."

Natural attrition had reduced the number of Lizzie's Girls to three, which was why in later years the gift had dropped to forty and then thirty dollars. Grace was the only one among the three who still lived in Findlay. None of the group had even seen Lizzie Monroe in person since their late teens.

"After she lost her family in that fire, she moved a coupla hours south to finish high school and live with her grandparents. She came back here once or twice … but after she went off to Oberlin, she never had reason to swing through Findlay again. But we understood. With all them bad memories, why would she have wanted to see this old town?"

But these childhood friends never let go of the kinship they felt toward my mother. "Knowing all she'd overcome by growing up in that family of hers … just hearing our little Lizzie was running for office was cause enough to celebrate."

My ears perked up. I thought about the old photo I'd found in my mother's personal files – of the four joyless faces posed on a front porch.

"I'm a firm believer in saying nothing about folks unless you have something good to say." That was Grace's response when I asked her what she recalled about the Monroe family. After a little prying, she nonetheless opened up.

According to Grace, Lizzie's father was a "mean-spirited drunk that everyone detested." Her brother was a "good-for-nothing hoodlum who should have been in jail on that horrible night he managed to burn down the whole house with his chain-smoking." Lizzie's mother "had no mind of her own, and that woman was too gutless to do anything about them bastards she lived with." And Lizzie, "Well, she was just too darned good for the whole lot of 'em."

Grace was glad to elaborate on this last point. "We were a bunch of girls the same age who got to be really close … there were maybe eight or nine of us. Now your mother, she was probably the smartest of the bunch … and she was a real live-wire … always in the middle of everything. She liked everybody, and everybody liked her back.

You could say she was our ring leader. We never did anything to get in much trouble, but we pulled our share of pranks and things. We were thick as thieves … that's what we were."

Grace Winfield smiled, allowing her thoughts to drift back to that group of friends and the fun they'd shared. Then suddenly her expression changed, growing coarse. "But we all recognized that if we ever did anything to get ourselves into serious trouble, poor Lizzie would have hell to pay. Her daddy slapped her around enough as it was. None of us wanted to go near that Monroe house because we were so afraid of that awful man … none of us except Lila, of course."

I interrupted her. "Lila?"

Grace responded as if I should have known. "Lila Henry … your momma's closest friend."

"I never heard my mother mention that name," I admitted.

Grace shook her head in surprise. "I would have thought Lizzie would have talked about Lila, of all people … the two of them were like sisters. But once Lila headed off to college, none of the rest of us ever saw much of her again either."

I reached into the oversized envelop I had brought along and pulled out one of the pictures from my mother's file drawer. "Is that Lila sitting at the picnic table with my mom?"

Grace took the old photo from my hand and studied it. Again, she smiled nostalgically. "That sure is. Those two were something special. Lizzie and Lila … even their names seemed to fit together. Just look how pretty they were!"

I moved on. "Did my mother date much in high school?"

This time, Grace chuckled. "She sure did … we all did. But look at our Lizzie in that picture there … she always had the most boys chasing after her."

"Did she have one special boyfriend?" I asked.

Grace pondered the question before answering. "I can't say there was. She kept the whole lot of 'em guessing and hoping they might be the one."

Winding our conversation toward a close, I asked Grace for phone numbers and addresses for the other two survivors among Lizzie's Girls. She gave me what I wanted but told me I needn't waste my time. "The three of us talk most every week by phone … we have for years. They don't know anything more than I already told you. Besides, Virginia, the one who has that address down in Alabama … she's gettin' to the point she barely can tell you what year it is."

Before leaving, I asked for directions to where the Monroe family home had stood before it burned down. I was hoping to see the neighborhood where my mother had been raised.

"Oh, it's just a mile or so north of here … but I can save you time on that one, too. All them houses have been gone for years … no one wanted to live up that way anymore. Now it ain't nothin' but vacant lots with a bunch of weeds and litter."

I told Grace I could see myself out, then bent down and gave her a big hug while she remained seated in her favorite recliner. When I stood up, she said, "I appreciate that, young man. This old lady don't get many hugs anymore. I think it's nice you're takin' such an interest in your momma's life. I'm sorry for your loss … we'll all be joining her soon enough. But when it's all said and done, our little Lizzie really turned out to be somebody, now didn't she? That always made me feel proud … like maybe we had something to do with it."

For much of my drive home, I reflected on what Grace had said. She was right. Lizzie Monroe really had turned out to be somebody. And, suitcase or not, I was becoming even more fascinated with the mysteries in my mother's life. Next up was Lila Henry.

Chapter 19

In recent weeks, I'd subscribed to three websites that located peo-ple for a modest fee. In no time, I was ranking these services among humankind's greatest advancements.

With little effort on my part, I discovered Lila J. Henry – born Findlay, Ohio (1940) – had majored in chemistry at Ohio State. She went on to receive her medical degree from Case Western Reserve, in Cleveland. In 1969, she married Angus T. Gilliam and became Lila H. Gilliam. She was granted a divorce in 1975. In 1981, Lila H. Gilliam married William B. Lemont and became Lila H. Lemont. She was granted a divorce in 1987, changing her name back to Lila J. Henry in 1991. She retired from Belkin-Watson Research Laboratories, in Baltimore, Maryland, at the end of 2004. Current residence: Oro Valley, Arizona.

I was anticipating a flight to Tucson as I punched in the phone number that had been provided for an added fee. Moments later, my mother's closest childhood friend told me, in no uncertain terms, that making such a trip would be a waste of time and money. She had no intention of meeting with me.

As soon as she answered, I'd turned on the charm – easing into a heartfelt preamble about my hopes of learning more about my mother's youth. I even complimented Lila on how pretty she'd looked as a teenager in the picnic table photo. She patiently listened until I got around to asking her whether she would be willing to talk face-to-face.

Her response to my outpouring was direct. "Yes, Mr. Davenport, I do remember Elizabeth Monroe … and yes, we were friends during our teen years. But as we approached college, we elected to go our separate ways. I appreciate your desire to hear more about your mother's past, but whatever she shared or didn't share while she was alive were choices she made. It is not my place to subvert another person's wishes now that she's dead. And besides, revisiting that period from my life isn't something I care to do. I wish you well. Good afternoon."

Like that, the phone call was over. I didn't even have a chance to try a fallback approach. Obviously, Lila Henry still carried memories of her relationship with my mother – memories that sounded rather ominous from her choice of words. But the conviction in her voice made it even clearer. Whatever those memories were, she would continue to carry them silently.

More than ever, I wanted to better understand the friendship between these two teenaged girls, but now I was stumped. Then later that night, tossing in bed, an idea hit me – a glimmer of hope. Lila's ex-husbands.

The next morning, I logged onto my locator websites. The first result was anything but promising. Husband number one, Angus T. Gilliam, could be found in Baltimore's Green Mount Cemetery – deceased since 2003. But fortunately, William Bowman Lemont, husband number two, was very much alive and residing in Mount Pleasant, South Carolina.

I wasn't sure how the conversation with a divorced husband might go, but it got off to an encouraging start. "Why sure, Troy, I recognize your mother's name. Beth Davenport was one of the finest senators I ever remember."

After the conversation with Lila, I wasn't sure what kind of response my next question might produce. But again, Mr. Lemont was receptive. "Yes, Lila told me that she and Beth Davenport had known each other when they were growing up in Ohio. Heck, she mentioned it almost every time we saw your mother on TV ... and Lila watched her on C-Span whenever she could. She was a huge supporter."

Strangely, that support was never financial. I'd checked the roster of contributors for all three of Lila's names. She hadn't given a cent to any of my mother's campaigns.

I plowed onward. "Did Lila say much to you about the nature of her friendship with Lizzie?"

Lemont suddenly seemed hesitant. "Yes, on quite a few occasions, she told me how close she was with Lizzie Monroe ... but I thought we were talking about your mother?"

Now it was me who hesitated. "Uhm, we are ... I was wondering if you might know anything about the type of friendship she and Lila had."

"But you just asked me about Lizzie Monroe, not Beth Davenport." Lemont sounded even more perplexed.

Then the reality hit me. "I'm sorry, Mr. Lemont ... I think I understand the confusion. Were you aware that before Beth Davenport got married, she was Elizabeth Monroe ... and that she went by the name of Lizzie as a young girl ... that they were the same person?"

"Oh, my word ... I never made that connection. I feel so stupid after your questions ... but Lila always talked about them as though they were totally different people. Why would she have done that?"

I couldn't begin to offer a reasonable answer. I'd learned logical explanations no longer seemed to matter. "So, Mr. Lemont, what kinds of things did Lila say about Lizzie?"

"I can't recall any specifics ... in fact, I don't remember hearing actual stories about their younger years. But Lila didn't hesitate to tell me that Lizzie Monroe was the best friend she'd ever had."

I moved on. "So, did the two of them stay in touch?"

"No, she and Lizzie hadn't seen or spoken to each other since sometime in the late Fifties, I think. Something bad happened between their families ... and that apparently split 'em apart. But Lila never said anything negative about Lizzie ... or Beth, I guess I should say."

My head was practically reeling. Lemont had turned out to be a wellspring. Before ending the call, I figured there was no harm in hitting this kindly gentleman with a question of a more personal nature. "I don't mean to pry, sir ... and you certainly don't have to answer ... but what happened between you and Lila? Why did you divorce?"

"I don't mind at all, Troy. I thought the world of Lila ... still do. She's a smart, interesting, fair-minded woman. We met at church and became good friends. We each were married before. After a couple years of spending time together, we both decided to give marriage a second chance. But it became evident a few years later that things weren't working out very well for either of us. You see, Lila isn't really the marriage-type ... and who knows, maybe I'm not either. She's got this buffer she keeps around her innermost feelings ... she doesn't let people get close to her the way families and married people are supposed to."

As William Lemont described his ex-wife, I couldn't help but think of my mother and the force field she'd erected around her emotions. I also thought of what Grace Winfield had said about Lizzie Monroe and Lila Henry just a few days before. "They were like sisters." How right Grace had been.

Chapter 20

The fire that destroyed the Monroe house in July of 1957, made headlines for several days in Findlay. Reading through those archived issues of *The Courier* that I purchased on-line, I noticed how the stories primarily dealt with eyewitness accounts of the blaze itself. Surprisingly little was written about the three individuals who died inside. Apparently, no one cared enough to go on the record about the significance of their loss.

The lone attributable comment about the Monroe family was made by the principal of the local high school. "We express our deepest condolences to Elizabeth, who will complete her secondary education in Troy, Ohio. At Findlay High, she has been a fine student and active leader among our incoming senior class. She will be missed by the faculty and entire student body."

I shifted my efforts to Troy and found that an alumni group had posted old copies of *The Gladiator* – Troy High School's yearbook. My mother was a member of the Class of 1958, which consisted of 144 students. There were no listed activities next to her picture.

Over the six decades since graduation, many of her classmates had passed away. Still, after just a cursory search, I uncovered active phone numbers for more than a dozen. After reaching five, I saw no reason to continue. What each recalled about Lizzie Monroe was pretty much the same.

They distinctly remembered my mother, because she was the girl who had lost her family and transferred into Troy at the beginning of their senior year. Most, but not all, realized she had gone on to become Senator Beth Davenport. Because of her performance in the classroom, they had recognized she was smart. Otherwise, Lizzie Monroe left little impression. She made no effort to become friends with any of them and didn't participate in sports or clubs. None of the five recalled her going on a single date during the year she resided in Troy. This girl they were describing sounded nothing like the popular teenager that Grace Winfield had known in Findlay.

Next, I began contacting individuals who attended Oberlin College during the same years as my mother. Their recollections were much the same. Elizabeth Monroe was a serious and ambitious student who had shown minimal interest in anyone else. She took an intensive course load and mostly kept to herself.

Oberlin was a highly-regarded small school located thirty-five miles southwest of Cleveland, just twelve miles from Lake Erie. Being the oldest coeducational liberal arts college in the nation, Beth Davenport's distinguished career as a female statesperson had become a source of great pride for the institution. A page on the Oberlin website was dedicated to her, and she had been awarded an honorary doctorate on the fiftieth anniversary of her graduation.

In view of my mother's strong ties, the school's development office was more than cooperative when I asked for assistance in locating alumni from the Class of 1962. Because of the small enrollment, it seemed students from that era had been familiar with virtually every student on campus. As one of those students went on to gain prominence in Washington, their memories of her apparently grew even more indelible.

Some called her Elizabeth while they were in college. Others knew her well enough to call her Liz, or even Lizzie. Still, none of these fellow students would have predicted a future of the stature my mother later achieved. They hadn't doubted her intellect, or the fact that she held strong points of view on a wide range of topics. The issue was her personality. Elizabeth Monroe was perceived as indifferent toward others. Detached. Almost anti-social. Not the type to pursue political office – let alone emerge as the Senator Beth Davenport they later came to admire.

One congenial woman who had occupied an adjoining dorm room claimed to have known my mother the best. Like others, though, she struggled to explain how my parents wound up married.

During our phone conversation, I asked, "Do you recall my father, Junior Davenport ... he graduated two years ahead of my mother?"

She responded, "Of course, I do. Tragic how he died so young ... he was well-liked by most everyone on campus."

"Were you surprised when he and my mother started dating?"

This time she wasn't as quick to reply. "That's difficult to say ... because if they were dating, none of us knew about it. Elizabeth hadn't said a word to anyone ... and then a few months after graduation, this announcement comes out that she and Junior were engaged. Apparently Junior had been returning for visits after he graduated, but we sure never saw them together."

Once again, I was getting knocked for a loop by oddities in my mother's past. "So, you never knew she was dating him?"

"Neither I nor anyone else ... we never knew your mother was dating period. Early on, some of us tried to fix her up with our guy friends, but she showed no interest. When we kept at it, she finally told us to stop ... that she had no intention of dating while she was in college because she couldn't afford to lose focus. Then, out of the blue, a few years later, she's marrying Junior Davenport. Troy, I guess you could say we were happy for her ... but we never understood how that whole thing happened. We all knew Junior came from big money, so we figured that might have had something to do with it ... since she always seemed so concerned about her future."

I moved to a subject I knew even less about. "What do you remember about my dad?"

Her voice softened, "Not a lot … because like you said earlier, Junior was two years ahead of me. But he was one of the kindest young men at Oberlin. He was more laid back than most the others. He was humble … never trying to outdo anyone. He wasn't especially outgoing, but you could tell he liked talking to people … not in groups, but instead getting to know a person one-on-one. He made you feel like he was genuinely interested in what you had to say. He was more than comfortable letting Cal Stratton grab all the attention … they always were such close friends."

My father and Cal had graduated from Oberlin the same year. Cal grew up in Dayton, Ohio, and was sent to Culver Military Academy, in the northern part of Indiana, for high school. That's where he and my father became best friends. "What more can you tell me about Cal and my dad?"

She chuckled, "Those two were joined at the hip. Cal Stratton was your typical 'big man on campus' … involved with everything. He played sports … he loved flirting with the girls … and that man was good at it. But Junior … he held his own in other ways … and that's probably why they got along so well. They never competed with one another."

Like many others I had contacted, this nice woman was generous with her time and probably would have talked much longer. I sensed these folks weren't simply being gracious. They seemed to experience a certain amount of satisfaction from finding that their memories still held up after fifty or sixty years. More importantly, there was an evident joy in the very act of reflecting – as though the passage of time assigned greater value to what they were remembering.

Chapter 21

"It sounds like you're persisting with your intrusions into your mother's past, Troy. Why can't you simply recognize that Beth would have had good reasons for being so guarded? If she had seen benefit in sharing more details with you, she wouldn't have held back. She was not a duplicitous person, by any means … and she loved you very much. Why can't you simply accept those realities?"

After our icy conversation about my mother's pregnancies a few weeks earlier, I'd anticipated Cal might be irritated by another round of questions. But having heard the circumspect nature of my mother's wedding announcement, just a few weeks out of college, I was left no choice. Only Cal Stratton could explain how my mom and dad found their way to the altar.

I wished I could accept Cal's premise – that my mother wasn't deceptive or deceitful, that whatever she concealed was done with my best interests in mind. But millions of dollars sitting in a storage locker suggested otherwise.

I didn't reply to Cal's questions for a few moments, as the two of us kept our eyes locked on one another. Finally, I spoke. "You're going to have to trust me, Uncle Cal … there are legitimate reasons I need to understand certain aspects of my mother's past."

Cal grimaced at my entreaty, then caught himself. "Stonewalling you appears to be pointless, but can you at least try to be less cryptic

... since, after all, it is you who is asking me for assistance?"

"Thank you," was all I said in response. I genuinely was apprecia-tive that this lifelong mentor had softened his stance, but I had no intention of becoming less cryptic.

I'd called Cal Stratton on Friday morning to ask if he could see me on Saturday. "I'm going to be staying with someone in the Palm Beach area this weekend, and I was hoping I might shoot up to John's Island for a brief visit."

I hated the thought of lying to Cal, so on Thursday evening I had invited Melanie to join me for a getaway to Manalapan, an oceans-ide town just south of Palm Beach. Sure, two days at a beach resort with this amazing woman should have been motivation enough for making the trip, but I figured it best to kill two birds.

I had been only slightly less cryptic with Melanie when I ex-plained the ulterior purpose for our weekend getaway. "As you know, I've been digging into my mother's past. I don't want you to think I'm turning into an obsessive nutcase over the loss of a parent ... but I've discovered a potentially unsavory skeleton in the family closet that I need to put to rest. If I'm able to piece together a legitimate explanation, I only hope I can share what I find."

After such an oblique explanation, most women I had dated, or for that matter most human beings I'd ever known, would have at once started grilling me for additional information. Not Melanie. She was content to let me handle my own business in my own fash-ion. "This must be hard for you. I hope you get the answers you're searching for ... and those answers aren't as unwelcome as you seem to fear. If you need to talk along the way, I think we're pretty good at it."

But now, I was face-to-face with Cal, who had every right to expect a more complete explanation of where my questions were leading.

"Let's go back to the subject I raised a few minutes ago, Uncle

Cal. How was it that my parents started dating in the first place?"

"I guess you could say I was the culprit … I encouraged them to go out … to give it a try," Cal said matter-of-factly.

I came right back at him. "My mother had shown no interest in dating while she was at Oberlin … she shut off everyone else who tried to fix her up with guys. Why were you successful?"

Cal smiled playfully. "Charm, of course. I'm surprised you need to ask." We were seated by the swimming pool adjacent to his condo building. Cal gave a quick wave to a group of women playing bridge across the terrace. All four waved back – far more enthusiastically than his casual gesture warranted. He looked at me with a see-what-I-mean shrug. He then leaned closer and uttered in a fake-whisper, "It seems you've been doing research into dear old Oberlin … I look forward to hearing what else you think you've discovered."

He held on to his reluctance at first, but then Cal slowly opened up. Finally, the details tumbled out. Based on other recent conversations, I was beginning to believe this was the way people from my mother's generation reminisced. If I managed to crack the ice, they would walk me through entire portions of their lives that now seemed frozen in time.

Cal admitted to watching Elizabeth Monroe with interest as soon as she arrived on campus at the beginning of his junior year. "Oberlin was small … how could I not? Your mother was extremely attractive. Plus, there was this mysterious presence about her." But she showed no interest in meeting young men, so Cal had allowed her the distance she seemed intent on maintaining.

Then many months later, during his senior year, he had his first real conversation with Elizabeth through a chance encounter – the details of which he barely remembered. "I just know Junior was there, too. The three of us hit it off and became fast friends. But you need to understand, Troy … your mother and I were just friends. She wasn't my type, and for sure, I wasn't hers."

Upon graduation in 1960, Cal accepted a banking position in Indianapolis, while my father went to work for Davenport Mining. Eighteen months later, in the autumn of 1961, he and Junior had agreed to meet up at Oberlin for Homecoming Weekend. My father wasn't seeing anyone special at that point, and he was unlikely to meet many women down in the coalmines.

"To be honest, your dad wasn't especially good at pursuing desirable young ladies … so I needed to push him when I thought an opportunity might be to his liking." Unbeknownst to my father, Cal had invited Elizabeth to join them for dinner on their first night back on campus.

"Halfway through dinner, I broke away to catch up with some other friends I hadn't seen in a while. I just had this funny feeling that the two of them would hit it off if I got out of their way." Cal chuckled, "And wouldn't you know, I was right. By the time the weekend was over, your mom and dad had found something special in one another."

While my mother finished college, these new lovebirds enjoyed a long-distance relationship, consisting mostly of letters and phone calls. She also joined Junior in Evansville a few times for social events. Soon after her graduation, they announced their engagement … officially tying the knot the following year.

He made the whole sequence sound rather poignant, dramatizing the fortuitous introduction he engineered, as well as the geographic hurdles my parents overcame during their courtship. Yet over the thirty-five years my mother and I coexisted, I'd barely heard a word about any of it. She apparently didn't think details of her early romance with my father had been worthy of mention.

Moving to Evansville proved to be a difficult adjustment for Elizabeth, due primarily to the heavy-handedness of my grandfather. According to Cal, the young newlyweds felt the constant presence of Senior Davenport in their lives, with him registering approval or disapproval on every decision they made or action they took. But aside from this one domineering influence, the young couple settled into a contented, caring marriage.

Senior quickly took to shortening 'Elizabeth' to 'Lizzie,' and she just as quickly converted to 'Beth.' Those kinds of games soon became the norm between daughter-in-law and father-in-law.

A second regular presence in their lives turned out to be Cal himself. Whenever he could, he drove down from Indianapolis to spend time with the two of them. The three were inseparable. "We loved each other like siblings. We did everything together, but I never once felt like a third wheel. I preferred to think I was part of a special glue that held them together. Those times I spent with your folks were some of the happiest years of my life."

Cal started tearing up as he reflected on that period, so I jumped to a different line of questioning. "How did you get along with my grandfather? Did he appreciate the special nature of your relationship with my parents?"

My volley of questions had the desired effect. Cal's mood hardened. "I don't think Junior's dad had much use for me, to be honest. He viewed any time that the three of us spent together as frivolous. If Senior could have had his way, Junior would have dedicated every waking hour to the business. Beth, too, once she eventually started working for the company. That's what Senior always had done ... so why shouldn't the next generation of Davenports?"

That sure sounded like my grandfather. I asked, "Was he ever confrontational with you?"

"Not at all," Cal shot back. "He saved his anger for more important matters. When it came to most things regarding Junior, or the three of us ... your grandfather's standard approach was to trivialize ... to belittle ... and all the while, flash one of his droll smiles."

Suddenly, Cal tensed up. "Troy, I'm so sorry. Here I am going off on your grandfather. That's terribly bad form on my part."

"No apology necessary … you've given honest answers to the very questions I've been asking … which I value. And, believe me, I'm under no delusions about what type of man Senior Davenport could be. I think I've always understood my grandfather was complex … that there was bad and good, and plenty of both to his personality."

Cal relaxed again, so I followed-up on his previous comment. "How would Senior trivialize the relationship between you and my parents?"

"Senior had a whole arsenal of wisecracks to draw from. He would call us 'the three musketeers' … 'the three stooges' … 'the three little pigs' … names like that. He had dozens more. He would toss them out to our face, or behind our backs. It didn't much matter to him."

As he spoke, the expression on Cal's face worked through a series of emotions, ultimately landing on resignation. "In Senior's mind, we were behaving like children … pretending we lived in Camelot. He would make his cynical allusions to Camelot ad nauseum."

His mention of Camelot took me by surprise. "What did he mean by that … that you were pretending to live in Camelot?"

Cal was unsure why that specific comment had caught my attention, but he did his best to explain. "I assume you're familiar with the legend of Camelot and King Arthur. Well, back in the Sixties, the musical production of *Camelot* was a huge success on Broadway … and eventually a popular movie was released … so the whole story was very top-of-mind – even in Southern Indiana. Senior thought he was being clever with his references to Camelot, because of the love triangle at the center of the story … you remember, I'm sure … King Arthur, Lady Guinevere, and Lancelot du Lac? He never understood how three adults like your parents and I could find so much enjoyment in each other's company … so it was easier to minimize our tight friendship with ridicule rather than understand any bond we might share."

One part of this explanation was troubling. "Love triangle? Uncle Cal, what are you telling me?"

Cal tensed up for just a moment, before responding calmly, "In no way did I mean to insinuate anything illicit took place. How careless of me. The comparison to King Arthur, Guinevere, and Lancelot was just a mean-spirited dig from a man who didn't have much capacity for softer human emotions. All of Senior's friendships were rooted in manly pursuits."

His explanation came as great relief, but the Camelot reference still nagged at me because of something I'd found among my mother's possessions when I was cleaning out her condo. When I returned to Indianapolis, I would explore the possibility of a connection further. But for the balance of my weekend in Florida, I would be occupied with other priorities.

I caught up with Melanie at the hotel in time to go for a late afternoon run along the shoreline. The run turned out to be a mixed blessing. I pushed myself harder than I had since my early twenties, but regardless, I couldn't keep pace with Melanie. She periodically would slow down and allow me to catch up, but invariably I would fall back again – which was when the mixed blessings part kicked in. Whenever I was trailing, the afforded view was beyond splendid, with her toned body on full display just a few yards ahead. However, this same view allowed me to notice that every male, and even most females, couldn't resist doing a double-take as she passed. It was like Chinese water torture. Each leering stare further confirmed the daunting reality of my current predicament. I was falling head-over-heels for a woman way out of my league.

Chapter 22

"Why, Mr. Davenport, you don't need to apologize. If you're having second thoughts about letting go of items that belonged to your mother, we understand. We deal with issues like this quite often. People choose to remember their loved ones in different ways ... you shouldn't feel embarrassed. If you give me a list of the books you'd like us to retrieve, we'll have them ready for you later this week."

I was starting to make headway. A few minutes earlier I had considered coming back on a different afternoon but couldn't stand the thought of starting over with another silver-haired volunteer at the welcome desk. With any luck, walking her through my explanation one more time would do the trick.

"Ma'am, that isn't necessary, I promise. I only am interested in the one book I mentioned. I'm quite positive Senator Davenport would have wanted the residents here at Heartland Village to continue enjoying the rest of them. I also know she would have been touched by your kind words. This was probably her favorite senior center in Central Indiana, if not the entire state."

The instant Cal had mentioned 'Camelot' during my weekend trip to Florida, I remembered the book. I'd found it in my mother's closet. On the top shelf, under a stack of sweaters. An odd place to find a book, but I figured she was just being clever. For most of her political career, social conservatives had labeled Beth Davenport a "closet Democrat."

The End of Camelot dealt with the Kennedy years. It looked like one of those commerative deals offered by *Life Magazine* or *The New York Times* – the kind people used to leave out on their coffee tables. I tossed it onto a stack of other books I was collecting from around the condo. I eventually boxed and donated that pile to Heartland. But once Cal described how my grandfather regularly referred to Camelot when he was disparaging my parents, I began wondering whether the hidden book might hold greater significance. Late on Monday afternoon, after a morning in the classroom, I was determined to find out.

Eventually, the well-meaning volunteer escorted me down the hall, to the senior center's reading room. I located the book on a shelf marked, People & Events During Our Lifetime. On this same shelf, I noticed there were books about the Great Depression, General Douglas MacArthur, and George Gershwin, as well as Facebook, Justin Timberlake, and Steve Jobs. I had to smile at the vast array, gaining new admiration for the woman waiting by the door, as well as the rest of the residents.

I resisted the temptation to page through the book during my drive home. Once inside my apartment, I began studying the book's cover. A blurb on the back explained that The End of Camelot was a compendium of photographs and newspaper articles published during the presidency of John F. Kennedy, as well as the weeks right after his assassination in November of 1963. The book was printed in 1973, to commemorate the ten-year anniversary of President Kennedy's death.

On the front cover, beneath the bold title, was a photograph of Jack and Jackie Kennedy holding hands on the White House lawn. Printed in an elegant script across the bottom was a brief excerpt from a quote – "For one brief shining moment …"

The Kennedy Era had ended long before I was born, but I'd seen enough documentaries to know how many people considered the youthful idealism of the JFK years as the Washington equivalent to Camelot.

The inside flap to the book's cover explained that Theodore White, a journalist and Kennedy biographer, wrote an article on JFK's presidency for *Life Magazine*, shortly after the assassination. In this piece, at the urging of the president's widow, White borrowed a lyric from the then popular musical, *Camelot*. "For one brief shining moment there was Camelot." Thus, began a comparison that wove its way into the fabric of a president's lasting legacy.

As I leafed through the pages, I became so fascinated by the overt political image-making of the 1960's that I lost track of my real purpose. After a lifetime of watching my mother in public life, I appreciated the amount of skill and talent involved. But toward the end of the book, I was jolted back to the present.

There, I came to a picture spread across two full pages. It was the iconic photograph of President Lyndon B. Johnson taking the oath of office on the inside of an airplane, with Jackie Kennedy standing behind him – still wearing the blood-stained pink dress she'd been wearing on the afternoon her husband collapsed onto her lap in that motorcade through Dallas. In the upper corner was a handwritten note. *"Lizzie, your little Camelot must end now. The affair with C.W.S. must cease. That was our deal!"* The note was signed, *"J.E.D."*

I read the note over and over. This book, concealed in her closet, had long ago been used to convey a message to my mother. It was a message that could have been written by only one person. One powerful man who was accustomed to getting his way, regardless of what methods were required. *"J.E.D."* Joseph Elwood Davenport, my grandfather.

He was instructing my mother – no, he was ordering her – to cut off an affair. An affair with someone who also could be but one individual. *"C.W.S."* Calvin William Stratton.

My mother and father were married in 1963. The book containing the note was published in 1973. That meant my mother and my parents' closest friend were carrying on an affair at least ten years into their marriage. Had they been cavorting all along? Had they managed to keep their affair a secret, or had my father found out? Or might he have accepted or approved of what they were doing? Worse yet, had he possibly taken part? Nothing was out of the question.

I remembered how careful Cal had been during Saturday's conversation as he tried to describe the special nature of their three-way relationship. Cal had flinched when I questioned him about the love triangle comparison with Camelot, before ardently disavowing such a possibility. He was lying. This man whom I'd admired for my entire life had been lying to me all along.

Did my grandfather's insistence bring their affair to an end? Had my father's death changed anything? Had my mother started seeing Cal again? Was that why Cal Stratton had remained such a regular presence in our lives? Was Cal the real reason our family moved to Indianapolis in the first place?

The ramifications were swirling inside my head. At first, I paid little attention to the last line of Senior's note – "That was our deal!" But eventually my mind slowed, and I processed those words more carefully. And that's when everything clicked.

"That was our deal!" It was an emphatic sign-off from a commanding tyrant who would do anything to assert his influence. A man with boundless resources. A man capable of filling a suitcase with millions of dollars.

The dates, the envelopes filled with money, the oddities and inconsistencies in my mother's past ... they all quickly fell into place. Everything seemed so obvious now.

The last time my mother had signed into the storage locker was early in July of 2008. My grandfather died of a heart attack later that month, so his monthly payments would have ceased immediately. With no new bundles to add to her stash, my mother no longer had reason to visit the suitcase. Senator Beth Davenport never entered Riley's-On-Raymond again.

The suitcase contained 543 packets of cash. I did the math, counting back from July of 2008. Five-hundred-and-forty-three months brought me to May of 1963 – the very month that Elizabeth Monroe and Junior Davenport were married. Her wedding vows were the commencement of a *"deal."*

Then there were the personal accounts I'd heard in recent weeks. My mother had seemed to lose all interest in boys after high school. Yet, out of nowhere, a surprising announcement was made that this same young woman was engaged to a young man from a wealthy family ... though she never had been spotted with him. I considered how my mother rarely spoke about the husband she lost, or the marriage they'd shared. I considered how she showed only marginal interest in being a mother at all.

The hard-cold facts were devastating. Since my mother's death, I had uncovered aspects of her past that provided encouragement. I had begun to wonder whether I'd been too quick to judge her behavior unfairly ... to question her innermost character. But now. Now, I was wishing the money in the suitcase actually had turned out to be a bribe or illegal slush fund. Then, I merely would be forced to accept that the late-great Senator Beth Davenport was a political phony. I could have lumped her in with all the others.

No, this reality was much crueler. A smart, attractive teenager had seen her world turned upside down by a family tragedy. Her personality changed dramatically. Then, as she progressed into adulthood as a hardened young woman, a wealthy and powerful man had deemed her a suitable spouse for his son. This man, my grandfather, somehow had preyed upon her and, worse yet, she had succumbed. In the end, my mother was paid $10,000 a month to marry and remain married to a man she barely knew.

Another important term to this unimaginable agreement was now screaming out at me just as loudly. This contracted daughter-in-law of Senior Davenport had committed to produce an offspring, a Davenport heir. But Elizabeth Monroe Davenport clearly had no intention of fulfilling that part of her obligation, which was why she conspired with the family's trusted doctor to stage three miscarriages. The young wife had no interest in motherhood. But for some reason, her false pregnancy ruse didn't work. And if my mother hoped to continue receiving those monthly payments … if she wanted to hold on to her privileged lifestyle … and if she ever was to leverage the family's powerful connections to launch a political career of her own … she was left no choice but to honor this pivotal term in the bargain she had struck. She must give birth to a child she desperately needed and truly didn't want.

Into this world was born Troy Joseph Davenport.

Part II
Unspoken

Chapter 23

The display on the laptop read, "93" – not even triple digit. It was a modest amount of email for late in the day. She went ahead and closed the screen.

She glanced down at the floor. A young staffer had loaded her briefcase with marked-up legislative drafts, plus at the last minute, she'd dropped in a folder with a dozen or so letters that merited responses. In due course, she would get to them all. But not now. First, she would enjoy a few moments of solitude and a glass of pinot. Overbooked calendars afforded her few such occasions.

Allowing her mind to wander well outside the Beltway, Beth Davenport once again eyed the Bottega Veneta briefcase at her feet. She probably had paid too much for it, but there had been little time to bargain when she snuck a way from the conference in Milan during autumn of 2011.

The bulge in the soft leather caught her attention. She reached down, then hesitated. Finally, she succumbed. Why not? If she was going to grant herself some "me time," she might as well indulge.

Beth unzipped the rear compartment and pulled out the single item preserved inside. The corners of the cardboard cover were rounded from age, but otherwise the book was holding up remarkably well. Though the journal was almost always with her, it had been months since she'd made a new entry. Beth closed her eyes and tried to remember the last time she revisited the nearly two hundred ink-filled pages that spanned back to 1953.

During her teens, when everyone knew her as Lizzie Monroe, she had discovered the simple act of recording experiences could help her cope with the complexities in her life. But over the many years since, she had learned that revisiting those same passages wasn't therapeutic at all.

She stared hard at the cover of the closed diary. *Go ahead.* She reminded herself that she could stop at any point. She opened to the first page and there they were. Like always. The scripted words waiting for her. Carefully crafted notations — each the final product of cautious deliberations.

During the 1950's, starting a diary had been very much in vogue among young girls progressing through adolescence. The thoughts and emotions captured on those early pages would have been interchangeable with those of thousands of other girls.

She reread her long-ago impressions of boys at school. She noted how her opinions about specific boys could change on a whim. There were cheeky observations about boys her age trying too hard to become men. Dreamier observations about a favorite male teacher. The frequent angst produced by shifting alliances among her close circle of friends. Worries about grades. The ebbs and flows of popularity. Her first bra and her first period. The embarrassment of being poor, of being teased about wearing the same faded outfits to school, day after day, week after week. Envious comments about how the other girls dressed. The eager anticipation of being asked out on a date. Her first date and dates that followed. Her first kiss and kisses that followed. Fighting off the groping hands of one boy after another.

How naïve she had been. Then and for so many years that followed. With the move to Evansville, at age twenty-two, Elizabeth Monroe had hoped to make a clean break, to distance herself from the realities of her youth. She was well past fifty before she finally accepted that discarding her past was a ridiculous fantasy. Yet even now, as Beth Davenport reflected on her Ohio childhood, she thought of young Lizzie in third person.

As she turned each time-worn page, Beth read meticulously constructed paragraphs that captured the joy and wonderment, along with the angst and anxieties, of a typical teenaged girl. The recorded events of her life seemed to be unfolding so predictably, so normally, until she reached that dreaded entry from the summer of 1955.

August 16, 1955

> *Tonight was the worst ever. He made me stand there much longer than the last time. I've never been so afraid of what he might do. His eyes were filled with pure evil. He kept walking around me and staring at my nakedness like some wild beast.*

After everyone else in the house was asleep, Lizzie had written down her feelings on that long-ago night. These were the only words she dared to put on paper, but they were enough. All the excruciating details from the horrid August evening came rushing back – etched permanently in her memory.

She had turned fifteen just a few months before. For as long as she could remember, her father had been spanking her whenever she stepped out of line. By age eleven or twelve, he had begun taking her into another room where they could be alone. The first few times, he had ordered her to pull down her skirt and underwear. It wasn't long before he was forcing her to remove everything. *"Bare yourself before God, young lady."*

As she'd moved into her teens, the spankings occurred more frequently. A disrespectful expression on her face, or the slightest agitation in her voice, was all the provocation he needed. When she was younger, she assumed all little girls received similar punishments. But as she aged and began sharing secrets with her friends, she realized her father was abusing her for his own pleasure. In time, he stopped trying to hide the bulge in his pants. He was spanking her for stimulation. At some point during the sick ordeals, he finally would bark at her to get dressed, and then quickly disappear into the bathroom.

Lizzie had gone to her mother repeatedly. Each time, the assurances were the same. She would talk to her father and convince him to stop. But nothing changed. Eventually Lizzie gave up trying, doubting whether her timid mother had ever confronted him. Frank Monroe was a physically mean drunk. On the nights he consumed too much cheap whiskey, which were often, the person who paid the harshest price was Theresa Monroe, Lizzie's mother.

Beth never could let go of those feelings of hopelessness she endured during her youth. In ways the rest of Washington couldn't possibly comprehend, she empathized with the physical and emotional pains experienced by victims of domestic violence. For decades, she had been one of the most outspoken activists in Congress on virtually every issue related to parental abuse. But back in her youth, there had been no place to turn beyond a mother who needed a haven of her own. During the 1950's, problems like theirs simply weren't acknowledged. No, it had been safer to sweep such dirty little secrets under a rug – especially among less-educated, working class families. At a stage when most young girls were awakening to the promise of their future, Lizzie Monroe only could dream about escape. Late into the night, she would bury herself in the books she brought home from the school library – fleeing to distant times in distant places. Then she would approach the next morning in fear, wondering what indignities she might face later that evening inside the walls of her own home.

After years of being slapped and shamed by a father she detested, her will finally gave way on that August night. Lizzie penned those words onto a page, breaking the vow she'd made to herself. She had intended never to write about those wretched experiences, terrified of what might happen if either parent were to find and read the journal she kept tucked under her mattress. Plus, recording the loathsome events only would make them more real, more inescapable.

That Tuesday was unusually hot and clammy. Late in the afternoon, she and Lila had gone to the public swimming pool as soon as they were done pulling weeds on the other side of town for twenty-five cents an hour. When Frank Monroe arrived home, more than two hours after clocking-out at work, the girls were sitting on the front stoop, still in their swimsuits. That was all it took.

"You girls are out here strutting your stuff like a coupla town whores to any carful of boys that happens to drive by. You go on home, Lila … and Lizzie, you get to your room until I call for you."

Lizzie and Lila both knew what that meant. Several hours and several shots of cheap whiskey later, she heard the knock on her door. "I'm out here waiting for you."

He was seated in the small dreary living room with the shades drawn. Lizzie's brother, Russell, was still at Findlay Country Club, where he worked nights washing dishes. Her mother had gone to bed early, as she always seemed to do when her father meted out punishment. He ordered Lizzie to stand in the middle of the room and remove her clothes. When she was down to her undergarments, she stopped – hoping he wouldn't make her strip further.

"Go on now. You know better than that."

She slipped off the bra and panties, awkwardly trying to cover herself. At age fifteen, her body was reaching maturity.

"Drop your arms to the side."

She obeyed, the tears rolling off her cheeks and landing next to her bare feet on the worn green carpet. He rose from his chair and stood behind her. Lizzie braced for the pain of his hand across her buttocks, for the unmistakable sound of skin hitting skin. But seconds passed. Even minutes. And there was nothing. Finally, he retraced his steps and faced her directly – his eyes frozen on her breasts. Reflexively, she started to cover herself.

"Don't you dare," he barked.

She dropped her arms back to her sides as he continued to stare. Slowly, he moved his gaze up and down her nakedness – the rate of his breathing increasing. Growing louder. Beads of sweat formed on his upper lip. He began pacing the small area in the center of the room, sometimes back and forth in front of her, sometimes making a complete circle around her. Taking his time, drawing out every moment of her debasement. She would never forget the vile expression on Frank Monroe's face.

"Isn't this what you and Lila wanted everyone to see?" he spewed in a low guttural rasp.

She waited for him to strike her. Worse still, Beth remembered how she had begun praying for her father to strike her. Absorbing the physical pain of his slaps would have been far less degrading than what she was being forced to suffer. Instead, her father kept pacing and ogling until his titillation piqued – at which point, he hurried off to another part of the house. She was left standing alone in the middle of the room, crying and completely humiliated.

As the entire episode played out in her head, Beth Davenport's eyes remained fixed on the short, handwritten notations she'd made later that night. She was jolted back to the present when a tear hit the open page of her journal.

For some reason, she thought of her husband. She remembered how often Junior had wanted her to open up about the events of her youth. Then her mind went to Troy and the thousands of questions he had asked over the years, and how she always managed to deflect them. Beth recognized that any son would be curious about his mother's childhood … that any son would want to know about his grandparents. But no son needed to hear the things she'd experienced as a young girl, or the things she had gone on to do over the years that followed. Some secrets were best left locked away forever.

Chapter 24

*M*aybe *I should just put the journal back in my briefcase.* Beth Davenport knew what waited a few pages later. She didn't need to see actual words to relive those vivid memories. After more than sixty years, the events of that night still lingered close to the surface, eager to steal whatever joy or sense of fulfillment a lifetime filled with accomplishments might merit.

October 6, 1956

Nothing will ever be the same after last night.

As school came to an end on Friday, the October weekend had held such promise. But by Saturday morning, Lizzie couldn't bring herself to write anything beyond a single sentence. "Nothing will ever be the same after last night." No other words were necessary. Even at sixteen, Lizzie Monroe recognized the events from the prior evening would remain with her for as long as she lived.

She'd first met Lila Henry in fourth grade, about a month after the new school year started. Lila previously was enrolled in a nearby catholic school – until her parents learned a nun had taken a ruler to their daughter's hand and dislocated one of her fingers. Lila matter-of-factly shared the details with everyone in her new classroom and, for once, Lizzie was glad her family couldn't afford to send her to parochial school.

The public school wasn't large, with each grade level assigned a single room. So, Lizzie progressed through elementary school with essentially the same kids. In the past, when someone new was inserted into the mix, Lizzie had been cautious with her judgements. She preferred to lay back and observe the kind of friendships a new student forged with other classmates. But something felt different with Lila. The two were drawn to one another from the moment they'd been paired as math partners.

In no time, they became inseparable. Lots of their friends still behaved like tomboys. But not the two of them. They were eager to become grown-up women. Lizzie and Lila enjoyed the same hobbies. They shared the same opinions on life's most vital issues – favorite movie stars, favorite TV shows, and favorite boys on the playground.

For the next six years, there was no Lizzie without Lila, or no Lila without Lizzie. Female classmates understood that inviting one to a party or sleep-over was tantamount to inviting both. Teenaged boys wouldn't dare ask either for a first date without lining up a friend to complete their standard double-date configuration.

While most friends grew wary of spending time at Lizzie's house because of Frank Monroe's mercurial temperament, Lila never balked. Lila once confided that she could tolerate the discomfort because hers would be short-lived – while her closest friend was forced to live with this vile man on a permanent basis. Fortunately, they spent most of their off-hours together inside the Henry household, where everyday life seemed like a storybook to Lizzie.

Lizzie lived in constant fear of her abusive father. Theresa Monroe was a quiet, mousy woman who worked during the day and usually came home exhausted. Lizzie's relationship with her mother was one of unending disappointment.

Her brother was three years older and always had been her father's pride and joy – "it is Russell who will carry on the Monroe name." Sadly, Russell Monroe was raised to perpetuate more than the family name. He was a dreadful student who bullied his sister and treated all females disrespectfully. Lizzie's brother also was the reason her parents rushed into marriage in the first place – arriving four months after a city hall judge pronounced them man and wife.

Lila Henry was more than Lizzie's best friend. She was even more than any sister might have been. Lila had been the one positive certainty in life. Their close friendship was her only secure foundation. The devotion they shared was the deepest, most genuine bond she'd ever experienced with another person.

Other than prom in the spring, the Harvest Ball was Findlay High School's most anticipated annual social event. Just six weeks into the school year, Lizzie and Lila were savoring their elevated status as members of the junior class. On Saturday night, they would be escorted to the dance by two seniors on the football team. To show their support for these popular young men, Lila and Lizzie suffered through most of the Trojans' lopsided loss on Friday, before retreating to Lizzie's house to try on a dress that Lila was loaning her for their big double-date.

Behind the closed door of Lizzie's tiny bedroom in the rear of the clapboard house, their conversation quickly turned to boys, as it often did. In this instance, the subject was kissing. More precisely, they were comparing experiences and commenting on which boys had demonstrated the greatest proficiency for "making out." After several rounds of back-and-forth teasing, Lila posed an unexpected question. "Wouldn't you agree that we're better kissers than any of the boys we've dated?"

Lizzie was somewhat befuddled with how to respond. "I don't know that I've ever given that possibility any thought." Then she laughed, "Lila, you do realize kissing is a two-person activity ... right?"

Her best friend wouldn't let go. "Think about it, Lizzie. You've already admitted how kisses with some boys are a lot better than kisses with others … which obviously means different boys have different skill levels. Well, I just happen to believe we girls have a more natural talent for kissing than they do."

Lizzie laughed again. "If you say so."

For a few moments, neither girl said anything. After Lila finished pinning the back of the borrowed dress, Lizzie took it off so they could alter the hemline. She was standing next to the bed, wearing only a bra and the half-slip that covered her lower body to the knees.

Before another word was spoken, Lila blurted, "We can prove it, you know."

"Prove what?" Lizzie asked.

"That we girls are naturally better at kissing," she replied.

The feeling in the room no longer was giggles and teasing. Lizzie had a sense for where things were heading, but feigned innocence. "How would we do that?"

Without saying another word, Lila smiled sheepishly, sidled up to Lizzie and put an arm around her best friend's shoulders. She waited, allowing Lizzie an opportunity to resist. After no objection was registered, Lila leaned forward and put her lips against Lizzie's. The kiss intensified as Lila wrapped her other arm around Lizzie's waist and pulled their two bodies tightly together.

Just moments before, Lizzie had been curious, but suddenly she lost all interest. Why had she allowed such a ridiculous conversation to go this far? They both should feel embarrassed, and she was certain they would.

But it was too late for mere embarrassment. The door to the bedroom flew open. "Hey, you little shit, I need a few bucks for …"

Her brother stopped mid-sentence. "Well, my, my, my … what is going on in here?"

Russell Monroe entered the room and closed the door behind him. Lizzie and Lila separated and stood next to one another, absolutely petrified. Lizzie tried to gather her composure, "Russell, what makes you think you can just barge into my room without knocking?"

He just looked at her and grinned broadly. She needed to say more. But what could she say? What explanation possibly would make sense to an imbecilic pig like her brother. Out of desperation, she made an attempt. "It isn't what you think. We were just trying an experiment before tomorrow night's dance." She recognized how lame the excuse sounded.

Russell's sinister smile turned even more gleeful. "Sure you were. I was never the student you are, Little Sister ... but tell me what crazy science experiment has you taking your clothes off and rubbing your bodies against each other with your lips locked together like a couple of queers?"

Lila started to cry, which only added to her brother's delight. "I imagine your friends at the high school will get a big kick out of knowing how close the two of you really are. I know my buddies down at the plant will want to hear every filthy detail."

After barely squeaking through high school, Russell now was working in a factory that produced brake parts for Detroit. He was nineteen with a full-time job. He shouldn't have been living at home anymore – which only added to the torment Lizzie was feeling.

He walked over to Lila, who stood completely docile out of fear and shame. "Are you interested in keeping this little incident between just the three of us, Lila? I've always had a hunch you'd be damned good at doing special favors for a guy."

She looked up at him, her eyes red and filled with tears. Her voice quivered. "What do you mean, Russell?"

He scoffed, "I'm sure you understand exactly what I mean. I would ask your little sweetheart over there to help you, but our dear old dad has her reserved for other things ... doesn't he, Lizzie? So, Lila, I guess you're gonna have to handle this all by yourself."

With that, Russell Monroe removed his belt and began unbuckling his pants. Lizzie watched as her closest friend sank to her knees.

Chapter 25

Such depravity would have been difficult to witness under any circumstance, but the scene on that Friday night was practically unbearable. The one person in the world on whom she'd always relied was forced to perform unspeakable acts by a brother she abhorred. The whole nightmare took place in her own bedroom – the one space which previously had afforded her sanctuary inside a living house of horrors. From that night forward, she couldn't even enter her bedroom without the repulsive images flashing through her head.

Before Russell reopened the door to exit the room, he had turned to offer one last indignity. "Lizzie, you can have your girlfriend back … I'm finished with her … at least for now. Your secret is safe as long as I have your full cooperation … who knows, maybe someday I'll ask you two lovebirds to put on a little show for me?"

Once he left, Lizzie raced to Lila, still kneeling on the floor. She tried to comfort her best friend with a hug, but Lila shoved her away, crying. "I don't want to be touched." With that, Lila pushed herself up, grabbed her coat from the bed, flung open the door, and bolted out of the house – allowing Lizzie no opportunity to discuss what just transpired. She had needed to console Lila and assure her she made the right choice in acceding to Russell's sick demands. If she'd refused, their reputations in Findlay would have been ruined.

Lizzie tried calling Lila the next morning, but Mrs. Henry

reported that her daughter was sick and didn't feel like coming out of her room. Independent of one another, both girls cancelled their dates to Saturday's dance. Lizzie stayed close to the phone on Sunday, hoping Lila might return her repeated calls. She didn't.

On Monday, Lila was absent from school. The same on Tuesday. On both mornings, Lizzie waited on the front steps until first bell. Finally, on Wednesday, she saw Lila walking slowly up the sidewalk toward the school's entrance. Lizzie hurried down to join her. "Lila, I've been so worried about you. What Russell did was disgusting … he is an animal. I will never speak to him again … from now on, we'll spend all our time at your house. It will be our secret … you'll just have to find a way to forget the things he said and made you do. We can't let him ruin our friendship."

Lila stopped walking and looked hurtfully at Lizzie. "Friendship? Is that all we have?"

Lizzie froze, as Lila turned away and headed toward the front door. Despite everything that had occurred in the aftermath of their ill-fated kiss, Lila instead was focused on the intimate exchange itself. For the first time, Lizzie realized there had been more to their embrace than prurient curiosity on Lila's part. Lizzie never had imagined having such thoughts about Lila. She couldn't have imagined such thoughts about any girl.

The two managed to avoid each other for the balance of the day. That evening, Lizzie made another short entry into her journal.

October 11, 1956

How could I have been so blind? Worse… how could I have been so reckless with my closest friend?

As she read and reread the passage, Beth Davenport relived those feelings of confusion and remorse she experienced as a teenager. Whenever she had thought back to her relationship with Lila over the sixty years since, she was overtaken with similar feelings. With no other person had she ever connected so intensely.

She still wondered. Did she and Lila enjoy a special kind of love? Perhaps. But as a naïve teenager, Lizzie wouldn't have perceived their bond as anything romantic. It was the 1950's. In Findlay, Ohio, no less. Such notions were out of the question. Having amorous feelings for someone of the same gender was viewed as aberrant behavior. Deviant. Demented. Persons demonstrating those tendencies were pariahs. Admitting to those kinds of unnatural feelings would have taken unprecedented courage. Far more courage than Lizzie Monroe could muster with a father who likely would have chained her to a post in the basement if he caught even the slightest hint.

But she'd never been able to shake the uncertainty. If anything, the ambiguity had intensified with each passing year. Were her feelings for Lila more than platonic? By not exploring them further, had she denied herself the deeper, more genuine passion that had eluded her ever since?

Retrospection only added to Beth's torment. Decades of cultural change had enlightened society to the complexities of interpersonal relationships – to passions and behaviors that once seemed unthinkable. During the dimmest chapter of her life, Lizzie hadn't allowed herself to even contemplate the possibilities.

With each passing year, hindsight became more haunting. She had seen her mother physically abused by her father dozens of times and never called the authorities. Repeatedly, she had been sexually abused and humiliated by this same father and never called the authorities. She had watched her brother sexually assault her closest friend and never called the authorities. Had she done the right thing just once, the horrifying events that took place over the ensuing months could have been avoided. The balance of her lifetime could have been dramatically different.

All Beth could do now was wonder.

Chapter 26

They tried to move on as though nothing had happened, and by outward appearances, Lizzie and Lila seemed as inseparable as ever to classmates. Both knew otherwise. The ruptures beneath the surface became harder and harder to navigate. Their natural chemistry couldn't be restored. Other than the brief conversation in front of the school, they avoided any discussion of the events from that tortuous Friday evening in Lizzie's bedroom.

Inside the Monroe residence, life continued to be a living hell for Lizzie. Her father's drunkenness and abusiveness toward her mother increased in lockstep. With each passing month, Theresa Monroe seemed to withdraw further and further from the human race. Somehow though, Frank Monroe must have reached his capacity for sheer evil, because he no longer paid much attention to Lizzie. He instead began treating her with total indifference, which came as welcome relief. Unfortunately, Russell picked up the slack in other ways. He rarely missed an opportunity to toss out teasing barbs laced with innuendo when people were around. In private, he wasn't nearly as clever with the insults and slurs he flung her way. *Dyke. Lezbo. Carpet-muncher.*

Each day became another tick mark in her countdown. Upon graduation from high school, Lizzie would be eighteen. Once she had her diploma in hand, she was going to leave home, leave Findlay, and never look back. She would apply for scholarships and work as many side jobs as necessary. She didn't care how many years it took, but she would earn a college degree and distance herself from every aspect of the life she had known to date.

Beth Davenport skimmed the journal passages written during the remainder of Lizzie's junior year of high school. They all were fluff. Boys. A prom. Car rides in the country. Nothing of substance. Nothing about what really was occupying her thoughts.

Beth remembered how she'd felt when the end of spring term finally arrived. With just one more year of high school remaining, it was to be her last summer in Findlay. During June and most of July, she worked as a summer girl for a family on the other side of town – in a stately home where she and Lila once picked weeds. Then, in late July, she caught the bus to Troy for a month-long stay with her mother's parents – something she had done every summer since she was a little girl. She carried no special memories of being there, but any time away from her parents and brother was a welcomed respite.

Both of her grandparents could have been described as stoic. Almost reclusive. Very much like her mother. They showed little emotion when Lizzie arrived for her annual visits, and little again when she departed. Her grandfather previously owned a small farm, but by the time Lizzie was a teenager he lived in town, working part time at the local hardware store. During those summer months in Troy, she was expected to assist her grandmother, who took in laundry and listened to church music on the radio from dawn to dusk.

On the bus ride south, Lizzie had given herself a pep talk. She would make the most out of the next four weeks in Troy. Because once summer was over, she had no intention of ever returning or seeing her grandparents again.

But her plans were soon to change.

July 29, 1957

This morning, three men came to the door and told me my whole family was dead. I think they expected me to be sad.

She'd heard the knock around ten o-clock. Her grandmother was ironing in the kitchen, at the rear of the house, so Lizzie went to the front door. Standing on the stoop were two police officers and a familiar figure wearing a clerical collar. She could tell from the looks on their faces. Someone in her family was dead. Beth remembered the thoughts running through her head at that instance.

Her father? Maybe Russell? As three grim-faced visitors stepped inside, she was mulling the options. *Which death would please me most?* Hearing the commotion, her grandmother joined them in the living room. Lizzie watched the local pastor move quickly to the elderly woman's side and wrap his arm around her shoulders. The compassionate gesture only amplified Lizzie's uncertainty. *For which death should I be praying?*

Moments later, the internal debate ended abruptly. Lizzie had hit the jackpot. Thanks to a fire, both disgusting men were out of her life forever. She suppressed a smile, though she did experience a tinge of remorse when she heard her mother also had died. But that may have been an impulse reaction to her grandmother, who sat next to her on the couch, absorbing the loss of a daughter. Over the months that followed, Lizzie gave little thought to the woman who had brought her into the world and done little else for her since.

The three dutiful callers seemed surprised and almost disappointed by Lizzie's tempered response to the tragic news about her family. Lizzie threw them a bone. "I hope they didn't suffer." She was lying, but it felt like the right thing to say.

The Monroe's small frame house would have been blazing in no time. Chances were good that Frank Monroe was drunk and passed out – denying him the opportunity to panic or suffer. Too bad. Her mother probably was curled up in a ball at his feet like some Viking dog. With any luck, Russell died a painful death. The only positive thing her brother managed to do during his entire lifetime was fall asleep on that very evening with a lit cigarette.

Over the years since, Beth Davenport often had wanted to punish herself for her cold and coarse reaction, but she honestly couldn't. Nothing could alter how she felt about her parents and brother. As a little girl and then as an adolescent, Lizzie had imagined her life would be better without them. She was right. It had been.

The final arrangements for her family were almost inconsequential. More than half the people who bothered to attend the funeral in Findlay were Lizzie's friends from school. Beth still could picture the small gathering and, pew by pew, name the indifferent faces inside that barren sanctuary. Because the Monroes didn't belong to the church where the service took place, no reception was held afterward.

To save money, her grandparents elected to inter the burnt remains of all three bodies in a single gravesite. It didn't matter. No one was likely to visit their cemetery plot. This father, mother, and son merely had been passing through. Their abbreviated earthly existence had produced no positive or lasting impact. If eternal life existed beyond, Beth was convinced her parents and brother wouldn't fare much better in the hereafter.

Recognizing she had nowhere else to turn, her grandparents invited Lizzie to live with them in Troy until she finished high school. With no viable alternative, she accepted their terms. They expected her to contribute $12.50 each week toward household expenses. But being sympathetic to Lizzie's situation, they agreed to advance the first few payments until she lined up a job in her new hometown.

As soon as the final prayer was offered at the gravesite, her grandparents had wanted to depart. They were intent on getting back to Troy by suppertime. They'd had little use for their son-in-law and weren't acquainted with any of the people who showed up to pay their respects. During the drive to Findlay the previous morning, her grandmother had summed up their sentiments. "Theresa was a good enough daughter to us while she was growing up. But from then on, she made her own bad choices … choices she had to learn to live with. And now, I reckon, she died because of 'em. God rest her soul." In the months ahead, Lizzie would gain similar insights into why her mother may have turned out the way she did.

Following the funeral service, Lizzie practically begged her grandparents to allow her some time to say goodbye to her friends. After a few rounds of quibbling, they granted her an hour. Lizzie hurriedly got around to as many of her schoolmates as she could, but finally resolved that she needed to spend the remainder of her allotted hour with Lila. Alone.

They walked to a distant corner of the cemetery and leaned against a split-rail fence. Lizzie took Lila's hand, "We've been through a lot together."

Lila looked at her as though she hadn't heard a word. Then she stared directly into Lizzie's eyes and asked, "Will you miss them?"

"I really don't want to talk about my family," she replied.

But Lila was determined. "A few weeks ago, before you caught that bus to Troy, you told me you wished you didn't have to come back here. You said you wished that all of them would simply disappear."

"But Lila, I didn't mean they should die."

"How else would you expect three people to disappear, Lizzie?" Lila sounded distressed.

"I guess I hadn't given that any thought." Lizzie was trying to get to other things she needed to say to her closest friend.

But Lila persisted, "You still haven't answered my question."

"What question?"

"Will you miss them? Are you glad your parents and Russell are dead?"

These were questions Lizzie didn't want to answer. At least out loud. There was an awkward silence. Finally, Lizzie started crying for the first time since she'd received the news of the fire. In a soft tone, she said, "Yes, Lila … I am glad they're dead … all three of them."

"Good … I needed to hear that." Her voice suddenly sounded more upbeat.

Lizzie's mind started racing. "My God, Lila, what are you telling me? Did you have anything to do with …"

Lila calmly cut her off. "Of course not, Lizzie. It was in the newspaper … the fire inspector already determined that the fire started from a cigarette in your brother's bed. Weren't you the one who always complained about how your house smelled like a tavern because of Russell's constant smoking?"

Now it was Lizzie who persisted, "Lila, you and I both know how much you hated Russell after that night in my bedroom …"

Lila cut her off again, her eyes growing animated. "Oh, I hated him all right … but it wasn't just that one night in your bedroom."

"What do you mean?" Lizzie asked with new alarm in her voice.

"Your brother wasn't done with me after just one night. He made me do the same thing to him two more times." Lila said.

"How … when?" Lizzie was dumbfounded.

Lila was surprisingly casual as she went into a lengthy description. "Findlay's not that big … so I imagine he followed me whenever he had nothing else to do. Twice he caught me when I was alone in places where no one else could see us. Once last winter, I was taking a shortcut home from school after dark. The other time was in the spring when I got mad at Chuck Tolson and left that bonfire early … you remember. All of a sudden, Russell was there in my path … he said, 'I'm still keeping that little secret for you and my sister … so why don't you get back down on your knees and remind me again why I should?' After the second time, I made sure I never went outside alone. But, Lizzie, do you know how horrible it is to live with

150

that constant fear ... wondering about the next time I'd be forced to do something so utterly disgusting?"

Lizzie did know. She had told her girlfriends how she routinely was whipped by her father over the years, but the more explicit details had been too humiliating to share – even with Lila. "Why didn't you tell me what Russell was doing, Lila?"

"What good would that have done? You already had enough problems just living in the same house with that bastard and your father. I figured I could manage the situation on my own. Besides, everything that went wrong that night in your bedroom was my fault ... and, as a result, everything that changed between the two of us was also my fault."

This last comment surprised Lizzie. "What would make you say something like that?"

They still were holding hands and Lila clasped more tightly. "It was me who lured you into that kiss ... and that kiss is what started the whole mess ... with Russell ... between you and me."

"We were just playing around!" Lizzie tried alleviating her guilt.

Lila didn't yield. "We both know better ... I'd been wanting to kiss you like that for a long time. I still do. Lizzie, surely you must realize I feel something you don't feel ... and it was wrong for me to put you in that situation ... whether Russell ever barged in on us or not. I am so sorry. More than anything, I want you to be happy."

Tears were running down the cheeks of both girls' faces. Lizzie was trying to process everything Lila had revealed. The possibilities were suffocating. She suddenly was convinced that her best friend somehow had been responsible for the fire that killed her entire family. Perhaps it had been an act of vengeance against Russell – Lila making sure he never could degrade another female. But more likely, it had been an act of love. Lila had committed murder out of devotion to her.

Lizzie no longer wanted absolute answers. There could be no

further discussion of Russell, her family, or the fire. Things were better left unsaid.

Instead, Lizzie moved on. "Lila, I feel closer to you than any person I've ever known … and I wanted to make sure I told you that. But now … now, I think this needs to be the last time we see each other."

Lila didn't say a word but smiled and nodded her head in agreement. On an impulse, Lizzie leaned forward and pressed her lips against Lila's, who immediately returned the kiss as she let out a short and barely audible moan. They pulled close and held that way for several moments.

When they separated, Lila continued looking into Lizzie's eyes and without making a sound, mouthed the words, "Thank you." With that, her closest friend walked off in the opposite direction, leaving Lizzie to head back toward her grandparent's car and a new life in Troy.

Lizzie took the bus to Findlay on two occasions over the next year to visit high school friends. But not Lila. She had said her final farewell to the friend who always would mean the most.

For Beth Davenport, the impetus behind that kiss had remained a mystery ever since. Had she intended the kiss as final punctuation to their long and extraordinary friendship? Was it meant as a gesture of reconciliation to Lila, who minutes earlier had apologized for tricking her into their first ill-fated kiss? Or was she expressing deeper feelings for Lila than she had been willing to admit previously?

In retrospect, the kiss itself wasn't romantically charged. No tingling electricity ran across her skin. No fireworks went off. No harps started playing. Beth Davenport never would fully understand what prompted her spontaneous act of intimacy. Yet something deep inside had impelled Lizzie to kiss Lila in the cemetery – and surrendering to her innermost desire at that precise moment in time was precisely the right thing to do. Not once had she regretted this long-ago act.

Chapter 27

"Though your unorthodox style could be described as unsettling, I do applaud your candor ... uh, Miss Monroe. That is your name ... am I correct?"

Before addressing her, the prim and scholarly professor moved back behind the rostrum to scan his roster of students. Dr. T. Reid Bingham had been a fixture at Oberlin College since before the Second World War, and clearly wasn't accustomed to being challenged – especially by a freshman taking his much-acclaimed course in world literature. Let alone on this, the first day of classes.

From its founding, when Oberlin's first president was an abolitionist who spoke against slavery, faculty members had been applying themselves in earnest to uphold the school's progressive reputation. On first impression, Professor Bingham didn't appear to be one of them. At least to Lizzie Monroe.

Their exchange took place shortly after he distributed the syllabus for the coming term. With her love for literature, Lizzie eagerly scanned the reading list – Thackery, Hugo, Hardy, Tolstoy, Balzac, Kipling, Cervantes, and Dostoevsky. Impressive authors all. The indicated titles were among the greatest works ever put to paper. Yet the selections weren't entirely to her liking.

"Excuse me, Dr. Bingham ... wouldn't you agree this list is incomplete?"

"I beg your pardon." He gazed across the thirty or so students sitting before him, searching for the source of such an audacious question.

She raised her hand from the back corner of the room. "I'm over here."

He tilted his head in her direction. "Name please?"

"Elizabeth … or Liz, if you prefer."

"I prefer neither … this is an institution of higher learning. In my classroom, we utilize surnames to address one another." He stared at Lizzie, expecting her to provide her last name.

She instead moved on to the issue at hand. "I don't see Wharton, Austen, or Alcott. There's no Virginia Woolf … no Charlotte or Emily Brontë among the authors you expect us to read and discuss."

"I'm sure you recognize there is a limit to how many books we can cover in a single semester. I'm sorry if we've omitted some of your favorites," Bingham responded dismissively. "Now, if you don't mind, maybe we can move on to …"

Lizzie cut him off, "You're missing my point."

"So, what exactly is your point, young lady?"

The legendary T. Reid Bingham appeared to be on the verge of exploding. Fellow students stared down at their desktops or shuffled awkwardly in the connected wooden chairs – registering their collective discomfort while trying to distance themselves from an insolent freshman. Lizzie was undaunted.

"We, no doubt, have much to absorb from the books on your syllabus, Professor. Through literary masterpieces like these, countless generations have gained insight into our own humanity from authors whose talents will continue to stand the test of time. But, taken as a whole, couldn't one argue that the views of the world expressed in these works are decidedly male … and if a class is to be entitled World Literature, it only could be beneficial to add female perspectives?"

Bingham stood silent for several moments, his eyes looking like they might burn a hole through the back wall of the classroom. Then he moved to the rostrum and ran a finger down his list of students. When he was confident he had the right name, he looked directly at her and nodded.

All these years later, Beth remembered the exact words he had spoken. "Though your unorthodox style could be described as unsettling, I do applaud your candor ... uh, Miss Monroe. That is your name ... correct?" Professor T. Reid Bingham paused again, before addressing the entire classroom. "A fair and considered criticism has been raised ... you can expect an updated syllabus at our next session." He then patted the rostrum twice with the open palm of his right hand, which must have made his proclamation official – because two days later, Thomas Hardy and Rudyard Kipling had been pushed aside for Edith Wharton and Jane Austen.

September 9, 1958
 First day of college. Today I tasted victory.

She made the simple notation in her journal as soon as she got back to her dorm room after classes ended that first day. Those few words adequately captured how she was feeling. Victorious. Anything more would have reflected unnecessary bluster. Beth Davenport had little tolerance for boastfulness, even as a young woman recording her musings in private.

She had challenged one of the historic school's most renowned and intimidating figures and won him over. Her fellow classmates were left gawking in awe after the exchange drew to a close. The performance most-definitely could be categorized as a victory. But that wasn't the conquest to which Lizzie was referring when she'd made her entry.

The acknowledged feelings of triumph were borne out of what

she had achieved merely by completing her first official day of college. Whenever she dared to raise the subject of furthering her education, Frank and Theresa Monroe had scoffed at the idea of a daughter pursuing anything more than a husband and a maternity dress – preferably in that order, but not mandatory. Expectations for their son were similarly low, and Russell had lived down to every single one of them. Her parents' narrow perspective on her future only had served to stoke Lizzie's ambitions of escape.

After moving to Troy for her final year of high school, she no longer was subjected to the base immorality that permeated the Monroe household. But her grandparents had been no less discouraging whenever the prospect of college was broached. In their minds, the menial part-time jobs she worked during high school were stepping-stones to a more permanent trade after graduation. They didn't fathom why Lizzie wanted to waste her weekends taking bus rides to different colleges and interviewing for scholarships. But as long as she was on-time with her share of the weekly household expenses, there wasn't much they could say.

The kids at the new high school in Troy had presented her a whole different series of issues. At first, she was embraced by them – with what she recognized as 'novelty sympathy.' These new classmates had been eager enough to express sorrow for a family they'd never met, but even more eager to hear descriptions of the horrific deaths and the pain Lizzie must be feeling over the loss. When she failed to regale them with details, the novelty wore off. Soon she was nothing more than an outsider inserted into a cemented group of locals who were intent on savoring their last year as kids before they strapped on the yoke of rural adulthood. No matter to her. Between college visits and various off-hour jobs, Lizzie had little spare time to assimilate. These new peers interpreted her disinterest as aloofness, but she didn't care.

This lonely transition to a new and temporary life in Troy had allowed Lizzie to focus even more rigorously on the years ahead.

College wasn't an aspiration. It was a necessity.

Her transferred grade average from Findlay already had placed her near the top of the senior class. As word spread that this outsider was applying for scholarships, the resentment built. Among the Class of '58 at Troy High School, less than half planned to attend college. Among females, it was less than a fifth. The notion of this uppity girl without a family going to college at someone else's expense was downright contemptable.

The bitterness among locals only intensified once she received word from Oberlin. The scholarship awarded Lizzie Monroe was granted to three Ohio seniors each year – none of whom could graduate from the same high school. She had beaten out another popular finalist from Troy, so from that point forward, her isolation was virtually guaranteed.

Two days after high school graduation, Lizzie boarded a northbound bus out of Troy for the last time. When she said goodbye to her grandparents, she meant it in the truest sense. She was grateful they'd conceded her a place to finish high school, and Lizzie truly wished them well. But she had no need or desire to see them ever again, and doubted they cared much one way or the other. They had met their family obligation and received payment in full.

She spent the summer in Oberlin, waxing floors in empty dormitories and classroom buildings during daytime hours, waiting tables at a local diner at night. Her scholarship covered room, board, and tuition, but she still needed money for books and living expenses.

Once classes started, Lizzie quickly realized a lot of her peers perceived their four years at Oberlin as a last retreat from the drudgery of adulthood that awaited them. Sure, they attended classes, but equally important were their fraternities and sororities, their football games, their nightclubbing in Cleveland on weekends. Lizzie was interested in none of that. She was there to advance her future, not delay it.

Lizzie Monroe was convinced she could jettison the shameful memories of her family. The beginning of college would set a new clock in motion and erase the first eighteen years of her existence. She was certain those feelings of exhilaration felt on that first day of classes marked a triumph over her past. Such was the naiveté of youthful optimism.

Chapter 28

From the outset, Lizzie felt good about her choice of schools. Oberlin professors were demanding. The required reading was endless. Writing assignments were rigorous and the ensuing discussions proved stimulating. But still, the most significant learning during her freshman year took place away from the classroom, because that was where Lizzie realized she had evolved into a different person.

Throughout her teen years in Findlay, Lizzie Monroe enjoyed healthy relationships with boys. Lots of them, in fact. She seemed better equipped than other girls. It all had come so naturally to her. The flirting, the teasing. The games of pursuit. Being receptive at just the right moments but knowing where to draw the line.

Now, with hundreds of eager young men sharing a campus, things felt different. A steady flow of freshman guys and upperclassmen, and even a few young faculty members, had made their attempts. But for Lizzie, the thought of a movie, study date, or walk in the park held little appeal. The desire for romance that once kindled inside her was extinguished somewhere along the journey. Maybe Frank Monroe had inflicted one too many humiliations. Maybe some switch in her brain had flipped when she watched her best friend being debased by her brother. Or maybe it had been Lila herself. Whatever the reason, Lizzie no longer was interested in male companionship.

Oddly, the same was true for female companionship. Once she treasured her many close friendships, yet now she routinely avoided social interaction. She was happier without it. Through her own volition, Lizzie had chosen to become a loner.

Fellow students tried bringing Lizzie into their circles of friendship. But she sensed life would be easier without the inevitable complications and so rebuffed them as politely as possible. Progressing alone into more serious adulthood felt safer. Smarter. She had much to accomplish and didn't need distractions.

As the end of her first year of college neared, Lizzie began making trips into Cleveland to line up a job for the coming summer. After devoting a great deal of thought to possible career directions, she was determined to land a job in the investment world upon her eventual graduation. In 1959, the banks and brokerage firms were populated almost exclusively by males – cloned and uniformed in dark suits and wingtips. And there lied the appeal. The challenge of penetrating this fortress of chauvinism.

Lizzie Monroe wanted to use the first summer between college classes to get her high-heeled foot in the door. In Cleveland, she went from one brokerage firm to another, resumé in hand. Mail room, receptionist, coffee girl. She didn't care. Any position that would place her on the other side of the walls. From there, she could start her climb against the odds.

Returning from a third unsuccessful trip to Cleveland, she made a surprisingly easy decision – at least that's how Beth Davenport now remembered it. While pounding the pavement, Lizzie had been offered a "special" opportunity at one of the brokerage houses. She mostly was cold-calling small to mid-sized firms, where she felt her chances were better. The gentlemen partners in these operations normally relegated the hiring of low-level office staff to an administrative manager of some sort. But in this instance, a young partner noticed her waiting in the lobby and, on a whim, decided to interview Lizzie himself. Over the course of their conversation behind the closed door of a conference room, he suggested they take their interview elsewhere. In fact, he made his suggestion several more times – each more blatant than the previous. Lizzie laughed off his invitations.

But on the bus ride back to campus, she began second-guessing her reaction. After all, she was applying to do grunt work for the sole purpose of gaining a foothold. Why should Lizzie Monroe care about upholding any moral standards? Based on her life experiences to-date, higher virtues didn't really exist. Whatever God-given talents or assets she might possess, they should be put to proper use. All of them. To her, that seemed like a truer, more virtuous behavior. If someone saw her as attractive or desirable, those were advantages to be leveraged. If bodily functions were required, what was the big deal? Romance was nothing more than a childhood fantasy. If faced with a second chance, a more prudent choice would be made.

On trip number four into Cleveland, she was accorded just such an opportunity. At thirty-nine, he was the firm's lone junior partner. Sitting in his office, where the mid-morning interview started, Lizzie noticed a picture of a wife and three kids on the credenza. The duplicitous asshole even joked about his wife's lousy cooking when he mentioned how hungry he was and invited her to an early lunch.

She was cutting her steak when he remarked, "Miss Monroe, it seems you have a great deal of ambition … and you also happen to be a remarkably beautiful young woman. I think both traits could serve you well in the years ahead … but you need to recognize there are lots of ambitious and attractive young women hoping to get hired by a firm like ours." He paused, leaned forward, and brought his leg up against hers under the table. "Can you think of some way you might differentiate yourself?"

Lizzie smiled. "I guess my response depends on the exact job that might be available."

He was surprised by her straightforwardness. He thought for a moment. "I'm pretty sure we could use another file clerk this summer."

She didn't flinch. "I'm surprised ... 'pretty sure' is the best you can do? I can't imagine that you'd really would want to hire a woman who was willing to 'differentiate' herself for something so vague and indefinite. That wouldn't speak well of her business acumen, now would it?" She stared at him across the table, moving her leg away from his and smiling coyishly.

He hesitated again, fumbling with his fork. Whatever level of authority he held within the company; she knew he would be over-stepping it by making her a firm offer. But he now was a dog in heat. She waited him out.

Finally, he broke. "You can start on the second Monday of June ... I'll see to it this afternoon."

The sex was unremarkable, at least for her. But she'd entered that small hotel room with no basis for comparison. Prior to her twenty-minute interlude with this Cretan, Lizzie Monroe had been a virgin. High school petting in Findlay was just that. Petting. With no idea of what to do, she fumbled her way through her first act of inter-course. Kissing him on the lips was the worst part. She viewed the rest as nothing more than bodily function – no different than brush-ing one's teeth. He, on the other hand, seemed to derive a great deal of pleasure from the ridiculous exchange. His animal urges had been satisfied by a desirable female half his age.

Lying next to him afterwards, she wasn't quite sure what to say. Fortunately, he made the transition easy. As soon as he caught his breath, he suddenly remembered another appointment.

As they rode down the elevator, they stood facing the mirrored doors and she watched him grow fidgety. When they reached the lobby, she reached out to shake his hand. "You have my word ... I'll make you look good this summer."

She hadn't been sure if she needed her insurance policy, but it was best to be safe. While still grasping his hand, she pulled him closer and leaned up on her tiptoes to whisper into his ear, "I forgot to mention what a nice job your surgeon did with your appendectomy. Eight stitches. Do you think your wife has ever counted them?"

May 12, 1959

> *Today I promised to make someone look good. I will. But I will do it for my own benefit. He was nothing more than a pig who served his purpose.*

Beth Davenport only could shake her head as she read the journal entry and remembered how she felt over the days that followed this first coital act. At peace.

Even today, she didn't regret what she'd done to land her first job in Cleveland. The senator only regretted that such degrading manipulations were necessary and rampant back then. A lot had changed since she was young and starting out. Over the course of her career, perhaps she'd helped level the playing field for aspiring women. She hoped so. Nonetheless, she didn't consider herself a feminist. At heart, Beth always had been a humanist, an equalist. She genuinely wanted every person to be treated the same, to be given the same opportunities.

True equality for women was unlikely to be achieved in her lifetime. But men in power finally were being held more accountable for the abuses they inflicted or simply tolerated. As for her own behavior through the years, Beth Davenport remained at peace. Idealism was for fools. She had been forced to become a pragmatist at an early age. Childhood taught her the folly of fairy tales and happy endings. To progress and have impact, one must adapt to the situation and play by whatever rules are in place at any given time.

Chapter 29

November 9, 1959

I was wrong. Love can be beautiful.

As the Fifties drew to a close, Lizzie Monroe had been exposed too often to the ugly side of humanity. How could she possibly believe people were capable of experiencing genuine love? Love was an overused hyperbole for the superficial fascination that two people might share for a temporarily convenient duration. This hardened attitude melded well with the no-nonsense approach she was adopting for life, in general.

But Beth remembered the balmy Sunday night when this mindset began to change.

Her summer in Cleveland had exceeded all expectations. She'd made a favorable impression on the senior partners inside the brokerage firm and received an offer to return the following summer with increased responsibilities. The louse who hired her was either too embarrassed, or too afraid, to say anything more than hello during the entire three months she worked there. So, Lizzie was able to avoid the awkwardness of rejecting further invitations to 'differentiate' herself.

By November, the rhythm of her sophomore year had been established. She again was fully engaged in the classroom and otherwise keeping to herself.

During this bygone era, strict hours and curfews had been in effect for college coeds. Women were required to be in their dormitories by 10 p.m. on weeknights, and 11 p.m. on Fridays or Saturdays. Nonetheless, three or four times each week, Lizzie would climb through a bathroom window to clear her head with a late-night stroll. One of the side benefits of being a loner was that no one paid much attention to whether she hung around the dorm or not.

She usually made a beeline for a heavily wooded area just off-campus, a few hundred yards from the residence halls. Once there, she would duck down one of the narrow paths and flip on her flashlight. On this memorable night, as she was scurrying toward the trees, she heard two male voices. Her eyes hadn't fully adjusted to the darkness, but as she surveyed the surrounding area, she saw two young men entering one of the familiar paths. Once inside the treeline, they did something unexpected. They put their arms around each other's waists as they continued walking.

She was overcome with curiosity. She waited a few moments, then hurried toward the path and followed them into the woods. Lizzie didn't dare turn on a flashlight, so she slowed her pace and moved as quietly as possible. Several minutes later she again heard the muffled voices. The twosome had left the path and sounded like they were thirty or forty yards away. She carefully wove through trees and brush, hoping to learn what this mysterious duo was up to.

When she neared, all she could see was a silhouetted pair, backlit by fragments of moonlight filtering through the trees. There was no stopping now. She crouched low and moved closer. First, she recognized Cal Stratton. His rugged handsomeness was unmistakable. The second figure most certainly was Junior Davenport. Once she recognized Cal, identifying his best friend had been easy. Everyone on campus knew they were close. But until now, she'd had no idea how close they actually might be.

The two of them were leaning against a tree, locked in full

embrace. They were kissing and running their hands over each other's bodies. She never had seen, or really thought about two men kissing – let alone someone with Cal Stratton's reputation. She couldn't begin to name all the girls on campus he had dated. Stratton always seemed to be front and center at Oberlin – with sports, student government, and fraternity life. Lizzie didn't know much about Junior Davenport. He tended to stay more in the background, which to her seemed a positive attribute.

She was fascinated by their total lack of inhibition. Soon she was completely transfixed by the intensity. Not just in what she saw, but also what she heard. Hushed voices. Belt buckles and zippers. Occasional moans or sighs. At one point, Cal couldn't help himself. In a louder than normal voice, he let out, "God, how I love being with you, Junior."

For Lizzie, this proclamation was the turning point. It no longer was sheer novelty. She now was watching with admiration, even reverence. For her, prurient interest was nonexistent – caring nothing about the body chemistry on display. She also wouldn't think to pass moral judgement on whether two males should or shouldn't be engaged in sexual intimacies. Who was she to judge what people might do in private?

Far more important to Lizzie Monroe was the beauty, the pureness, that these two individuals were experiencing. Despite the risks posed to two young men. Despite the stigma that would be attached to them if they were caught. She could see their unbridled passion for one another. The raw emotion was unlike any she'd ever witnessed, or even imagined. Then, inexplicably, her thoughts turned to Lila. Soon, she felt tears running down her cheeks. When she reached into her coat pocket for a glove to use as a handkerchief, she dropped the flashlight. It struck the ground with a thud.

Cal and Junior stopped what they were doing at once. The whole world seemed to stop. Lizzie scooped up the flashlight, hurried through the trees, and started running down the path. It wasn't long before she heard a pounding pace behind her. She needed to get out of the woods ahead of them. She had no idea what they might do to protect their secret.

She was away from the trees and heading across a clearing when Cal caught up to her. He showed no sign of anger as he slowed down to run alongside her. Only fear. He implored her, "Please stop. We need to talk."

She kept running toward her dormitory.

"Please, Elizabeth, I'm begging you to stop."

He knew her name. Of course, he did. It was Oberlin. Everybody knew everybody. But hearing her name made his plea sound more desperate. She stopped running and turned to face him.

"Thank you," he said. He made no move toward her. Instead he gave a slight, sheepish smile. "I suppose you might want an explanation."

Lizzie smiled back. "Oh, I don't think any explanations are necessary."

At this point, Junior reached the spot where the two were standing. He was out of breath and attempting to slide the end of his belt through a pants loop. He looked at Cal, then at Lizzie, not sure what to say. Finally, he held out his hand to her. "Hi, I'm Junior Davenport."

She looked down at his hand and stared. He suddenly remembered where his hands had been just a few minutes earlier. "I guess not. I'm sorry … that was pretty stupid."

She laughed. How could she not? In an instant, Junior Davenport was red-faced. He was blushing over a thwarted handshake. Not because he'd been caught "in flagrante delicto" with another man. And that's when Lizzie felt her first meaningful connection with the man who eventually would become her husband.

To avoid being seen, the three of them returned to the edge of the wooded area. They hadn't anticipated how long the resulting conversation would last. And they couldn't possibly have anticipated the enduring friendships that would take root on this memorable night.

Cal wanted to make sure Lizzie knew she was the only person at Oberlin aware of the "special relationship" that he and Junior had forged. "In fact, you're the only person anywhere. We've never been able to talk about our love for one another." Junior rapidly nodded his head to affirm what Cal was saying.

She was taken aback by how easily they expressed their feelings. She wouldn't have expected two men to speak openly of love. They seemed almost relieved to be sharing their secret with someone. After a few tentative questions from her, the floodgates opened. There was so much they at last could reveal.

The two had met as freshmen in high school, soon after their arrivals at Culver Military Academy. They hit it off immediately. A few months later, a first late night of experimentation "just happened." Soon they realized their secret late-night activities were more than curious adolescent urges. They felt something for each other. Something deep and extraordinary.

Cal and Junior made it through four years at Culver without anyone suspecting – and even mixed in a few summer visits to their respective homes. When senior year at Culver rolled around, they both applied to Oberlin – intent on remaining together for another four years.

They understood how military school and college offered them unique environments for time together in private – as long as they remained careful. Sadly, they also recognized their situation would change dramatically once those eight years had run their course – which now was a mere seven months away. Junior grew somber as Cal opened-up about the looming deadline.

"It's hard to imagine what things will be like when we aren't able to see one another, but we can't throw the rest of our lives away. Junior will someday run his family's business ... he'll be an extremely wealthy man. My parents have invested a huge part of their savings to send me to school ... they expect great things from me. Our families could never appreciate or accept the feelings we share. Hell, no one could. We'd be outcasts ... seen as nothing more than a couple of fairies ... queers. These realities have hung over our heads since the beginning ... which is why we're spending every moment we can together now."

Lizzie saw the anguish in their faces. She could see the deep devotion they shared when Cal put his hand on Junior's shoulder and they looked into each other's eyes. Their love was real – more genuine than any feelings she'd ever witnessed between two people. Later that night, when Lizzie made her journal entry – "Love can be beautiful" – she was remembering those touching moments of conversation, not what she'd observed in the darkness of the woods.

She promised Cal and Junior that their secret would remain safe. She had no intention of telling anyone. She even laughed, "I barely communicate with the other students here ... you have nothing to worry about."

Junior, who had done little of the talking, spoke up. "Our future is very much in your hands, Elizabeth Monroe ... and for some reason, I feel okay about that."

The three of them shared a long, heartfelt hug before starting back to campus. Cal and Joe moved to either side of Lizzie, flanking her as they walked. After a few steps, she reached out and put an arm around each of their waists. In turn, each put his arm around her.

Beth reread the passage, then closed her eyes – trying to hold on to that long-ago memory of their walk in the moonlight. In just such a fashion, Junior, Cal, and Lizzie would continue a shared journey for many years to come.

Chapter 30

Whenever the three were together during the balance of the school year, Cal would make teasing references to their November encounter – calling it "our adventure in the woods." Junior invariably turned as red as he did that first night. Cal's good-natured humor and Junior's boyish bashfulness were just part of their charm. Lizzie couldn't meet up with them as often as she would have liked, but their reunions soon became the high points to her college memories.

In June, Cal and Junior graduated and headed off to the respective careers for which they'd prepared. Lizzie spent the summer in Cleveland, taking on more and more responsibility from men eager to reduce their workloads by pushing tasks onto someone more junior with proven competence – even if that person happened to be female. When she returned to campus for junior year, Lizzie missed the camaraderie and chemistry of these two "special friends." Even with herself, she wasn't sure how she should refer to Cal and Junior. Were they a couple? Were they lovers? Soulmates? In the bold new decade of the Sixties, no one had come up with an acceptable label for two males in their situation.

During her junior year, Lizzie received periodic notes from Cal, who had promised to stay in touch. Predictably, she heard nothing from Junior. Nonetheless, she penned several letters to both.

She returned to Cleveland during the last summer of college. By the end of August, she was offered a full-time position at the firm as a market analyst upon graduation the next spring. Inside the dark-suited fraternity of brokerage firms, such an opportunity was practically unheard of.

Perhaps even more unexpected, and equally welcomed, was an invitation from Cal to join Junior and him for dinner on the Friday evening of homecoming weekend during the autumn of 1961, when they returned to campus for the first time. They promptly brought her up to date on their budding business careers. Cal had completed his full year of training rotations inside the Indianapolis bank that recruited him at Oberlin. He was now an assistant loan officer.

Junior was shuttling back and forth between Evansville, Indiana and various coalmines in a three-state area. His father had plans for Junior to someday run Davenport Mining, but first he needed more coal dust under his fingernails.

From there, the conversation took an unanticipated turn. Since graduation, Cal and Junior had managed to coordinate schedules to allow them several weekend rendezvous. One had taken place over the Fourth of July holiday, when Cal travelled to Riceville, Kentucky – which was where Junior had been sent to oversee the fortification of a borehole shaft in one of the company's oldest mines. It was a small community without secrets, and they'd been careless. Word traveled back to Joseph Davenport, Sr., that his son and a visiting male were sharing Junior's motel room – a motel room with only one double bed.

A month later, Junior had been called into his father's office and ambushed. As soon as the door was closed, the elder Davenport unleashed. "Listen, Junior, if you ever expect to run this company, you have to stop whatever disgusting things you do with this Cal Stratton character and start dating women … you need to start dipping your wick like a man, for Christ's sake. I can't have people down in my mines thinking I've raised a faggot for a son … wondering whether they even can trust being alone with you down in a coalmine while they try to teach you our god-damned business."

Junior had been caught totally off-guard. When he tried to interrupt, his father cut him off. "Don't waste your time trying to lie about it. I've suspected you and your sweetie pie, Cal, for a long time. You've always been a softy … and he's such a pretty boy. All my folks down there in Riceville knew the two of you were shacking up … and it didn't take long for me to hear about it. After that, I paid someone to do more digging. If you want to see the pictures from your trip up to Indianapolis last week, I'll see that my source gets you a set. I just can't believe a son of mine has turned out to be a pansy."

Though Junior had been the target of his father's rage, it was Cal who provided most of the details during the dinner conversation with Lizzie. She wasn't surprised the pair had continued seeing one another. Though they'd intended to move on with their lives in separate directions, she had recognized their feelings were far too intense for them to stay apart. Still, what Junior's father had said was horrifying – and she had a unique perspective on the cruelties a father could perpetrate. As details poured out, she reached across the table and took Junior's hand. She pressed it tightly for a few moments. He gave her an appreciative smile, but otherwise showed little reaction while Cal continued to lament the messiness of their situation.

She realized then that she'd been mistaken about one important aspect of the unusual relationship between these two young men. Since that fateful night in the forest, she had assumed it was Cal who was the stronger, more steadfast personality – the stable influence. But now she watched as Junior maintained an even keel and Cal took them on an emotional rollercoaster ride. Funny how she had missed that before. Cal might be the face, voice, and outward energy in their relationship, but Junior provided the solid foundation.

Cal sounded off with a final tirade about Senior Davenport before pausing to regain his composure. Junior looked at Cal and calmly asked, "Are we ready to move on?"

Cal shrugged, then laughingly added, "I think so ... but I reserve the right to tear into your father again later."

Junior nodded a playful okay to Cal before directing his attention to her. "Lizzie, since the meeting in my father's office, Cal and I have devised a plan that would allow us to avoid future dilemmas ... that is, if we are to continue seeing each other ... which obviously we want to do." Now, it was his turn to reach across the table and grasp Lizzie's hand. "And this plan is very much dependent on you."

She listened attentively. In fact, due to her astonishment over what soon was proposed, the sentences felt like they were coming at her in slow motion. She absorbed and dissected each and every word, trying to assess whether Junior and Cal possibly could be serious.

Junior had no intention of dating the young women of Evansville, or anywhere else. He long ago had recognized girls were of no interest to him, at least romantically. They wanted Lizzie to pretend she had become Junior's girlfriend back when he was a student at Oberlin, and that the two of them still were involved in a long-distance relationship.

They were hoping she might agree to write a few schmaltzy letters which Junior would leave lying around for certain people in Evansville to read. They could take some pictures that weekend at Oberlin – showing she and Junior frolicking around campus, doing things a normal dating couple might do. Junior would make sure those photos also were conveniently visible to his father and his father's inner circle.

Plus, they wanted her to make a few trips to Evansville – joining Junior at social functions where Senior Davenport and his cronies would be present. "With you at my side, Lizzie, I'll be able to display the appropriate amount of lovey-dovey behavior to make people believe we're for real."

What's more, they expected to pay her – and pay her well. In addition to covering her travel and other expenses, she would receive a thousand dollars each month for participating in the charade. It was an exorbitant amount of money for the early Sixties, but a mere pittance to Junior, who had gained access to a sizable trust fund at age twenty-one.

After the entire plan was laid out, Lizzie started laughing. "Surely, you must be joking."

Their resulting pleas convinced her they were completely serious. Junior was the one who finally posed the question. "Lizzie, we entrusted you with our deepest secret those many months ago … and you've been true to your word. Once again, our future together … and my future inside a company that carries my family's name … depend on you. Will you help us out … or will you at least think about it for a few days?"

She sat silently as they stared anxiously across the table at her. She closed her eyes and thought about what they were proposing … about their predicament and the fact they had conceived such a ludicrous plan. With her eyes still closed, she began to smile.

When she opened them, Junior and Cal were practically jumping out of their skins trying to decipher the meaning of her smile.

"Gentlemen, I don't need time to consider a response … and I certainly don't want any of Junior's hush money. You two have become my closest friends … you simply should have offered to reimburse me for my expenses. That said … of course, I will help you. Your love for one another is very special … not only to you, but also to me. It needs to be protected and preserved."

Before the evening was over, Junior and Cal convinced Lizzie to accept the thousand-dollar monthly payments. She later would regret that aspect of the masquerade. Otherwise, she never once sec-ond-guessed her consenting to the arrangement.

October 21, 1961

Last night, I signed on to the most foolish plan I've ever heard. Today, I feel spectacular.

Chapter 31

Beth Davenport may have been feeling the effects of a second glass of wine. Or perhaps her prolonged nostalgic ponderings had triggered an unfamiliar mental state – since, after all, she'd never ventured this intensely into her journal. Whatever had come over her, she now was committed to reading the passages from cover to cover.

Throughout her lifetime, her personal diary had become a convenient place to record and bury memories, not revisit them. But strangely, she was feeling a contentment, a calmness about the events of her life. This type of serenity was foreign. She normally didn't allow her mind to delve very deeply into the past. She preferred to avoid the cringes and winces that accompanied the assorted remembrances. But, taken as a whole, she was finding unexpected peace in the complex mosaic.

The three of them indeed had been foolish to believe their farfetched scheme might work. As soon as Lizzie met Senior Davenport, she knew the plan was destined for failure. Junior and Cal had been deluding themselves. Yet now, these many years later, recalling their naïve hopefulness made her miss seeing the two of them together even more. Granted, she still saw Cal when she was in Indianapolis and he had remained a positive force in hers and Troy's lives. But he never was the same after losing Junior. Sadly, the same could be said for her. Life never again seemed as full.

At age twenty-one, she hadn't been on a date since she was a seventeen-year-old in Findlay. The only time she'd even conceded to be alone with a male over that period was to sacrifice her virginity to the gods of commerce and ambition. She'd lost interest in having a romance of any kind and wasn't sure she could or wanted to feel otherwise again. She was a markedly different young woman than the teenager who loved the constant cat-and-mouse games with boys.

Once she got her mind around the bizarre proposal, committing to an artificial dating relationship seemed like the ideal substitute. All the trimmings, none of the entanglements. That first weekend in November, she and Junior romped around campus posing as ersatz lovebirds while Cal took dozens of Polaroids. Then came the weekly letters, which turned out to be even more of a lark. She chronicled made-up details about made-up times together – expressing made-up longings for made-up intimacies. She might as well have been writing a paperback book for a rack in the drug store.

In early January, she received a phone call. That's when she learned their day of reckoning was approaching. February 10, 1962 – the Saturday night leading into Valentine's Day. Evansville's biggest charity gala would be held in the city's swankiest hotel, and this year's chairman was none other than Joseph Elwood Davenport, Sr. – which meant the evening was a command performance for Junior. The event was made-to-order for a son looking to showcase a college sweetheart in front of his father, his father's colleagues, and the whole of Evansville, for that matter. With any luck, she and Junior would see their faces plastered across the society page of the local newspaper.

She entered the weekend filled with preconceptions – having listened to Cal and Junior bemoan Senior Davenport's iron-fisted style and closed-minded viewpoints. When she at long last was introduced to Junior's father, he made an attempt at charm. His kind of charm. Not the kind that would put a woman at ease.

He was standing in a crowd near the center of the ballroom, surrounded by a throng of friends and wannabe friends – everyone decked out in evening gowns and tuxedos. Junior held out his arm as they worked their way toward the scrum. "Strap in," he said to her.

As people shuffled about, Lizzie caught glimpses of the man of the hour. Though only forty-four at the time, his closely cropped hair was silver, which made his head stand out among the crowd as it bobbed up and down in animated conversation. He appeared average in height and had the skin of a television cowboy – well-worn and permanently colored from the elements. He was broad-shouldered and had a barrel chest that seemed to push out whenever he spoke to one of the females among the gathering.

When he finally saw them approaching, Senior motioned for those around him to clear a path. His gaze riveted on Lizzie. He waited until they stopped directly in front of him. "So, this is Elizabeth," he said for all to hear.

She extended her hand, but instead of taking it, Junior's father stepped back two or three paces. "Let's just take a look at you." He eyed her up and down, even extending his neck to either side, so he could view her from several angles. Lizzie summoned every ounce of inner strength she could muster to retain her composure. At that moment, she felt like she was back in Findlay, standing before her father with the drapes pulled – his eyes moving lewdly over her body. But she wasn't going to give Junior's father the satisfaction of seeing her tear up, or worse yet, dash from the room.

Senior Davenport smiled and slowly shook his head back and forth for several seconds. Eventually, he moved closer and took the hand that by now had dropped to her side. He brought it up to his cheek, feeling the softness of her skin against his face, before placing her hand to his lips and giving it a light kiss. "Now aren't you something? Our little Junior goes all these years without ever bringing a girl around … and now he shows up with a gal like you on his arm. My, but you are exquisite … a vision of beauty, I have to say." He looked around to see how many of his friends were within earshot. Convinced his audience was sufficient, he said in a noticeably louder voice, "Elizabeth here must have taken a liking to his daddy's money!" Then he let loose with a bawdy laugh, and the assembled ranks quickly joined in.

Lizzie did the unthinkable. She dug deep and laughed along with them.

Until that moment, Lizzie had been regretting the monthly payments she accepted from Junior – mad at herself for not putting up more resistance. Suddenly, she felt like she was earning every penny.

Joseph Davenport, Sr., was even more of a self-centered brute than she'd anticipated. If he had been anyone else, she would have said something unseemly and hurried away from Senior and his whole smarmy enclave. But her primary objective was winning him over. Only then would he believe her when she spoke about the devotion she felt for his son.

Later in the evening, she and Junior were having an enjoyable conversation with a group of younger people in attendance – friends with whom Junior had grown up. From behind them, one of Senior's toadies appeared. He was there to 'fetch' Lizzie away. Shortly, Junior's father would be dancing his only dance of the evening, and he had ordained that Junior's girlfriend be his partner. She met him in the middle of the dance floor, and to her surprise, they were alone – surrounded by open space. The other guests were crowded around the perimeter of the ballroom, watching their every move.

He smiled as he once again ogled her from head to toe, his eyes lingering in all the places they shouldn't. "Thank you for joining me. It is time for the Chairman's Dance … it's a long-standing tradition. Everyone else will join us after a few minutes."

He held up his arms in dance position and she stepped into place as his partner. With a nod, he signaled the bandleader. As the music began, he slid his face close to her ear. "I'm a huge Sinatra fan ... I hope you don't mind. I've requested one of my favorites." With that, the band's male vocalist began singing *The Lady Is A Tramp*.

Throughout the balance of the song, as well as the balance of the evening, Senior never said another word to Lizzie. Meanwhile, it seemed like the rest of Evansville couldn't wait to meet her. Junior received hardy pats on the back from a steady stream of males and she was obliged to dance with most of them.

On Sunday, Junior took her to the airport where she boarded a plane for the second time in her life. The first had been Friday afternoon, when she'd flown into Evansville from Ohio. Junior had met her at the gate and driven her to a hotel where she was checked into the nicest room she'd ever seen. There had been no pretense about her staying with him at his apartment. In those days, no proper gentleman would have dared to place his girlfriend in such an indelicate situation.

The two walked to dinner at a nearby restaurant. Previously, she and Junior had spent no meaningful time alone. Cal always had been present. Their meal lasted several hours, and she came to appreciate what a caring and sensitive soul he truly was. She began to wonder if she really could fall for a guy like Junior Davenport.

She drank more wine than intended, so when he escorted her back to the hotel, she was feeling playful as they stood in the lobby. "Would you be interested in coming upstairs? Maybe we could be more believable as a couple if we threw caution to the wind and ..."

He cut her off. "Lizzie, you are so incredibly beautiful ... and you are amazing even to suggest you'd be willing ... but please, please stop. I can't."

Junior once again was turning red from embarrassment. She no longer felt impish, as something about his reaction caused her concern. "I'm sorry, Junior ... I'll stop. But why 'can't' you ... is it because of Cal?"

He stammered slightly, "I guess so ... yes. I want to be loyal to him."

She was digging deeper than she should but couldn't stop herself. She wanted to understand what rules applied when two men were carrying on a secret relationship. "You do remember that Cal dated plenty of girls while he was at Oberlin ... and that he had a reputation for doing a lot more than simply holding their hands? Are you saying he has stopped his sleeping around ... that he has lost interest in women?"

Junior became frustrated as he tried to respond. "I don't know ... I hope so ... but probably not."

"Then why do you feel obligated to maintain your fidelity if he doesn't?" she asked.

"It's not just fidelity ... and not just about Cal. I truly cannot be with a woman. How can I say this? Lizzie, there are parts of my body that won't do what they're supposed to do."

She felt horrible for pressing the issue. "Don't say another word, Junior. I understand. Please forgive me for being so persistent ... and for being so dense." Like a mother protecting a child, she wrapped her arms around him and pulled his head into her shoulder. "We're going to have a wonderful weekend together ... I promise."

She kept her promise. Her first visit to Evansville was a memorable time for both of them. Discovering such genuine goodness in another human being made Lizzie Monroe feel better about the world as a whole and Junior had been certain that Saturday night's charade was a total success. She decided to keep her misgivings to herself.

February 12, 1962

From the moment I met him, I had this feeling he was seeing right through us. He is a disgusting human being. But he's also very savvy, and that is a frightening combination. I fear there are tough times ahead for my two dearest friends.

Beth read the entry a second time. And then a third. In hindsight, those ominous feelings from 1962 were more than warranted. Tough times for Junior and Cal soon followed. In fact, her "two dearest friends" navigated difficult circumstances for the balance of their relationship. Yet still, they managed to focus on the positives, to celebrate the joy of working through their obstacles together.

But what really struck Beth as she studied the passage, was the manner by which she had distanced herself. It was an aspect of her journal writing that never had dawned on her until now. In making countless entries like this one, she never once had cited a name or noted specific details. Whatever her thoughts and emotions had been during these seminal moments in her life, she was able to condense them into concise, almost impersonal observations as she recorded the events.

For a teenager, this practice made sense. How could any child feel comfortable writing the name of a parent and attaching it to the abhorrent acts that took place in the Monroe house? Plus, she'd lived with the risk that her journal might be found by a family member. Keeping things vague and anonymous was pragmatic.

But why had she continued to be so cryptic as an adult? These were messages written only to herself. No other person ever would read her journal.

Rationales for this patterned behavior fell neatly into place. She could see that now. The abuses of her father. Her brother's deviant demands of Lila. The obliteration of her entire family, most likely at the hands of her dearest friend. The scorn to which Junior and Cal were subjected. The eventual tragedy that took Junior's life. She simply had shut off her emotions each time, distancing herself from the pain of any given moment. But as years rolled by, the remorse and resignation never left her.

So what if she had endured a litany of unspeakable secrets? Her life turned out fine. She shattered too many glass ceilings to count. She was a respected United States Senator. She had championed scores of worthwhile causes. There was no reason to dwell on scar tissue, on the gaps in her relationships, on the gaps in her emotions. Detachment and dispassion were developed skills. If she had hoped to succeed, they were requirements.

But now? *What a crock.* She stared at words scrawled onto pages by a young woman in her early twenties. As the most important experiences in her life unfolded, she had discarded names and details like candy wrappers. Even now, as she reflected on these events from her distant past, she still visualized them in third person, somehow pretending Lizzie or Elizabeth was a separate person. *Who have I been kidding?*

Chapter 32

S he hurriedly leafed through the next few sections of the journal – as though skipping over the upcoming June entry might make it disappear. But jumping ahead would be futile. She already was reliving the numbness she felt that day. Beth flipped back to the page that marked a critical crossroad and the choice she had to make. Whether she read the words or not, the outcome was etched indelibly into her being. Her ultimate decision altered every aspect of her life from that point forward.

> _June 20, 1962_
>
> My instincts were right. He did know all along. Unfortunately, the man is even more vile than I imagined. But now I'm left wondering if I am any less vile.

Following the charity ball in February, Lizzie spent March and April focused on schoolwork and lining up a small apartment in Cleveland for after she graduated. She tried to forget about Senior Davenport – the feelings of angst and disgust he stirred within her. But in May, Davenport Mining would celebrate its tenth year in Evansville with a weekend of festivities. Her presence was required once again.

Cal also drove down from Indianapolis, hoping he might score points with Senior by being there. As it turned out, none of their attendance really mattered. Other than a few contemptuous glances, Senior Davenport ignored all three of them for three days. Junior finally realized his make-believe romance with Lizzie was working with everyone but the one person he needed to convince. The next day, he and Cal decided they should stop seeing each another until they devised a better plan. Lizzie flew back to Ohio believing her faux fling with Junior was over. Little did she know, her experience to-date merely had been the training phase.

After graduating on the first Saturday in June, Lizzie started with the Cleveland brokerage firm two days later – not wanting to waste even a day before she launched her real career. At the onset, she informed her coworkers that she no longer wanted to go by Liz or Lizzie. Henceforth, they should refer to her only as Elizabeth – a name that would cause people to take her more seriously. And Elizabeth Monroe had every intention of being taken seriously for many years ahead. She was determined to become the firm's first female partner.

She was less than three weeks into her ascent up the corporate ladder, when she received a call from one of the executive secretaries. The firm's managing partner needed her in his private conference room at once. Having met this imposing man but once, she hadn't been sure he even knew what she looked like.

When she arrived at the closed door adjoining his office, she heard laughter on the other side. She knocked lightly. No response. Just more laughter. Male laughter. She knocked more emphatically.

The laughter stopped. "Please come in, Elizabeth."

She pushed the door open and the managing partner rose from his chair to greet her with a warm smile and handshake. Another gentleman was sitting at the small conference table facing the opposite direction. He did not rise.

Even from behind, she recognized the cropped silver hair. Her stomach sank. What possible reason could he have for being in Cleveland? For visiting the place where she worked?

"I believe you know, Mr. Davenport. So, if you don't mind, I'll leave the two of you alone." In an instant, the senior-most executive in the firm was hurrying from the room and closing the door behind him.

Her world felt like it was turning upside down. She didn't move – having no idea what was happening.

Slowly, Senior turned his chair around to face her, choosing to remain seated. He signaled for her to take the chair directly across the table from him. "We have a lot to talk about, Elizabeth. Or maybe, you would prefer I call you Lizzie." He drew out her nickname with an almost venomous tone.

As a display of confidence, she took the chair at the head of the table – the one just vacated by the managing partner. "I think Elizabeth will do just fine, Mr. Davenport. Thank you." Despite her outward gestures, she was spinning out of control on the inside. Whatever awaited, she needed to exhibit strength. "It would seem you have friends here. To what do I owe the honor?" she asked with a polite smile.

"Rest assured, young lady … with a simple phone call or two, I can create instant friendships at any institution that invests money. But I'm not here to discuss investments … at least with you."

"I see. Well then, I guess I should tell you before you say another word … I have no interest in working in one of your coalmines." She deadpanned the delivery, hoping her attempt at humor might ease the tension in the room.

He was caught off-guard and momentarily baffled by the non-sequitur. As he thought about the absurdity of her comment, he began to grin. "You are a clever one … and I like that. In fact, it's your cleverness that brings me here today."

She looked at him without saying a word, trying to gauge where the conversation was headed. Finally, she said, "I'm sorry ... I'm not sure what you mean."

"Oh, come on, Lizzie ... I mean, Elizabeth ... you're a smart girl. You know exactly what I mean." He leaned in closer, stretching his arms and hands across the table that separated them. "You didn't really think I would buy that bogus bullshit that you and Junior were dishing out, now did ya? Not long after I confronted him about the disgusting things he and Cal were doing down in Kentucky, he started leaving your phony pictures and letters laying around. Hell, I'm not a complete moron ... I knew what he was up to. But I had to hand it to him ... I sure liked what I saw in those photographs. If he was going to rent himself a fake girlfriend, he might as well hire a pretty one. Ain't that right? Anyway, I just wanted to see how far he'd push his bogus little game."

She wasn't ready to admit anything, so Elizabeth just kept looking at him in silence – able to maintain a calm façade out of sheer determination.

He rambled on. "It took a few months before I knew for sure he was paying you ... but my people figured it out ... they always come through for me. I don't pay Junior squat in salary ... and what little I do pay him is still more than he's worth. But based on the activity in his trust fund, they tell me he's probably been sending you something in the neighborhood of thousand dollars a month. Does that sound about right?"

He waited two or three seconds for an answer. "I guess the cat's still got your tongue, huh?" In total command, he was enjoying himself. "You know, missy, I've got people on my payroll who can get me whatever kind of information I ask 'em to. For a couple years, they've been bringing me reports on Junior and his faggot boyfriend. I never much liked what I heard ... but when he got careless down there in Kentucky, I had no choice but to step in and put a stop to it. I've worked too damned hard to make the Davenport name mean something ... I can't just sit by and let him destroy it. You know I'm right ... now don't you? Actually, I'm sure you do ... why else would you have agreed to help him fool folks into thinking he was a real man who liked to stick his pecker inside a real woman?"

She swallowed hard to suppress her disgust. If not for her concern for Junior, she would have slapped him and stormed out of the room.

He saw how she was struggling, so he paused to watch – savoring the effect he was having. Finally, he moved on. "Funny thing ... I had those same people do some checking on you. You've got quite an interesting background, now don't you Miss Lizzie Monroe? Oops ... there I go again. I don't think I'll ever get used to calling you Elizabeth. You just seem more like a Lizzie to me."

He placed his hand up to his heart, in mock sympathy. "But I gotta give you credit, pretty lady ... you've overcome a lot of adversity for someone so young. Your dad was a drunk and your brother was scum. Your family was nothing but dirt-poor white trash ... and then they went and got themselves burned up in a fire. Now that kind of background might make a mess out of most people. Not you, though ... you studied and earned yourself a full scholarship ... and then a highfalutin job here at this firm. What you've done is mighty damned impressive. But despite all that success, you still couldn't resist the money my son was willing to pay you to make him look like a man. I guess growing up poor, some people are willing to do just about anything for a buck."

For the first time since he'd started his diatribe, she interrupted him. "I didn't do it for the money. I did it for Junior and Cal ... they have a very special relationship and deserve the chance to be together. I care a great deal about both of them."

He scoffed. "Sure you do, honey ... you cared so much about

them that you charged my son a grand a month to become part of their lives."

Her calm, confident demeanor cracked – or maybe it shattered. Lizzie was fighting back tears. "It wasn't like that ... not like that at all. I didn't want to take the money. They made me ..." She stopped, realizing how pathetic she sounded – realizing how foolish she had been. Why hadn't she just refused those payments?

"Don't you worry, Lizzie. I admire folks who seize an opportunity. I have great respect for someone with your brains and beauty, who also happens to have what I like to call an enterprising nature. I've been giving our Junior's situation a great deal of thought, and I've come here today with a proposition of my own for you."

Over the next twenty minutes, Elizabeth Monroe felt like she was having an out-of-body experience. She couldn't possibly be hearing him right. Senior Davenport wanted her to marry his son. He would pay her well, and make sure she had whatever kind of career she wanted down in Evansville. She would be expected to keep Junior on "the straight and narrow" with his personal life – which meant no more sex with men. If he had strange urges that she didn't want to tend to ... then let him go to a hooker like any normal man would. Most importantly, he expected she and Junior to produce children. Ideally several, and at least one of them a male to carry on the Davenport name.

It was 1963, not the Middle Ages. The whole idea was preposterous. She didn't know if she should laugh, cry, or call the authorities. That was, until he finally got around to the amount he proposed to pay her. Ten thousand dollars a month, for as long as she remained married to Junior and abided by the contractual terms he'd laid out. What's more, Junior already had agreed to the outrageous arrangement if his father could convince Lizzie to go along.

This last part threw her for a loop. What was Junior thinking? Why would he agree? Could his father possibly wield that much control over him? After Senior left, she would get Junior on the phone. But at that moment, she was fixated on the amount Senior Davenport casually had thrown out.

Ten thousand dollars a month. One-hundred-and-twenty-thousand dollars a year. The average annual income across the country was under five-thousand dollars. She had just graduated from college near the top of her class and was earning four-hundred-and-eighty dollars a month at a respected brokerage house. The President of the United States was earning only a hundred thousand each year. Baseball players were the highest paid athletes in the world, and their average annual salary was twenty-thousand dollars. The staggering sum offered by Senior would place her among the highest paid people on the planet … she'd be breathing the same thin air as corporate tycoons and a handful of movies stars.

Even as a little girl, she had been obsessed with the idea of someday earning lots of money and shedding the vestiges of her childhood. She had been one of the poorest kids in her school. Day after day, she had worn the same tired clothing. If she wanted a new outfit, she usually was forced to alter her brother's hand-me-downs. She had seen how the families on the other side of town lived – only to return to a hopelessness that hung like a foul vacuum inside the Monroe house. No matter how hard she worked over the many years ahead, she might never earn anything close to what Senior Davenport was willing to pay her for the rest of her life.

Beth Davenport focused on the last line to the journal entry she made later that night in 1962. "But now I'm left wondering if I am any less vile." Had she been any less vile? She still wasn't sure.

By current standards, Junior's father had offered her the equivalent of millions of dollars per year. Plus, there had been the power and prestige of the Davenport name. For an ambitious young woman, her possibilities for the future suddenly were limitless.

Lizzie did what any sane person would have done. She asked

Senior how much time she could have to consider her decision. He smiled like a Cheshire cat. He gave her a deadline of one week, but he already knew the answer. They both did. Otherwise, she would have turned him down on the spot.

Chapter 33

It was only three days before Lizzie got back to Senior with her response. Her resolve was strengthened by a heartfelt conversation with Junior, who was totally in favor of Senior's proposed arrangement. After a final night of self-reflection, her choice was an easy one. As soon as she admitted to herself that she had no interest in romance, and likely never would, all emotional considerations quickly fell to the wayside.

Lizzie reduced the issues to simple black and white. Or more simply, green. What was in it for her? On that measure, both the short and long-term benefits were practically incalculable. As a last-minute precaution, she reached out to Junior one last time before placing her call to Senior.

"Lizzie, though not for reasons my father possibly could understand, it's the most decent thing he's ever done for me. I don't even have words to describe what your agreeing to go along means to me. With all the swirling rumors about my personal life, Senior has decreed that any future I have inside the family business is contingent upon me being married ... contingent upon me being perceived as a normal 'red-blooded' male. Well, considering my situation in the bedroom department, I'm not inclined to date eligible women and waste their time ... let alone ask one of them to marry me. But you're fully aware of my physical limitations and willing to proceed regardless. You will become a wealthy woman as a Davenport ... as well as a successful businesswoman in your own right, I'm sure. You'll enjoy a wonderful life in Evansville. Correct that ... we'll enjoy a wonderful life together. Whatever interests you might pursue, I won't stand in your way ... and that includes other men, if those needs were ever to kindle inside you. If you happen to fall in love with someone else, the choice will be yours. I'll grant you a divorce anytime you ask ... no questions asked."

Junior was going into the contracted marriage with his eyes wide open. Sure, she cared a great deal for him as a friend. But one didn't commit oneself to marriage and a tyrannical father-in-law out of friendship. For Lizzie Monroe, their union was principally a business deal, which Junior fully accepted. In fact, he was encouraging her to take full advantage of the family name and fortune in whatever ways she saw fit.

She pressed him on the terms his father had specified. First, she reminded Junior, "He expects us to have children. That could become awkward."

Junior had wrestled with this delicate topic and grown comfortable with the prospects. "At some point, my father will simply have to accept we're unable to have children ... that I'm incapable. We'll convince him I have fertility issues ... he doesn't need to know about my real problem."

She added, "And maybe in time ... with the right medical experts, we can do something about that. I'm willing to try if you are."

His only response was silence, so Lizzie moved on to a second, more complicated issue. "Junior, your father has had people watching you for several years ... he's not going to stop. We'll be living under a microscope. If you plan to keep things going with Cal ... to keep sneaking away together ... how do you expect to pull that off?"

The answer was the same as when she first broached the subject three days earlier. "We'll figure something out." The reply didn't provide much comfort, but because of her feelings for Junior and Cal, Lizzie Monroe was willing to live with this uncertainty.

When she informed Senior of her decision, he was true to form. "I knew you were a smart girl … and now you're going to be a rich one, too. But you'll earn every nickel trying to make a man out of Junior. I sure as hell never could."

She couldn't resist. "Oh, don't be so hard on yourself. I think you did an excellent job. Junior is a much better man than some people I can think of."

Lizzie heard a muffled growl on the other end of the phone. Then he proclaimed, "I suppose you're gonna want a written contract."

She hesitated before yielding to her instincts. "I hadn't really considered that possibility. I'm assuming you're a man of your word." She did figure he was a man of his word, and she worried a written agreement would carry more risk for her than for him – since she was clueless as to how she and Junior were going to fulfill certain aspects of the bargain.

Her response pleased him. "Good … cuz I wasn't sure how to explain our arrangement to my attorneys." He chuckled at his own attempt at humor. "I'd say we have a deal then … and that I'm gonna have me a daughter-in-law. You better start thinking about what you're going to call me … at least to my face." He chuckled again.

"I think 'Senior' will do just fine. Good day, sir." With that, Lizzie hung up the phone – not giving Senior Davenport the opportunity to beat her to it. And so began their on-going test of wills.

May 18, 1963

It won't be the wedding of my dreams. But of course, I had no dreams of getting married in the first place.

Lizzie assumed that she and Junior would be married later in the summer, but Senior had other ideas. The wedding would take place the following May, and her monthly payments would commence once she and Junior were man and wife.

The delay was unrelated to the money. Senior had different reasons that surprised Lizzie. He prided himself in being his own man, in parading through life as though he didn't notice or care what others thought. But a major crack in his crusty armor was revealed as wedding plans began to take shape.

"You two need to have a proper engagement period. Being raised in the coalmines doesn't mean we're a bunch of red-necked hillbillies … and I won't have folks around here questioning how we go about things. So, Junior, you and your new fiancé go off and pick a date for the spring or summer of next year … the way the son of some doctor or lawyer would."

They settled on May 18, and it was the last decision connected to the wedding that she and Junior were allowed to make. A high-priced New York woman was hired to handle every detail – in concert with Senior alone. The black-tie reception was held under a gigantic pergola constructed out of imported Spanish cedar – on a bluff overlooking Senior's beloved Ohio River. Newspapers from Cincinnati, Louisville, and Indianapolis sent reporters to cover the event. The articles described it as the most elegant affair in Southern Indiana in more than a decade. Joseph Elwood Davenport, from the coalmines of Kentucky, had made his desired statement.

Since they weren't burdened by wedding preparations, Junior and Lizzie devoted their energies to other priorities during the eleven-month engagement. Most notably, they became better acquainted with one another – figuring a deeper familiarity might come in handy while they were spending the rest of their lives together.

Lizzie gave two-week's notice in Cleveland and moved to Evansville, eager to restart her nascent career. Senior volunteered to secure her a position inside a local brokerage house that handled a significant portion of his investments. She took him up on the offer. After accepting Senior's money for commissioned wedlock, she wasn't inclined to stand on principle and reject his assistance in other areas. Meanwhile, Junior helped her find a studio apartment and presented her with the keys to her first car – a white Thunderbird convertible.

She didn't mean to sound ungrateful, but she was unable to quash her immediate reaction. "Do you really believe I want to drive around in something that flashy?"

His answer surprised her. "Not in the least. But Evansville's a small town. Seeing someone who looks like you, in a car like that, is sure to get talked about. And whenever folks say, 'there goes Junior Davenport's future wife,' it'll be a reminder that I'm actually getting married ... despite any rumors they might have heard about my personal life. If we're going to put on a show, then let's put on a good one ... wouldn't you agree?"

Lizzie took the keys and kissed him on the cheek. "I think I'm going to enjoy being married to you."

Her words couldn't have been more prophetic. By the time Lizzie and Junior walked down the aisle, their close friendship had deepened into a very special bond. Not the romantic feelings of traditional newlyweds, yet in many ways much stronger.

In the days leading up to the wedding ceremony, Lizzie recognized how much she truly did look forward to being married to Junior Davenport. As a companion to her unusual lifestyle, he was near-perfect. As a human being, he may have been the most genuinely caring person she'd ever known.

There was a softness to him – a subtlety. He was possessed with no hard edges. Inside or out. Unlike Cal, his looks and physique were unlikely to draw much attention. He was average in height and weight. His brown hair was in constant need of a comb. His facial features had a cushiony, baby-like quality. But the combination of those average looks with Junior's shyness and understated charm produced a boy-next-door appeal.

Over the course of their engagement period, Junior was sent away on job assignments for weeks at a time by his father. When he returned to Evansville, he wanted to spend as much time as possible with his future bride. Dinners. Movies. Long walks. Picnics in the park. To the outside world, they were doing the things a couple in love should be doing. And in the end, they weren't putting on appearances.

Their conversations ran a wide gamut. Junior was remarkably well-read and unquenchably curious. At times, the two of them might go off on an intellectual tangent that lasted for hours. But he also possessed a dry sense of humor which unveiled itself at unexpected moments, so they just as easily could spend an entire afternoon laughing and being silly – diversions Lizzie hadn't allowed herself since her early teens.

By the day of the wedding, Lizzie completely understood why Cal had fallen in love with the man she was marrying. As their vows were exchanged, she was elated to be standing at the altar with Junior Davenport, a man she admired and for whom she profoundly cared. Yet she also harbored a plaguing sadness, ever mindful that Junior's one true love was standing a few feet away as the best man.

Chapter 34

After reliving the mixed emotions of her wedding day for a few moments, Beth turned the page in her journal. At first, she was puzzled by two blank sheets staring back at her, but then she remembered why they were there. Junior had surprised her with a month-long honeymoon on the Amalfi Coast of Italy – a trip filled with experiences she wouldn't have thought possible as a young girl in Findlay. She associated such sights and luxuries with books of fiction. But this new life with Junior was real and she was intent on savoring every moment.

When she returned to Evansville, her belongings had been moved into Junior's apartment on the fourth floor of a well-preserved historic building. Before the honeymoon, Elizabeth had packed hurriedly and thrown her journal into the bottom of a box, and during the move that box was stowed in the back of a closet and soon forgotten. As months passed, she figured her personal diary and been lost and experienced a sense of relief. In starting a new life, she was more than ready to close the book on her past.

But she eventually found and unsealed the missing box. Inside, she saw a portion of the familiar dark green cover lurking beneath a few old photos. Elizabeth "Lizzie" Monroe immediately realized she only had been fooling herself. No one received a free pass. Fate. Destiny. Whatever one called it; she had no choice but to live with her memories. As well as their consequences. Lizzie already had endured more subplots than Cervantes, Hugo, or Dumas would dare put into a single storyline. She had weathered a tumultuous childhood and sold herself into marriage – to a man not capable of consummating their union. Yet ironically, she cherished this good man, her new husband – fully empathizing with his private plight, as societal norms and a tyrannical father denied him the one relationship that brought him the greatest happiness. No, not even Shakespeare could have concocted the everyday realities to her life. She considered destroying her found-again notebook, but instead slid it beneath some clothing in a dresser drawer.

To mark her one-year wedding anniversary, Lizzie decided to pull out the journal and pen a long overdue entry. That was when she decided to leave the two preceding pages blank – intending to go back and record a few of the more significant memories from her first year as a Davenport. But ultimately, she didn't bother. Whatever milestones she thought she had experienced eventually became commonplace.

May 18, 1964

Happy anniversary to us! Today we celebrate our shared capacity to adapt.

Beth Davenport closed her eyes and allowed her mind to once again drift back. Despite the insanity of their situation in Evansville, those early years with Junior had been filled with happiness. As a young couple, they experienced genuine joy just by being in each other's company. They also savored the momentary pleasures of victory. Victories won alone. Victories won together. None big, by any stretch. Yet each was made more satisfying because the two of them were outmaneuvering the evil-most forces of the universe – or at least their own small universe. All those forces happened to emanate from one individual, of course. Senior Davenport.

Lizzie's career took off as soon as she started her new job in Evansville. She was engaged to a Davenport. The family name opened doors in Southern Indiana and across the Ohio Valley. She didn't hesitate to exploit this inside track to build a portfolio of investment clients. Back in the Sixties, no one thought to keep records on such matters, but some in the financial world believed she may have been the highest producing female in the entire Midwest.

In no time at all, the commissions were pouring in. As a result, she refused to open the envelopes that contained even larger amounts from her father-in-law – and her stubbornness did provide a modicum of relief. For indeed, she had struck a deal with the devil. Her stomach churned whenever she thought about the dreaded packets he delivered in person at the beginning of each month. "Here you go, Lizzie dear ... ten more crisp thousand-dollar-bills. I hope you're givin' Junior his money's worth."

For Mrs. Junior Davenport, the arrangement presented a monthly paradox. She was the one being held ransom, but she also was the one receiving the ransom payments for abetting Senior in the oppressive manipulation of his son. Disgusted by her own weakness, she had done the worst thing an investment adviser ever could imagine. She allowed those unopened envelopes to accumulate in a safe deposit box – drawing no interest, generating no gains. This dormancy didn't eliminate her ever-present guilt, but she wasn't going to add to the anguish by watching the soiled money multiply.

Her new life also brought another name change. She now went by Beth. The freshly minted Beth Davenport. A few weeks before the wedding, Elizabeth felt a need to change more than her surname. She was working at her desk one April afternoon in 1963, when the phone rang. Picking it up, the familiar voice on the other end of the line barked at her, "We need to talk. Dinner at the Kennel Club ... seven o'clock." Senior hung up before giving her a chance to reply. He didn't need to hear whether her schedule was free. It was a command performance – the first of many. Junior was out of town. Whatever plans she might have had, her future father-in-law expected her to cancel them.

When she arrived, he was seated at his favorite table by the window, nursing a whiskey. His sips were slow, which meant he now was on his second glass of Old Overholt. His first would have been downed in two or three gulps. The immensely popular President Kennedy was rumored to prefer the same brand of rye. It was the only facet of the whole Kennedy mystique that Senior could stomach – though not without commenting. "I've heard that drinking with JFK is like drinking with a little girl because he puts so damned much ice in his booze."

To her amazement, Senior rose from his chair as she reached the table. Manners weren't something to which he paid much attention. "Good evening, Elizabeth. You're looking as beautiful as ever … that dress you're wearin' sure shows off your pretty shape. I like how you're never shy about using the assets God gave to you." Respect for women also was low on his priority list.

She had been escorted into the restaurant's dining room by the club's manager – who personally tended to the Davenports at every opportunity. After properly seating her, he vanished. No other parties were anywhere near them, which wouldn't have been by accident.

Before speaking, she made a sweeping gesture with her right arm – drawing attention to the empty tables. "Good evening to you, Senior. I'm guessing you have something you'd like to discuss in private. Though it would have been nice if you had allowed me to order something to drink first."

The self-made millionaire turned red – embarrassed that he had neglected such an obvious nicety. She repeatedly experienced red-faced reactions from Junior but seeing the elder Davenport blush was something new. Who would have imagined that heredity could be so adorable? Senior instantly waved an arm, holding one finger up, and a waiter practically sprinted through the dining room in their direction.

They made small talk until her cocktail arrived – a double scotch, straight up. Senior didn't waste another second. "Do you think I'm a fool?"

He wasn't being playful in the least, but that didn't stop her from wanting to joust. "Answering a question like that is rather subjective … so I'd prefer to have a little more context before offering you an opinion."

Senior failed to see the humor. "Do you know where Junior was the day before yesterday?"

She thought for a second, "He was in Kentucky … Jack's Creek, I think."

He didn't bother acknowledging that she was correct. "And how about yesterday?"

She had a sinking feeling about where his questions were leading, but she played along. "I believe he needed to get to Ohio … maybe Millfield?"

He leaned forward, snarling. "And who do you think was with him in both of those towns."

The answer was obvious, but she wasn't willing to give Senior an inch. "I have no idea. But if it's vital to the future of Davenport Mining, I can do some checking."

"Don't get cute with me, Liz-z-z-zie." He drew out her name, as he had a habit of doing when he was trying to get under her skin. His tone sounded especially noxious this time. "I've promised to pay you a shitload of money to become Mrs. Junior Davenport … and I'm letting you use my name in whatever ways you see fit to make yourself a bloody fortune on top of that. In return, you're supposed to keep my son away from Cal Stratton. I don't care what you have to do in the bedroom to satisfy his perverted urges … but you sure as hell better start doing your job."

She knew the best way to irritate Senior was to keep her cool and go on the offensive. "First off, we're not married yet, and you haven't paid me a dime. Second, what happens in our bedroom once we are married will be none of your business. And third, I never agreed to keep Junior from seeing Cal ... only that I would keep your son from being sexually intimate with him. Those two have been best friends since they were fifteen years old ... and I have no intention of discouraging their friendship from continuing. So, if Cal chooses to take a few days off work and travel with his lifelong friend, then good for him ... in fact, good for both of them. So, unless you have any deeper knowledge that you're eager to share, I suggest we talk about something else."

She had been caught totally off-guard by the news that Junior and Cal were traveling together. Junior certainly was aware of the need to be careful. She couldn't fathom that the two of them would take chances in either of those towns, where practically everyone was loyal to Senior Davenport. She suspected Junior and Cal had stayed in separate rooms, but she was flying blind as she stood up to here future father-in-law. Now she waited to see his reaction.

Senior's face went beet-red, though not from embarrassment this time. He clearly wanted to lash out at her but was struggling with what to say next. In exasperation, he finally hissed, "You always think you're so damned clever ... well, little lady, you don't want to declare war with me ... I happen to possess all the best weapons. If I need eyewitnesses or even pictures to prove my point, I'll get 'em, by God. So, I'd suggest you convince those two lover boys of yours that they don't want to put themselves in a similar situation ever again."

Senior stopped talking and sat back in his chair. It was evident he had more to be say, but he seemed to be wrestling with whether to keep going. Elizabeth likewise sat back in her chair and waited – curious to hear what else he had on his mind.

With his anger piqued, Senior couldn't resist. "Listen, Miss Lizzie Monroe, I can understand how growing up the way you did, that sexual perversion may not bother you much ... but it ain't normal for Junior to want to do those disgusting things with another man. Knowing what I did about you and your daddy, I hope I didn't make a mistake by coming to you in the first place."

To Elizabeth, it was like her mind immediately stopped functioning. She was worried her heart might explode. Hearing the words as they came out of his mouth had been difficult enough, but once she absorbed the totality, she felt like throwing up. For nearly a year, Senior had been holding his heaviest artillery in reserve. She somehow managed to form words. "What did you say?"

Senior could see that he had registered a deep blow. He suddenly turned jovial. "I'm sorry, I just assumed with you being so smart and all ... you would have figured that my people filled me in on what a disgusting man your daddy had been ... about what Frank Monroe liked to do with his daughter when they were alone. It must have been strange to stand there and have him look at you the way he did."

What she was hearing couldn't be possible. No one had been aware of what her father made her do. She'd never told a soul. Sure, her friends had known that Frank Monroe beat her when he came home drunk. But that was it. Her mother and brother may have figured out the rest, but those family secrets died in a fire.

She tried to retain her composure, but it was hopeless. With tears in her eyes, she caved. "No one knew the horrible things he made me do. Please, Senior, you have to tell me ... how did you find out?"

He'd won and now it was time to gloat. "Like I said a few minutes ago, I possess all the best weapons. Not only was Frank Monroe a disgusting pervert ... he had a big mouth when he was out getting drunk with his buddies. You know, Lizzie ... you had quite a fan club of twisted minds who liked to hear your daddy describe how his pretty, teenaged daughter looked with all her clothes off ... her perky tits ... her round little ass. It didn't take long to find the rest of 'em once my folks got pointed toward the right tavern. Findlay's a nice town, but you know, it ain't very big. Funny thing though, I have this feeling you won't be planning to go back there anytime soon."

He reached down to pick up his empty glass, then held it above his head. Immediately, the waiter on the other side of the room made a beeline to the bar. Senior was going to enjoy a celebratory drink. "Would you care for another?" he asked with a chuckle.

She excused herself. But instead of going to the restroom and gathering herself as Senior presumed, Lizzie went straight to the parking lot and drove home to her rented room. On this night, she would grant the man his victory – because for now, her thoughts were elsewhere. She was reliving the indignities her father had forced her to endure – now made worse by the knowledge he was sharing those lurid details with his sick, drunken friends. Waves of revulsion overwhelmed her.

During the sleepless night that followed, she arrived at two decisions. There was nothing she could do to erase the scarred memories, but she at least would further dissociate herself from them. The next morning, she ordered new business cards and letterheads so they would be ready when she returned to work after her honeymoon. From that day forward, she would go by the name, Beth Davenport. As far as she was concerned, Elizabeth Monroe would cease to exist. She hoped never to hear "Lizzie" slithering out of Senior Davenport's mouth again.

Secondly, she committed that she never would touch any of the money she soon would begin collecting each month from Senior Davenport. She considered rejecting the money entirely, but ultimately decided the ruthless prick should pay for the pain he inflicted. In cash, and in whatever ways she might conceive over the years ahead.

The next night, Junior returned from his business trip. She met him in the lobby of his apartment building, kissing his cheek before she took his hand and escorted him toward the elevator. She had much to get off her chest. For several hours, Junior mostly listened.

Beth described, verbatim, the prior evening's episode with his father. Junior interrupted her when she reached the part about Cal, trying to explain how his arrival in Jack's Creek had come as a surprise, and to assure her "no lines had been crossed" during their two days together. That conversation could hold. She had more important issues on her mind.

Using Senior's revelations about her own father as an entry point, Elizabeth Monroe launched into full disclosure. She didn't want to hold a single secret from her future husband. For the first time, Junior heard the sordid details about her family life and the abuses she suffered from Frank Monroe. She told him about Lila and the abuses her closest friend had suffered from Russell. She tried to describe the significance of the two kisses she and Lila had shared, and the realization that Lila was probably responsible for the fire that killed her family. She previously hadn't uttered a word about any of these subjects to anyone. She even confessed about how she'd secured her first summer job in Cleveland. She wanted everything out in the open between Junior and her. If the two of them were to outmaneuver and outwit their common enemy, there could be no secrets. Nothing was ever to be withheld from Junior again.

Chapter 35

B eth Davenport was never one to give up without a fight. The more difficult the odds, the more she savored an opportunity to defy them. As a new bride, she carried her competitive spirit into the bedroom, confident she and Junior would prevail over the psychological or physical adversaries residing there.

During the early years of marriage, she made one unsuccessful attempt after another at eliciting, inducing, or provoking the most basic of anatomical reactions from Junior. Though he was convinced their combined efforts would prove futile, he had been game to keep trying. Family name and fortune weren't nearly as important to Junior as they were to his father, but he still harbored hopes of propagating the family's lineage by producing a Davenport son or daughter. Together, the young couple would shrug off each failure and look for the stars to align on some future attempt.

As the pair aired out skeletons from their respective closets, Junior confided how certain "bodily parts" had been more cooperative in his earliest years with Cal. "But whenever we were done, I would feel this awful shame because we'd allowed ourselves to do things that two boys weren't supposed to do. It was strange. I never felt worse about Cal … only about myself … about my lack of restraint. Then we'd be alone somewhere, and our urges would take over again. But by the time we finished high school, all that stopped

... at least for me. Maybe out of guilt, I willed my own impotence."

"I don't understand," Beth responded. "I saw you in the woods that first time. If you were incapable of ... you know, ... why did it look like the two of you were ... uh ..." She couldn't find a tasteful way of asking her question.

He made it easier for her. "We still were able to enjoy what I guess you would call heavy petting ... him more than me, you might say. But I also recognized my lack of interest wasn't fair to Cal. He still had needs ... almost insatiable needs. Which is why he dated so many women ... that was the deal we struck. We declared other guys off-limits."

She noticed how he talked about the intimate aspects of his relationship with Cal in past tense, which meant he intended to abide by the demands his father imposed. She wondered how many of Junior's insecurities or dysfunctionalities could be attributed to Senior – a man who dealt out shame and guilt as standard currencies.

But Beth also knew the vagaries of biology and psychology applied to more than just her husband. Now, in her mid-twenties, she'd yet to experience the physical or emotional fulfillment such acts were purported to produce. But to her, this void was inconsequential. She felt no such needs.

Since the lamentable exchange with Senior at the Kennel Club, she had given much thought to Junior's situation. Intense thought. She had come up with a plan. It wouldn't necessarily remedy her husband's impotence. In fact, the plan wasn't likely to address that problem at all. But physical capacities aside, Cal and Junior wanted and deserved to enjoy their intimacy. Plus what she had in mind was sure to infuriate her father-in-law – which was just as important.

She and Junior invited Cal to Evansville over Independence Day weekend. Ever since their engagement, Cal had stayed in hotels whenever he came for a visit. This time, they offered up their apartment's second bedroom. The threesome went out for dinner on

Friday evening, drinking more wine than usual. Returning home, they enjoyed a nightcap. She noticed how naturally and easily Cal and Junior completed one another. She remembered thinking that all men and women deserved one such person in their lives. An hour or so later, Beth rose from the couch she'd been sharing with her husband. Yawning, she proclaimed in almost script-like cadence, "Why, I do believe I've overindulged … and fear I'm going to have a restless night ahead. It may be best for me to sleep in the guest room instead of Cal. I do apologize for any inconvenience this might cause … but you two will figure something out. I'll see you in the morning … here in the living room. I imagine I'll be up and around by nine."

Cal stood and gave her a good-night hug with a look of disbelief on his face. Not fully understanding the ground rules, he didn't want to say anything to violate whatever veiled scheme she was initiating. Beth kissed him on the cheek, then did the same to Junior. Heading down the hallway toward the bedrooms with her back to the two of them, she added, "I love you both very much."

July 24, 1964

And so begins a new era.

This journal entry from 1964 signaled the escalation of Beth's efforts to subvert her father-in-law. But her words also suggested a new optimism.

Indeed, gratifying times did lie ahead for Junior, Cal, and her. They would refer to this memorable period of their lives as "our Camelot years" – a label they credited to a most unlikely source, Senior Davenport.

A few weeks after his July visit, Cal drove down for another weekend stay. By Thanksgiving, the three had established a regular routine that required no further discussion of sleeping arrangements. Beth's temporary moves into the guest room were understood.

Considering the realities of their marriage, what might have seemed peculiar was the desire Beth and Junior shared for sleeping in the same room, and even the same bed, on the nights Cal wasn't a guest in their apartment – which was most of the time. The pretense of faux matrimony certainly didn't require such measures behind closed doors. As far as the outside world was concerned, they could have been hanging like bats from the ceiling once the lights went out. But awake or asleep, she and her husband enjoyed each other's company.

Whenever Cal was in Evansville, they became an inseparable threesome – in every sense of the word except one. A conversation about the economy. A daytrip to Louisville or Lexington. A jigsaw puzzle, or a game of monopoly on a rainy day. Any activity was made better by the natural chemistry that took root on a night in a forest adjacent to Oberlin's campus.

Conversely, these regular visits from Cal became a living nightmare for a certain family patriarch, which delighted Beth to no end. When Cal first stayed in their apartment the previous summer, she anticipated the news would reach Senior quickly. He had eyes and ears everywhere. Surely, Senior had been seething over the steady stream of similar reports ever since. But short of busting down the door to their apartment in the middle of the night, he couldn't prove Junior and Cal were even spending time alone.

The irony was inescapable. For years, Senior had envisioned wanton acts between his son and Cal Stratton – acts he couldn't erase from his mind. Images that disgusted and enraged him. Yet since Junior was a teenager, he hadn't been capable of any such acts – a secret that she would protect at all costs. She wanted Senior's imagination to run wild. In the on-going battle with her father-in-law, Beth would find satisfaction in the oddest of circumstances.

As expected, Senior registered his objections about Cal's frequent presence in Evansville. Prior to Cal's regular overnight stays,

Senior hadn't paid a single visit to Beth and Junior's apartment. When he'd wanted to see either or both, it always was on his turf, at his appointed time. But suddenly he developed a new habit of popping in to say hello – though only when Cal happened to be in town. Early in the morning. Late at night. The middle of the afternoon. It didn't matter. There would be a series of loud knocks. And wherever the three might be in the apartment, or whatever they might be doing, they quickly reunited in the living room before one of them answered the door.

He would saunter in, pretending to be cordial. "How are my three little love birds today?" He had a full repertoire of remarks, and each revealed how truly irritated Senior was by the whole situation. He clearly understood the three of them weren't going to allow him to see anything they didn't want him to see, but he liked reminding them. Others still were watching and reporting back to him.

Just prior to one of his unannounced visits, Senior had traveled to New York City with a lady friend. While there, they had taken in two plays. The second was a musical – *Camelot*. Normally, his interests in the performing arts were confined to strippers and lounge singers. He clearly was expanding his mind, because now Senior Davenport felt a need to expound upon the impact that the theater was having on him.

"If you three haven't seen *Camelot*, you really should. I had myself a god-damned epiphany ... sittin' right there in the middle of Broadway. You see, I realized we've got our own little love triangle ... our own little Camelot ... right here in Evansville, Indiana. Problem is, I can't figure out which one of you is King Arthur, and which one is Lancelot." He walked over to the couch and stood in front of Junior. "But I'm pretty sure I got Guinevere pegged ... ain't that right, Son?"

Senior was especially proud of himself for delivering his soliloquy. He chortled for half-a-minute before he turned and made his way to the front door, whistling the title song from the hit musical as he headed toward the elevator.

For months thereafter, Senior would work in snarky references to Camelot as part of his endless onslaught. Beth, Junior, and Cal had learned not to let any of his comments get under their skins. But his repeated mentions of Camelot brought smiles to their faces. The three truly were living a modern-day love triangle. And now, courtesy of the individual who most resented their triumvirate, they'd been handed a name for this halcyon period in their lives. *Our Camelot years.* Beth remembered them like they were yesterday.

Chapter 36

Nothing lasts forever. Senator Beth Davenport had learned the truth to this adage many times during her seventy-eight years. Regardless of what she achieved in politics; another question would always be left unanswered. How far might she have gone if she had remained in the private sector?

At twenty-seven, she already had earned the title of assistant vice president inside the Evansville brokerage firm – an almost unthinkable position for a female of any age in those days. A male with her track record would have been sitting on the management committee. The growth rates inside the investment portfolios she managed for clients often outpaced the rest of the organization by more than double. Long before desktop computers enabled data-driven financial advisors to develop their own multi-variate models for timing the market, Beth was conceiving effective models with pencils and old-fashioned spreadsheets. The biggest challenge was handling the deluge of business that came her way. Clients served elsewhere in the firm clamored for results like those produced by Senior Davenport's daughter-in-law.

Without question, Beth's career in Evansville benefitted greatly from the head start of a family name, but eventually, even her most chauvinistic and resentful detractors had to recognize her prodigious talent for investment strategy. In late 1968, while rapidly progressing toward a full vice presidency, Beth was confronted with a harsh reality. She had agreed to reside within the boundaries of a limited universe – a universe operating under a single power source. Senior Davenport.

As such, she was reminded many times. Senior Davenport could giveth. Senior Davenport could taketh away.

The career struggles of her husband offered a stark contrast to Beth's meteoric rise. No matter what responsibilities his father assigned Junior, he repeatedly fell short. Indeed, Senior did place unrealistic demands on the son who was destined to inherit the reins of Davenport Mining. But even Junior recognized his actual performance was lackluster. It was hard to produce results when he hated going to work every morning.

Junior had been raised on a perpetual diet of his father's shoptalk. Unfortunately, nothing about coalmining, deal-making, or corporate structure had been remotely interesting to him since earliest childhood. During adolescence, Junior harbored hopes of becoming a journalist, a museum curator, or maybe a teacher. Senior refused to listen to such nonsense. Junior was dutybound to oversee the corporate empire being built by his father for legions of unborn Davenports.

If Junior hoped to continue accessing the trust funds bearing his name, to say nothing of the enormous wealth his father someday would bequest, he was given no choice. During high school and college, his summers were spent in servitude – cleaning equipment in the bowels of a coalmine or raking up loose chunks of coal that fell out of railroad cars in a loading area.

After Junior graduated with honors from Oberlin, his more serious rotations began. Degree in hand, he was sent for two-month stints to various mining operations as an apprentice to miners, drillers, pump men, tram operators, and just about any position ever conceived in a coalmine. The only consistency across these bootstrap assignments was that Junior detested them all. He was treated poorly by anyone to whom he reported – almost assuredly at the instruction of his father. Senior wanted to toughen-up his namesake.

By observing the conditions, complexities, and dangers of underground operations, Junior truly gained a healthy respect for coalmining and coalminers. But as with any profession, some level of inner passion was required for success. He felt none.

Eventually, Senior started rotating Junior through a series of white-collar positions in Evansville – hoping his son might take to the managerial side of the enterprise. Accounting. Purchasing. Training. Government relations. Transportation. The list went on and on. But no matter the assignment, the outcome was the same. Nothing struck Junior's fancy or stirred anything inside him. He made repeated mistakes. Each department head would report his mediocrity up the line – and each time Junior would be called into his father's office for a verbal accosting.

Beth continually encouraged her husband to throw in the towel. She was more than willing to forego Senior's monthly envelopes filled with cash. After all, the money was gathering dust in a safe deposit box. With or without the full imprimatur of the Davenport name, she and Junior were capable of moving on with their lives. They could relocate from Evansville and she could sign on with another investment house. She would support the two of them while he explored career paths that better suited him. These conversations helped them realize how strong their unusual marriage had grown.

Regardless, Junior remained adamant. He couldn't abandon the family business. To Beth, he seemed as concerned about the future of Davenport Mining as Senior did. Against the context of her own impoverished childhood, she couldn't reconcile her husband's convictions with the agonies they brought him – but she continued to capitulate to his wishes.

October 23, 1968

Today I became a man.

The first time Junior showed the slightest hint he might consider leaving the family business was during the spring of 1967. He and Beth were at their favorite new pizza place, a couple miles from the three-bedroom home they'd recently purchased. Earlier that afternoon, Senior had come down especially hard on Junior because the company was outbid on the acquisition of a coalmine Senior coveted. Junior was part of the due diligence team and therefore the most natural scapegoat for his father's rage. In this instance, the team had done nothing wrong. Another buyer simply had overpaid by a ridiculous amount. For Junior, this episode was more demoralizing than usual because his father unleashed his fury in the busiest section of the executive floor. Dozens of employees listened uncomfortably while Senior berated his son.

"Beth, it would be so much easier for everybody involved if you would just come to work for the company … you could be the Davenport my father needs to lead the company someday."

She chuckled at the proposition. "Wouldn't that be perfectly wonderful … your dad and me at each other's throats from dawn til dusk."

He offered a slight smile in response. "I know … maybe I'm just blowing off steam. But you have no idea how much my father thinks of you … and not simply because he likes staring at your rear end." Senior rarely missed an opportunity to leer at her.

Junior continued, "He repeatedly tells me that he wishes I could be half the man you are when it comes to business. He won't admit it … but the old goat is completely in awe over what you've accomplished … and he also can't admit how proud he is to have you representing the Davenport name around town."

She let Junior's comments pass and changed the subject. But

over the ensuing months, he offered up the same suggestion with increased frequency – no longer raising the possibility in exasperation or jest. He seriously wanted her to consider a career change. Senior could groom her to run Davenport Mining after he eventually stepped down, and Junior could move into some innocuous position way down the totem pole, outside the crossfire … or better yet, leave the company entirely and pursue a career that stimulated and better suited him. He was convinced she would thrive inside the organization and the organization would better thrive because of her. "Beth, it is the only way forward I can envision for the family's business. Otherwise, my father will someday be forced to sell Davenport Mining to one of our competitors … and our name will come off the sign and disappear from the industry."

At the time, this whole issue about a family name was beyond Beth's comprehension. For most of his life, Junior had been treated like dirt by his father. The prospects of their marriage producing an heir to carry the name forward were practically nil. Still, Junior felt an immense obligation to preserve the legacy of the Davenports. But now, as she approached eighty and had seen her own accomplishments attached to this same family name, Senator Beth Davenport was a great deal more empathetic.

"If it wasn't for all the embarrassment it would cause me and the whole blasted company, I'd fire your sissy ass." That was how the meeting ended on a Monday afternoon in October of 1968, when Junior finally stood up and walked out of his father's office. From behind the desk, Senior flung this last insult just as the door was closing behind Junior. An unwarranted accusation from the field had escalated into the most heated argument ever between father and son, and the damage to their tenuous relationship looked to be permanent.

The company had fired a miner from Vigo County, Indiana, for failing to show up for multiple work shifts. Now, that miner was claiming senior management had been out to get him since 1962. "Those big shots in Evansville have been looking for a way to nail me to a cross ever since I refused the advances of that fruitcake son they sent up here for us to train. But I didn't care who he was, I wasn't about to let another man try anything with me."

The conversation had begun with Senior slamming the door and presenting Junior with a letter from the union rep who was filing a complaint on behalf of the ex-employee. "See the shit I have to deal with because you can't control your perverted urges."

Due to rumors and speculations about Junior's private life, five other complaints had been lodged through the years. Each time, Senior would place the growing folder of allegations on his desk for Junior to see. Most came from the field, but one also was submitted by a mid-level bookkeeper in corporate accounting, who accused Junior of sneaking glances as they stood next to one another at a urinal. Not a single grievance could be corroborated by a third party. Most importantly, Junior knew there wasn't an ounce of truth to any of them. By virtue of his name, Junior Davenport had become a sitting duck for opportunists.

The real facts meant nothing to Senior once his fuse was lit. Junior had no choice but to sit and listen as his father tore into him. Again and again.

This time, however, his father had taken an unprecedented action. Senior Davenport hated the unions. Even more, he hated paying-out claims to union members. His standard response to potential lawsuits was to fight tooth-and-nail. Then afterwards, retaliate. But in this instance, Senior acquiesced to the union representative and upped the severance amount originally paid to the fired miner in Vigo County. Further, he committed to placing Junior Davenport on probation for inappropriate behavior in the workplace. If another valid claim was to be filed in the coming year, his own son would be terminated.

From bits and pieces of their one-way dialogue, a fuller picture emerged. Junior heard how a variety of other complaints related to production quotas also had been filed against Davenport Mining by the same union, and after several months, the mediation process was going nowhere. Thus, to achieve an overall settlement, Senior had used his son and his son's reputation as bargaining chips. Junior was beside himself. For once, he pushed back. Vehemently. By the time they ran out of steam, the already precarious working relationship between father and son had suffered irreparable damage. The next day, Junior refused to go into the office – unsure whether he'd ever go back.

As Beth remembered the anguish Junior experienced those many years ago, she found solace in the many societal changes that had taken place since. Much work still was needed in Washington and elsewhere, but in those days, even the faintest rumor of homosexuality laid one bare to ridicule and accusation.

With Junior at wit's end, Beth decided to step in and attempt a reconciliation. She paid an unannounced visit to Davenport headquarters, where she was told Senior couldn't be disturbed. Mr. Davenport was holding his weekly budget meeting inside his private conference room. She nonetheless demanded an audience – first with the receptionist, and then Senior's secretary. Because Beth was a family member, neither woman was comfortable denying her access. When each hesitated, she barged right past them. Without knocking, Beth opened the door to the conference room, stood in the doorway, and looked directly at her father-in-law. In a soft voice, she said, "You and I need to have a conversation." She gently closed the door and went down the hall to Senior's corner office and waited.

Sure enough, he arrived a few moments later. "You have a lot of nerve, young lady," he said, hovering next to the chair in which she was seated.

Beth calmly looked up. "Oh, you have no idea. But let's not waste our time talking about me, and instead focus on you and your son."

Over the next twenty minutes, she gave the family's formidable patriarch a lot to ponder – telling Senior in no uncertain terms that she and his son were prepared to revoke all affiliations with him, his precious mining company, and the city of Evansville. Granted, she may have taken license with how she was representing Junior's intentions, but her point needed to be made. Once she'd said what she came to say, Beth stood to leave. "The next step is yours, Senior."

Later that day, as she was working away in her own office, Beth received a call from Junior. "My father wants to have dinner with us tonight … at the Kennel Club. Something strange is going on with him. He was wondering if he and I might be able to forget yesterday's argument … he even admitted that he was wrong to put me in such a compromised position with the union. Beth, in my entire life, I don't remember my dad ever admitting a mistake to me … or anyone else."

Just like the last time Beth had been beckoned to the Kennel Club, no patrons were seated in the proximity of Senior's favorite table. But in this instance, he wasn't lying in wait. There would be no angry tirades. In fact, during dinner, he couldn't have been more conciliatory – not once lashing out about hippies, Democrats, or uppity Negroes. Finally, over a bottle of port, he revealed the true purpose of his invitation.

"After a great deal of soul-searching, I've come to a number of conclusions I probably should have reached long before now." His carefully chosen words would open a new chapter in their lives.

He directed his next comments to Junior. "Let's be honest, Son. The three of us recognize you're not cut out to run Davenport Mining, or any other company, for that matter." These were harsh words, but the tone suggested Senior wasn't trying to be hurtful. He continued with uncharacteristic sensitivity, "Telling people what to do just isn't your thing … and you know what? It doesn't need to be.

You're better at helping people … and I'd be a fool if we didn't use those skills. The time you did the most good for our company was when I put you over in Personnel. I think Davenport Mining would be much better off if we planned on you running that part of the business from now on … and you sure as hell would like coming to work a lot more."

Beth and Junior reacted with careful optimism – each giving a slight nod to Senior. It was obvious, he had more to say.

Senior continued. "There ain't no secret about what I've always wanted … having Davenports at the top of my company until hell freezes over. Until now, this dream of mine has put a lot of pressure on you, Junior. But just because we agree you'd be happier doing something else, we don't have to start rethinking the whole future of our family's business. We've got another Davenport who would be perfect for the job. A lot of experts out there keep saying that women are gonna be running big companies someday. Now, wouldn't we surprise everyone of 'em if we made Davenport Mining one of the first?"

He stopped talking and allowed awkward silence to set in. Senior studied Beth's face, then Junior's, and then Beth's again. Remembering Junior's many previous attempts at convincing her to join the company, Beth wondered whether father and son had started secretly colluding. If so, she probably deserved it. That very morning, she had gone to see Senior behind her husband's back.

Junior finally broke the silence with a broad smile. "Dad, I can't believe those words just came out of your mouth. I've been talking to Beth about the same idea for months. She would be brilliant at running Davenport Mining."

The look on Senior's face revealed his surprise. "It seems you have a keener instinct for personnel matters and the company's future than I might have realized."

Attention shifted to Beth. She knew what they both were hoping, but she wasn't prepared to tell them what they wanted to hear. She needed time to think. Ever since Junior began making his pleas to her, she had been identifying the pros and cons in her head – with the cons outnumbering the pros by a wide margin. But her previous contemplations had been hypothetical. Now the very real opportunity was being presented to her.

She reached for the bottle of port in the center of the table and refilled three glasses. "How refreshing it is to see the two of you playing nicely together in the same sandbox … considering how you were at each other's throats less than twenty-four hours ago. At least we can celebrate this new peaceful accord. As to the other matter … I need to sleep on it."

Surprisingly, Beth did sleep. The next morning, she was of sound mind. The negatives still overwhelmed the positives. She already was making a name for herself in the investment community – a genteel club of white-collar men that needed a shake-up. From the standpoint of personal wealth, her current career path looked to be long and well-paved. Staying in the investment world, she wouldn't have to contend with a domineering father-in-law, his personal fiefdom, or a mining industry that basked in its own testosterone. How could she possibly tolerate such a raw, one-sided culture? Why would she want to? How could she expect to make Davenport Mining into anything more than an extension of the founder's heavy handprints? A founder who placed himself at the heart of his own corporate empire as chairman, president, and essentially the only person entitled to make any decision of importance. The notion of a woman effecting a meaningful transformation was preposterous.

Beth's deliberations may have been swayed by her loyalty toward Junior and his concern for family legacy. But in the end, a deep-seeded thirst for attaining the unthinkable was the deciding factor. Each of the daunting challenges she had been able to enumerate were like a beckoning call.

Chapter 37

B eth Davenport joined Davenport Mining in early December of
1968, just in time for Senior's annual deer hunt. This invitation
for a weekend in the woods was a holiday tradition for his senior
management team, of which she now was part. She couldn't be sure,
but her presence probably put a damper on some of the yuletide
rituals these men might otherwise have enjoyed while their wives
remained in Evansville.

For two decades, the performance and expansion of Davenport
Mining had stood out among mining companies. Senior Davenport
had built an impressive track record by engineering a continuous
flow of acquisitions and improving the productivity of those acquired
mines. Still, some years produced better bottom-lines than others.
Spikes and dips were to be expected from a privately-held enterprise
eager to extend its footprint. Overall, the profits from good years
more than made up for the periods when growth was slower.

With Beth on board for 1969, Davenport Mining started a
string of thirteen years that would establish new standards for operating efficiency and overall profitability, as well as expansion. The
peak-and-valley charts inside the Davenport boardroom were replaced with graphs that, quarter after quarter, plotted steady upward
slopes on every key metric. This sustained performance was unprecedented not just for the company, but for the mining industry in

total. To the investment community, Senior Davenport was viewed as an entrepreneurial genius – in great part due to the phenomenal growth of the company he founded, but even more so for his foresight in bringing in a woman of his daughter-in-law's caliber to alter the pervasive barroom culture of a coalmining operation. Inside and outside the organization, Davenport Industries was lauded for innovations being systematically introduced into its business practices. Unsolicited bids to buy the company for extraordinary sums became common occurrences.

On occasion, Senior would let his frustrations show if too much of the acclaim was heaped on Beth. As she moved up the corporate ladder, others among the management team learned to deflect their praises. Instead of singling her out, they applauded Senior for nurturing a new appetite for change – which just happened to coincide with Beth's arrival.

Internally, her strongest ally and collaborator in transforming the most seminal aspects of the corporate culture was her husband. With personnel now his permanent domain, Junior asserted a newfound confidence in how he went about his daily responsibilities. By the end of 1970, Junior was made Senior Vice President of Personnel – a title he deserved regardless of the last name on his business card. In 1976, Davenport Mining became one of the first companies in the country to change the name of its Personnel Department to Human Resources, to clarify a heightened priority for developing its human capital.

Externally, Beth redefined the landscape on which Davenport Mining conducted business. She gradually brought in a string of management consultants, who in turn assisted her in methodically reorienting Senior's single-minded vision. From his earliest days in Kentucky, he had wanted to dominate the coalmining industry by simply aggregating the largest number of coalmines. No one could deny this approach had served Senior Davenport well. Beth and the consultants were quick to extol him for masterfully executing his 'vertical strategy' – whereby all resources were concentrated on developing and dominating a single business sector. With the same visionary focus, many of the country's most respected corporations had achieved a critical mass necessary to transform themselves into huge conglomerates.

With its expanded base of coalmining, Davenport Mining was now poised to evolve to a more 'horizontal strategy.' One-by-one, Beth presented the management team opportunities to diversify the company into contiguous business sectors. The end-result produced enormous synergies and significant competitive advantages. Davenport bought its own railroad cars for transporting coal. Then it purchased even more railroad cars and leased them to competitive coalmines, as well as other types of mining. Next were companies that manufactured and serviced mining drills – and soon, other heavy equipment. Followed by safety equipment – first for mines, but eventually safety equipment for other industries. And so went a systematic and horizontal expansion that ultimately led to a name change. Davenport Mining became Davenport Industries.

Business analysts and journalists viewed the company as the mining industry's most fascinating success story of the 1970's. Insiders recognized that Beth had become the driving influence, and she ended the decade as the organization's only executive vice president. But the countless external reports on the Davenport family business still focused on the company's founder, chairman, and president. Beth made sure of it.

Over this period, Senior's personal wealth increased exponentially. And to his credit, he liberally shared the financial benefits with his employees – and particularly his management team. Beth remembered how effective her father-in-law could be at procuring loyalty, or, in some cases, souls.

In 1973, she and Junior used some of their increased wealth to move into an even larger home – the one she still owned and rarely visited. At most, she returned to Evansville once or twice a year, and then only out of a sense of duty to the people who had supported her in politics for more than three-and-a-half decades. Beyond those voters, Beth felt little attachment to the city she associated with a single individual who during his life had cultivated the best and worst in her.

December 31, 1979

Mr. Dickens, are these the best or worst of times?

Beth was amused by the literary allusion she had made in her journal those many years ago. She'd always treasured the timeless nature of classic literature. For she and Junior, the decade that was drawing to its close truly did represent the best and worst of times. It also was a time when she had discovered the best and worst in herself. Sure, her father-in-law may have been a master manipulator – bullying her, his son, and scores of others at will. But who was she to condemn him? Hadn't she manipulated Senior, the company he founded, and every available advantage to serve her own ambitions? To create a name for herself?

As Beth was pushing new envelopes for the company, and Junior was settling into a productive role inside the organization, their unusual marital bonds continued to strengthen. The love she felt for Junior was more than she ever might have experienced with another man. She was sure of it, and he seemed to feel the same about his relationship with her. Completing this odd utopian existence was Cal.

Cal Stratton's banking career in Indianapolis had progressed rapidly, but more and more of his weekends were spent in Evansville. Plus, when schedules permitted, the three would vacation together in faraway places, or book long weekends at more accessible destinations.

As Beth's indispensability to the company grew, fewer cautions were taken. They became less concerned about how often they went out in public, or who saw them when they did. They weren't thumbing their noses at Senior, by any means. But years were ticking by and they were determined to enjoy themselves. It was a high stakes game of poker and because of her importance to the company, Beth now held an upper hand that she played with moderation. With her father-in-law's unpredictable temperament, she recognized how quickly the deck could get reshuffled.

Meanwhile, one major sticking point persisted on the home front. Progeny. Senior still was waiting for his heir to the Davenport throne. Junior's impotence had been kept a closely guarded secret. Even if his son's sexual appetites "ran against the grain," Senior presumed this ersatz husband and wife could make an accommodation. After all, bearing children was part of the marriage agreement he'd struck with the former Lizzie Monroe.

Senior would threaten repeatedly to stop his monthly payments. Beth would give him a shrug and standard reply. "Do what you have to do." She really didn't care. Beth was earning plenty of money inside her father-in-law's company. But Senior never pulled the trigger. He didn't want to kill, or even injure, the golden goose his daughter-in-law had become.

Beth especially remembered one episode stemming from Senior's unrelenting harassment about grandchildren. The unexpected confrontation sparked another turning point. There was no entry in her journal to mark the occasion, but she was pretty sure it all started on a Thursday during March of 1974. That evening, after a long day of work, she and Junior were exiting Davenport Headquarters and walking, hand in hand, toward their car in a far corner of the parking lot. Senior also happened to be leaving when he spotted them. He redirected his latest new Cadillac to intercept them. Lowering the window, he probed, "Where have you two been ... I haven't seen either of you all week?" His tone had started pleasant enough.

"We were down in New Orleans for a few days," Junior responded.

Senior instantly turned feisty, "I suppose 'pretty boy' tagged along ... I wouldn't want the pair of you ever goin' somewhere alone ... like a normal married couple. God forbid that you might wind up making babies or something."

"Anything else?" Beth asked, trying to cut the conversation short.

"Come to think of it, there is." Now Senior was getting worked up. "Since when do two of my direct reports take time off without my approval?"

Beth bristled, "You know, Senior, we're not inclined to come to daddy and ask for permission every time we go to the bathroom ... but I did send you a memo several weeks ago. If you were concerned about us being out of the office, you should have said something then."

He didn't like being challenged. "But your note didn't say a damn thing about New Orleans." He stared directly at Beth. "But I guess I can understand why you omitted that detail ... you didn't want me to know you were going to Mardi Gras with Lancelot and Lady Guinevere there," he said, pointing toward Junior. "With all them drunkin' freaks and faggots down on Bourbon Street, the three of you must have felt right at home."

Junior spoke up before Beth had a chance to retort. "Dad, we're under no obligation to tell you where we go or what we do on our own time. So, please, let's call it a night ... and we'll see you in the morning."

Senior scowled at Junior and began to roll up his window. Then he stopped and rolled it back down. He wanted to make sure he fired off the last word. "You know, boy, I'd feel a lot better about calling it a night if I thought you were heading home to screw your pretty wife like a real man would. But I imagine the three of you used up all your energy in New Orleans ... doing whatever sick things the three of you do when you're alone. No wonder there aren't any grandbabies. The Good Lord ain't about to grant children to a coupla sexual deviates … you and your godforsaken Camelot."

After he'd said his final piece, he rolled up the window, and sped off with tires screeching. In a moment that Beth always would remember, she and Junior looked at one another and shook their heads in unison. Seconds passed before he spoke. "Well, my dad was right about one thing."

She couldn't imagine what Junior meant. "Excuse me?"

He stepped closer, bent down, and kissed the tip of her nose. "I do have a pretty wife."

The next morning, a large unmarked envelope was waiting on the desk chair in her office. Apparently, Senior hadn't been ready to let go of his anger. Inside she found a book – a pictorial produced in magazine format. As soon as she read the title, she'd known who left it. The End of Camelot. The book had been published the prior year, on the tenth anniversary of the Kennedy assassination, and it chronicled his abbreviated term in the White House.

A handwritten note was scrawled into the corner of a page marked by a paper clip. "Lizzie, your little Camelot must end now. The affair with C.W.S. must cease. That was our deal!" It was signed, "J.E.D."

She threw the book into her wastebasket. The audacity of the man. No, the lunacy. Joseph Elwood Davenport thought he could intimidate her with a conveniently titled book and an idle threat. And to revert to calling her "Lizzie" after all she had accomplished for his sacred Davenport Mining. Her father-in-law was a Neanderthal.

For nearly fifteen years, Beth had been tormented by the feelings she harbored about the "deal" – about the ten thousand in cash she accepted each month. This money was meant to compensate her for marrying a man who had no interest or prospects for marriage. Yet she and that man were able to find unexpected love and settle into an unconventional marriage that could endure on its own accord. Being married to Junior hardly had been a sacrifice. So, each month, she tried unsuccessfully to transfer the nagging guilt into a safe deposit box inside an Evansville bank.

But at that moment, all the shame and remorse vanished. How many times had she tried to convince herself that she was earning every cent by tolerating the oppressive presence of an arrogant barbarian? His influence on her daily life was inescapable. And now, a clever little package waiting on her chair had pushed her over the line. Moving forward, for as long as "J.E.D." drew breath, she would relish the extraction of those monthly payments. And she would make sure Junior and "C.W.S." – Calving Willian Stratton – spent as much time together as they damn-well pleased.

She reached into the wastebasket and pulled out the book she'd discarded just moments before. She inserted <u>The End of Camelot</u> into a row of books on the credenza behind her desk – as a keepsake. She wanted to remember when her revised plan for the future first took shape.

Chapter 38

The game was on. By spring of 1974, Beth was taking full advantage of every connection she made through her father-in-law's company. She expanded her personal network – building a power base from which she could launch her new career when the time was right. The next big move would jettison her from the family business and the sacred realm of its founder. She had no intention of hanging around until Senior was ready to hand over the reins. Hell, the surly bastard was likely to live to be a hundred.

Until the time was right, Senior Davenport and his precious company could benefit from her intensified ambition. During this interim period, he needed to believe that she and Junior also were serving his best interests away from the office. Or at least giving it their best efforts. Senior was relentless with his assertions about their failure to have children, certain their inability to produce an heir was a result of Junior's aversion to good old-fashioned screwing – the kind a real man would want as often as possible with a woman like Beth.

She had a plan to satisfy Senior's growing expectations. But in the end, he would be forced to recognize his Davenport lineage had run its course. And the fault would be hers, not Junior's. Senior would have to accept that the woman he purchased as a wife for his son was incapable of carrying children. Of producing the grandchild he desperately coveted.

The plan would mute Senior's threats and harangues until Beth Davenport was ready to transition to the next phase of her life – a transition that would free her and her husband at last. She was optimistic Junior would join her on this eventual leap, but those conversations were yet to come. First things first.

Beth had met Elliot Reynolds soon after moving to Evansville. He was one of Senior Davenport's oldest and dearest friends. The man's word was as good as gold to her father-in-law.

Elliot also happened to be one of the city's most respected physicians. He was married with three children – which surprised Beth when she first learned the details of his personal life. She would have ranked him as one of the plainest, dullest individuals she'd ever known. In hindsight, these many years later, she was sure Doc Reynolds would have held his own with any of the lumps of clay who populated the landscape of Washington DC – and that was saying something.

She was even more astounded when she eventually met his wife. How this man convinced a living, breathing female to go on a first date was mystery enough, but he somehow had managed to convince a charming, attractive woman to commit to matrimony and conceive three offspring with him. Those facts alone suggested this unobtrusive figure possessed a sexual drive of some sort. Of more relevance to her situation, Beth had noticed the doctor's lascivious stares whenever she was near him. She needed a proper accomplice to pull off a ruse that would fool Senior, and his most trusted friend was practically raising his hand to volunteer.

Over the ensuing months, Beth directed a great deal of special attention toward Doc Reynolds whenever the opportunity arose. Idle chatter at cocktail parties, as he stole glances down blouses she'd buttoned too carelessly. Sitting next to him at a charity gala and repeatedly leaning forward in her most revealing evening gown.

Asking him to dance late into the evening at a mutual friend's wedding – after several rounds of cocktails afforded her an excuse for rubbing against him during a slow foxtrot.

In the summer of 1976, she finally felt the time was right. Beth phoned Dr. Reynolds' office and made an appointment for a physical – claiming to be disappointed with her previous doctor. A week later, she was waiting in his examination room when she heard a knock on the door. The timid doctor opened it a few inches and asked, "May I come in?"

"Of course, Elliot ... it wouldn't make much sense for me to be here if you didn't," she teased.

Doc Reynolds pushed the door all the way open and Beth watched his eyes widen when he saw her sitting on the examination table completely disrobed.

Once he was able to speak, his voice cracked. "Good afternoon, Beth. Wouldn't you prefer to put on an examination gown?" he asked, pointing to the cloth cover-up draped over an adjacent chair.

"Oh, I'm sorry, Elliot ... your assistant instructed me to remove my clothes and I didn't even notice the gown." She giggled, "Now I feel like a complete idiot ... but I guess the damage is done." She shrugged and made a gesture with her arms and open palms, as if to tell him he'd seen everything there was to see. "I'm comfortable if you are ... let's get started."

His gaze dropped to the clipboard he was holding. He began ticking through a standard list of questions, nervously making notations when she answered. She watched with amusement as he tried to maintain his professional decorum. But he couldn't help himself. What started as occasional glimpses became more frequent. Beth periodically shifted positions to offer views of her nakedness from different angles. It wasn't long before she knew he was wrapped in her web.

When they proceeded to the actual physical exam, he sounded

almost out of breath. Whenever she saw an opportunity, she brushed one body part or another up against him. The moment of truth arrived while he was listening to her heartbeat with his stethoscope. She allowed her hand to fall off the side of the table and sweep lightly across his crotch. He was startled but didn't back away. A moment later she nonchalantly moved that same hand a few inches and left it there, resting casually against his zipper. His body responded accordingly.

She feigned embarrassment. "Elliot ... I believe your mind might be wandering." With her hand dangling by his crotch, she looked him in the eyes and smiled like an embarrassed schoolgirl.

He stood trance-like until common sense kicked in. He hurriedly stepped away from the examination table and buttoned the medical coat he wore loosely over street clothes. "You can put your clothes on, Beth. I'll be back in a few minutes." He started to open the door, then turned to her. "I must apologize for what just occurred. You are an incredibly beautiful woman ... but there is no excuse for my lack of professionalism."

He allowed her enough time to get dressed, but he still was flustered when he reentered the small examination room. She behaved as though nothing unusual had taken place, letting him off the hook. Or so he thought. Her mission for that day had been accomplished. A month later, she would call for another appointment.

All these years later, Beth Davenport still cringed when she thought about her conduct that spring. She had abused her sexuality to exploit a wonderfully nice human being. It was one of the few conscious choices Beth ever made that she genuinely regretted.

Her planned subterfuge was a series of pregnancies – or alleged pregnancies. Each would end with a miscarriage. She would stage them twelve or fifteen months apart to convince Senior that she and Junior were undeterred by persistent struggles with fertility. Senior was bound to be skeptical, which was why the participation of Doc

Reynolds was paramount. As her doctor and Senior's lifelong friend, no one was better suited to make off-the-cuff remarks while they were out on a lake fishing. "Senior, I feel so bad about what Beth is going through." Or, "I'm glad to see Beth and your son haven't given up … but you eventually may have to accept that some women just aren't meant to go full-term."

During her second session with Elliot Reynolds, Beth let the doctor in on a secret. She informed him that she and Junior had been trying unsuccessfully to have children since the earliest years of their marriage. More recently, they had visited a fertility clinic in another city where they learned Junior's sperm count was unusually low. A close friend like the doctor surely would recognize that such a disclosure only could widen the already tenuous chasm between Senior and his son. Thus, she was determined to redirect responsibility for their problem onto herself. She wanted Senior to believe that she was the reason their marriage hadn't presented him his prized grandchild.

"After all, Elliot, it is my body … and it is my reputation. If I want people to think I'm the one with pregnancy issues, it isn't like anyone else will be hurt."

If he had shown reluctance, she was prepared to politely remind him of what occurred during her previous visit. He wouldn't want Mrs. Reynolds, the medical authorities, or his good friend, Senior, to hear he was unable to control his biological impulses during a routine medical exam. But no such prompting was necessary. The doctor had turned sheepish as soon as she entered his office. He offered no resistance whatsoever to the proposal. If anything, he seemed eager to comply – expressing genuine empathy for the complexities she and Junior confronted due to Senior's intimidating ways.

After he agreed to participate, Beth promised Elliot Reynolds that she someday would return the favor. At the time, he must have thought she was blowing smoke. But all those years later, after his brand-new regional hospital was up and running, she proved true to her word.

On Thanksgiving Day of 1976, she and Junior delivered their first good news to Senior. They were expecting a child. His jubilation was practically uncontainable for the three months they allowed him to believe she was pregnant. If her father-in-law hadn't provided so many reasons to feel otherwise, Beth might have regretted his pending disappointment. In mid-February, they informed him of the miscarriage and their intention to keep trying.

Pacing was important to the overall plan. She needed time to gain the support and political capital required for the years ahead. She and Junior waited until early 1978 to announce a second pregnancy, then dashed Senior's hopes with news of a second miscarriage in May. Doc Reynolds played along, confirming the difficulties Beth was having, and at the same time cautioning Senior not to get his hopes too high. "Your daughter-in-law is approaching forty ... let's face it, Senior, not every woman is meant to carry children."

To keep Senior at bay, she and Junior went to the well one last time. In late 1979, they announced a third successful conception – then a few weeks before Beth's fortieth birthday, in the spring of 1980, they played out the final miscarriage. Senior was devastated. As far as Beth was concerned, the issues around children and a family heir were behind them. Her deceitful ploy had bought her the necessary time. Very soon, she and Junior would be free and clear.

What she hadn't counted on was Junior coming up with a deceitful plan of his own. But in her mind, it was the most beautiful act of deception ever to be perpetrated.

Chapter 39

B eth would forever remember the looks on their faces when she blurted out her response. So many memories with her "two special men" seemed frozen in time as she paged through the journal.

Cal had arrived in Evansville late on Friday afternoon. He and Junior hadn't seen each other in over a month because Cal was closing a bank deal in Buenos Aires. As a reunited threesome, they grilled steaks and enjoyed a bottle of Argentinian wine before Beth headed up to bed. On Saturday, they went boating in the morning and she even tried water skiing for the first time. Somehow though, it suddenly felt like Junior wanted to be alone with Cal, which was unusual behavior on his part. But Beth could put the time to good use. She still had lots of details to nail down for the week ahead. On Sunday, she would share her plans with the two of them – before Cal shuffled back to Indianapolis. They'd been aware of her intent to enter politics, but now Beth Davenport was ready to make a public announcement. On Monday morning she would pay a visit to Senior, who was totally in the dark.

June 21, 1981 - Father's Day
Insane. Unthinkable. MAGNIFICENT.

How shocked she was when they completely turned the table on her. Junior and Cal had been cooking up their own plan, which they unveiled first thing Sunday morning. Any political ambitions suddenly paled by comparison.

Her two special men didn't recognize how far ahead of their time they were with their thinking. That realization would hit many years later, at least for Cal and her. But in 1981, such an idea from two persons of the same gender was preposterous, if not downright immoral. Since that time, a wave of societal transformations made a wide array of new parental constructs acceptable. Sadly though, Junior died before he could see surrogacy go mainstream with improved techniques for transplanting eggs and embryos. On that Sunday morning, however, the notion of a child being somehow shared by two same-sex individuals was still a decade away. Because of the unique bond they shared, Junior and Cal had allowed their imaginations to run wild.

"Beth, how would you feel about delving into uncharted territory this morning?"

It had seemed like a peculiar question when Junior emerged from the bedroom for his morning coffee. Even more peculiar was watching Cal emerge a few steps behind him. Cal was a notoriously late sleeper on weekends.

"I guess I'm willing to tackle a new adventure or two ... what do you have in mind?" she responded playfully. She was wide awake and more than ready to attempt something new on a warm summer Sunday, having already enjoyed her early morning work-out and first cup of coffee.

Junior joined Beth at the kitchen table. "Good ... let's hope you feel the same after you hear what we're about to propose." They both watched as Cal filled two mugs with coffee and brought them over to the table, handing one to Junior and grabbing the chair on the opposite side of Beth.

"Did you two boys get in trouble with the principal again?" she asked in jest – mostly to ease the tension she instinctively began to feel.

Junior smiled for a brief second. Then, his expression turned serious, "Beth, Cal and I have been discussing a possible idea for several months ... and it very much involves you."

He paused to gather his nerve. She nodded, encouraging him to proceed. There was a slight tremor in his voice. "You know how much I love you ... and how much Cal also loves you."

She nodded again, sensing their obvious awkwardness. Where was the discussion heading? "And I love the both of you," she said in bewilderment. "Please tell me you're not going to break up with me," she smirked.

Junior was oblivious to her attempt at light-heartedness as he continued, "Well, you certainly recognize how much I've always wanted children ... and not just because my father has applied constant pressure on this issue. No, deep-down I've wanted it for myself. Maybe I feel I should play my role in the future of civilization and all that tripe ... but more to the point, I'd like to see the Davenport name live on after I'm gone." He watched for her reaction, hoping to see a sign of receptivity.

Instead, she was confused and interjected, "Yes, Junior, I know ... and I respect those sentiments. But I think you may be forgetting ..."

He cut Beth off before she could complete her thought. "Cal and I want to have a baby."

He had said it so matter-of-factly that she wasn't sure she heard him correctly. Junior saw her puzzled expression and started blushing with embarrassment. "I know ... I know. I took biology in high school. I should have said that Cal and I were hoping the three of us might together have a baby."

Like that was supposed to clear things up. "An interesting concept, guys. Please, do go on."

Junior was undaunted by her sarcasm. "If you hate what you're about to hear ... then just point your anger at me. I dreamed up this idea months ago ... and yesterday Cal finally agreed to go along ... that is, if you also agree." As if on cue, she and Junior gazed over at Cal, who nodded his affirmation. So Junior continued. "We all know the problems I have in the bedroom ... and we also know, only too well, that Cal doesn't suffer from the same affliction."

All at once it dawned on Beth where the conversation was leading. Her eyes grew big and her body bolted upright in the chair. Seeing her reaction, Junior began talking faster.

"It's not as crazy as you might think, Beth. I'm your husband ... and I have no problem with the two of you ... uhh ... you know ... doing what needs to be done. Heck, I'm the one who's pushing for it. And isn't it fair to say that you and Cal genuinely love each other ... and have for a long, long time? Okay, maybe it's not the kind of love one normally correlates with the intimate acts we're suggesting ... but no one will ever know. You and I could raise the baby like normal parents ... yet at the same time, this child would be the product of the three of us ... a lasting symbol of the uncommon affection we've shared for twenty years. You are the only person who understands the special feelings Cal and I have for each other ... and you've been a part of us over all these years."

She watched with admiration and amusement as Junior struggled to convey what was in his heart. "Well, as I see it ... somewhere along the way, the compassion you originally felt for us underwent a metamorphosis ... it turned into its own unique form of love." His energy intensified, "And then somehow, your love added to our love ... and we've wound up with this strange blended love that is almost magical ... a love shared by three people that the rest of the world couldn't possibly understand."

Junior looked pleadingly at Beth. "Okay, maybe I'm making a mess of all this ... but you know what I mean, and you know that I'm right. Anyway, with all these special feelings swirling around us ... it just seems like having a baby is the perfect way to perpetuate what we mean to one another."

Barely pausing to take a breath, Junior reached over and took her hand. "Beth, we understand what a ridiculous thing we're asking ... considering the physical strain of pregnancy and the sacrifices required for motherhood ... plus the potential impact on your plans for entering politics ... not to mention, the impact on your life in total for many years to come. And we know the necessary acts between you and Cal would no doubt be awkward for all of us. But Beth, if we don't raise the possibility now, I'll be kicking myself forever. This whole crazy concept depends on you ... and let's face it, your biological clock will be running out soon."

He froze momentarily, his face turning red. "Oh, God, I can't believe I said that ... it's just ... it's just ... it's just that it's true. So please, Beth, forgive my clumsiness ... but please also tell us you'll think about what we're asking. Don't give us an answer right away ... just promise you'll take a few days and think about it."

At last, he ran out of words. Beth was stunned. To think that her dear Junior had envisioned something this implausible, this outlandish, and not uttered a word to her until now. She had never seen her husband this unabashedly hopeful and excited. Yet, at the same time, desperate. What he and Cal were proposing sounded like pure madness. But oddly, her first instinct was one of inward reflection. How had she not once considered the same insane, impractical proposition during all their years together?

Junior and Cal had come to her once before with an implausible proposal, and once before they had asked her not to give them an immediate answer. She had ignored their plea then by instantly agreeing to pose as Junior's girlfriend. She never had lamented that decision.

Here she was again. She looked at Junior, her eyes moist. She looked over at Cal. Both were leaning forward with their elbows on the table and their hands scrunched under their chins. Turning her head toward Junior, she finally spoke. "You have my word ... I will take a few days and think about this rather unconventional idea of yours. But I must warn you ... my mind already is made up. What you're suggesting is beautiful ... beautiful and totally magnificent."

Chapter 40

"We can start by pinning down your menstrual cycle and determining the midpoints between your periods over the next few months. Then we can tell Cal which weekends he needs to be here."

So much for appropriate table talk. The two of them had been enjoying a leisurely dinner on their patio when Junior decided he could wait no longer. It already had been thirty-some hours since Beth signed onto his crazy plan. Her biological clock was ticking.

Junior could think of little else. As soon as Cal left on Sunday, he rushed to the mall and purchased books on every imaginable topic related to childbirth. On the way home, he stopped by the hospital and picked up schedules for upcoming Lamaze classes. He immersed himself in the tiniest of details concerning pregnancy and delivery. Conception, too – though his role would be limited to bystander during this first leg of their upcoming baby journey.

"As I recall, your cycles are fairly regular ... coming every twenty-eight to thirty days. If Cal can block out his calendar accordingly, we should have you pregnant by the end of summer." After a pause, Junior grinned and added, "But Cal may want it to take longer."

She laughed and threw a napkin at him. Meanwhile, her mind was a mishmash. After Junior's comments, she wondered if the impending appointments might be better scheduled in a barn. For sure,

Cal was stepping into his role as stud. She just wasn't sure if she should consider herself a mare or a cow.

Of greater concern was the fact that Cal was well-practiced for playing his part. At forty-two, he was handsome, fit, and socially active. He had been intimate with many women over the years. She, on the other hand, was a sexual bumpkin and frightened as hell about the carnal acts ahead.

During the entirety of her forty years, only four men had even seen her naked. An abusive father. A snake of a man to whom she'd sacrificed her virginity for securing a job. Junior, during their failed attempts at "raising the dead." And of course, poor Doc Reynolds – a guilt-laden memory that still made her cringe with guilt. These experiences hardly provided a solid foundation for healthy intercourse.

Very soon her ineptitude in the bedroom would become obvious. Within minutes of signing-on to the secret surrogacy pact, she warned Cal about her lack of experience and asked him to be patient. "You are rumored to be an ideal mentor ... so I'll try to learn fast," she'd teased nervously. But then Junior threw out an even bigger curve ball.

He wanted to be present for every stage of the baby journey. "In for a penny, in for a pounding," he quipped. If this infant was to be the 'love child' they hoped it to be, both males in the triangle believed his full participation was vital. Junior should be in the room, and even in the bed, during conception. On what basis could Beth possibly put up an argument? Morality? Common decency? Beth had crossed through that looking glass many years earlier and now was convinced she would never experience normal sex.

The circled weekends on their calendar were labeled 'bedding sessions.' Beth found Junior's choice of words rather humorous. Whatever peculiar acts Senior might have believed these three close friends had been committing all along, they finally would get around to at least some of them. Sexual threesomes on a monthly basis.

As the rest of that summer unfolded, their bedroom efforts scarcely could have been referred to as lustful. Most often, they were light-hearted. Even comedic. These shared acts became the ultimate consummation of their Camelot triangle. With each monthly attempt, Beth's feelings for both men deepened – as did her self-doubts. She seemed to be missing the sexual curiosity and capacity other women wrote and talked about. She felt no urges to let loose or experiment.

But in fairness, different people might have different proclivities. Kicking-off a session in the center of a mattress with Cal and Junior taking their assigned positions on either side of her may have been a turn-on for some. Just not for her. Regardless, their interludes became lovingly functional.

As each month passed, they waited and hoped. By the time Christmas arrived, they'd begun to worry Doc Reynolds had been prophetic when he cautioned Senior. *"Your daughter-in-law is approaching forty ... she may not be meant to carry children."* Beth viewed such looming prospects as Shakespearean justice.

With the possibility of pregnancy on the horizon, she'd placed her plans for entering the political arena on hold. As they progressed toward January, Junior finally encouraged her to delay no further. "At least we gave it the old college try," he said with a shrug.

1982 would be an election year. She couldn't waste time. She needed to inform Senior of her intentions. Meanwhile, they would continue their monthly bedding sessions until summer, but mother nature looked to be getting the last laugh.

She had been contemplating this meeting with her sixty-three-year-old father-in-law for so long that the words practically were scripted in her head. As satisfying as it would be to free herself from Senior's tentacles, her political aspirations would be better achieved if she could gain his support. She needed him to believe that any political success she might achieve would be part and parcel to the powerful reputation he personally had created around the Davenport name.

Senior unleashed endless strings of profanities when she told him she was leaving the company to pursue public service. She wanted to bring him along slowly, so she sat back and patiently absorbed the anticipated fireworks. After he was done ranting about the amount of time and energy he had invested in her future with the company, he turned somewhat sullen.

"Beth, I was counting on you to take over when I ... to take over down the road." He couldn't even mouth words that suggested he someday would step down, or worse yet, perish. His mortality was forbidden territory.

With his anger momentarily spent, she began leading him along an upward climb – before his rage returned. "Senior, you have taught me so many things since I joined the company ... and Davenport Industries is poised to expand in whole new directions. You're still a young man ... you don't need me inside the company. Imagine how much more I could do for the company ... for the Davenport name ... if I were working from the outside ... if I were to become Mayor of Evansville. Maybe someday I could run for Congress. I'm forty-two ... if I were to become a city councilman this year, by the time the next mayoral election rolls around, I think my chances would be reasonable with your help. After that, who knows? The Davenport name carries a lot of influence around this state."

She watched his eyes light up as his brain began to churn. He was taking the bait. He sat frozen, staring in her direction for several minutes. Not at her, but through her. His mind was traveling down a continuum of possibilities. He always had fashioned himself as a powerbroker – a modern-day kingmaker for the coalmining states. Finally, he spoke.

"Beth, you know how much regard I've always held for you. You have more balls than any man in this whole gutless city or county ... except for me. But by now, you should have learned an important lesson. It's one thing to underestimate your own potential ...

just don't ever underestimate mine. Why would you want to lower yourself and this family's name by running for some piddly-ass city council seat ... or even mayor for that matter? If you're intent on becoming a congressman, let's not waste my time and money by running for anything less. Let's kick this public service bullshit of yours into high gear ... and we'll have you in the United States Senate in no time at all. We gotta think big. You mark my words ... someday there's gonna be a god-damned lady president ... why shouldn't she be a Davenport?"

She couldn't have agreed more. In somewhat different words than she might have used, he articulated everything she'd been thinking and planning for more than seven years.

Beth was neither Democrat nor Republican. In the past, she only had bothered to vote in elections when she felt especially positive or negative about a specific candidate. Before launching into politics, she faced an important decision. With which party should she affiliate? The choice she made was rather expedient. Her largest available power source, Senior Davenport, was an entrenched Republican. Also, the district's incumbent congressman was a Democrat who had failed to distinguish himself during two terms in Washington. He was especially ripe for defeat in November due to the soaring popularity of Ronald Reagan and the broader momentum swinging to the Grand Old Party.

Two veteran Republicans from the area had thrown their hats into the ring over the prior six months, but neither was making a meaningful connection with the electorate. As a late entry, Beth Davenport was a new face – and an attractive one, at that. In 1982, the expense of television advertising was a daunting proposition for candidates seeking congressional seats in Southern Indiana. Senior never hesitated. He phoned a few cronies, raised the necessary funds, and for two solid weeks leading up to the early May primary, voters were regaled with details about the meteoric accomplishments of a local businesswoman. Top executives from the area and across the country served as spokespersons, attesting to the impact this talented Beth Davenport could have in Washington. Meanwhile, Beth honed her campaigning skills with endless personal appearances. She carried the primary in a landslide.

The next day, she and a team her father-in-law assembled began strategizing a new and bigger campaign for November's election. Her opponent recognized the powerful storm heading his way and made the mistake of challenging Beth Davenport to a series of four debates – figuring her lack of political experience would sink her. He was wrong. She kept her answers short and simple, conveying a confidence that suggested greater depth on issues than she really possessed as a novice. Meanwhile, the incumbent repeatedly became entangled in his own long-windedness when she probed him about his inconsistent voting record and poor attendance at committee meetings. After the first two debates, which were broadcast on local radio stations, the Democratic incumbent decided all relevant topics had been adequately covered and cancelled his participation in the remaining two.

Beth was well on her way to victory when her campaign hit a speed bump. Or, more accurately, a tummy bump.

September 23, 1982
 "Fate will find a way"

When she read this journal entry, Beth Davenport couldn't help but think of her son. The pregnancy that would result in his birth was confirmed on that date – September 23, 1982. But the date above the entry wasn't the only reason her thoughts turned to Troy. The quote – *"fate will find a way"* – could be attributed to Virgil. It came to her as she was sitting in the waiting room outside Doc Reynolds' office. Even as a boy, Troy had been drawn to the ancient poets and philosophers of Rome. The Greek ones, too. She wondered if he still might wind up teaching humanities instead of sociology someday. Troy's interests and passions always had been varied. But whatever he taught or did in life, she hoped he eventually would find the contentment he sought. He was so much like his father – or at least the man he thought to be his father.

On the prior September weekend, candidate Beth Davenport had completed a 5K run for charity and was changing clothes in the bathroom of a VFW hall, where she would be speaking to a full house. Fastening the skirt was tougher than usual. With her frantic schedule of public appearances, she couldn't imagine that she'd put on weight. She slid her hands over her abdomen, felt around, then smiled. Her period was long overdue, but her menstrual cycles had become highly irregular since the beginning of the year. Round-the-clock campaigning had wreaked havoc in all sorts of unexpected ways, so she had given it little thought. After the primaries, there had been two more bedding sessions before Junior decided to throw in the towel completely in July. For a year, they had attempted the impossible. Pregnancy wasn't in the cards and Beth's schedule until November was now in the hands of her campaign team. "At least we tried. It was a long shot from the beginning." What none of them knew was Cal's visit in May had done the trick. *Fate will find a way.* Beth was four months pregnant.

Doc Reynolds barely could contain his excitement. "You tell that husband of yours that those big city fertility clinics aren't always right. But I guess we know that now."

He seemed unusually giddy for a doctor who probably had told hundreds of women they were pregnant. As Beth was preparing to exit his office, he confided, "I can't tell you how relieved I am to see things turn out the way they have. Since that embarrassing incident in my examination room years ago, I've had this burden hanging around my neck. I hated how the two of you couldn't have children

... and how you felt the need to cover for Junior because of the way his daddy treats him. And to be honest, what I hated most was lying to Senior about those phony miscarriages. That man can be a pain-in-the-ass sometimes, but he's been a close friend to me and my family since he first came to Evansville. Today all that weight has been lifted. My blessings to you and Junior."

Under normal circumstances, Elliot Reynolds might have come around from behind his desk and hugged the daughter-in-law of a lifelong friend. But Beth understood why he wouldn't want to have physical contact of any kind with her. She had manipulated his loyalty to the Davenports. She hoped someday to make amends.

Beth swore to herself that she was going to shoot straight and play fair once she was serving the people who elected her. If called upon, she knew she could play dirty. The entirety of her life to-date had been a testament to deceit and underhandedness. At last, she would break the cycle. Or very soon she would. First, she needed to win.

Back in 1982, announcing a pregnancy during the run-up to an election would have been political suicide for any female candidate. Perhaps Beth owed the voting public the truth about her situation. But no such rule was written anywhere.

For six more weeks, she was careful with what she wore. She confined her discussions about the baby to Junior and Cal – who had gone over-the-top with excitement. And, of course, she told her father-in-law.

Senior had seen his hopes dashed three times previously. But this time, Doc Reynolds assured him she was well past the danger zone. Senior Davenport finally would have his grandchild. What's more, his gritty daughter-in-law was hiding this fact from a voting public on the verge of sending her to Washington. His girl Beth wasn't about to let the prospect of motherhood turn her soft. She truly was a Davenport.

Chapter 41

The baby arrived on the last day of February in 1983 – just two months into her first congressional term. Beth spent most of January in Washington, but Doc Reynolds insisted she stay off airplanes during the final month of her pregnancy. Six hours of labor was short compared to many first-time mothers. Junior stood, sat, or paced at her bedside for every second of it. Cal peeked in from time to time, but mostly camped out in the waiting room.

Senior stayed away from the hospital until he received word he had a healthy grandchild. Minutes later he arrived, passing out cigars to everyone in sight. Because his grandchild happened to be a boy, he also saw that cases of champagne were delivered and distributed to every floor of the building.

As it turned out, Troy's birth had provided a second big reason in just four months for the Davenports and everyone associated to celebrate. The first was election night, November 2. The weeks between were anything but celebratory. Only days after giving an acceptance speech, Beth Davenport confronted her first political controversy and it was explosive.

Word leaked out that she was expecting a child – and thus would be absent from Congress for two or three months in the early part of the upcoming year. The Democrats, as well as her Republican opponents from the primary, stirred up the media. Beth's telephone rang non-stop. How could the citizens of her district be properly served by a mother tending to a newborn? What could have possessed her to keep such an important consideration from the public?

Exactly one week after her election to the United States House of Representatives, Beth Davenport requested several minutes of airtime during the evening news on Evansville's most-watched TV station. She would read a prepared statement that ignored the advice of the same campaign advisers who had helped her get elected. As the backlash continued to snowball, speculation among local pundits fell into two camps. Beth Davenport, the first female ever elected from Indiana's 8th District, was going to resign before she even took the oath of office. Or, Beth Davenport would appear deferentially before the camera and read an emotional apologia.

She did neither.

Her remarks were replayed many times over the weeks, months, and years that followed – providing vibrant context to a powerful new wave in the feminist movement. Before Beth Davenport made her first appearance in the halls of Congress, she already was earning a place on the nation's political landscape.

In her comments, she explained that she had not been pregnant when she entered her name into the Republican primary race, back in January. She confided how she and her husband had tried unsuccessfully to have children for many years, and thus, at age forty-two, wasn't anticipating this likelihood to change. Upon learning she was expecting a baby, just six weeks prior to Election Day, her first instinct had been to concede the election.

"My thoughts quickly turned to motherhood and raising our child. I would put my career, political or otherwise, on hold for a few years and focus on family matters. But soon I began to realize how wrong that was. Not the raising of children and the prioritization of family … as those concerns always should be imperative. No, what suddenly hit me as horribly wrong was that I automatically felt an obligation to place essential parts of my life on hold ... all because I was a woman who was bearing a child, and society therefore would presume I should be satisfied with a partial existence for some appropriate period of time. So, I stand before you tonight to confess I made a conscious decision to withhold the announcement of my pregnancy – knowing full well that my work and travel schedules were to be compromised soon after I took office.

"I would like to believe that not too many years from today, a woman will be able to divulge such details in any circumstance without fear of repercussion. You can judge for yourself, but I submit we have not yet reached that stage of gender equality. If I had made my condition known, I fear the election would have been lost ... and what a travesty that would have been. Whatever the outcome for me personally, I wanted votes to be cast on issues and merit rather than biology. I don't deny my motives and ambitions are somewhat selfish. I want to be your congresswoman ... to serve you effectively in Washington for many years to come. But when I made that decision six weeks before Election Day, I was not thinking of myself. I was thinking about the millions of girls and young women in this country who will confront similar choices ... and the many generations to follow. On their behalf, I now have much to prove. In two years, you will have the opportunity to grade me accordingly."

She ended her appearance by smiling into the camera. No cliched "good night" or "thank you." Beth Davenport projected the non-traditional attitude that was to become a seminal part of her public persona. When the camera shifted back to the news desk, the anchorman sat speechless for several moments, contemplating whether he should comment on what he'd just heard. He wisely moved onto his next story.

By the end of the evening, a firestorm had broken out on Evansville's largest call-in radio station. Editorials filled the next morning's paper. In no time, the story went national. Looking back,

Beth remembered how exhausting those weeks were – fielding non-stop calls from reporters from across the country as she prepared to take her seat in Congress. All during the final months of a pregnancy. In hindsight, she was fortunate the cable news networks weren't around yet.

From her vantage, not a soul in the universe had been at a loss for a strong opinion. She was being glorified and excoriated simultaneously. An enlightened egalitarian voice. A feminist Nazi bitch. Welcome to the world of politics. Each time she was captured on camera, the contentious debate over the validity of her position was refueled by the enlarging protrusion of her midsection. Adding to the controversy were the various medical experts who weighed in, opining on how her repeated trips to Washington during December and January were irresponsible for a forty-two-year-old woman in her condition.

Now, three and a half decades later, Beth had gained an appreciation for how the passage of time could reshape history. Today, her detractors chose not to remember attacking her as a rebellious agitator. Her once unconventional perspectives had been normalized. In the years since, Beth Davenport had been proclaimed widely for her relentless courage and for advancing central issues of gender equality. But she also realized how those same passing years had allowed her to delude herself. Yes, in her own way, she had been concerned about feminist causes as a young woman. On some level, she probably was reflecting her innermost beliefs when she stood before that television camera those many years ago. Whether she made the decision to keep her pregnancy secret in the precise manner she'd related to her constituents was now immaterial.

February 28, 1983
 Victory in the Name Game.

She was hoping for a girl. Beth never expressed this preference to anyone – before or after Troy was born. In a maternal sense, she didn't have a fondness for girls over boys. If anything, she'd been worried about experiencing a fondness for either.

Many times throughout her pregnancy, she'd felt like a vessel instead of a soon-to-be mother. Her emotions were a tangled mess. Didn't the child inside her body really belong to Junior and Cal? This unborn baby was more a product of their love than hers. How much of her truly was vested in this son or daughter? What kind of mother would Junior and Cal even want her to be?

Regardless of the anxieties she experienced, all three parental parties were resolute on one point. Boy or girl, this child never was to know the role that Cal had played during conception. On the birth certificate, and for life ever after, only Elizabeth Davenport and Joseph Elwood Davenport, Jr., were to be identified as the parents. Hence, Senior Davenport would be the baby's grandfather. And that was the reason Beth had hoped for a girl.

Her father-in-law never uttered a word. He didn't have to. Preference for a boy was as an accepted component of Senior's constitution. Men ruled the world. Males were the ones who transported names and testosterone across generations. The presence of a grandson allowed Senior to believe his personal Davenport dynasty would be carried into perpetuity.

Junior understood the complications associated with naming a baby, especially a Davenport baby, so he opted to sit on the sidelines. Whatever his wife chose would be fine with him. For Beth, selecting a girl's name would have been easy. Lila.

The naming of a boy offered up a minefield. As much as she might have wanted Calvin as the first or middle name, she thought it best to avoid drawing attention to their unusual friendship with Cal. The more notable complexity was Senior. He simply had assumed his grandson would be labeled, Joseph Elwood Davenport

III. No further discussion required.

But in the hospital, as he held his cherished grandson for the first time, Beth seized the moment. Junior watched with amusement. In a loving voice, Beth said, "So you and Troy seem to be hitting it off rather well."

He almost dropped the baby. "Who?" he asked.

Beth feigned innocent surprise. "Troy Joseph Davenport ... your grandson, of course." Then she waited and watched.

"You're kidding ... right?" He chuckled lightly, hoping to see Beth and Junior join him in laughter.

Beth savored every second of the interchange. "We figured you'd be thrilled with his middle name ... you know, 'Joseph' ... after his father and grandfather."

This man who had been coveting thoughts of a grandchild, a family heir, for the entire twenty years she had known him, now was turning angry just minutes after finally being presented with one. "Thrilled my ass! What kind of name is Troy?"

The scene was playing out just as she'd imagined. Just as she'd hoped. Beth pretended not to notice the change in temperament, "Troy is a wonderful name for a boy. It also happens to be the name of a small city in Ohio that played a prominent role in my life. Troy is where my grandparents lived ... where I spent time every summer ... and it is where I lived after my parents died in the fire."

Out of respect, Senior dialed back his irritation, but the frustration still was evident. "That's nice, Beth ... but why do you need to saddle your son with all that? In the years I've known you, I don't remember you once talking about your grandparents ... or this legendary town of Troy."

She was finding it hard to keep a straight face. "Perhaps you weren't listening carefully enough. But either way, wouldn't you concede that as the mother, I played a role in the birth of this baby ... at least a minor one? And you do recognize that your side of the family is well-represented in the name department … with both Joseph and Davenport. Wouldn't it seem fair to also reflect a mother's identity?"

Senior wanted to avoid this whole thorny issue at any cost. He'd watched his daughter-in-law take on most of the free world in recent weeks on the subject of women's rights. "You're right, Bethie dear … like you always are when it comes to fairness. But how about we change the order a bit … to say, Joseph Troy Davenport?"

"Troy Joseph Davenport," she responded, showing no room for negotiation. She hated to see the lopsided skirmish drawing to its close.

In a meek voice, he made one last plea. "Can we at least call him Joe … or maybe T.J.?"

"We'll call him Troy," she said with an easy smile. Game, set, match. On this day, complete victory was hers.

Lost amid this on-going battle of wits had been the insignificance of the name itself. As a young girl during her summer visits, or later when she lived inside their home for a final year of high school, Beth felt no attachment to either grandparent. Plus, what memories she carried of those drawn-out months in Troy were mostly negative. Purely for the sake of argument, she'd needed to glom onto something from her past. Their son would never know he was named to spite his grandfather.

Chapter 42

As a political novice, Beth's first term in the House of Representatives would have been a high-wire act under any circumstance. But because the congressional freshman just happened to be a freshwoman already placed in the national crosshairs, she wound up walking a tightrope with no net underneath. Only a shark tank. Each meeting that Congresswoman Beth Davenport missed or attended was duly noted by reporters throughout the Midwest and elsewhere. Each vote or abstention. Any opinion expressed. Over the next two years, being second-guessed at every turn was totally exhilarating for her.

She surprised critics by not falling neatly in-line with the conservative dogma of the Republican Party. In charting her own course, Beth attracted a growing base of support that pulled in moderate voters from both parties. Her early notoriety from the pregnancy had made her a media darling, so she needed to pick her issues judiciously.

Proving disparagers wrong about her ability to balance a political career with motherhood and marriage proved especially satisfying. Her achievements on this front were enhanced greatly when Senior purchased a second corporate jet for Davenport Industries – making this new plane and its pilots available to her on a moment's notice. He was committed to Beth Davenport's success in Washington and still wanted her spending as much time as possible with his grandson back in Evansville. Unfortunately, any goodwill he created with Beth could be quickly offset. "I worry that if you're not around, Junior will turn our little Troy into a sissy like him."

Whenever circumstances allowed, Beth made local public appearances with Troy in her arms. Junior and the baby even flew to Washington on several occasions so she could do the same in front of larger crowds. To many, she became a symbol for working moms with young children. As for herself, the lines often blurred. Was she doing all the visibly right things in raising her child as a caring mother, or as a savvy politician hell-bent to outwit her detractors? Fearing the real answer, Beth chose not to dwell on such distinctions.

By the time 1984 rolled around, Beth Davenport was a shoo-in for reelection. Shortly before the primaries, she surprised both political parties by declaring herself an Independent. The Republicans didn't even bother to prop up a last-minute candidate. The Democrats put only a token effort behind theirs. When Congress reconvened in 1985, she'd earned a position on the desirable Ways & Means Committee, as well as Education & Labor – where she advocated social reforms that further secured her popularity among voters.

Strangely enough, during these first two terms in the House, Beth began to recognize she truly did care about important aspects of public service. She wanted to see the playing field leveled for regular citizens of every race, ethnicity, and gender. She no longer was simply mouthing words. The first forty-plus years of her life had been so consumed with overcoming obstacles from her past and winning at all costs, that she really hadn't explored her innermost appetites. Perhaps she had feared what she might find. Sure, she still was driven by a personal need to overcome adversaries, but to her surprise, she sometimes felt tugs of responsibility toward a greater whole.

Beth had enjoyed huge success as an investment advisor, and then again as a corporate strategist and senior executive inside the family's mining businesses, but nothing compared to the skyrocketing notoriety and achievements she now was experiencing. Fulfillment on a professional level was climbing toward maximum capacity.

Away from politics, behind the facades she toiled hard to erect and maintain, sacrifices were being made. At home, there was little time to feel connected to her husband and Troy. Luckily, Junior had taken to fatherhood from day one. They'd hired a daytime nanny for when Junior was at the office, but otherwise he and his son were practically inseparable.

These many years later, Beth only could wonder how this tight bond might have grown and flourished if Junior had lived. How sad that Junior couldn't watch his little boy mature into the balanced and caring young man Troy became. Sadder still, her son had lost the most important influence in his life – the one parent who naturally and lovingly gave of himself – seeking or expecting nothing in return. Beth couldn't pretend otherwise.

As to their relationship with Cal, the 'Camelot Years' most definitely had come to an end. After Troy was born, Cal cut back his visits to Evansville during the early months – to eliminate any potential awkwardness surrounding Troy's parentage. He had no intention of meddling. He wanted Beth and Junior to establish their own turfs, their own rhythms, as married parents.

But soon, he started making the drive downstate more regularly again. Unfortunately, the chemistry was never the same – at least for Beth. Junior and Cal remained as close as ever – maybe even closer due to their secret bond of surrogacy. But Beth no longer had time to idle away hours with these two men who meant everything to her. Lost was the easy spontaneity of afternoons canoeing down a river, strolling through an art fair, or perched in front of a fireplace. In the void left by her growing absence, a new triad took shape during Cal's visits. Together, Cal and Junior would fill Troy's weekends with playgrounds, swimming pools, amusement parks, sledding hills, or countless other excursions. She still remembered the mixed emotions she experienced whenever Junior related the details to her – usually by phone.

During these early years in politics, the dichotomy between her sense of accomplishment on a professional level versus a personal one became an everyday reality. She would awaken each morning, energized by new horizons to be explored, new envelopes to be pushed, and new balances to be struck, if government was to better serve its tax-paying public. Yet, on too many evenings when her head hit the pillow, her last thoughts as she slipped into slumber were of duties she again had neglected as mother and wife. Of the growing disappointment she was to the people most important to her. Of the parental experiences she was denying herself, but regrettably didn't miss.

Whatever the reason, Beth was wired differently than other people. Her emotions and instincts didn't click in like they were supposed to. She, at times, had condemned herself for not trying harder. But even those feelings of self-reproach were conveniently banished to some recess of her brain where they failed to alter behavior.

In another year or two she would turn eighty. But as she read through the diary, Senator Beth Davenport was amazed by how few of her feelings had changed with time. She detested her parents and brother as much as she did sixty years earlier. She still wrestled with what Lila might have meant to her. She still got agitated when she thought about Senior. She still got melancholy when she reflected on her indifference toward romance, toward sexual fulfillment, and yes, toward motherhood. Over the course of her lifetime, she had done little to overcome the bile she carried inside. She had done little to understand the shortcomings that probably denied her a fuller, richer life. It had been easier to accept them and proceed along other dimensions.

November 4, 1986

Election Day. A new chapter begins.

When Beth entered politics, she was anticipating a run for Senate after her fourth term in the House – when the most vulnerable of Indiana's two senators would come up for reelection. The other senate seat was to be contested four years sooner, in 1986. Two stints in the House had seemed inadequate for knocking-off a popular incumbent who handily won his three previous terms. But who could predict the fortunes of politics? There was only one certainty. A viable candidate needed to seize an opportunity when it was presented. Commissioned surveys among voters had virtually guaranteed her a victory.

A few weeks after her second election to Congress, Beth Davenport began organizing a campaign for Senate two years later. With popularity soaring, she announced her candidacy as an Independent well in advance – during the summer of 1985. With the prospect of Beth Davenport's name on the ballot, other Indiana notables decided to save their ammunition for 1990. By mid-March of 1986, with the popular congresswoman pulling away in the polls, the incumbent Democrat announced his withdrawal from the primary – claiming he had wanted to return to his law practice all along. When votes were tallied in November, Beth carried a staggering seventy-seven percent. She wasn't merely Indiana's first female senator. The former Evansville businesswoman received the largest majority ever by a female running for either chamber of Congress from any state.

With the advent of 1987, she not only entered the United States Senate, but she also entered the final stage of a carefully crafted plan that would exact her full revenge on Senior Davenport. Beth had needed her father-in-law's influence to launch and sustain her early political career. But no longer. At last, she could even the score with a man who had toyed with her deepest vulnerabilities since 1960, when he lured her into a loathsome marriage arrangement. A year later, he had ambushed her with the horrible things her father had done to her. It had been thirteen years since the threatening inscription inside his oh-so-clever book about Camelot. And so much more over twenty-seven years.

Under a pretense of practicality, Beth now would extricate Senior's family from his private kingdom. Her principal senatorial office obviously needed to be in Washington. But she was going to relocate her home state operation to Indianapolis, taking along the man's son and grandson. By the end of the year, Senior Davenport would be left alone in Evansville. Alone with the company that carried his beloved family name. He would have no Davenports to strongarm and abuse. No Davenport to eventually run the company. At last, she would have her retribution.

But as Beth was soon to learn, retribution came with a price.

Chapter 43

O ver the years, many of Indiana's senators had opened offices in the state's capital and largest city. Indianapolis offered obvious benefits. Access to resources ... synergies with other agents of government ... a location in the exact center of the Indiana map. No one questioned Beth Davenport's decision.

Her local supporters in Evansville were unconcerned when the media reported that she and her husband had purchased an upscale condominium 175 miles to the north – a block off Monument Circle in downtown Indianapolis. After all, the couple was retaining their stately home in the most prestigious part of the city that first elected her. This busy woman couldn't be expected to shuttle back and forth from Southern Indiana on a routine basis. Surely, she and her family would return home for holidays and whatever weekends they could. Only her father-in-law was suspicious. "I don't understand why you just can't rent a simple apartment up there and let Troy and Junior stay put?"

This time, she left it to her husband to handle Senior. "Dad, we struggled to make this whole arrangement work while Beth was in the House ... and now her schedule demands are going to multiply. If she, Troy, and I are to have any semblance of normal family life, I'll need to spend more time in Indianapolis and Washington. Having me heading up Human Resources is no longer practical. But thanks to Beth, I'll be in an advantageous position to look out for the company's best interests at the state and federal levels of government. Why don't we create a new office of government relations … a one-person office consisting of me?"

Senior had been painted into a very distasteful corner. He hated to admit how his son had evolved into a valued member of his executive team. Due to many of Junior's initiatives, work force satisfaction was at an all-time high, and Davenport Industries often was cited as a model of progressive employment practices. Even more, Senior hated to admit that the idea of a well-placed government relations officer was a savvy one. No doubt, Senior would have leapt at the concept if he had conceived it himself. Instead, he needed a couple days to come around.

In the early summer of 1987, Junior and Troy quietly packed up and joined Beth in the Indianapolis condo. This meant Junior and Cal were living in the same city for the first time since college. They could see each other as often as they liked. Beth was confident they would exercise appropriate discretion to protect all concerned – which now included a son, as well as a wife with a public image.

What no one anticipated, however, were the petty squabbles this constant proximity soon produced. Both men were approaching fifty and accustomed to their own individual lifestyles. The easy comfort of prior weekend rendezvouses was replaced with tension. Junior enjoyed sedate evenings at home with Troy, while Cal found a steady diet of fatherhood mundane. The bigger problem was his active libido. Junior couldn't quench Cal's sexual appetite, but he'd failed to appreciate the depth of it. Cal had remained true to his word about other men, maintaining gender monogamy with Junior for three decades. However, Cal's interactions with women were more plentiful and essential than Junior ever had conceived. On his home turf, Cal Stratton was a well-respected banker by day, and middle-aged playboy by night. On the two, three, or sometimes four evenings a week when Cal was out leading his double life, Junior grew increasingly resentful.

As Beth was juggling cities, appointments, and public appearances, she noticed a change in her husband's temperament. For the first time since she'd known him, he'd become high-strung and, at times, volatile. In early November, Junior informed her that he needed a week away from Troy, Cal, and everyone else in Indianapolis – a week on his own, to regroup. She agreed and they arranged for one their regular babysitters to stay with Troy so Junior could fly off to the Florida Keys. Months later, Beth learned Cal had flown off that same week to Barbados – with one of his girlfriends. Junior merely had been evening the score.

The flu symptoms started in mid-February. Some days were better than others, but Junior couldn't shake them. After three weeks, his strength seemed to be waning instead of rebuilding, so Beth finally convinced him to see a doctor. Two days later, he received a call about the blood work from his physical exam, but the results only could be shared in person. Junior strapped four-year-old Troy into his car seat and drove to the doctor's office that same afternoon – promising his son ice cream on the trip home. He and Troy never made it to the ice cream shop.

An elderly general practitioner, Dr. George Talbert, was recommended by a friend, and Junior had met him for the first time just a few days earlier, when the blood samples were taken. Thinking back to that horrible period, Beth still empathized with how difficult that discussion must have been for two men barely acquainted. But at the time, her focus solely was on Junior. Because Senate was in session, her husband had no choice but to relay the devastating news to her over the phone.

When he was sitting in the doctor's office, the reality hadn't registered at first. Talbert told Junior his blood tests revealed a severe infection was causing his symptoms of recent weeks. The doctor seemed somewhat distressed as he went on to explain how the infection had begun breaking down and destroying his body's immune system. "Unfortunately, Mr. Davenport, these damaging effects are almost certain to intensify over time and we have no effective means by which to counteract them."

Junior calmly tried to process the vagaries of the medical jargon. Meanwhile, the silver-haired doctor on the other side of the desk grew visibly more uncomfortable. Suddenly, everything registered. "Are you telling me I have AIDS?" Junior asked abruptly.

Dr. Talbert spoke softly, with genuine sorrow in his voice. "I'm afraid I am. We ran the tests several times. The results are conclusive. You have an acute HIV infection, which will inevitably advance to AIDS. I am very sorry, Mr. Davenport."

Junior Davenport had been delivered a death sentence. In 1987, AIDS was an epidemic. The diagnosis was almost certain to be fatal. This disease was so feared and misunderstood that seasoned medical professionals, such as Talbert, still were struggling to understand its transmission and treatment.

The experienced physician admitted to having had no prior experience with an AIDS case. That same morning, he had run over to the hospital, met with a specialist, and picked up informational literature. He walked Junior through the materials and gave him copies. With his mind reeling, Junior only managed to absorb bits and pieces.

Little could be done for him in those days. Based on the accumulating data, Junior could expect to live several years – maybe as many as ten if he was extremely lucky. But a lesser number was a more likely outcome. Life expectancy would depend upon how rapidly the HIV virus attached itself to a particular type of white blood cell, called CD4.

Beth remembered how the tragedies continued to compound over the ensuing weeks. First came Junior's revelations about his trip to Key West, the previous autumn. To hurt Cal, he had selected a destination known for its "wide open" gay community. Shortly after arrival, he'd met up with a random group of revelers and partied late into the night. He hung with them through the balance of the week, experimenting recklessly and allowing himself to be used in ways he was too embarrassed to discuss. His omissions left little doubt about how he contracted HIV.

By mid-July, Junior's condition worsened dramatically. The doctors at Methodist Hospital determined the virus was destroying his immune system faster than anticipated. His CD4 cells were unusually conducive. He was unlikely to live until the end of the year. In September, they checked him into the hospital's isolation ward. He was allowed limited visitors and those that did come were required to wear disposable suits over their clothing, plus face masks and latex gloves.

Junior's visitors did not include his father. Beth had called Senior the day after the diagnosis. She thought she heard his voice crack with sadness upon hearing the news, but moments later he hardened. "That boy has nobody to blame but himself. I gave him one opportunity after another to step up and do what was right, but he wasted every last one of 'em. You just make sure none of this gets out. I won't have people ridiculing me or my company because Junior didn't have what it takes to be a man."

Junior tried in vain to reach out to his father. Senior refused to take his phone calls. Beth periodically updated her father-in-law on his son's deterioration, but he showed little interest or compassion. His only concern was keeping Junior's condition a secret. Senior never saw or spoke to his son again.

Over all the time she had known Senior Davenport, Beth had come to expect despicable behavior. But during those months, she became just as disappointed in her own. In the arena of public opinion, AIDS was synonymous with homosexuality. Acknowledging that her husband was dying from AIDS would have raised endless questions about his lifestyle, and therefore the stability or legitimacy of their marriage. The stereotyping and prejudices were entrenched. Regardless of what explanation she might offer, she was sure to lose a large portion of her loyal voter base. Washington's newest golden girl would be tarnished severely. Maybe irrevocably. She found it much too easy to fall in-line with Senior on the need for secrecy.

To outside parties, Junior's illness was described as a complicated blood disease. The family wished to elaborate no further. In the meantime, Senior was anything but discrete about his two-million-dollar donation to myeloma research – a cancer that attacked plasma cells. The media quickly made the connection he was seeking.

Compounding the sadness of this overall situation was Troy. He and Junior always had been demonstrative with their affection, exchanging dozens of hugs and kisses in the course of a normal day. Following the diagnosis, physical contact was restricted to random pats on the head. A five-year-old hardly could be satisfied by the explanations he received. "Daddy has a sickness that is contagious … meaning we don't want you to catch it." Round-the-clock nannies were inserted into his life, and it soon became obvious how much Troy missed their time together.

Troy last saw his father in early September. They both wore masks. Beth tried to convince him he was dressing up like an astronaut as he donned the sterile cover suit and latex gloves. None of it was easy to explain. Afterwards, Junior was the one who made the decision. No more visits. He didn't want his son to watch as his already emaciated form withered down to skin and bone. Troy didn't need to see the extensive bruising that eventually covered his body. The small scabs that spotted his face. The bald spots where splotches of hair fell out. The proliferation of tubes attached to his body. Until his final few days, Junior relied on Beth and Cal for a daily exchange of messages with Troy.

Junior Davenport's body gave out in October of 1988, just seven months after the diagnosis. Fortunately, he slept most of the time as he waited to die over those final weeks, surrounded by machines and monitors. Without a doubt, the brightest light during this whole ordeal was Cal.

Junior and Cal found their own special Camelot once again. Whatever difficulties the two had experienced since Junior's arrival in Indianapolis were all but forgotten. With limited time available, none was to be wasted on apologies. Their feelings for one another were as genuine as when they'd been young students at Culver Military Academy. Cal always had been Junior's one true love. He was the person who completed Junior Davenport. Beth never pretended otherwise. Whenever Cal wasn't at work, he was at Junior's bedside, sharing memories, reading favorite books aloud.

Beth arranged her schedule to spend more time in Indianapolis. Whenever she was in town, she would join Cal at Junior's bedside. There were occasional glimpses of the chemistry the three once shared. But more often, she felt like an interloper. The love between Junior and Cal was still the genuine article. Her affection for them, like theirs for her, was something entirely different. As it always had been. But now, she truly was a third wheel. She experienced a profound jealousy. Not because they purposely excluded her. But because they were savoring every ounce of something pure and beautiful she was incapable of experiencing.

During the hours she spent alone with Junior during those months he battled AIDS, the discussions weren't anything like the ones depicted in literature. In the great novels she cherished, the act of dying could be poignant. It could be dignified. It could be courageous and romantic. But reality had been none of those things. Junior didn't try to hide his fear of dying, or the resentment he harbored because his life was being stolen from him by a disease that wasn't even recognized just a few years before. Or the anger he felt about his own recklessness during that vengeful week in the Keys.

Junior Davenport never forgave his father for forsaking him or regretted that he was unlikely to see him again. If anything, his greatest remorse was that he had wasted so much of his life trying to gain the love of a man who was incapable of loving anyone but himself. "I don't pretend to understand the human psyche, but maybe that's why Cal's love always was so important to me."

Junior was grateful to Beth for staying by his side for their many years together, and for agreeing to the odd arrangement that had produced Troy. When he talked about the son they shared and his hopes for Troy's future, her role seemed to be minimized. Sadly, his perspective wasn't wrong.

Their deepest, most memorable conversation took place only a day or two before he died. They were holding hands – shielded by latex. He had been drifting in and out of sleep. All at once he awakened and looked up at her, flashing a remnant of his old boyish smile. "Beth, I can't imagine another marriage quite like ours. I've often thought about how fortunate I was to have someone like you … someone who could provide a semblance of normalcy to my life. But as I look back, I'd have to say the same could be said for you. Our marriage provided you that same semblance of normalcy. Neither one of us was really cut out for all that 'boy meets girl' stuff. Perhaps it was providence when you walked into the woods that night at Oberlin."

His clasp on her hand tightened as they smiled at each other in silence for a few moments. Then he said something completely unexpected. "You should reach out to Lila. Life is preciously short, Beth. Don't leave things unsaid." Once again, she felt his grip tighten as he drifted back to sleep.

She was amazed Junior even had remembered Lila. It had been years since she'd opened-up to him about the horrors of her childhood, and the close friendship that had once given her refuge. It had been years since she'd confided to him about the kiss in her bedroom, and the subsequent kiss at the cemetery, after her parents' funeral. Neither he nor she had mentioned Lila's name ever again. Yet now, lying on his deathbed, Junior suddenly was urging her to revisit those conflicted emotions from her teens. Clearly, he had sensed something unresolved in how she had spoken to him about Lila. Based on his own life experiences, he perhaps was uniquely qualified to offer advice on such matters. She rose to leave, but first slid the protective mask away from her mouth, leaned forward, and kissed Junior on the forehead. When the time was right, Beth would think about Lila and what her husband had urged her to do.

A small group gathered for the funeral in Evansville. Even the media honored the family's request for privacy. Senior attended, but for the most part stood off to the side as a much better man was laid to rest.

When Beth returned to Washington, a statement of sympathy was read on the floor of the Senate at the opening of her first session back in the chamber. She looked around as she listened to this brief tribute to Joseph Elwood Davenport, Jr., and noticed how few of her colleagues were paying attention. Most of them were shuffling through papers, preparing for the day's agenda. Once such "perfunctories" were completed, the real games could begin. Some of her colleagues would be grandstanding on pet issues. Others would be lying-in-wait.

Something struck her at that moment. Hearing Junior's name in that hallowed hall where history and laws had been made for 129 years, she became reflective. Soon a new normalcy would take root for Beth Davenport. A normalcy that would reshape the next thirty years and make her a national icon.

November 12, 1988

Another new chapter. But this time a better chapter.

Having reached the Senate in 1986, everything was progressing perfectly as Beth played out the final moves to her lifelong chess game with her father-in-law. She, along with her husband and son, would live happily ever-after outside the tentacles of Senior's money and influence. Checkmate. But twelve months later, she was wishing she could turn back the clock. How could anyone have foreseen the sequence of events that were triggered by the relocation to Indianapolis?

Remorse. Repentance. Contrition. Words couldn't begin to capture her feelings. Over the entirety of her adulthood, she had been consumed by ambition and rancor. Whatever latent virtues she might have possessed, Junior had been able to bring them out in her. The strongest counterbalance to the darkest sides of her personality now was gone.

She readily could admit her early election successes were the result of well-conceived, careful manipulations. She had been adept at determining which opinions or perspectives would win the most votes and then finding fresh, seemingly genuine, ways for voicing them. Much the same as many other successful politicians, she figured. But elections aside, she had begun discovering something new since arriving in Washington. Thus far, she'd only scratched the surface.

There indeed were issues worth fighting for. Real issues, affecting real people who deserved real representation. With each passing month, she felt stronger affiliation with the important causes she championed and influenced. Still, given an ignoble history of advancing her own selfish agendas, she remained skeptical. Was she really capable of acting on higher principles, of behaving altruistically? Or had she merely reached an even higher pinnacle of self-absorption by manipulating herself into believing she'd changed?

The irony was inescapable. She was a woman born and bred for politics because of her ability to ignore rules, say whatever was necessary, and fend for herself. She was a woman whose outward warmth and charm camouflaged an inner emptiness. Since first learning her family died in a fire, she had been devoid of conscience. Yet, out of some inexplicable sense of gratitude to a man to whom she'd been married in the most unpredictable of circumstances, she suddenly saw her future differently. On the day she returned to Washington as a widow, Beth Davenport decided to go all-in. Moving forward, she would pay little heed to the politically expedient and little mind to popular opinion. Henceforth, Senator Beth Davenport would strive to do the right thing only because it was the right thing to do.

Chapter 44

The more Beth downplayed the praises she received for courage and fortitude in the months following Junior's death, the more she was heralded by virtually everyone. She didn't want to exploit the tragedy, but journalists, commentators, and congressional colleagues were determined to single her out. The op-ed pages of newspapers were filled with letters from readers lauding the senator from Indiana as a positive role model. The President only added to the awkwardness she felt during his State of the Union address. "Beth Davenport has displayed the kind of mettle our nation's voters deserve and should expect from their elected representatives ... male or female. In this instance, we're fortunate to have a very talented woman setting a much-needed example." A standing ovation followed as every eye in the auditorium turned toward the section in which she was seated.

January 25, 1989
Can one truly atone? Time will tell.

In a few short years, she had become one of Washington's most recognized and respected figures – in great part due to a string of events of which the full truth would never be known. She was launched onto the national scene because of an undisclosed pregnancy she used to her advantage. Consequently, she soon became a poster child for parenthood in the workplace – despite having negligible skills for parenting. Her husband hadn't even been her son's biological father. Voters would have abandoned her in droves if they'd understood the deceptive manner by which Troy was conceived. A huge percentage of the Midwestern electorate would view her entangled relationship with Junior and Cal as utterly repugnant – and even more so, the disease that killed her husband and the manner by which he contracted it. If the true cause of Junior's death were to be leaked, she would have been subjected to persistent innuendo and mockery instead of universal sympathy. No doubt, the complicated secrets in her personal life had contributed mightily to her political fortunes. Clearly, much of her success and stature was unwarranted. But the past was the past. Moving forward, she needed to put those ceded advantages to proper use.

Over the ensuing years, Beth Davenport became the political equivalent of King Midas. Every stance she took with the public turned to gold. It was immaterial whether people or opinion polls agreed with her position on an issue. Her thoughtful and nonconfrontational approach in asserting a point of view could be admired from all sides. Her calm, inquisitive voice screamed out to voters through its softness – offering stark contrast to the din of grandstanders filling the airwaves. By the early 1990's, her name was being bandied about for Vice President, with leaders from both parties hoping she might shed her Independent middle ground. Though once such an opportunity would have appealed to Beth, she now was committed to serving out her political career in the Senate for as long as the folks of Indiana found benefit.

During the summer of 1993, one of those Indiana supporters paid a surprise visit to her Washington office – showing up unannounced. Since Junior's death, her relationship with Senior Davenport had evolved into an unspoken armistice. She'd lost all appetite for jousting and volleying with him. He had wrought enough misery upon himself, though he never would admit to it.

Several times a year, Beth accompanied Troy to Evansville for holiday visits with his grandfather. Their interactions were tepid and cordial. Each July, she arranged for someone to drive Troy down for a lengthier stay on Senior's newest farm – a property he allegedly purchased for spending time with his grandson. These annual two-week visits were something Senior had requested just days after Junior's passing.

Amidst the wooded and rolling hills, Senior asserted that he would teach his grandson how to fish, hunt and "get his hands dirty." But from what Troy reported back each summer, he and his grandfather spent little time alone. The guestrooms in the large farmhouse usually were filled with Senior's contemporaries. After dinner, a collection of men would sit inside the large screened porch and drink late into the night, while Troy retreated to his bed and read or watched TV.

Beth didn't know what to make of Senior dropping by the Dirksen Building unannounced. When she greeted him at the doorway to her office, he leaned in to kiss her cheek. She backed away and extended her had. "This is a surprise … what brings you to Washington?" Her tone was one of polite indifference.

"I'm in town on business, so I thought I should stop in and pay respect to my daughter-in-law." This explanation didn't fly because Senior Davenport had little familiarity with respect of any kind.

Not since his surprise visit to Cleveland in 1962, when their unholy alliance was struck, had Senior Davenport deigned to meet with her anywhere but on his own turf. He loved to wield the power he held over people. Maybe he finally was acknowledging that she had achieved equal footing as a second-term United States Senator.

As things turned out, he was planning to take Davenport Industries public. He had flown "out east" several days before and was shuttling back and forth between Washington and New York with a "whole damned flock of overpaid bankers and lawyers" to get the deal done. As wealthy as Senior already was, he soon would become a great deal wealthier. "They tell me I'll wind up a billionaire. Not bad for a Kentucky coal miner who never saw a day of college."

She sat back and allowed him to ramble, and soon his real purpose revealed itself. Reality finally was forcing him to surrender his dream of seeing a succession of Davenports at the top of Davenport Industries.

"With the reputation you have here in Washington, you ain't ever gonna leave the Senate and come back to run my company ... heck, you'd be a crazy fool if you did. Plus, if I had to guess, you're prepared to do everything possible to stop young Troy from moving down to Evansville and learning the business from me. So, let's not kid ourselves about any of that, Bethie." Oddly, his assertions contained no outward bitterness or resentment. He simply was relating the truth as he saw it. Beth said nothing to persuade him otherwise.

He continued, "The commission-hungry bankers tell me it's a good time to come out with a stock offering ... because apparently there are plenty of investors who'll pay a premium price to own a piece of a company like mine. Well, who am I to stand in their way? I'll take their money ... then I'll give myself a big fat raise for sticking around and runnin' things for 'em. Since no one in my family gives a shit about me or my company, I'd be a damned idiot not to take advantage of all that greed out there. Wouldn't you agree, Senator?"

Despite the spicy language, Beth still couldn't detect the slightest hint of acrimony in his voice. She was baffled by Senior's complacency. His whole life had been wrapped up in building a business that would be owned and operated by Davenports for generations to come. His legacy was to be their destiny. His patriarchy was to live-on in perpetuity. A man like her father-in-law didn't give up easily on such grand dreams.

He went on to describe plans for a huge chunk of his upcoming windfall. That's when she finally understood how Senior had found peace with the prospect of thousands of faceless shareholders controlling the fate of Davenport Industries. He was making preparations for his name to live on in other ways. Family disappointments weren't about to stop Joseph Elwood Davenport, Sr., from leaving his lasting mark on civilization. But an unexpected detail had cropped up, and that was the real reason he was sitting in Beth's office.

Years before, Senior had established a charitable foundation to gain tax advantages. The legal paperwork required that he name two directors for the foundation beside himself. Without notifying either, he had instructed the attorneys to list Junior and Beth, who at the time were harmonious members of his executive management team. The Joseph E. Davenport Foundation was now central to the new legacy Senior wanted to sculpt for himself.

During the 1990's, most large family foundations were shifting their focus away from bricks and mortar projects and instead channeling their resources to social programs, scholarships, and medical research – choosing to invest in lives over structures. Senior was determined to do the opposite. He was doubling down on architecture. The family attorneys had drafted a revised charter for his foundation, which soon would be the receptacle for hundreds of millions of dollars from his Davenport stock. Moving forward, the charter specified that any and all assets could be used only for the endowment of buildings. Beth understood his dilemma. The buildings Senior intended to erect through his foundation would conveniently bear the name of Joseph E. Davenport on each of their exteriors, and he needed her signature to put his plan into motion.

Senior envisioned edifices that would stand the test of time. Community centers. Recreational complexes. Campus halls. Each would address some identified void, and Senior would build those buildings one by one, provided his name stayed on top of them for decades and centuries to come. Every move in this man's life had come with strings attached. Why should his afterlife be any different?

Beth took her time reading and rereading every paragraph in the document. She had no intention of refusing Senior his request, but he at least should be afforded a few moments of uncertainty. Regardless of how little regard she had for her father-in-law's character, Beth never would deny his accomplishments. He had built a prosperous enterprise from the ground up and passionately looked out for the welfare of tens of thousands of employees over the course of his lifetime. If he wanted to reward himself by plastering his name on a few buildings, who was she to stand in his way? When she acquiesced without a fight, he seemed almost disappointed. Now in his seventies, maybe he missed the sparring contests from their past.

As Senior rose from his chair to leave Beth's office, he reached into the pocket of his suitcoat, withdrew an envelope, and placed it on her desk. "With this month's cash, I figured I'd spare the expense of a courier. You gotta admit one thing, pretty lady … when I struck that deal all those years ago, I sure knew how to spot talent. Not only did I pick my son a nice piece-of-ass, but I also got myself a U.S. Senator named Davenport out of the deal." Then he chortled, hoping to get a rise from her.

Instead, she smiled and walked him to the door. "Funny how things turn out, isn't it? Nice to see you, Senior." Once the door opened, a staff member whisked him away and Beth turned to stare at the white packet he'd placed on her desk. Not once over the years had she bothered to open a single envelope. When she returned to Indianapolis for the upcoming weekend, she would make her monthly trip to the storage unit and open the vintage leather suitcase – the same suitcase Junior had purchased a year prior to his death, just days before he flew down to Key West.

Now, as Beth stared at her journal and remembered Senior's Washington visit, she couldn't help but shake her head disappointedly – much the same as she had when he left her office that day in 1993. Why had each of them allowed their original bargain to persist? The son she was paid to marry was no longer even alive. And while he had been alive, she'd upheld her end of the arrangement only by the loosest of interpretations. She had toyed around the edges and infuriated her father-in-law too many times to count. All the while, she had exploited the Davenport name for her own career and financial benefit, making her more than secure in her own right. The monthly payments meant nothing to her. Yet, Senior Davenport still had felt obligated to make them – as she had felt obligated to accept.

It was like blood money. Her disgust for every detail in the arrangement had intensified with every turn of the calendar. She would bristle when the unmarked envelopes filled with cash arrived like clockwork at the beginning of each month. Senior's courier would wait patiently for her signature. Then there were the slow elevator rides to the third floor on Raymond Street. Stepping into that barren storage locker. Opening that suitcase on the table – poor Junior's suitcase. Month after month, watching those envelopes accumulate inside. She carefully would place the latest atop a mounting stack. Before leaving, she would make certain the thirty measured columns were perfectly uniform before closing the lid. Her actions were almost ritualistic, every meticulous step serving as penance for her craven compliance. Beth Davenport would never be rid of Lizzie Monroe.

Chapter 45

*L*ife is preciously short, Beth. Don't leave things unsaid. His words
had stuck with her for five years. Not in a haunting or eerie
way. It was more like Junior had stayed by her side, trying to help her
make sense of the feelings she once held for Lila Henry. But at age
fifty-three, she still couldn't.

When Junior urged her to reach out to Lila, just hours before
he slipped into a final coma, Beth made a vow to herself. She would
track down Lila and let this treasured friend know what she had
meant to her.

Yet, on the last day of 1993, she still hadn't followed through. It
wasn't that Beth changed her mind or forgot this commitment she'd
made to herself. She just didn't know what to say to Lila. She'd been
unable to discern what Lila Henry had meant to her as a seventeen-
year-old girl, or over the ensuing decades of adulthood.

Troy was spending the holidays with his grandfather, so Beth
was toasting in the New Year inside her condominium, with Virginia
Woolf and a snifter of cognac. The book was folded open on her lap
and she had allowed her mind to wander. She was thinking of Lila.
Of the sanctuary their friendship provided during the darkest chapter of her life. Of the comfort she felt when the two of them were
alone. Of the momentary stirring she felt as Lila pulled her close and
kissed her that first time. She needed to let Lila Henry know.

January 1, 1994

Caution to the wind.

The next morning, as best she could, Beth put her thoughts in writing to Lila. The night before, the words had fallen neatly into place inside her head. Now, she wasn't so sure. But she could wait no longer. Life was preciously short.

As a personal favor, her most trusted staff person, Annabelle Jenkins, did some legwork and learned Lila Henry was living in Baltimore. Alone. Twice married, twice divorced. She was a doctor, working for a medical research company.

Beth mailed the letter on a Thursday. Or maybe it was a Friday. No matter. Lila Henry's response never came.

Chapter 46

Beth leafed through the subsequent pages of her journal with a more knowing calmness, in much the same way she'd been able to approach the subsequent stages of her life. Soon, she came to an entry that caused her to stop and stare at the date. Sophie Mullins would have lost her Jamie four years earlier – which meant it would have been five-plus since Junior's death.

> *April 8, 1994*
>
> *A coward once. A coward again and again.*

Beth did the calculations. If Jamie Mullins were alive today, he would be a thirty-four-year-old adult – just seven months younger than Troy. Junior would have turned eighty by now. Over all those years, Beth and Sophie Mullins had carried the same tormenting secret.

Regrettably, during their most recent afternoon tea at one of her downtown private clubs, Beth still had lacked the courage to share her own story. She was content to once again have the conversation center on Sophie's travails. Beth could pretend she was protecting the secrecy she'd promised Junior, but who was she fooling? Sophie had made the same promise and nonetheless confided in her, disclosing the real cause of Jamie's death.

While Junior was dying of AIDS, Beth once raised the possibility to him – though admittedly as a half-hearted question. "Are you convinced we shouldn't acknowledge your illness and help draw attention to the plight of AIDS victims?" At the time, there was a dire need for research funding. Greater awareness and understanding were needed to help educate people on taking the necessary precautions in avoiding contact with a virus that led to this lethal disease.

Junior had been unyielding. "I'm sorry, Beth ... this decision must be mine alone. Do you think I want to be remembered for one thing, and one thing only? Because that's exactly what would happen. I'd be forever remembered as 'that Senator's husband who died from AIDS' ... and be labeled with all the demeaning associations. I wish I could be more selfless, but I can't. I don't want my whole existence to be condensed down to nothing more than punchlines for sophomoric jokes. Plus, think about the potential impact on Davenport Industries ... all those people we worked with. Think about your own future in politics ... the speculations that would kill your chances of ever getting elected again." It was the answer she needed to hear to alleviate her inner cowardice.

Ultimately, Beth wielded her influence in Indianapolis to call in a favor from the hospital's senior administrator. Junior's detailed medical records were placed in a highly protected file, while his condition was categorized as a rare blood disease inside the hospital's central system.

To demonstrate that her request was properly addressed, the administrator invited Beth into his office and pulled up the relevant section from the general file on his computer. It showed a short list of hospital patients who were being treated for HIV or AIDS. Probably because she was a respected senator, he didn't bother masking the names. As Beth scanned the list to confirm her husband's name had been removed, she noticed the age of one of the other patients. James Mullins recently had turned five. That afternoon, she asked Annabelle to monitor the young boy's condition.

Fifteen months later, Annabelle phoned her in Washington with somber news. An obituary ran in that morning's edition of *The Indianapolis Star*. James Mullins had died. A heart condition was listed as the cause of death, which surprised Beth. That fact gnawed at her for several days. Finally, she decided to do a little digging, and soon Beth learned the young boy's father was a rising star in the teachers' union. She instantly understood the decision that the Mullins family had faced. She felt a need to reach out to the unfortunate mother.

During their first meeting, Sophie Mullins became teary-eyed as she described the heartbreak of losing her son. She clearly needed a compassionate shoulder. Before the two-hour conversation was over, Sophie broke down and conceded that her Jamie had died from AIDS. He contracted the HIV virus through a blood transfusion. Her sorrow was worsened by having to keep those tragic details to herself. She had hoped Jamie's death might help the public confront the realities of the AIDS epidemic, but she'd succumbed to her husband's wishes. He was paranoid about his own reputation and the damage that could be rendered by any association with AIDS. Sadly, in the late 1980's, Senator Beth Davenport could fully empathize. The man's concerns were legitimate.

During every year since, Beth had spent meaningful time with Sophie Mullins. The two had formed a genuine friendship. It still was obvious these annual sit-downs were cathartic for Sophie. But even more so for Beth.

In the years since Junior's death, Beth had become a forceful advocate for AIDS education and AIDS research. Likewise, she frequently had taken strong positions to advance same-sex benefits, same-sex marriage, and overall same-sex equality. Other such currents from her past had helped shape her public stances on parental child abuse, sexual harassment in the workplace, and a multitude of gender issues. Having lacked the fortitude for properly contending with the negative influences that permeated her own life, Lizzie Monroe had found her voice in Senator Beth Davenport.

Chapter 47

B eth found herself hurrying through the final third of her journal. It all seemed less important now. The landmark bills that consumed her weekends and late nights. The vaunted committee assignments she never took lightly. The endless awards and distinctions, so often undeserved. The repetitiveness of election cycles. The fund-raising. The victory celebrations.

Away from politics, there had been the lucrative take-over of Davenport Industries by a global mining conglomerate. And Senior's ill-fated attempt at the eleventh hour to avert the sale – behaving like a pigheaded anachronism for the whole world to witness. Then there'd been the final years of Senior's life – filled with bluster and bravado, but mostly loneliness. Even in death, Senior had fired a final salvo at the family that so often disappointed him. He left everything to his cherished buildings. Joseph Elwood Davenport had remained bitter to the very end. Despite all the concrete monuments, Senior's stubborness would stand as his most lasting legacy among the people who knew him best.

Breezing through passages, Beth paid little attention to thoughts and events that seemed important enough to record while she was living through them. None of them mattered now. Nothing in those words could change a thing. Deciphering cryptic entries in hindsight wouldn't lift her soul with newborn contentment. The ironies were profound. So many of her loyal supporters might look back on her lengthy tenure in politics and credit Senator Beth Davenport for a life well led. She knew otherwise.

But as time had passed, Beth Davenport did stay true to "doing the right thing," and the Indiana electorate had stayed true to her. Her votes and oratory didn't always please those who stuck by her side. But she thoughtfully considered issues as they surfaced, and only then articulated meaningful perspectives. Her conscientious approach had been enough to satisfy an ever-changing and growing voter base.

With more and more seniority, her popularity at home and in Washington afforded Beth Davenport a ready platform to opine on whatever matter she deemed important. But instead, she'd avoided opportunities to grandstand as though they were radioactive. She refused to deal in pithy sound bites. Consequently, any opinion she did choose to offer was given greater credence and more intensive media coverage.

She increasingly had been described as a statesperson, or better still, a stateswoman. Sure, the designation pleased her, as did the enviable array of committee assignments and her overall status inside Congress. But the satisfaction from all her successes still felt hollow. "Doing the right thing" in public life stood in stark contrast with how she had conducted her personal life. No amount of outwardly good intentions could camouflage what she knew deep down.

Beth Davenport would continue giving her best efforts to the nation, and to the people of Indiana, for as long as her health held out. She had nothing else to do with whatever years she had remaining. But on the inside, the emptiness was unlikely to be filled.

Beth wanted to believe she once had been a normal teenager, equipped with all the desires and emotions that other kids experienced. Too often, she had rationalized that these inner qualities had been robbed from her by her parents, by her brother, and by her upbringing. But with the passage of time, more questions formed. Was she ever truly normal on the inside? Had she all along been trying to suppress and repress her way into normalcy?

Reflecting on the totality of her adulthood, Beth recognized she had enjoyed the greatest emotional fulfillment during her "Camelot years" with Junior and Cal – the three of them leading their secret lives in secret unity. Disregarding the expectations of others.

She had felt most energized and spirited when she was engaged in her undeclared warfare with Junior's father. For Beth, bucking the system always produced the greatest satisfaction. Contrary to the temperate public persona, her natural tendencies were to disrupt and destroy. In the months following Junior's death, she finally had seen the lunacy, the wastefulness. Over the thirty years since, she had been overcompensating for the twisted quirks and voids in her personality. At least as a senator.

With time, her incapacity for motherhood had become even clearer and more disturbing to her. While pregnant, she had accepted her role as third-person surrogate. Sadly for Troy, she never was able to shed that mindset. He deserved better. Every child born into this world was a miracle of nature, but Troy's existence was especially so. He was the product of a forbidden love. With Junior gone, she had provided for Troy in every way but the most important one. True devotion required a person to share her innermost self. For her, that was impossible. She never could have allowed Troy to see or sense what she was like on the inside – to recognize the conflicting forces that steered her behavior. Fortunately, busy schedules and geographic separation provided a convenient cover for her many inadequacies.

Nonetheless, Troy had grown into a young man with a vast array of positive qualities – most of which she envied. Like any teenager or young adult, her son may have lost his way a few times – but considering the parental circumstances to which he was subjected, those momentary blips might have been far worse. Watching him develop, almost as an outsider, Beth had been relieved to see Troy cultivate passions and desires she could not. The balance to his personality reflected a sound moral compass and inner strength. She took little credit. Their relationship was respectful and supportive, but regrettably, little emotional connection existed between them. Among the many deficiencies that constantly nagged at Beth, this missing bond was the most hurtful.

Chapter 48

Leaning back in her seat, she ran her fingers along the worn edges of the now closed journal placed beside her. Beth Davenport glanced at her watch, then closed her eyes. She had lost track of the hours. How could she possibly have spent so many of them traipsing through the past, retracing the timeline of her life, lost in memories? She couldn't remember ever allowing her mind to run so free. How long had it been since she last read the cryptic entries that Lizzie began penning as a teenager?

She smiled a wry smile, amused by her continued penchant for pretense, even with herself. Beth Davenport was completely aware of when she last took the time to read the musings from her journal. The answer was never. For more than sixty years, she dutifully had recorded thoughts and reactions to the events of her life, but not once did she turn back those pages. From the earliest years, ever onward had been her philosophy. She chose to focus on the present and future, on issues or events she could do something about. The approach had provided her a suitable justification. She'd always been adept at rationalizing.

Dwelling on the past could only unleash an "unholy trinity" inside her – shame, guilt, and uncertainty. That was the cold, hard truth. Any attempt at introspection was harrowing for Beth, so she'd been content to avoid rather than confront her demons. Yet hours earlier, she had surrendered to a momentary impulse after she opened her briefcase and saw the bulge of her journal in the rear compartment. In the hours since, she had reflected on the events of her life more deeply than ever before. Now, to her surprise, she felt a calmness, a wistful combination of nostalgia and sentimentality. More surprising, she was completely at peace. For the first time in memory, she was at peace with herself. With her past.

Sure, the selfish decisions had been plentiful. The truths, the incongruent and sordid actions were still inescapable. But throughout every phase of her life, Beth had accepted full responsibility for her misdeeds. She had refused to consider herself a victim from the very first time her father came home drunk and lowered his hand to her naked buttocks. She knew as a ten-year-old that she was better than him, and that ultimately, she would prevail. Maintaining control over her own destiny had been and still was paramount to Lizzie Monroe. So, yes, there had been many mistakes and her most troublesome acts were no less troubling.

Somehow, though, the totality now seemed more acceptable than the sum of its parts. Apart from the tortuous burdens, there also were moments to cherish and celebrate. Moments she too easily had pushed to the back of her mind. Dozens of them. No, hundreds, or maybe even thousands of them. Laughable moments. Poignant moments. Even proud and profound moments.

Beth recoiled. She shouldn't allow herself to become saccharine or mawkish just because she had managed to suppress her anxieties long enough to read a journal that she lugged around as some form of sacrament. Yet, something felt different. A new sense of liberation had brought her an unfamiliar serenity.

A few moments later, she was on the verge of slipping into a contented slumber when her thoughts returned to Troy. Undoing the mistakes of her past was impossible. Apologizing for her feeble efforts at motherhood hardly seemed appropriate at this stage in their lives. But she suddenly recognized one important step she could take.

Soon after Troy was old enough to talk, he began asking basic questions she deflected pleasantly, ignored willfully, or at best, answered superficially. Regardless, he persisted with his questions well into adulthood. Only in recent years did he accept the futility and stop trying. His questions never were unfair or unreasonable. His curiosity was only natural. He wanted to know about his mother's family and childhood. About the fire that killed his grandparents. He wanted to understand how she reacted and adjusted to such a devastating tragedy. He wanted to hear about her subsequent decisions on college … and then the early years of her career. And how the romance had unfolded between his parents. What their wedding was like. About her adjustment to the wealth and influence of the Davenport name. He wanted to hear what his parents' marriage had been like before he was born. About why they waited so long to have a child.

So often Troy's queries would cross into her forbidden territories – of which there were many. But every son or daughter surely craved the same sort of information. His questions deserved answers. She would see Troy later that month, upon her return to Indianapolis. She could begin to right this indefensible wrong.

As she pondered how their conversations might go, Beth realized she again was wide awake. An adrenaline-mix of fear and excitement, she presumed. Certain aspects of these pending discussions with her son would be difficult – for both of them. But she was committed to follow through. Nonetheless, she fully recognized a pattern of behavior. In a few days, her outlook might shift. Another wave of convenient rationalizations might overwhelm the current good intentions. This time, though, there could be no turning back. Bolstered by her newborn tranquility, she decided to commit herself in writing.

She reached for the briefcase next to her feet, placed the journal back into its zippered hiding place, and pulled out a legal pad. Beth looked at her watch. She had just enough time to write a long overdue letter.

My dearest, dearest Troy,

More than you possibly could realize, I look forward to seeing you in the coming weeks. We have a great many things to discuss when we're together - far more than you might anticipate. It is time I begin to right a horrible wrong. In fact, a lifetime of horrible wrongs.

You are a remarkable son. More importantly, Troy, you are a remarkable young man. I have played but a small part in both outcomes. I have not been the mother I should have been, while you have lovingly and graciously accepted my shortcomings since your earliest childhood. I regret that I cannot undo the many mistakes I have made.

I do, however, promise to make one amends to the best of my ability. Throughout your life, I have avoided the many conversations we should have been having. I have evaded your legitimate questions. Troy, for both of our sakes, it is time we talk. Truly, truly talk.

There is much you deserve to know about my past, as well as your father's. Some aspects of our conversations will be quite difficult for me to share and for you to absorb. I will do my best not to hold back.

You deserve to hear the unvarnished realities of my childhood. No son wants to hear that his mother was molested by a grandfather he never knew, but that is where I must start when we sit down. I wish

I could say the revelations will get easier, but there are many more hard truths.

I think it only fair that you be told in advance, so that you might prepare yourself for hearing how ...

Chapter 49

"Senator Davenport, we'll be landing in ten minutes, so you'll to need to wrap-up what you're working on."

The interruption startled her. She looked up at the uniformed young man standing respectfully in the aisle next to her seat. "Thank you, Lieutenant … as it turns out, I'm just about finished."

She completed the last sentence, signed "Mom" at the bottom of the page, and carefully tore four perforated sheets from her legal pad. The letter was longer than intended, but there could be no retreating now.

When she met with Troy, Beth would pull no punches when it came to Frank Monroe. The abuses he inflicted on her. The drunkenness. The cruelty. Or likewise, her mother's dereliction and cowardice. Or her brother's gruesome behavior.

Her letter made reference to Lila and the sexual assaults she'd endured from Russell. When discussing Lila with Troy, she would describe the unusual closeness of their friendship, and even share her suspicions about the role Lila had played in the fire that wiped out her family.

Troy would learn about Lizzie's loveless relationship with her own grandparents. About her lost interest in social life and dating. About how she lost all interest in making friends, in general, as she finished high school, attended college, and lived out the rest of her life.

For no other reason than sheer catharsis, she acknowledged in the letter that she had secured a first serious summer job in Cleveland by knowingly degrading herself. She was hoping the old-adage would prove accurate – that confession truly was good for the soul.

The letter also committed her to revealing the secret of Junior's and Cal's relationship, and the relationship that the three of them went on to forge at Oberlin – though she foresaw no reason to disclose the details of how she first came upon them in the woods. Confident of her son's open-mindedness, Troy would learn of the love his father shared with another man for more than thirty years.

Perhaps the most difficult admission she faced was the deal she'd struck with Troy's other grandfather. Besides her, only Junior had been aware of the outrageous sum she was paid each month by Senior for her complicity. She and Junior hadn't even revealed the full terms of the arrangement to Cal. For the first time, Beth ran a total in her head. That suitcase, hidden away in Indianapolis, contained five-and-a-half million dollars. If that money had been invested, the amount easily would have been four or five times that total by now. This self-imposed penalty was the least of her regrets.

She further planned to describe the lifelong tension that existed between Junior and Senior – as well as her own difficulties with her father-in-law. As best she could, she would present Troy a balanced perspective on his grandfather.

In one paragraph of the letter, she purposely cited the Camelot Years she enjoyed with Junior and Cal. The peculiarities of this unconventional relationship would be fascinating to Troy as both son and sociologist. Beth wasn't sure if she adequately could capture the utopian existence of their many special weekends. But she would try.

One important item she planned to withhold was the bizarre nature by which Troy was conceived. Hearing about Junior's impotence would serve no purpose. Exposing Cal as his biological father would do a monumental disservice to both Junior and Cal, as well as to Troy.

Twenty years later, Cal Stratton's loyalty to the man he loved hadn't faltered an iota. He had guarded the secrecy surrounding Beth's pregnancy. For close to sixty years, Cal had been a rock in her life, and now her son's. Troy would never know the truth. Junior Davenport would remain his father in every sense.

Somehow, nobody ever had noticed. All one needed to do was see Troy and Cal standing close to one another. To her, the resemblance was so obvious – their towering height, the broad shoulders. The squared-off chins. And mostly, the laughs. When Troy and Cal laughed, the likeness was unmistakable.

Ironically, the issue of paternity no longer mattered from a practical standpoint. She and Junior had worked hard to contrive an heir for the Davenport fortune. Yet in the end, Senior's buildings were more important to him. When he died, the whole issue of bloodlines was rendered moot. Their disinheritance had been difficult for Troy at the time, but he seemed to have adjusted well.

Boarding the transport eleven hours earlier, Senator Beth Davenport was planning to catch up on paperwork and sleep. She had done neither. Instead, her entire life had been brought into new focus. She couldn't help but marvel at the unpredictability of any given day. The measure of a lifetime was more than buildings or legislation with one's name on them. Thankfully, she still had time to mean something more to Troy.

Beth evened up the pages and neatly folded the letter. As the plane made its final descent for landing, the handsome young lieutenant assigned to her was preparing to take his own seat across the aisle. She asked if he might happen to have an envelope. He scurried to the front of the plane and returned moments later. "Here you go, Ma'am. By the way, a helicopter will be waiting on the tarmac in Doha. You'll be airlifted immediately and flown to Al Udeid for their morning briefing ... but one of the officers has promised to have you back here in the city by mid-afternoon ... which will allow you enough time to freshen up for tonight's dinner. It has been a privilege flying with you, Senator."

He straightened his spine and saluted. She acknowledged his gesture of respect with a nod and a smile. "Thank you, young man. For the envelope ... but most importantly for your service to our country."

She inserted the letter, then sealed and addressed the envelope, before placing it in the outside pocket of her briefcase. Once she arrived at the base in Al Udeid, she would drop the letter into a pouch going back to the States. Her tour of Mideast military installations would consume the balance of the week. Another week of meetings in Washington would follow. By the time she saw Troy in Indianapolis, he would have had time to digest the letter and arm himself with all kinds of new questions for her. She looked forward to answering all of them. At last.

Part III

Closure

Chapter 50

The main highway between Crawfordsville and Indianapolis was closed because of a jackknifed semi and all the side roads were layered with ice. The drive home took nearly three hours and that gave me more time than usual to obsess. To grow agitated. For over a week, the time in the car, the free periods between classes, and the sleepless hours in the middle of the night had been consumed by one haunting question. How had my mother lived with herself?

When I pulled into the carport, my eyes and mind were weary from squinting through a slushy windshield. So maybe I'd sleep for a change. With any luck, I could drift off before the nagging thoughts resurfaced and left me staring at the ceiling again, wondering why an educated, attractive woman would have sold herself into marriage and motherhood. It wasn't like she'd grown up in the Dark Ages or needed asylum from some third-world authoritarian state.

I hadn't bothered to pick up mail for several days, so entering the building, I swung by the communal row of mailboxes on my route to the elevator. Out of habit, I tossed the assorted junk mail and catalogues into a giant recycling bin that some eco-fanatic resident kept placing in the center of the passageway as a roadblock. I then began shuffling through the balance of my pile. A few bills. An academic newsletter. More bills. I came to a curious envelope with no return address. "Troy Joseph Davenport." My full name and address were hand-lettered on the front.

Riding up in the elevator, I slid a fingertip under the flap and opened the top of the envelope. Peering inside, I saw what looked to be a handwritten letter. As I removed and unfolded the enclosed pages, my arms and hands stopped functioning. All I could do was stare. Nothing made sense. It was her script. The precise lines – every word the same height, tilting neatly at the same angle. How could my dead mother possibly be sending me a letter?

I instantly checked the postmark. The letter was mailed from Arizona the prior week. I looked again at the handwritten pages, and that's when I noticed the date. My mother had written this letter before she died. Long before. I also saw that the two enclosed pages had been written to someone else.

Recognizing the name of the original addressee, I slipped the opened letter inside my coat pocket. Restful sleep was now an impossibility. Once inside my apartment, I poured a tall vodka and plopped down into my favorite chair. I didn't want to be empty-handed for this journey into the past.

As I began to read, my eyes widened. There was no end to the mysteries that had pervaded my mother's life.

January 1, 1994

Dear Lila,

I start this new year with a letter that should have been written long ago. In fact, it is a conversation I wish we could have in person, but I admit to lacking the fortitude. I fear what emotions might be stirred. Maybe someday, but not yet.

I would imagine you have an idea of where the years have led me. I am proud to serve in the United States Senate. I am prouder, still, of having a son, Troy – who is the greatest joy and accomplishment of my life. As you perhaps know, I lost my beloved husband to an unfortunate illness, and doubt I will marry again. I've come to understand such relationships are not in my nature.

I hope, with all my heart, that the years have treated you kindly. I still remember the moment I met you, when you transferred into our school in fourth grade. From that first day, your talent, enthusiasm, and unique qualities were evident to me. You deserve much success and happiness.

When we last were together, in the cemetery after my family was buried, you said things that caused me to conclude we shouldn't see each other again, for our own peace of mind. I wish I could say I found that peace of mind about what we meant to each other, but I have not. Without question, you remain the most positive memory from my youth. In a family such as mine, I desperately needed an emotional safe haven, and you were that for me. But much, much more. I wish I could better describe my special feelings for you, but still, I am unable — just as I was as a teenaged girl. Maybe someday I'll better understand that period in our lives. However, you should know I've always felt the manner by which you expressed yourself to me was courageous and noble. With each passing year, I've respected you more and more for acting on what you felt in your heart.

As importantly, Lila, I've always wanted you to know that what you revealed to me in the cemetery has remained, and will remain, a secret. Not once have I experienced anger or hostility toward you for what I believe you did, in great part on my behalf. Did I experience gratitude? Of that, I cannot be sure. But you forever changed my life, and I firmly believe for the better. I never have had a dearer or truer friend.

Please let me hear from you.

Lizzie

Chapter 51

"What kind of woman would do the kinds of things she did?" The exasperation in my voice was approaching anger.

Melanie could sense where the discussion was headed. We'd been enjoying a comfortable morning together and she didn't want to see me get worked up. Again. So, she tried humor. "If you mean getting elected six times to the United States Senate from a state like Indiana, I would say not many women in all of history have been capable of doing the things your mother did."

"That's not fair ... and you know it," I grumbled. "Forget all that crap about her public life. How my mother conducted herself in private is indefensible. Quit trying to stand up for her, Mel."

Her humor didn't work on me and I was letting her know in no uncertain terms. As a kid, Melanie Reynolds had resented how most everyone at school considered her a tomboy, and to this day she hated being tagged with a decidedly male nickname. Mel. She'd even admitted to bloodying one older boy's nose on the playground after he dared to call her that.

"So, you're willing to resort to petty labels, are you? I warn you ... paybacks can be hell." Melanie's response sounded mischievous – which was just one more of the qualities to which I'd grown exceedingly partial.

Her hand slipped under the sheet and gave me a firm squeeze

in a place I wasn't expecting. Her grip tightened until I promptly yielded. "Okay, you win. I'll play nice."

Her resourcefulness worked to our mutual advantage. I rolled onto my side and put an arm around her waist, pulling her body tightly next to mine. Soon we were making love for the second time since the early sunlight had awakened us.

When I finally slid out of bed and tiptoed toward the shower, Melanie couldn't resist. "Next time you get testy, I think I'll just skip the joking around and jump right to the sex. Your stamina between the sheets is about the only attribute that makes you tolerable these days."

I turned with a half-smile and saw her watching me with her head propped against a pillow. She could look so blasted sexy and angelic at the same time. I back-tracked to the edge of the bed and knelt beside her. "You must really love me to put up with all my moodiness these past few weeks." I leaned forward and kissed her gently. "Despite the disturbing discoveries, trudging through my mother's past is the best thing I've ever done."

She looked at me quizzically, and I completed my thought. "Otherwise, I wouldn't have found you … and my world has never felt this full."

She took my hand and held it against her cheek as we gazed at each other in silence. I wondered how it was possible that two forces in my life could be operating in such opposite directions.

Since childhood, I'd recognized the relationship between my mother and me was different than those with other kids and their moms. In time, I accepted our emotional gap as a by-product of a complex personality that propelled Beth Davenport to become one of the nation's most respected figures. Life was a series of trade-offs. As compensation, I learned to focus on her positive features, and there had seemed to be an abundance. Her integrity. The leadership strength for which she was universally acclaimed. Her many accomplishments in Congress that bettered the lives of millions. But a suitcase filled with cash could shake one's beliefs.

When I first unlocked this remnant from my mother's past, I still had been reeling from the news of her death in a helicopter crash half-a-world away. As it turned out, that tragedy merely marked her departure from the physical world. For me, the emotional separation had been occurring ever since.

The puzzle pieces weren't falling neatly into place. The picture was anything but clear. If my mother had just been willing to share portions of her past with me, I might have been able to make sense of her life and come to grips with how I really felt about this woman who had given birth to me. Was she truly my mother? Biologically, yes. Apparently, she'd fulfilled one of her contractual obligations and produced a son. Beyond that, how was I to know? In a letter, she told Lila Henry that this same son represented her greatest joy and accomplishment, but those words read as though they'd been written by a shrewd politician playing to her audience.

My mind already was muddled enough from the note my grandfather scribbled to his daughter-in-law on the pages of a book about the Kennedys. Reading that note was like uncovering the Rosetta Stone. Gigantic curtains fell away, and with them, granite pillars crumbled like clay. My mother had sold her soul for ten thousand dollars a month. Worse yet, this paragon of virtue and integrity wasn't even able to uphold her end of the bargain. She'd been caught in an affair with her husband's closest friend – a man whom I had admired my entire life. I was being forced to rethink everything. My father. The marriage between my parents. Cal Stratton. My own birth, and the presence of my mother in my life. What had any of these relationships and roles meant to a woman who never revealed her true feelings? A woman who seemingly possessed no feelings at all?

But then a letter shows up in my mailbox, presumably sent by Lila Henry – who is but another enigma from my mother's past. This

Lila Henry includes no explanation or context. Just the letter. When we'd spoken by phone in the fall, she had confirmed her teenaged friendship with my mother before abruptly cutting off our conversation. She had been adamant about not reopening that chapter from her life. But then months later, she searches out my address and sends me an old letter she received from my mother. A letter she had kept for quarter of a century. For some unknown reason, this Lila Henry ultimately decided I should read the thoughts my mother was carrying around since her family had been buried in 1957.

The secrecies surrounding my mother never seemed to narrow. The unanswered questions invariably led to few answers and more questions. What was my mother trying to communicate in her letter to Lila Henry? These closest of friends hadn't merely drifted apart. Something happened between two teenaged girls to break off a very special relationship. Was a boy involved? Had Lila confronted Lizzie about a mutual love interest? Had Lila warned Lizzie about someone she was seeing? Is that what might have changed her life for the better? Whatever occurred, my mother carried no grudge toward Lila. Yet still, they had parted ways.

Which portion or portions of this letter did Lila want me to read? That my mother loved me as a boy of eleven? The open acknowledgement of her troubled childhood and family life? That my mother had forgiven Lila for some troubling act from their past? Or that my mother was willing to express uncertainties about her own feelings, about her own shortcomings when it came to relationships? Maybe none of these, maybe all of these. What had Lila Henry understood about Lizzie Monroe that she wanted me to better understand?

As was typical of my mother, her letter to Lila had been written in cryptic fashion. She touched on subjects without expressing exactly what was on her mind – leaving most everything open to interpretation. I wondered whether my mother received a response from Lila, as the letter's closing encouraged. Lila had told me she didn't care to "revisit" that part of her life. But maybe this letter had allowed them to rekindle their friendship, if only briefly. To express feelings which needed to be expressed. For both their sakes, I hoped so.

I was trying to be sympathetic. My mother hardly could be blamed for the difficult start she was dealt in life. The household in which she was raised was dysfunctional, at best. And whatever flaws or weaknesses she saw in her parents and brother, they still had been her family – and she lost all of them on a single tragic night. How could I possibly understand what that period in her life must have been like?

After high school, the mosaic became even harder to piece together. By the time she entered college, the popular and fun-loving Lizzie Monroe had transformed into a loner. The descriptions were universal. She detached herself from the people around her.

But soon after graduation, to the surprise of everyone who knew her, Lizzie announced she was getting married. As it turns out, that union was the result of an unimaginable arrangement that reeked of medieval insanity. She wedded a desirable young man from a wealthy and powerful family, and those family connections ultimately provided her the launchpad she needed for a meteoric political career.

The amounts paid to my mother by my grandfather were mind-boggling. Ten thousand dollars a month during the 1960's would have provided her anything money could buy. Yet, bizarrely, it appeared as though she never spent a dollar from those payments. The millions of dollars paid to her by a manipulative father-in-law had done nothing more than collect dust. Yet, she had been eager, or at least willing, to sell herself as part of some unholy bargain. To then turn around and ignore the money was completely irrational.

In the meantime, she faked a series of miscarriages before finally giving birth in her early forties – while on the side, enjoying some form of sordid relationship with her husband's closest friend.

I realized that virtually every son since the beginning of time probably harbored mother issues of one type or another, but this was a lot to absorb. I wasn't much for self-pity but starting with that call from the White House about a helicopter malfunction, I'd been pelted with a steady barrage of tough realities.

On the other hand, over those same months, I'd fallen head-over-heels in love. As devotion to my mother's memory dwindled, affection for Melanie was soaring far beyond anything ever thought possible.

On an almost daily basis, I kept recalling something this same mother had said to me as I cycled through one meaningless relationship after another. "Troy, I hope someday you might be lucky enough to meet that special person who truly completes you." When she'd uttered them, her choice of words sounded peculiar. Until Melanie. The paradox was now inescapable.

Melanie was both my sounding board and wailing wall. Few days passed when we didn't speak at least three or four times by phone. We texted at all hours. Most every weekend was spent in Effingham because her place took me away from the conflicting signals I'd begun to associate with Indianapolis.

If I hoped to achieve closure on my mother's past, I needed to pay one more visit to Cal Stratton and confront him about their affair. Melanie was encouraging me not to cross that boundary. "What can you hope to resolve, other than recognizing your mother was human and susceptible to the same temptations as everyone else? Troy, we all have baggage."

As soon as she'd said it, she wished she could pull it back. The double-meaning played right into my hand. I didn't bother reminding Melanie that most people's baggage wasn't filled with millions in cash. I allowed a smug grin to speak on my behalf.

She pretended not to notice. "Your mother was elected to the

Senate, not elevated to sainthood. Don't force your way into Cal's past and ruin a relationship with someone who means a great deal to you. Why not give him the benefit of the doubt?"

I wasn't totally convinced, but for now I would postpone any immediate next steps with dear old Uncle Cal. I instead would focus on the unusual arrangement my mother had struck with my grandfather.

Chapter 52

If Senior Davenport had forked over ten thousand dollars a month to his daughter-in-law for forty-five years, there was one person likely to know something about it. With annual payments equating to a hundred-and-twenty-thousand dollars, Kendall Ackermann surely must have been involved.

The hours I invested with the head of the family office, downing martinis inside Riverbank Tavern, paid dividends. The normally cantankerous Ackermann picked up the phone on the second ring. "Young Mr. Davenport, to what do I owe the privilege?"

After an exchange of pleasantries, I jumped right to the point. "Kendall, what do you know about the $10,000 secret payments my grandfather made every month for nearly half-a-century?"

The silence from the other end of the conversation was deafening.

"Ackermann ... are you there?" I asked.

"I'm still here," he said softly. The welcome tone in his voice had vanished. "I'm struggling with how to answer your question."

I didn't want Kendall Ackermann to clam up, so I proceeded cautiously. "Let's start with your reticence ... the fact you're a bit tongue-tied suggests you were aware of the monthly payments. Is that correct?"

After a pause, Ackermann responded with no elaboration, "Yes."

It was like a game of Twenty Questions. "Can I assume these

monthly payments were always made in cash … bundles of cash placed inside sealed envelopes?"

This question was met with another, even longer pause. "How could you possibly know that?" Ackermann finally replied suspiciously.

"Because I've seen the envelopes. All 543 of them," I informed him. "In fact, I'm holding one of the empty envelopes right now … plus a currency strap that would have been wrapped around the hundred-dollar bills inside."

"How did you end up with those? Who was Senior paying all that money to?" He quickly blurted out his questions. Now it was the measured Kendall Ackermann who sounded eager for answers.

I tried to process what he had just asked. "You're telling me you didn't know what my grandfather did with five-and-a-half million dollars over all those years?"

Ackerman wasn't the least bit sheepish with his response. "That's exactly what I'm telling you. When Senior first asked me to arrange for those monthly envelopes … sometime back in the Sixties … I questioned him about why he needed so much cash. He told me it was a private matter and I was better off not knowing the details. He assured me he wasn't doing anything illegal and since the money was coming out of his personal account rather than the company … I didn't need to hear anymore."

"But you had to wonder what he was doing with that much cash?" I probed.

"I sure as hell did, Troy. But I'd learned early-on with Senior … one shouldn't push him on things he wanted to keep to himself. He insisted on receiving the ten thousand in cash every month … in thousand-dollar bills … and I had no choice but to get it for him … no questions asked. When we couldn't get thousand-dollar bills any-more, he had to settle for hundreds in those envelopes I gave him."

"But, Kendall, you must have had some idea of where all that money was going. Who did you think he was giving it to?"

"Need I remind you, we're talking about your grandfather," It sounded like Ackermann was smirking, but then he caught himself. "I'm sorry … it's best I choose my words carefully. During his younger days, Senior sowed a lot of wild oats when he was out on the road … making the rounds to all his coalmines. From time to time, we had to pay off a few folks because of his indiscretions. To be honest, I figured somewhere along the line he must have fathered a kid or two with one of his gal friends … and he'd promised to do the right thing by supporting some hidden family he was keeping in one of those coal towns. It would've been just like him to make a promise like that … and then honor his word over all those years."

I said nothing and waited – knowing Kendall Ackermann would start up again whenever he was ready. Which he did. "Well, based on what you said a few minutes ago, someone must have been keeping all those empty envelopes and money wrappers as proof for some reason … and they told you the amount your grandad instructed me to seal inside every one of 'em. Who was it that reached out to you, Troy … are they hitting us up for more money? What in God's name did Senior do to those folks? Should we be contacting the police?"

If nothing else, I liked how quickly Ackermann's mind shifted gears when it came to protecting the family interests. But now I found myself in a tough position. How much could I share about who really had received five-and-a-half million dollars in 543 installments?

"You can relax, Kendall … no one contacted me. It's nothing like that," I assured him. "Since my mom's funeral, I've been sorting through her stuff. I came across the envelopes among her belongings … but there was no explanation as to how she wound up with them, and certainly no reason to be concerned. I guess we'll just have to assume someone wanted her to hold onto those envelopes for reasons we aren't likely to understand."

I prided myself in telling the truth – if only partially. I left out the part about the cash still being inside those 543 envelopes. I rationalized I was doing him a favor. Kendall Ackermann might have suffered a coronary if he'd heard that five-and-a-half-million dollars had been collecting dust instead of interest.

"Did you have any reason to think my mother might have been aware of my grandfather's mysterious payments?" I decided to try one last indirect angle, in case some random fragment jarred loose in Ackermann's memory.

He thought about my question for several seconds before responding. "No, I can't imagine such a thing. Your grandad had way too much respect for your mom to involve her in any of his dirty little secrets. I remember him once telling me he admired Beth because he could deal with her straight up … 'man to man,' he said. And let's face it, Troy … Senior didn't feel the same way about your dad. He kept Junior out of his private life for a whole other set of reasons."

Then there was a long pause on the other end of the phone. Finally, Kendall reiterated, "No, I can't imagine your mom being involved at all." But his voice sounded like he was still processing everything he'd heard during our call. Perhaps, my last bit of digging had backfired. "For sure, she was a damned special woman," he said with a sigh. I couldn't tell if that final remark was meant for my benefit or his.

Chapter 53

By mid-spring, I was running out of ideas on where to gather even random morsels of information about my parents' relationship. I had been five when my father passed away. I still held onto surprisingly vivid memories of many things we'd done together – reading at bedtime, flying kites in the park, spending afternoons at the Children's Museum. But I had only vague recollections of spending time with both my parents together, of watching them interact.

Shortly after my arrival on the scene in 1983, a first nanny was hired – Jenna Claire Dorsey. She lived in our home until we left Evansville for Indianapolis in 1987. Well into her eighties, Jenna Claire had attended my mother's memorial service. She and my mother stayed in touch over all those years. In fact, Jenna worked as a volunteer for every one of Beth Davenport's reelection campaigns.

In Indianapolis, my nanny was Sofia Fernandez. She resided in the extra bedroom of the condo until I was almost ten – four years after my father passed away. Sofia left our family's employ when my mother convinced the then twenty-six-year-old to open the cake shop she and her sister had fantasized since childhood. Today, specialty cakes created by Fernandez Sisters can be found in high-end grocery stores across a five-state region.

When I phoned, each ex-nanny was delighted to share memories of my parents. Their two descriptions sounded almost identical.

Neither remembered an argument, or even a cross word being uttered between my mom and dad.

Jenna Claire observed, "Your mother and father were the best folks I ever worked for … they were different than any married couple I've ever known … and at my age, I've known plenty. They were like the best of friends … always eager to hear what the other was up to, but they also gave each other lots of space. I can't imagine any couple having more respect for one another. I tried to be more like your momma when I got married for a brief spell … but you know, it just ain't natural to be that patient or understanding … especially with a man. I'm sure you recognize how special the two of 'em were. It makes me sad to think that their life together was cut so short."

I was curious about whether my parents had demonstrated outward physical affection toward one another but thought it best to probe this matter with the younger Sofia. At first, my question stumped her. "I never gave that aspect of their relationship much thought, but now that you ask, I'd have to say no … no, they didn't. Neither of them seemed to need much physical contact … occasional pecks on the cheek … or quick hugs when someone was leaving the condo, but that's about all I remember. It could be they were just being modest around me … but I honestly think their love was a different kind than most. They met each other's needs in other ways. Both had separate lives to lead, but they definitely complemented one another whenever they were together."

In describing the final months of my father's life, Sofia recounted, "I don't know how your mother managed the way she did … all that coming and going between Washington and here. She was a strong woman, and your dad showed so much courage in the way he dealt with his blood disease. Thank goodness for your Uncle Cal. Once your dad went into the hospital, Cal was able to spend lots of time with him … and that freed up your mom to spend more time with you when she made it back to town. She had a big gap to fill …

because it was your dad who devoted the most time to you. I may be out of place saying this ... but being a parent didn't come as naturally to Mrs. Davenport."

Cal's involvement was another facet of my parents' relationship I hoped to better understand. After my father died, my mother must have entertained hundreds of acquaintances. She gained the respect of practically everyone with whom she came in contact. But I couldn't recall Madame Senator having deep personal attachments to anyone other than a few of her loyal staff members. Anyone except Cal Stratton.

I asked the two former nannies about this special friendship. Jenna Claire Dorsey laughed as she responded. "I hate to think of all the miles that poor man had to drive just to spend time with your folks. I bet he came down here to Evansville a weekend every month ... and some months, it might have been two or three weekends." I had remembered Uncle Cal being around, but this level of frequency came as a surprise.

"What did they do when he visited?" I asked.

Jenna Claire's answer was simple. "The same things your parents would have done if he hadn't been in town ... he was just part of their normal routine." She hesitated, then added, "Except Cal was kind of funny about you. When you were a baby, he never wanted to hold you. Yet with me, or anyone else who came to visit, he would go on and on about you ... like you were the perfect child. It's odd how some people can be about kids."

I took my inquiries a step further, "Since Cal stayed at our house so often, did he have his own room?"

Jenna Claire replied, "I guess you could say the extra room upstairs was his ... no one else ever used it. Your folks turned the other bedroom on the second floor into a nursery for you, and I lived in the bedroom on the first floor. When I took the job, I thought it was kind of odd that they didn't want me sleeping in the room next to the baby, like other folks I'd worked for. But if your mom was home from Washington, she wanted to be the one who tended to you during the night. In fact, your folks didn't want me coming upstairs at all unless they called for me."

My curiosity was piqued. During Cal's stays, would my mother have been brazen enough to slip into another man's bedroom? Could my father have been complicit in an extramarital affair between his wife and closest friend – an affair that had drawn the attention of my grandfather? I didn't want to go near those questions with Jenna Claire.

Sofia could shed only a sliver of light on my parents' relationship with Cal. "When I first started working for your parents, after they got settled here in Indianapolis, Cal would drop by the condo a lot. But then his visits spread out more. I think something happened for a few months ... he and your folks might have had a falling out or something. That is, until your dad got sick. Like I said earlier, Cal Stratton was a godsend during Mr. Davenport's final months."

To a follow-up question, Sofia responded, "No, I can't remember Mr. Stratton ever spending the night at the condo ... or even staying late if he came for a visit."

Wondering whether my mother might have continued or re-kindled her affair with Cal after my father's death, I asked a second follow-up. Sofia's reply was equally unsuspicious. "No, Mr. Stratton didn't come around more often once your father passed away. If anything, it was the opposite because of your mom's busy travel schedule. Funny though, occasionally he would stop by unannounced when she was out of town ... just to check on you. To me, that showed what a special friend he was to the whole family."

I thought of one last person who might offer additional perspectives on my parents' relationship. Annabelle Jenkins. It was a long shot, because Annabelle started working for my mother just a year before my father died. Their interactions would have been mostly job-related during those early months. Further, I couldn't imagine my mother sharing details about her personal life with Annabelle, since she was so reluctant to share them with anyone else. But if I was being honest with myself, I had a separate reason for calling Annabelle on a Sunday morning in late April to see if she'd be receptive to an afternoon visit. I wasn't planning on driving to Logansport alone.

I wanted Annabelle Jenkins to meet Melanie. With my mother gone, these were the two most important women in my life. To me, both were miracles of nature. They should know one another, and I couldn't wait to experience the fullness of the universe in seeing them together.

Within minutes of our arrival, I wondered why I even was needed there. Becoming fast friends was one thing, but the bond between Annabelle and Melanie was instantaneous. After handling initial introductions, I gave up trying to be part their rapid-fire conversation and quickly became a passive observer. A passive and contented observer. The chemistry between them conveyed a joy for life and life's adventures. Their optimism was boundless. If forced to choose a moment in time in which to be frozen for perpetuity, my search could have been declared complete.

Melanie was thoroughly amused when Annabelle recounted episodes from my younger years. The various mischiefs I would get into when my mother brought me to the office. The way "The Senator" allowed me to sit at her desk while she took her mail folder and worked from an adjacent couch. The extra efforts required to keep me occupied backstage at political rallies … as well as my occasional refusals to join my mother onstage for a final ovation. And later, as a teenager, when my mother honored my wishes and allowed me to skip the rallies entirely. Melanie kept asking for more stories and Annabelle didn't disappoint.

Her recollections seemed to contain two consistent threads. My petulance and my mother's patient tolerance. At first, I attributed the one-sided skew to Annabelle's unflinching loyalty to her former boss and mentor. But as the examples wore on, I eventually realized what a pain-in-the-ass I must have been for everyone involved. Fortunately, her chronicles turned a lot more positive once Annabelle got around to more recent years.

Somewhere along the line, Annabelle inquired of Melanie, "What can you tell me about this attractive pair sitting here in my living room?" Her tone may have been playful, but her interest was genuine. She had delivered on her side of the equation with stories about me from my youth. Now, the discussion took on an unmistakable aura of *quid pro quo* – with me serving as both *quid* and *quo*. Melanie detailed our six-month history, remembering to work-in my sappiest and most embarrassing romantic gestures. Annabelle grinned from ear-to-ear as she took it all in.

Upon hearing I had driven two hours to Effingham on a cold winter night to bring Melanie a container filled with hot soup when she was suffering the flu, Anabelle looked at me. "I always told your mother you'd be a charmer once you found the right girl … and the Senator didn't disagree with me. I probably shouldn't repeat this in present company … but, Troy, when you were dating all those other 'unique' and 'interesting' young women over the years, your momma wasn't sure you really cared about finding the right one." She turned her gaze to Melanie, "But our Troy here, he done good … the Senator would have loved seeing the two of you together."

Melanie wasn't the least bit insulted or irritated by Annabelle's allusion to my previous dating regimen. She instead accepted the compliment as it was intended and seemed especially touched by how Annabelle felt my mother would have received her.

As for me, the whole exchange was surreal. Who had I been fooling? How many psych classes had I taken in college … in grad school? Of course, I'd been eager to introduce Melanie to Annabelle.

I wanted Annabelle to adore her as much as I did. Through the years, Annabelle Jenkins had become a principal figure in my life, so now I wanted her to become a central part in my life with Melanie. But I couldn't deny an even deeper reason for this sudden trip to Logansport. No woman had been closer to my mother, or better understood my mother, than Annabelle Jenkins. In my mother's absence, she alone could provide the surrogate affirmation I subconsciously had been seeking.

I knew with certainty I had "done good" by falling in love with Melanie and convincing her to fall in love with me. Collecting outside endorsements was utterly unnecessary. If anything, it was gratuitous overkill. Just the same, I would never forget the satisfaction of hearing those wonderful words tumble out of Annabelle's mouth.

When I got around to questions about Madam Senator's relationship with my father, Annabelle had little new to offer. "I barely knew Mr. Davenport. A few months after I began working for the Senator, you dad was diagnosed with that horrible disease. I occasionally would run magazines and other things over to your father at the hospital, when your mom was in Washington ... but that was no way to get to know the man. He always was appreciative ... he always remembered to ask me about my Byron ... but he seemed so sad and scared."

She went on, "Those were tough times for the Senator. Imagine what it must have been like to head off to Washington every week while your husband was back home failing from some rare disease. It was a dark period in her life. Once she almost resigned her position so that she could stay in Indianapolis and be with Mr. Davenport ... but he and Mr. Stratton talked her out of it."

I treaded carefully, "Did you get to know Cal very well?"

"Oh, sure. He came to your mother's office quite a few times," she replied.

This revelation surprised me. "Do you know why?"

Annabelle seemed confused by the question. "You do remember that Mr. Stratton ran the finances for two of your mom's reelection campaigns? He also was one of her biggest fund-raisers."

I had forgotten the obvious, so I tried a pivot. "I meant besides the money part ... did they have other reasons for meeting? As a close friend, did he help her in other ways?"

Annabelle shook her head. "I wouldn't have any idea about anything like that ... you know how private your momma was. You'll have to ask Mr. Stratton. I just remember that whenever he came into the office, it was a special event."

"Why was that?" I asked with sudden interest.

This time, Annabelle smiled broadly. "Mr. Stratton was one of the best-looking and most sought-after men in the whole state of Indiana. The ladies in the office loved it when he would show up ... and he never disappointed them. That man could flirt like no one else."

I pushed one step further. "Did my Uncle Cal ever flirt with my mom? Do you think they might have dated after my father passed away?"

Annabelle's gleeful smile turned somber. "The Senator wasn't built that way. Pretty as she was, I can't imagine anyone flirting with that woman. I wish she and Cal had seen fit to start dating ... it might have done her some good. There was a void in her life I never understood, and it wasn't my place to pry ... she was such a great woman in so many other ways. I just hope she was able to enjoy the kind of happiness with Mr. Davenport that the two of you have found in each other ... and that I had with Byron. When I draw my last breath and leave this earth, he's the memory I'll be taking with me."

I drove away from Annabelle's house in a state of euphoria. The time spent together with her and Melanie had been a glorious reminder of how much good there still was in the world. Perhaps it was time to stop chasing through my mother's past.

Besides, I had run out of places to turn. If I hoped to find resolution on any of the issues still haunting me, I would need to confront Cal Stratton with some very difficult questions. In our previous conversations, Cal had tried to dissuade me from digging further – convinced my mother had kept the doors closed to her past for good reason. Melanie also was urging me to let go – to accept the memory of my mother on my mother's terms.

For the time being, I would heed their advice. Deep down, though, I knew it was only a matter of time.

Chapter 54

"You led me to believe we'd be roughing it."

I shrugged sheepishly, "Well, we are going to be sleeping in a tent."

The only thing I had told Melanie in advance was that we would be staying in a camp on the fringe of Ranthambore National Park, near Sawai MaDhopur, in Northern India. But camping hardly described the luxury accommodations into which we'd just been ushered.

"Tent? Troy, this place has three ceiling fans and a wet bar."

"Not to mention a private open-air shower through that door over there in the corner." Now I was goading her. "A shower might come in handy. We're likely to work up quite a sweat photographing tigers ... or maybe we can come up with a few other ways if we put our minds to it."

"I already can see where your mind has gone." We were nine or ten feet apart and she stood staring at me in mock disgust for several seconds. Then she dropped the backpack she was holding and began unbuttoning her blouse. "Let's check out how private that shower really is."

I had wanted everything to be perfect. I needed it to be. I was taking a huge risk. A monumental risk. A risk to end all risks. Early in our relationship, Melanie Reynolds had confessed that she wasn't the marrying type. At the time, those words seemed like music to my ears, because I, too, had been averse to matrimonial permanence. But that was before she took ownership of my mind, body, and soul. Now I couldn't imagine life without her.

Since the end of spring term at Wabash, I'd been bouncing between Indianapolis and Effingham. My campus duties would ramp up again in mid-August, so I convinced Melanie to take-off on a ten-day adventure with me before the start of classes.

I spent many of my summer hours planning the trip. The first imperative was choosing a place that would be new to Melanie – some exotic location that could take on special meaning for just the two of us. Coming up with an appealing destination that she hadn't explored was no easy task.

I was a sociologist, not a finance professor. I settled on Ranthambore without bothering to consider the costs. The required upfront payment wiped out my checking account and a huge chunk of my savings – that is, the savings I'd managed to squirrel away on my own. Inheritances were another matter.

By now, my mother's assets had been transferred into my name and were parked in various bank accounts – drawing basic interest, I presumed. Until I knew for sure how I felt about my mother, I wasn't going to spend or invest a single dollar of her twenty million. In my mind, everything about my mother was tainted.

As to the money left to me by my grandfather, the exact sum still was a moving target. According to Kendall Ackermann, those funds were riding the wave of a "bull market." The four hundred million from September had climbed another fifty million. But until otherwise notified, this amassing fortune remained in a legal state of suspended animation. The terms and waiting periods stipulated by Senior Davenport were more complicated to untangle than the attorneys who drafted them had anticipated – which was fine by me. I had no idea what I might do with all that money, and fortunately,

Melanie didn't care either way. If anything, she balked at the complications of wealth.

My plan was to ease into the subject of marriage during the last evening of our stay. I would lay the groundwork by being on my best behavior for an entire week – which was no small feat. To symbolize the longevity of a successful marriage, I had arranged for a secluded candlelight dinner under a banyan tree that was more than two-hundred-and-fifty years old. Our own dedicated chef would prepare seven gourmet courses – none of which I'd either heard of or could pronounce. All the while, we were to be serenaded by a flute and a lute-like instrument called a veena.

As it turned out, all my meticulous preparations went for naught. Eight thousand miles from home, and just four hours into our first afternoon at this remotest of remote retreats, Melanie surprised me. Once the dust from our journey was showered off, we had crawled under the sheets for some rest and recreation – but not in that order. We were awakened a short time later by a knock at the door, reminding us of our 4 p.m. safari. At first, Melanie didn't stir. Then she rolled over, lifted her head, and looked down into my eyes. "We should always wake up next to each other, Troy Davenport. Why don't you marry me?"

Chapter 55

Now that he was retired, Cal Stratton was enjoying one of his typical Indianapolis summers. Morning golf, endless cocktail parties, and escorting women of every age to restaurants or the theater. I was staying true to my plan of not prying further into the past. As a result, the two of us had enjoyed lunch with no agenda on a pair of occasions. Then, shortly before our trip to India, I introduced Cal to Melanie at a cook-out we hosted for a small group of friends. Not surprisingly, Uncle Cal and Melanie hit it off immediately. Cal even remembered her father from his many trips to Evansville.

His first question to me was an obvious one. "How is it that the two of you started dating when you live in different states?"

I kept my response vague, not wanting to open up a conversation that might prove too tempting for me. "When I was going through my mother's things, I came across some information pertaining to Doc Reynolds, so I tracked down Melanie and gave her a call. One thing led to another ... and you know how that goes."

My answer seemed sufficient. In keeping with his convictions about leaving the past behind, Cal showed no signs of curiosity about the information I'd referenced.

During the return flight from India, Melanie and I made a short list of people we wanted to inform about our engagement. At the top were her sister and brother, whom we contacted by phone within hours of landing. Next up was Uncle Cal, and we chose to handle this announcement in person.

We met for dinner on the terrace of Woodstock, an "old money" golf and tennis club to which Cal Stratton belonged. I wasn't sure who turned more heads as we made our way to the table. Melanie looked stunning in her bright orange sundress, and Cal was as dashing as ever in a yellow linen sports jacket. I, on the other hand, felt like a loaf of stale bread in my standard-issue blue blazer.

As soon as we sat down, I motioned to our assigned waiter. "Mr. Stratton would like to order us a bottle of your finest champagne."

Cal nodded approval to the waiter and looked at me with amusement. "It appears you're adapting rather well to your newfound wealth."

Melanie spoke up, "Hardly. Most of his socks still have holes in them."

Cal hadn't needed extrasensory powers to understand the need for champagne. Nonetheless, he showed how much he cared for us by keeping his reactions in check, so as not to rob us of a very special moment.

After champagne was poured, I began a rambling oration. "As you know, Melanie and I returned from India a few days ago. When I told you about the trip I was planning, Uncle Cal, I failed to mention what I expected to do there. As you have duly emphasized to me in private, I've managed to fall in love with a rather remarkable woman … and somewhere along the line I realized I wanted to spend the rest of my life with her. So, I drove up to Chicago one day in July, where I purchased the ring you now see on Melanie's left hand. Over the course of several weeks, I spoke frequently with the manager of the resort camp where we were to be lodged amidst the splendor of India's Ranthambore National Park. I did this to arrange a romantic dinner for our final evening in one of the world's most magnificent and undisturbed jungles. With the arrival of dessert, I had every

331

intention of dropping to one knee and professing my undying devotion as I asked Miss Melanie Reynolds to become my wife."

I paused and feigned a grimace before continuing, "However, much to my surprise, this woman to whom I was willing to chase to the far end of the earth, turned out to be a killjoy. On our first day in this distant land, she asked me to marry her with no more forethought than if she'd been asking me to pass the salt. And I, being raised a gentleman, had no choice but to accept. So, let us raise our glasses to a woman whose bountiful talents and supreme beauty are surpassed only by her unbridled spontaneity."

Cal rose to his feet and offered a slight bow to the two of us before putting his champagne flute to his lips. After taking a sip, he lifted his glass once more in our direction. "Notre soif la plus profonde est satisfaite à la fontaine de l'amour."

He spoke in what sounded to me like perfect French. I sat motionless, clueless as to what had been said. Then I gawked upward at Cal, transfixed by the man's timeless elegance. I noticed how people seated in the immediate vicinity were likewise spellbound. A moment later, Melanie added the final punctuation to what had transformed into a Hollywood movie scene. She responded in equally proficient French, "Vos paroles sont belles. Merci." After which, she stood, walked around the table to Cal, kissed him on the cheek, gave him a long hug, and told him how important he was to both of us. A woman at the next table started applauding. Soon others joined in.

By the time Melanie and Cal returned to their respective chairs, I was able to regain my composure and speak again. "While you two were speaking, I kept looking for subtitles, but there didn't seem to be any. Can someone tell me what I just missed?"

Cal made a hand gesture toward Melanie and she took his lead. "Cal toasted us by saying 'our deepest thirst is satisfied at the fountain of love' … and I expressed our gratitude for his beautiful words. And they are beautiful, aren't they?"

I hesitated for a few seconds, trying to come up with a witty retort. Ultimately, I recognized this moment should stand untarnished. "They are indeed." I then tipped my glass toward Cal in genuine appreciation.

From there, the conversation turned a great deal more lighthearted. Cal commended me on snaring a wife so far out of my wheelhouse and probed Melanie on whether she'd previously suffered from similar bouts of temporary insanity. He especially wanted to hear more specifics surrounding my thwarted marriage proposal. Laughter abounded as Cal celebrated our happiness in full.

At several points, when the three of us were laughing, I noticed Melanie eying me curiously, and then doing the same with Cal. Something seemed to fascinate her as she shifted her gaze back and forth between the two of us. Finally, I asked, "Is everything okay?"

Her response pleased me. "At this moment, life couldn't be grander. What a joy it is to share our happy news with someone so dear." She looked at Cal, "You always have been like family to Troy … and now you are to me."

Moisture formed in Cal's eyes. "His parents meant the world to me. Remaining close to Troy helps me hold on to a special relationship. Junior and Beth would have been very pleased this evening."

Cal's unconstrained sentimentality caused Melanie to well up. She smiled lovingly and nodded her head several times, "I'm sure that's true."

I avoided tears, but their emotional exchange did have an effect on me. Seeing the devotion this man continued to exude toward my parents was enough to cement my conviction. Whatever past arrangements might have existed among three special friends, their relationship should be respected as private and left undisturbed.

Leaving that dinner with Melanie on my arm, I experienced an inner calmness, an unfamiliar sense of serenity. Since childhood, I'd become accustomed to the veils of uncertainty. Of wondering why things couldn't be different with my mother. Of wondering how and why I might be disappointing her. Suddenly, all the weighty angst had vanished. As the anniversary of my mother's death approached, I was sure I could move forward without looking back.

Over the prior year, I had uncovered one surprise after another. Many had been unsettling – including the question of my own existence. Had my birth been nothing more than a bargaining chip between my mother and grandfather? The deeper I delved, the blurrier the picture of my mother had become. Yet, time and again, I'd also had stumbled upon behaviors that warranted heightened admiration for this woman. Senator Beth Davenport was and would remain a complicated being. I would have to accept the unanswered questions. My mother had carried many secrets to her grave by choice. There they should continue to rest.

This prospect was made easier because providence had intervened with a seemingly flawless spirit who changed my life forever. Melanie brought new meaning to everything I thought or touched. To every sight I saw, to every smell I smelled. With Melanie in my future, I really didn't need to understand any of the complexities from the past. She had made me whole.

Chapter 56

Since first laying eyes on a towel-clad Melanie Reynolds at the front door of her house in Effingham, I had learned to expect the unexpected. Hardly a week went by when I wasn't discovering some new interest she harbored, or some new skill she possessed. Two nights before our wedding in October, she surprised me once again. She wanted to discuss something that was likely to change the plans we'd made for our future together. It related to her physical condition and the consequences of a choice which predated me by several years.

Soon after her fortieth birthday, Melanie's menstrual cycles had become unusually irregular and infrequent. She appeared to be moving into menopause earlier than most women. As a result, she felt that continued use of birth control pills would pose an unnecessary health risk and ceased taking them. As soon as our relationship turned intimate, she informed me of her decision and we elected not to take alternative precautions. Due to the frequency with which we conveyed our passions over the ensuing months, with no resulting signs of pregnancy, we assumed mother nature had rendered any discussion of children unnecessary. We'd never bothered to have a serious conversation about having or raising a family. Two days prior to matrimony turned out to be the perfect time for our first.

The small wedding ceremony was to take place on Saturday

afternoon in Indianapolis, where Melanie would relocate her career and move into my apartment. Her Effingham ranch home already was on the market. Before heading out of town, Melanie made one last appointment with her doctor – mostly to bid a proper farewell. Her female physician was one of the first friends Melanie made when she was starting her counselling practice after graduate school.

Thirty minutes into the appointment, Melanie was presented a wedding gift like no other. "You most definitely are pregnant … about two months would be my best guess."

She wanted to share the news with me in person, which provided her a full day of adjustment to the this altered state. One year earlier, Melanie Reynolds had believed she was averse to marriage. Suddenly, she also was facing parenthood.

I likewise needed time to absorb the unanticipated wrinkle in our plans. I'd been envisioning an unstructured lifestyle with Melanie that would stretch us into our golden years. Just the two of us. Adventurous excursions. Romantic dinners and lost weekends. Nowhere in my thoughts had there been diaper bags and parent-teacher conferences.

Maybe because of the relationship with my mother, I had never thought that having children was important to me. Oddly enough, as the focus for my upcoming years took a startling turn in those final hours of bachelorhood, I found myself feeling even more jubilant about our pending nuptials. Starting a family and raising a child with Melanie could only be one thing. Spectacular.

Chapter 57

Beth Davenport had been forty-two when she gave birth to me. The coincidence seemed almost eerie. Melanie would not turn forty-three until our baby was three months old. I was certain the comparisons ended there. Since psychology textbooks first were printed, shrinks had been opining on the inclination that men have for marrying women like their mothers. But Melanie wasn't anything like my mother. Melanie was far too generous with her emotions, and she was completely transparent with every facet of her life.

Knowing what I knew about her troubled childhood, I was willing to concede that my mother had given parenting her best shot on many fronts. While on others, she hadn't made much of an attempt at all. Now it would be my turn, and I was committed to hold nothing back as husband and father.

I continued to wrestle with what to do about the wealth that awaited me. Until the past year, I hadn't given much thought to the source of whatever money I might spend. I'd been willing to squander any available wages that wound up in my checking account.

The prism through which I viewed the world began to change the day my mother was killed in the helicopter crash. In an instant, this all-consuming presence in my life was gone. Round-the-clock media coverage followed. Then the funeral service. And the endless tributes ever since. All of it had been about her. Of course, it was.

Troy Davenport didn't even register as an afterthought. As the son of Beth Davenport, I had lived, and often basked, under her vast halo. All the while, feigning my independence and pretending to forge my own trail. Suddenly, I really was on my own. At age thirty-five, Troy Davenport finally had been forced to confront his full adulthood.

Now in hindsight, at thirty-six, my transformation had been swifter than I ever should have expected. I suddenly felt more accountable for decisions I made. The option of falling back on my mother's position or influence no longer was available to me. Strangely, this cord-cutting produced an inner confidence. The view of my future seemed crisper, less daunting, when I was standing on my own two feet. Especially with Melanie at my side.

Together, we needed to decide if we wanted to go on the family dole. Perhaps, with time, I could get my mind around the incomprehensible sums left to me by my mother and grandfather. But the thought of crossing over that Rubicon still spooked the hell out of me.

Plus, there was another amount which hardly qualified as insubstantial – $5.4 million parked in a storage unit. I didn't understand why my mother would have allowed so much capital to sit idle. Yet all these months later, I had done the exact same thing. Somehow it just felt like those envelopes filled with cash belonged in that suitcase.

Though I'd vowed not to pry into my parents' past, I was compelled to pursue one important issue related to my father. The blood disease that shortened his life. With childbirth on the horizon, our selected obstetrician was working with Melanie and me to identify any and all hereditary concerns. When discussing my father's blood condition, my mother always had been vague – leaving me awkwardly ignorant on relevant facts.

A copy of the death certificate indicated my father died in Methodist Hospital, so I placed a call. To my surprise, the retrieval of his medical records would require a face-to-face meeting and a slew of legal forms. By the time I arrived for my appointed time, more barriers had gone up. My father's file had been sealed. It only could be accessed by the hospital's chief administrator, and then solely at the direction of one individual. Senator Beth Davenport.

After several more days and a string of phone calls between attorneys, I discovered a skeleton my mother had taken great pains to hide in a closet. Joseph Elwood Davenport, Jr., had been diagnosed with a human immunodeficiency virus (HIV) in March of 1988. In October that year, he died from acquired immune deficiency syndrome (AIDS).

From materials I'd read in the past, I understood the two principal means by which HIV was likely contracted. One was the exchange of bodily fluids with a person already carrying the virus, which typically occurred during sexual intercourse. Second was the possibility of an infected hypodermic needle, which most often occurred among illegal drug users sharing non-sterile paraphernalia. Either way, I no longer could let the doors to the past remain locked. I needed answers that only one man could provide.

Chapter 58

The temperatures up north were turning cold, so Cal Stratton had flipped the seasonal switch and returned to his Vero Beach lifestyle. Melanie volunteered to make the trip with me, but I thought a one-on-one conversation was best. This time there would be no clever repartee or French aphorisms. Just unadorned truth. Hard, cold facts which had been kept from me for thirty-six years. I hoped not to alienate Cal, but I wasn't leaving Florida without real answers.

On the phone, Cal had suggested we meet at the John's Island Beach Club. I declined the invitation, opting instead for the privacy of his condo, and this request alone created an undercurrent of tension when Cal greeted me at the door. "Hello, Troy. I don't suppose this is a friendly visit."

"It certainly can be … if you're willing to finally open up with me." I continued talking as I stepped inside and slid past Cal. "I had a rather surprising meeting at Methodist Hospital on Wednesday. I thought you might be interested."

I wanted to catch Cal off-guard, and now watched for his reaction. In an instant, the ever-present smile was gone – replaced by an expression of anguish. For the first time I could remember, Cal Stratton suddenly looked his age. My assumption immediately had been confirmed. Beth Davenport wasn't the only person who knew the real cause of my father's death.

Cal shepherded us into his spacious living room, where he took a seat on a couch and gestured for me to sit in one of the opposite chairs. Cal was making no effort at pretense. "Where do you want to begin?"

At last, the blanks from my parents' past were going to be filled. I took a deep breath, now wondering if I really was prepared to hear the missing truths. "Let's start with my father's illness. Do you know how he wound up with AIDS?"

Cal closed his eyes for a moment, as though gathering strength for the conversation ahead. When he opened them, he spoke with a somberness. "It was my fault."

I hadn't expected that response. My voice cracked as I came back sharply at Cal. "He got it from you? You are HIV positive?"

Cal shook his head. "No, not from me directly. But because of me."

I tried to calm myself, recognizing how much ground we still needed to cover. But my attempts were futile. I let loose with a litany.

"I'm sorry, Cal. Maybe we should back up a little ... and here are just some of the issues where I could use a little help. My mother was paid by my grandfather to marry my father and have children with him. They stayed married until he died twenty-five years later – from a disease my mother went to great lengths to conceal. During their marriage, my mother faked multiple pregnancies and miscarriages, and she was confronted by my grandfather about an affair she was having ... an affair she happened to be having with you, her husband's best friend. And that best friend now is claiming responsibility for his death. You can just imagine the questions I might have ... and Cal, I've got all afternoon ... so why don't you enlighten me?"

Cal looked like he'd received a sucker-punch to the gut. The rapid-fire revelations and allegations had come at him from out of nowhere. He was searching for a proper response. Finally, he spoke.

Rather slowly at first, selecting his words carefully. "You obviously chose not to heed the advice from our previous discussions. You just couldn't leave the past alone." As much as Cal tried to remain neutral in his tone, he couldn't disguise the disappointment.

I felt obliged to explain. "Cal, I really had decided to put all this out of my mind ... to file-away every last obscurity, ambiguity, and absurdity that riddles my family's history, and never dwell on them again. But with a baby on the way, it became important to understand the medical history in my family ... and thus the nature of my father's blood disease. And since my mother never went into much detail with me, I was left no alternative but to contact the hospital where my father died. I wasn't expecting to get broadsided by another Davenport bombshell."

The expression on Cal's face brightened slightly. "That makes sense, Troy. Thank you for telling me." Then it was his turn to take a long, deep breath before continuing. "As to what you've learned about your mother and father, or what you think you've learned about them ... I guess it's time we set the record straight. But before we begin, I want to be clear ... Junior and Beth Davenport were two of the finest people ever to grace this planet. I always will love them immensely, and I'm hoping when we're done here today, you will have gained new admiration for both your parents. They made decisions in their lives that might seem odd to others, especially by today's standards. They each contended with complicated realities and did so with utmost discretion and dignity. Having watched you grow up, I am confident you will do the same."

And so our journey back in time began.

Cal Stratton started with the first time he and Junior Davenport met – as high school freshmen at Culver Military Academy. He described how they became fast friends. Soon they had realized there was something different, something deeper to their friendship. They both felt it. As teenaged boys, they were experiencing bodily urges and impulses. Late one night, these urges and impulses led to experimentation.

The next morning, Cal was overtaken by embarrassment and guilt because of the boundaries they'd crossed. But when he walked into the dining hall and saw the tranquil look on Junior's face, the awkward feelings disappeared. He instantly realized their explorations in a storage closet hadn't been deviant, or even reckless. He also recognized then that other intimacies were sure to follow.

For the next four years, the two were inseparable. Other students would tease them about how close they were or toss derogatory epithets at them in jest – as teenage boys were prone to do. But no one suspected the truth. They'd been careful. Exceedingly careful. It would have been scandalous for two adolescents from respected families to be outed in the 1950's.

During his summer and holiday breaks, Cal would date girls when he returned home to Dayton. Lots of girls. Junior similarly pursued a few young women in Evansville, but with far less enthusiasm. He was more of a loner who contented himself with books and music until classes resumed. Neither showed interest in other males – physically or romantically. Cal maintained that the feelings he shared with my father were unrelated to gender. Their connection was ethereal. They were young soulmates who wanted to share and explore everything life had to offer.

Hence, they applied to the same colleges and ultimately settled on Oberlin. For another four years, the environment of a campus made it easy for them to slip under the radar. In actuality, there had been less and less to hide. Physical intimacies between the two of them became less and less frequent. Junior had lost interest in that aspect of their relationship, but he encouraged Cal to address his lustier needs among a growing number of coeds who found him desirable. Cal was more than willing to comply and quickly gained a reputation as a ladies' man – a reputation he still was cultivating more than sixty years later. Yet all the while, the only person for whom he ever felt genuine love and loyalty was Junior Davenport. Watching Cal express his sentiments, I knew he wasn't exaggerating.

Periodically, human biology prevailed, and Junior would crave bodily contact. One such occasion was an unusually balmy evening in November, during their final year of college. The two of them snuck off to a secluded spot in a forest near their dormitory, where they were discovered in a compromised position.

At his point in the narrative, Cal paused and closed his eyes. When he opened them, he was smiling. "You know, Troy ... as things turned out, some unknown deity was sending us an angel. The person who happened upon us was a girl we recognized but really didn't know. Her name was Liz Monroe ... your mother."

I became more and more mesmerized with every detail. The unexpected chronology was unfolding like a fairy tale. And something in Cal's demeanor promised a happy ending.

He recounted the empathy and compassion my mother exhibited on that very first evening, following their unusual introduction to Lizzie. A bond formed immediately between three new friends. A lifelong bond like no other – of that, Cal was certain. A bond that would protect their secret for years to come. A bond that would prompt my mother to come to their rescue more times than he possibly could enumerate. A bond so deep and intense that she was willing to redirect the entire course of her life. From Cal's perspective, he indeed was describing an angel. As I listened to him, I couldn't disagree.

But every such story also contained a principal villain. That role fell to Senior Davenport. "I wish I could tell you otherwise, Troy, but your grandfather made childhood a living hell for your father. He would have ruined the rest of Junior's life, too ... if your mother hadn't intervened."

In conversations about my grandfather, I always had sensed my mother was holding back. My mother was a rarity among politicians, because she wouldn't make disparaging remarks about her adversaries. It was one of her attributes I long had admired. Cal's revelations about Senior served as testament to how firmly my mother had held to that principle.

"Those two men may have been father and son, but Junior wasn't cut from the same cloth as Senior. Junior should have been a doctor, or a counsellor ... or a professor, like you. He loved helping people, and he was always hungry to explore new things. Your granddad didn't care about any of that.

"Sure, Senior, was driven to succeed ... and because of his ruthlessness, he made a lot of people rich ... most notably himself. But he also was a hate-spewing bigot. If people didn't see the world the same way he did, he had no use for them. And that was the case with Junior. In his heart, Senior had no use for his own son ... but he couldn't just turn his back the way he would with other folks. The Davenport name was too vital to him. He wasn't going to live forever, but his legacy could. For that to happen, he needed Junior to conform to his expectations.

"Hell, the whole reason Junior was sent to Culver for high school was to toughen him up. Most kids would have resented being shipped off to military school like that. Your dad was ecstatic though. It allowed him to get away from his father and the constant feelings of falling short.

"Junior didn't care much about football or basketball ... or sports in general, for that matter. He hated guns and hunting. As a kid, Senior would take him along on fishing trips with all his old cronies, but Junior mostly stayed in the cabin and read. In Senior's eyes, all those tendencies made your father a sissy ... and he never was shy about calling him that. As Junior grew older, the labels grew harsher."

For close to an hour, Cal went on and on about my father and the hardships he endured from my grandfather. In the telling,

Junior's anguish became Cal's anguish. The poignancy was not lost on me. Thirty years after my father's death, these two men were still soulmates.

By the time Junior was out of college and working in the family business, he had lost his appetite for false pretense. The only relationship he cared about was the one he had with Cal, and he was tired of going through the motions of dating local women to keep up appearances – mostly for his father's sake. Meanwhile, Senior had picked up on rumors about his son. Cal had joined Junior while he was touring coal mines in Kentucky. They'd shared motel rooms. "Ironically, nothing of a sexual nature even occurred behind those closed doors. By then, Junior was disinterested, and my sexual interests were strictly heterosexual. We just enjoyed being alone together, being in each other's presence … talking late into the night until one of us fell asleep, then in the morning, picking up where we'd left off. Our feelings for one another transcended into something that defies explanation."

Senior confronted Junior on the reports he received from Kentucky, and my father tried to make him understand that his relationship with Cal was different than what people assumed. Senior would have none of it. He threatened to disown Junior. If they didn't stop seeing each other, he also would see that Cal's reputation was ruined in Indianapolis, where Cal was launching his banking career.

Soon thereafter, Cal came up with an idea. Lizzie Monroe. She already was aware of their relationship and Junior's awkward situation with his father. If she would pretend to be an out-of-town college sweetheart, Junior could dispense with his charade of dating other women. More importantly, he might convince Senior that his son wasn't the "pansy" he believed him to be. All Lizzie needed to do was pose for a few pictures with Junior, write an occasional letter, and attend one or two social events in Evansville. Junior would cover all the expenses and even compensate her for the disruption to her study schedule. She was reluctant to agree to the payment part, but the rest of the scheme turned out to be an easy decision for her. Cal explained, "Your mother told us that a close friend once had gone above and beyond for her ... when her own father was making life desperately difficult. She welcomed the opportunity to do the same for someone else."

Unfortunately, after several months, it was clear that Junior's father wasn't falling for the smoke screen. But instead of confronting his son, he upped the ante in what became a high-stakes game. Senior paid a visit to Lizzie and struck his own deal. He used his checkbook to structure an arrangement that would provide him everything he needed from a son – the semblance of a normal marriage between a man and woman, an attractive and talented daughter-in-law, and the promise of Davenport progeny.

Cal didn't know what Senior said or promised to secure Lizzie's agreement – to lure her away from the "big-time job in Cleveland" she had landed after graduation. Cal wasn't aware of how much money Senior offered her, or how long after the wedding she continued to be paid. Cal wasn't even sure if she'd shared that information with Junior. "You know how your mother could be. Nothing was going to stop her from doing what she believed was the right thing to do. Yet, she never would open-up about her past ... about people or events that might have helped her or hurt her before she arrived at Oberlin. So much about Beth always remained a mystery, but if we just focused on the end results, none of that really mattered. She was an extraordinary woman, Troy."

Regardless of how the arrangement between my mother and grandfather originated, the outcome seemed to be fortuitous for everyone involved. Senior was able to squelch the speculations about his son's sexual leanings – his "perversions." He wound up with a daughter-in-law who played a prominent role in the success of the family business and took the family name into the upper echelons of national politics. And, of course, with a grandson, Senior got the continuation of the Davenport name he so greatly coveted.

As for my parents and Cal, the three of them achieved levels of happiness they likely wouldn't have experienced otherwise. "Face it, Troy, none of us were programmed to be normal. Your dad ... he always beat to his own drum. Your mom ... she carried scars the rest of us never understood. And me ... I'm like a bee or hummingbird that flits from flower to flower. The only lasting relationships of con-sequence in my entire life have been those I shared with your folks ... and now you."

His expression turned serious. "Remember, Troy, we're talking about the 1950's, 60's and 70's ... two men who demonstrated open love with one another would have been declaring themselves pari-ahs." Cal allowed that to sink in, before chuckling. "So, I owe your granddad, the old goat, a huge debt of gratitude. All three of us did. For a good many years, our weekends together were like having our own private utopian society. I can't imagine any three people caring more for each other, or enjoying one another's company, as much as we did. And your mother, your wonderfully open-minded mother ... she was the most amazing person I've ever had the privilege of know-ing. She truly loved her husband, but she understood how Junior and I still needed our time alone. Beth never resented that ... in fact, she went out of her way to encourage it. Senior didn't mean to, but with one of his favorite taunts, he even provided us a name for all those times we spent together. They truly were our Camelot years."

The unexpected reference reminded me of something I needed to tell Cal. "I bet you never saw the book."

Cal had no idea what I was talking about. "You've lost me, Troy."

"I found a book my mother kept hidden ... it was about the Kennedys and their Camelot years in the White House. It contained a note from my grandfather that was written at least ten years after my parents were married. The note was a warning to my mother that the affair with you must cease. I had assumed he was referring to an affair between you and her. Now I realize his focus was you and my father. The man never let go, did he?"

Cal smiled. "He did not. It was something we all learned to live with. That's why your family's relocation to Indianapolis seemed so important ... Junior and Beth were finally getting out from under Senior's constant badgering." The smile disappeared. "Who could have imagined how badly this escape to freedom would backfire?"

The conversation had landed on sensitive ground. I probed carefully. "Was it something my grandfather did?"

Cal shook his head. "Hardly. Senior finally seemed to surrender. He had his grandson. Whatever strange friendships his son might have, and whatever he might do in private, Junior at least wouldn't be doing those things in Evansville anymore. No, Senior wasn't the problem. The problem was me." Cal stopped – his mind locked in the past.

"What do you mean?" I asked.

"I was a hypocrite ... a hypocrite who failed your father. Fully sharing my love for him had been easy enough when it only meant weekends in Evansville ... or when your parents and I took vacations together ... away from anyone we knew. I didn't care what total strangers thought. But now they were living on my home turf in Indianapolis. I had a reputation to protect. My calendar was full ... I saw lots of women. I now was confronted with fitting your parents into my lifestyle ... instead of them fitting me into theirs. By then, your mother's schedule as a senator was crazy ... she spent most of her time in Washington. Meanwhile, I became possessive of my own availability and increasingly cautious about where I was willing to be seen with Junior.

"We'd known each other since our teens, yet for the first time we started bickering. The downward spiral was rapid. The more we bickered, the less I wanted to be with your father at all. Then one night we had a huge blow-up. Out of anger, I called one of my girl-friends and took off to Barbados, just to spite your father. He knew what I was doing, so he did the same. But he took it one step further. He flew down to the Florida Keys ... to a gay community that was known for wild partying in those days. He threw himself into the middle of the raucous behavior to get back at yours truly. Half-a-year later, Junior was diagnosed as HIV-positive."

Tears were rolling down Cal's face and he made no effort to wipe them away or conceal his crying. "Excuse me for being direct ... but even during our younger years, when Junior and I had been physi-cally involved, we never committed the kinds of acts that led to his death. He wouldn't have been interested in pushing new boundaries. Only as punishment to me, he allowed men he'd barely met to take unprotected liberties. He, of course, denied I was the reason ... but I always knew otherwise."

My eyes also started to water as I thought about the final months of my father's life. About the conversations he and Cal must have had. About how their Camelot years with my mother had ended so abruptly. About where my mother had fit into this tragic equation, as her husband lay dying in a hospital. No wonder she'd felt such a strong connection to Sophie Mullins when she'd learned her son had died from AIDS.

I thought it best to shift the focus. "Earlier you alluded to scars my mother was carrying from her past. You're saying that she never described what her life was like before college ... before you and my father became acquainted with her?"

Cal reflected before responding. "Not with me ... not a word about her parents, her childhood, or even her high school years. But I don't have to tell you, facts about a person's past always find their way to a college campus. We all knew that she'd had it tough while she was growing up ... that she'd lost her whole family to a fire. Anyone acquainted with her family believed the world was better off without them … especially her dad. He apparently was one horrible human being. We only can speculate as to why she didn't want to talk about any of them."

I had arrived at Cal's condominium three hours earlier. The sitting area, surrounded by windows, now was considerably darker with dusk approaching. I still had one more issue to pursue – a line of questions I hadn't even anticipated before the visit. There was no easy way to broach the subject, so I went directly at it.

"Cal, from what you've said today, it sounds like my father turned apathetic, or possibly even became averse to sexual intimacy. Considering the pressure he felt from my grandfather, combined with the mixed signals his own mind and body might have been sending him, it wouldn't be unprecedented for a person in his situation to become impotent. Is that what happened?"

Cal shrugged and shook his head slowly. "I never saw evidence to suggest that was the case … you're the one who studies human conditions. With Junior and me, our lack of interest in continuing that type of relationship was mutual. As for me … let's just say I learned my biological urges skew heavily toward the opposite sex. But despite this realization, I still knew Junior was the truest love of my life … we just didn't need or care about those particular acts of love."

Cal was right. I had studied the nature of human relationships. Ad nauseam. I knew there was no accepted category or classification for the feelings that existed between my father and Cal. That fact pleased me. I'd never believed love should fall into neat and tidy boxes.

"How about with my mother?" I asked.

The confusion registered on Cal's face. "I thought we already covered that. I never was interested in a sexual relationship with your mother."

I held up both hands in apology. "I'm sorry … I didn't mean you and my mother. I was asking about my father. Did they enjoy a normal sex life?"

Cal waded into this subject cautiously. "You're raising questions that are highly subjective. Who am I to say what was normal or what wasn't ... or what others might have considered enjoyable?"

I tried a different angle. "Okay, let me ask your opinion. Why would my mother have felt the need to stage three false pregnancies ... with each ending in a false miscarriage? It sure seems like she might have been covering up for my father's impotence to keep my grandfather at bay."

"My young friend, I think you've watched too many soap operas," Cal teased. "I was aware Junior and Beth were pursuing a variety of methods to become pregnant. They weren't the first or last couple to deal with issues of this sort. Whether it was bouts of impotence, low sperm counts, ovarian problems, or the sheer alignment of the cosmos, I can't tell you. Their situation just happened to be more complicated than most because of Senior ... so I give your mother a great deal of credit for finding a way to buy them more time. Whatever she did, it worked. You're sitting right here in front of me."

We locked eyes in silence for several seconds, neither of us feeling a need to avert the other's stare. We both smiled – Cal first, then me. My questioning was over. Some inner sense told me there was nothing more to be gained. I rose from the chair and extended my hand. "Thank you ... today has meant the world to me." As Cal stood and grasped my hand, I added a postscript. "And you were right about what you said at the start."

Cal looked at me enquiringly. "What was that?"

"You thought I would gain new admiration for my parents." I released our hand shake. "I have done that, Uncle Cal ... as I have for you." I wrapped both arms around this dignified octogenarian. As we hugged, a line from my mother's memorial service popped into my head. *"How fortunate we are that people with genuine honor and nobility can have such influence on our lives."* I didn't remember which political robot had uttered those words from the lectern, but they couldn't have rung truer than they did at that very moment. *Honor and nobility.* Indeed, these were the most enduring monuments.

Beth Davenport had been a more remarkable woman than I, or any of her legions of supporters, ever conceived. My mother's long journey through life was like a gigantic jigsaw puzzle. I reflected on the letter she wrote to Lila, trying to explain the confusing thoughts about their relationship she carried into adulthood. Random pieces always would be missing, but enough now fit together for me to understand the unspoken complexity of her past, and the continued impact those complexities would have had on all future relationships. Whatever disappointments or regrets I might have experienced from her relationship with me, those feelings now had vanished and been replaced with a comforting admiration.

After exchanging goodbyes with Cal Stratton, I headed to the airport, to Melanie, and the rest of my life. The irony was not lost. My journey had started with a mysterious key, and over the thirteen months since, a suitcase filled with millions of dollars in cash turned out to be the least significant thing I unlocked.

Epilogue

"Where's Monroe?" I asked as I entered the kitchen through the swinging door.

Melanie was sitting at the table alone, enjoying a cup of tea in solitude. "She's with Annabelle ... outside on the patio. If we ever hope to hold our daughter again, we may need to pry her out of Annabelle's arms."

"Well, we'd better find a crowbar ... because there's someone else here who wants to see our little bundle of joy," I said, pointing behind me with a thumb.

Following me through the door was Cal Stratton – handsome as ever, and clumsily steering an enormous stuffed elephant into the kitchen. "Surely, Melanie, you didn't think I could stay in Florida when there's a brand-new princess up north who needs to be spoiled?" After several failed attempts, he managed to sit the elephant upright on the floor. "Don't worry, the giraffe and panda are on their way ... they'll be delivered tomorrow afternoon."

I watched my wife hurry across the room and greet Uncle Cal with an enormous hug. It had been almost five months since he'd flown up to join us for Christmas dinner in our apartment. Joy and peace had filled the holiday season, and every day thereafter. I was convinced Melanie and I would usher in thousands of New Years together, because the love I felt for her couldn't be diminished by mere mortality. I still looked at her with astonishing awe. This magnificent woman, this all-around perfect human being, really had married me.

In January, we'd purchased a house on North Delaware – not far from where I called on Sophie Mullins those many months ago. The listing sheet indicated the English Tudor had been updated multiple times since its original construction in 1922. If that was the case, I wanted to know how.

Renovation on the second floor already was underway, with our family of three now sleeping in what eventually would become a first-floor music and yoga room. Melanie had other plans that were likely to introduce whole new architectural concepts to one of the city's most historic districts.

The move added a half-hour to each leg of my daily commute to Wabash College – but only until the end of the school year. I had accepted a position as a full professor at nearby Butler University for the coming fall. This one-time rolling stone was strapping in for the long haul. The glorious, glorious long haul.

I shuffled Melanie and Cal through the backdoor to get them out of my way. In our wedding vows we had promised to hold "no secrets." But I'd been granted one exception. The recipe for my signature margaritas. Pitcher in hand, I finally joined the others on the brick patio and the scene was pure Norman Rockwell.

The four of them were surrounded by tulip trees in full bloom. Cal sat in a wicker rocker, holding one-week-old Monroe and performing a fascinating medley of baby sounds. Annabelle Jenkins and Melanie were standing behind him to either side, giggling at his silliness and soaking up the magic of the moment.

Cal looked up and noticed me. Beaming, he said, "I wish your dad and mom could have seen this precious angel."

I didn't miss a beat. "I wish they could have seen their distinguished banker friend, Calvin Stratton, babbling and jabbering like an infant!"

Everyone laughed, as all eyes focused on our swaddled newborn. Finally, Cal spoke again. "You know, Troy, I couldn't have been more wrong. Back in December, when you and Melanie told me you weren't keeping any of Senior's money, I encouraged you to strongly reconsider. But as I look around here today, I'd say the two of you have everything you'll ever need in life."

Before responding, I moved closer to Melanie and put my arm around her. "We aren't likely to second-guess ourselves ... but, Uncle Cal, that comment still means the world to us. We think the decisions we've made will serve everyone's best interests."

Annabelle was trying to follow the discussion and finally gave up. "Hello, people ... if you want to have a private conversation, I'll just go inside. Otherwise, could someone please tell me what money and decisions you're talking about?"

Cal and Melanie quickly looked in my direction, making their preference clear as to who should handle the explanations. I gave a sigh of resignation. "Maybe we all should sit down."

The women sat in two wrought iron chairs left behind by the home's previous owner, and I pulled up a lounge chair, taking a seat on the end. Looking at Annabelle, I started slowly and somewhat hesitantly. "None of what I'm about to tell you has gone public, and as it relates to Melanie and me ... we're hoping to avoid any media attention. Plus, as a final side note ... Kendall Ackermann and his team in Evansville already are convinced we've lost our minds, so please don't feel you have to hold back with your opinions on our account."

I gradually picked up the pace. "As you know, my grandfather amassed a rather sizable fortune over the course of his lifetime. For a host of reasons, he wanted to make sure my mother didn't benefit from a dime of his money after his death. So, when he died, we were led to believe that all his billions went to his beloved Davenport Foundation. Well, that turned out not to be the case. Unbeknownst to anyone other than his attorneys, a sum of more than three hundred million dollars out of his estate was held back." I paused, then added, "It was held back for me."

Annabelle Jenkins leaned forward, amazed by what she'd just heard. Her surprises were just beginning. I continued. "I wasn't told about the money until after my mother died, per the explicit instructions in my grandfather's will. By then, the amount he left me had grown to over four-hundred-million ... and according to last week's statement from the family office, the most recent tally is $463 million.

"Funny thing though ... since inheriting his money, I've learned a great deal about my grandfather ... and I've concluded that all the wealth he accumulated didn't do much for him. He was a cold-hearted, self-serving son-of-a-bitch who alienated the very people who should have been most important to him. I take no pride in being his heir, and don't want to be anything like him ... or feel obliged to honor the memory of Senior Davenport in any fashion. Taking that money would be the most hypocritical thing I could do with my life ... and I'm fortunate, because I'm married to a woman who understands how I feel."

Annabelle and Cal turned their heads toward Melanie, who instantly became embarrassed by the attention. She flipped her head to one side and threw up her hands. "What can I say ... I'm a sucker for men with virtues."

Ever the gentleman, Cal chimed-in to take Melanie out of the spotlight. "Annabelle hasn't heard the best part."

"I was getting to that," I acknowledged. "So ... once we decided to forgo a life of luxury, we needed to give my good friend, Kendall, some form of instruction on where the money should go. Now, one could argue that this $463 million should be reunited with the rest of my grandfather's coalmining booty. The Davenport Foundation could erect another shrine or two in his name. But, it's a funny thing ... that sounded like a crummy idea to us.

357

"Instead, we thought the best way to honor the Davenport name was to give this sizable sum back to the person who did the most to distinguish the family. Ironically, my grandfather went to great lengths to make sure that couldn't happen. While my mother was alive, there was no way for her to receive even a portion of the money that Senior set aside for succeeding generations ... however, now that she's gone, Melanie and I have arranged for her to receive all of it. Hers is a memory worth perpetuating ... so we've established a charitable foundation in my mother's name."

Annabelle Jenkins clasped her hands and raised them above her head to register overwhelming support for the idea. No one had been more loyal to Senator Beth Davenport.

I nodded my head appreciatively and continued the explanation. "When we sat down with the attorneys to start drafting a charter for this new foundation, our first stipulation was to prohibit the use of any of these resources for the construction of buildings ... my grandfather pretty well cornered that market for the Davenports.

"Since her death, I think I've finally gained a proper perspective on how remarkable my mother truly was. She endured abuses inside her own home during a childhood that ended abruptly due to a family tragedy. That combination produced a young woman filled with uncertainty and angst. But ultimately, she was able to dedicate her life to helping others ... to helping others overcome their own obstacles. So, we're launching a program that will do the same. It will address inequities and prejudices that many confront merely because they're perceived as outside the mainstream. These were the types of individuals Beth Davenport fought for in Congress ... and as it turns out, she did the same in her private life. Well, now my mother is going to keep battling on their behalf through the Beth Davenport Be-Who-You-Are Initiative."

As soon as I mentioned the name of the initiative, Annabelle began vigorously nodding her head. In recent months, I'd been experiencing similar reactions in a series of meetings with many of my mother's largest campaign donors, as well as her closest allies in Washington. 'Be who you are' was a phrase that became synonymous with Senator Beth Davenport after her death.

Two weeks before her ill-fated trip to the Middle East, she made a brief impromptu speech from the floor of the Senate, in what turned out to be her last public appearance. That evening, all the major networks had included Beth Davenport's comments among their lead news stories. In the immediate hours after her death was reported, the same clip began running practically non-stop.

A bill related to transgender bathrooms had been advanced to the Senate and was being debated. My mother hadn't planned to speak at all, but as tongues kept wagging about public policy being too heavily skewed toward the special interests of the LGBTQ communities, she was compelled to step up to the microphone.

"I couldn't agree more with my esteemed colleagues here today," she began. "We spend far too much time in Washington talking about the L's, the G's, the B's, and every other segment in a growing rainbow of initials. What a pity we must waste our collective energy granting all these groups their special privileges ... since they already were granted those privileges by our forefathers in the Constitution. But I guess until we're truly able to guarantee the same rights to every individual, we'll be obliged to assign names, and yes, even initials, to segments of people who don't quite fit our definitions of mainstream ... just as over our nation's history, we've been forced to recognize women and minority groups of every race, religion, and ethnicity."

The chamber went silent as the senator from Indiana spoke. The usual undercurrent of noise subsided. Throughout the cavernous auditorium, side conversations came to a halt. One by one, junior staffers who had been scurrying through the aisles, stopped and knelt – their eyes focused on the woman at the microphone.

"You know, I have a vivid imagination. I imagine a time when labels will not be required. I imagine a time when any young girl or young boy, progressing toward adulthood, won't worry about which definition they might fit or box they must check … when she or he won't have to be concerned with possible stigmas assigned to them. I imagine this time as someone who loves this country. I imagine this time as a wife … as a mother … and as a one-time young girl who still remembers the complex challenges of coming into one's own. How wonderful it would be if we … as parents … as friends … as an American people … could put our hand on the shoulder of that young girl or young boy, look them in the eye, and simply say to them … just be who you are. Your life ahead will be so much grander because all of us want you to be exactly who you are. Now, can't you all just imagine that?"

Beth Davenport had said her piece. She didn't utter a word about the bill on the floor – a bill that ultimately passed by a wide margin. Silence hung in the air. In unison, everyone watched her step down and head back toward her seat. As she finally sat down, the persons nearest her began to clap. Within moments, the entire chamber was engulfed in a thunderous ovation.

I had been hoping to give a shorthand description of the initiative named for my mother, but Annabelle insisted on hearing every minute detail. Cal didn't help. Though he was fully aware of the specifics, he slowed me down at several junctures. "You'd better get used to telling this story, young man … it's one that a lot of folks will want to hear."

I knew Cal was right. In every meeting thus far, the reaction to the "Beth Davenport Be-Who-You-Are Initiative' had been overwhelming. Our idea was to offer people a chance to sign-on to a movement bigger than any single faction or special interest. The initiative would prompt people to do more than voice passive support from the sidelines for groups who were challenged by discriminatory social and legal standards. The initiative would cause individuals to take action ... to become part of something bigger than any single cause. Males, females. Gays, straights, transgenders. Persons of any skin color ... of any background. Among every group or classification, basic desires were the same. What persons didn't want to be allowed to be who they truly were? What persons didn't want to pursue the lifestyle or ambitions that brought them the greatest sense of fulfillment?

By signing on to Be-Who-You-Are, persons could affirm this most basic need and right for themselves, and thereby for everyone else. In advocating for themselves, they also were advocating for every hue in the rainbow and every checked box in the census. No longer just watching and rooting from the sidelines.

The Beth Davenport Be-Who-You-Are Initiative was to be launched with high schoolers, through social media and live rallies. Literature and merchandise would follow. A number of big-name singers, rappers, and bands already were expressing keen interest in staging kick-off concerts. In time, this grass roots effort would extend to college campuses, and eventually across broader segments.

For me, the most amazing part was the money. Pledges were pouring in – ten, twenty, and thirty million at a time. By year's end, I anticipated the foundation's treasury would surpass the billion-dollar mark ... with no sign of slowing down. An executive director had been hired and a small office was taking shape in Washington. The White House was prepared to throw its full support behind the initiative. The announcement would be made near the end of summer, on the second anniversary of Beth Davenport's unplanned speech on the Senate floor.

As the final details were shared on the patio, I noticed the gleam in Annabelle's eyes. I saw the same in the eyes of Melanie and Cal. Inside, my heart was bursting. Just a few months before, the possibilities for such an initiative seemed far-fetched. Watching them come to fruition had been magical.

I'd saved one last surprise. "As it became clear to us that the Be-Who-You-Are initiative was going to be a homerun, Melanie and I started wondering how my mother would have felt about the whole idea. We concluded Beth Davenport would have put everything she had behind it. And, you know … that's exactly what we decided she should do … put everything she had behind it. So, a few weeks ago, the proceeds from my mother's estate were transferred into her new foundation … almost twenty-one million dollars. And like I said earlier, Kendall Ackermann and his gang already think we've gone off the deep end … so I want to clarify something. This latest wrinkle was my wife's idea."

Once more, all heads turned and looked toward Melanie. And once more, she responded by throwing up her hands. "What can I say? I'm also a sucker for poverty."

Cal again came to her rescue. "Troy, you make a half-billion dollars of inheritance sound as trivial as old bowling trophies left to you by a distant cousin."

He paused, but I could tell he wasn't finished. Though he previously had endorsed our decision to forgo the money from my grandfather, he was hearing the part about my mother's estate for the first time. At heart, he still was a banker. Cautions on matters of finance were to be expected.

"Are the two of you sure you don't want to reconsider and pull back a portion of your mother's money? You do have a daughter now. Who knows what college will cost by the time she's ready … and Ivy League schools won't be cheap? Plus, looking at Monroe here, I'm already envisioning law school. Don't you think Beth at least would have wanted to cover the cost of her education … or set up a trust to create some form of special connection with her granddaughter?"

Melanie reached over and lightly placed her hand on Cal's knee. "That's a sweet thought … and, by the way, I'm figuring on med school for our daughter." She then looked at me. We had failed to discuss one obvious detail in advance. Fortunately, as an official married couple, we now had mastered the art of communicating solely through facial expressions. With our eyes, we were able to agree on how much more to divulge.

Melanie continued, "And Cal, you make a great point … Monroe should have something to remind her of her grandmother. As it turns out, Troy came across an old suitcase his mother kept around … and it contained a surprising number of items she collected over the years … rather interesting ones, in fact. When the time is right, her granddaughter will be given that suitcase exactly as the Senator left it."

Cal seemed satisfied by Melanie's response. I knew I was. Sure, my mom could be hard to read, but I think she also would have been satisfied.

Other novels by Mitch Engel

Deadly Virtues

Stephanie Burton is a trusted voice that pierces the din of television news. Attractive and charismatic, she eventually is hailed as "America's Moral Compass." Privately, she contends with emotional scars as sordid as the stories on which cable networks feast. In this psychological mystery, the dissonant behaviors of an unlikely murderer unfold to a surprising conclusion.

Noble Windmills

Milo Peters has climbed to the upper echelons of corporate life but is headed for a mid-life nuclear meltdown after battling twenty years of misdirected ambition. Now his closest, lifelong friend wants him to become a whistleblower for the government. His first-person account of what ensues is an emotional rollercoaster. You'll probably laugh, maybe shed a tear or two, but definitely fall in love with this irrepressible character.

Crimes of Arrogance

Webb Tremont has spent much of his life disentangling himself from the complications of being a billionaire's son. His career as a cop is cut short by unforseen circumstances, so he does the next best thing. He writes about crime stories. After eleven popular books, he sells the rights to a television network – and that's when the lives of everyone close to him are thrown upside down. Six tech geniuses have banked hundreds of millions from a software company and are hungry to prove their intellect on a different plane. The anonymous group commits weekly parodies of the crimes enacted in prime time, except their crimes have no real victims. At each mock crime scene, they leave high-bound messages and envelopes filled with cash for popular causes. The public falls in love with them – at least until their crimes take a dark turn. The group has been manipulated from within by Anthony Lafferty, who harbors a vendetta against Webb Tremont and his wealthy family. You'll ride with Webb on a roller-coaster journey as these unknown adversaries continually confound the FBI. The events prompt him to reexamine the resentment he long has harbored toward his father and finally step into a serious romance.

364

2/22

CPSIA information can be obtained
at www.ICGtesting.com
Printed in the USA
LVHW111252040320
648972LV00001B/26

9 781977 222657